Flicker & Burn

T. M. GOEGLEIN

G. P. Putnam's Sons

An Imprint of Penguin Group (USA) Inc.

G. P. PUTNAM'S SONS • An imprint of Penguin Young Readers Group.
Published by The Penguin Group.
Penguin Group (USA) Inc., 375 Hudson Street, New York, NY 10014, USA.
Penguin Group (Canada), 90 Eglinton Avenue East, Suite 700, Toronto, Ontario M4P 2Y3,
Canada (a division of Pearson Penguin Canada Inc.).
Penguin Books Ltd, 80 Strand, London WC2R 0RL, England.
Penguin Ireland, 25 St. Stephen's Green, Dublin 2, Ireland (a division of Penguin Books Ltd).
Penguin Group (Australia), 707 Collins Street, Melbourne, Victoria 3008, Australia
(a division of Pearson Australia Group Pty Ltd).
Penguin Books India Pvt Ltd, 11 Community Centre, Panchsheel Park,
New Delhi–110 017, India.
Penguin Group (NZ), 67 Apollo Drive, Rosedale, Auckland 0632, New Zealand
(a division of Pearson New Zealand Ltd).
Penguin Books South Africa, Rosebank Office Park, 181 Jan Smuts Avenue,
Parktown North 2193, South Africa.
Penguin China, B7 Jiaming Center, 27 East Third Ring Road North,
Chaoyang District, Beijing 100020, China.
Penguin Books Ltd, Registered Offices: 80 Strand, London WC2R 0RL, England.

Design by Marikka Tamura. Text set in Calisto.

Library of Congress Cataloging-in-Publication Data
Goeglein, T. M. (Ted M.)
Flicker & burn : a Cold fury novel / T. M. Goeglein.
pages cm
Summary: Still searching for her missing family, sixteen-year-old Sara Jane battles new pursuers
and discovers more about her cold fury and more about the past murders and vendettas of
the Chicago Outfit. [1. Secret societies—Fiction. 2. Missing persons—Fiction.
3. Violence—Fiction. 4. Chicago (Ill.)—Fiction. 5. Mystery and detective stories.] I. Title. II.
Title: Flicker and burn.
PZ7.G5533Fl 2013   [Fic]—dc23   2012043305
ISBN 978-0-399-25721-6
1 3 5 7 9 10 8 6 4 2

For Michael and Dora, with love

PRELUDE

MY NAME IS SARA JANE RISPOLI.

It's not my birthday and I haven't eaten cake since I turned sixteen, but I'm plagued by ice cream.

If anyone offers me a cone, I'll break his nose.

I've been chased for the past month by a creepy black truck that sells frozen treats, and just when I've shaken it, the little nightmare comes tinkling around the corner again.

I have a movie-obsessed sidekick with a roller-coaster weight problem, and an ill-tempered Italian greyhound that's not really my dog but I love him anyway, sort of.

I have a classic 1965 Lincoln Continental convertible in dire need of bodywork and a badass 2000 Ferrari 360 Spider that's like driving a fuel-injected comet.

I have a boyfriend who's finally, actually my boyfriend and who accommodates this decidedly non-petite nose and these braces, but has no idea who he's really dating.

I also have an ancient, worn leather notebook that chronicles a century of Chicago's most valuable criminal secrets but refuses to yield the secret I desire most—ultimate power—holding it mute and indecipherable within its last chapter,

"Volta." The whole thing is held together by rubber bands and masking tape, while my last measure of sanity is held together by an unyielding determination to track down my missing parents and little brother. Every breath I take is fueled by a cold flame of fury that burns in my gut with a need for vengeance and revenge.

I'm alive because I have the notebook.

What I don't have is a real clue where my family is.

They're not dead, but there are ways of being alive that are worse than death.

I hold no mercy for my enemies because mercy is for suckers.

I don't have any plans for the future other than to continue breathing.

I throw a hundred hard combination punches at a heavy bag every day, and it never feels like enough.

When I'm not being chased, I chase back. And when I'm not studying the notebook, I roam the streets of Chicago, where one day soon I'll either catch the people who have my family or be caught by them—either way I'm ready to fight to the death.

As long as I have the notebook, I have a weapon.

As long as the possibility exists that my family's alive, I'll keep looking.

Every violent, unspeakable step I take to save them makes me into someone else. I remember the other Sara Jane, but it's no longer completely me, and that's okay.

She would've only slowed me down.

1

I WALKED FROM ROOM TO ROOM THROUGH GRAY midday light, inhaling the odor of stale floor wax and dust, listening to a grandfather clock tick into the void. A thin sunbeam shone weakly at the bottom of the staircase, and I stepped into it, feeling no warmth. The home I grew up in, stripped of the people I loved, crowded my heart with unbearable loneliness.

My family was violently kidnapped four months ago.

Then, slashed photos smiled from shattered frames. Gutted couches yawned next to splintered chairs, and muddy-bloody handprints and footprints of strangers smeared the walls and floor. Today, the living room stood bare before me; I'd had the remnants hauled away, but the emptiness was even worse than the torn and battered furniture that had seemed so wounded. Now the room was plainly dead, and it made me feel dead inside. With one hand on the banister, I looked into the hall mirror, seeing my dark hair pulled into a careless ponytail, my usual attire of worn Cubs T-shirt and beater jeans hanging limply from my body. An aggressive nose, lip-stretching braces, and high cheekbones—my face looked back, dominated by blue eyes flecked with gold, and I noticed something missing from them. Where there had once been hope, even in the darkest moments, now there was only tired despair. It seemed as if for every true fact I discovered, two lies followed, stoking a hatred that has simmered for months.

It's hard to admit, since it's directed at my parents.

Their disappearance and that of my younger brother, Lou, was a result of the duplicity baked into the Rispoli family history. My mom and dad showed me only one of their two faces, and by omitting the full truth, they lied to mine every day. The despair in my eyes—they put it there, and it isn't fair. And then the idea of fairness reminds me that no matter what they didn't tell me or how much damage it caused, no one deserves their tortured existence. The hatred fades and I love them again, completely.

I looked away from the mirror and creaked upstairs to the second floor.

My unconscious will and heavy feet led me to Lou's room, where I shut the bedroom door. Overcome by a weary sense of desolation, I lay on his bed, flipped on his rocket ship clock, and looked at a green, glowing moon on the ceiling intersected by a faint *1:58 p.m.* My family felt farther away than that cold, distant satellite.

As empty as the house was, it paled next to Rispoli & Sons Fancy Pastries.

Our family business had not churned out a cake, pie, or molasses cookie in months. It occurred to me that regular customers would notice that the place was perpetually dark, so I papered over the windows and hung a sign that read REMODELING! PLEASE PARDON OUR DUST! My greater concern was that the Outfit would grow suspicious—if just one nosy thug linked my dad's absence as counselor-at-large (while I fill in for him, my excuse is that he's ill) to the bakery's closure, every crook in Chicago would start whispering "rat." For my family's survival and the preservation of my own neck, I can't allow anyone to assume that he's become an FBI informant.

Closing my eyes, yawning deeply, I tried to picture my family's faces as a song tinkled outside the house like an off-key kiddie piano, and Frank Sinatra crooned along—

Chicago, Chicago, that toddling town,
Chicago, Chicago, I'll show you around, I love it!

My ex-nanny turned assailant, Elzy Zanzara, used to belt it out when I was small, and it startled me awake. I blinked up at the moon intersected by a flashing *2:15 p.m.*

Outside the door, wooden stairs creaked softly as someone tried not to be heard.

I stared at the doorknob turning slowly, silently, and leaped like an insane linebacker, throwing all of my hundred and five pounds against the door and twisting the lock. Someone on the other side hit the ground hard as I flew to the window and looked down at the Mister Kreamy Kone truck blocking the Lincoln. Moments later, a shoulder assaulted the door like a battering ram. Wood groaned, hinges complained, but the lock held; another shot like that and I wouldn't be so lucky. I yanked open the window and grasped the frame, my hair moving in a humid breeze, filling me with the paralyzing memory of a slow-moving Ferris wheel. But then adrenaline trumped fear and I scrambled out, inching along the narrow ledge toward a maple tree's creeping branches. It was too far away, so I stretched, slipped, grasped at empty air, and then desperately pushed off with my other foot, hoping to reach the tree, which I did. In fact I hit every branch on the way down, kissing earth with a thud, feeling like I'd been tenderized by hockey sticks. The bedroom door split and shattered above me as I rolled to my feet, ignoring waves of nauseating pain, poised to sprint for the car, when something in my gut made me stop. It felt like a mistake to look up at the window but I couldn't help myself.

It was leaning on the ledge with both hands, staring back.

I say "it" because the gender was indistinguishable.

Maybe it should be simple to discern one's sex when he or she is covered in something skintight, but this thing's body was model-thin and androgynous—a life-sized is-it-a-Barbie-or-a-Ken? It wore a weirdly militaristic uniform in the same fathomless shade of black as the ice cream trucks, so taut and glossy it could have been latex, complete with a jaunty cap and elbow-high gloves. A thick leather belt cinched its non-existent waist, and when it perched a foot on the ledge, I saw its pants tucked into tall boots. The only other color in the ensemble was red letters, *MKK,* encircled by the red outline of an ice cream truck, stitched on its breast and shirtsleeve. Even stranger, something silver and shiny hung from its neck. Its rigid face was composed of delicate, sexless features covered in snow-white flesh with a thin blue line for a mouth, giving it the appearance of a death mask.

And then it removed its sunglasses.

Its eyes pulsated like electric cherries.

So shiny, so red, and so sickly wrong.

I was stuck in the ghoulishness of it, my feet magnetized to the ground, when the thing leaped from the window. It fell quickly and landed deftly on both feet, and I turned and sprinted for the Lincoln, jumped inside, and locked the doors. I fumbled keys into the ignition and cranked the engine just as the thing threw itself onto the hood like a vampire-monkey. We were inches apart, its wet breath steaming the glass between us. Fear and injustice flooded my chest as a cold blue flame flickered beneath it; I was calm but furious, seeing the demonic thing for the very first time. It had been chasing me for a month, hidden behind its own impenetrable black windshield. Mister Kreamy Kone trucks were windowless vending machines on wheels with no way to see inside; customers deposited money, made a selection, and out it popped. Until I'd learned that a small fleet of them surrounded my home the night my family disappeared, I'd never noticed them around Chicago; I had no real idea how long they'd been on the streets or where they came from. The truck that pursued me was always in motion, and I'd even wondered if it was unmanned and remote-controlled.

Now I had an answer as my burning blue eyes locked onto its glowing red eyes.

We were face-to-face, and I deployed ghiaccio furioso with a vengeance, searching its psyche for its very worst fear, but—nothing. I blinked again and cold fury bounced back, stinging my brain like a cloud of angry bees. The windshield wasn't the problem—I'd conducted experiments of ghiaccio furioso on (poor) Doug, trying to ascertain its power, and I knew glass was no barrier against my concentrated rage. I still couldn't summon cold fury at will, but when the intense emotion kindled deep in my gut, I'd learned to control it in the same way that a stovetop flame can be turned up or down.

The thing's eyes widened, showing fat clusters of veins pumped full of blood.

Its pupils pulsated in time to its heartbeat, nearly thump-thumping out of its skull.

It drew its head back, hammered it against the windshield, shook it, and did it again even harder.

Broken glass rained down as I leaned on the gas, tearing through a hedge onto Balmoral Avenue. The creature flew up and over the top of the car while I cranked the wheel, hauling ass onto Clark Street and up Lawrence Avenue at eighty miles per hour. I was sure I'd thrown it free. I sat back cautiously listening to the world hum past, which became a violent slitting of fabric, a determined ripping of seams as I was sliced in the neck by a hunk of windshield as sharp as a surgical tool. The creature slashed through the convertible top, swinging at my face, missing, and gashing my shoulder while I swerved crazily, trying to shake it off. Car horns screamed, more glass bit and tore at my neck, and I remembered the loaded .45 in the glove compartment. I scrabbled for it with desperate fingertips, bumping it to the floor, and lunged for the cold metal with one hand on the wheel and the seat belt gagging my neck. The frantic wail of a vehicle brought me upright. I veered out of the oncoming traffic lane just as the creature stuck its alabaster face through the convertible top and I squeezed the trigger, blasting once, twice, three times. The thing shrieked and rolled onto the trunk, trying to grip it with all fours as I accelerated, yanking the steering wheel from side to side. First one black glove slipped, then a boot, and then it disappeared as a moving van veered awkwardly and failed to brake, followed by a sick, wet *thunk!*

In an instant the creature was gone for good.

A couple blocks later I pulled to the curb and gulped air, shocked to be alive. I shouldn't have survived, yet there I sat in (almost) one piece, heart hammering in my chest, blood oozing down my neck and raging in my ears. The creature's demise was good because I was safer, but bad because it was a link to my family, but good because I wasn't dead and could still try to find them, but bad because—

Because a piano began to plunk and a voice began to croon. *Chicago, Chicago, I'll show you around, I love it!*

My eyes darted to the rearview mirror as the black truck materialized on the street behind me, slip-sliding through traffic. It wasn't possible—I'd seen the thing get hit by a van with my own eyes, or at least thought I had, or at least I'd *heard* it—and yet it was six cars back, then two, gaining rapidly, and without thinking my foot fell like lead on the gas. The back tires shrieked as I tore across lanes, eyes filling with tears as I saw the sign:

CONSTRUCTION AHEAD—WILSON AVE. CLOSED—NO LOCAL TRAFFIC

I made a lunatic right turn, cars screeching and biting curbs behind me as I squinted into the rearview mirror. There was the truck, on two wheels then bumping onto four, on my tail as I sped past the wooden barriers and hit chewed-up Wilson Avenue, which was waiting for new concrete to be laid. It was like driving through the Grand Canyon, all deep craters and ragged potholes, and just as deserted—there were no other cars, sidewalks were empty, construction equipment was unattended and idle. There was an end-of-the-world quality to it—I was in one of the largest cities on earth rocketing though an uninhabited wasteland, pursued by a relentless creature— and the bleakness of it all made me miss the sign posted at the cross street where the road rose up.

WILSON AVE. BRIDGE RECONSTRUCTION— NO ADMITTANCE!

Or maybe I did see it and just sped up.

Maybe I'd finally had enough of searching for my family, which was as futile as chasing shadows, and enough of that childish emotion, hope. A whispered notion occurred to me then, that today was a fine day for *me* to die too, and that an easy way laid just ahead.

Flying up the incline, knowing the Chicago River lurked on the other side, I realized what a relief death would be. All I had to do was keep rolling! And there it was, my side of the bridge—a steel skeleton with girders wide enough to drive on but nothing underneath except a seventy-foot drop. The other half of the bridge was gone. After a long span of air, Wilson Avenue continued on the opposite side. I looked out at the gap of nothingness and wondered how it would feel to be a part of it—to float for a split second with the wheels spinning and then plummet headfirst into the dark, churning water. Solving my problem in one fell swoop seemed unquestionably correct, like doing myself a favor. My foot wavered between gas and brake; gas won, and I floored it thinking of freedom, of peaceful resolution. Except there would be none without knowing what had happened to my family—no peace, no resolution, only an eternity of unanswered nothingness—and I jammed on the brakes. But the steel was slick, and the car skidded to a slow, slippery stop with the front tires at the very edge of the last girders to nowhere.

In front of me, the summer wind whistled.

Below me, deep brown water swirled.

My heart hammered at my chest, and somewhere far away a duck quacked.

For a moment all I could hear was my own disjointed breathing. And then, quietly, Sinatra began crooning behind me as the truck crept up the bridge, eased to a halt, and the creature slid out from behind the darkened windshield, staring intently. I looked into the rearview mirror, wondering why it wasn't torn and bleeding, when its mouth moved and it ferociously licked at pinkish soft-serve ice cream. When it was done, it flicked its hand like shaking liquid from a cup. Something silvery glinted as the thing climbed back into the truck, and I knew it would come for me now, or, more accurately, my brain. Months earlier, Lou told me the captors had invaded my dad's head. It would be the same for me; besides invaluable gray matter, the rest of me was just gristle.

Some days really are fine to die, I thought, stepping out of the car and onto the bridge. *But maybe it requires some help to do it.* I moved carefully, slipping a bit on the slick steel, regaining my balance as I glanced through the girders beneath my feet. All I could see were construction cables and, farther down, the river, and I stopped only when I was equidistant to the truck and the edge to nowhere behind me. The creature now had a clear shot. Standing perfectly still, I pointed at it and then touched my head with the same finger. "You want this? What's inside?"

The truck revved its engine, dying to burst forward.

I closed and opened my eyes, exhaled, and said, "Well then . . . come and get it."

Back tires squealed as the thing barreled straight for me—fifteen feet, ten—and I smiled, extended a middle finger, and stepped between a gap in the girders. I fell a few feet before grabbing a cable and swinging like a pendulum while the truck roared above me. Its brakes complained, searching for traction, but the slick girders rejected them. I hauled myself up just in time to see the truck slide over the edge of the bridge and come to a precarious, tilting halt. I sprinted for it, determined to shove it into space, as a gentle gust of wind blew past. The truck teetered once and was gone. I heard it hit the river before I saw it, and when I looked over, it was already sinking. Water pressure blew out the windshield as cold brown liquid rushed into the truck. The creature stared up at me, clawing at the seat belt, convulsing like it was an electric chair, trying to scream while its mouth filled with water. Grimly, feeling no joy, I murmured, "Fine day, isn't it?"

The river covered its face, the red eyes flickered once, and it sank slowly away with Frank Sinatra gurgling to silence.

I rose to my feet, watching an eruption of fat belching bubbles and stringy motor oil, experiencing the same conflicted feeling as when I believed the thing had been run over by a moving van; I'd saved my own life but lost a connection to my family. The last trace of the truck swirled away and I turned from the river, seeing something shiny lying nearby. I picked up a small ice cream cone the size of a Dixie cup; it was hewn from silver, its conical shape crisscrossed with a waffle pattern. It must have been the object hanging at the creature's neck from which it lapped up the disgusting soft serve. Looking closer, I saw how the creature had lost it—a broken chain hung from a loop—and an engraving on the inside. After two years of high school Spanish at Casimir Fepinsky Preparatory (known as Fep Prep) I was able to read, "*Soy belleza y belleza es yo.* I am beauty and . . ."

"Beauty is me," a voice whispered.

I jumped back, shocked at the creature nearby, its eyes on the cone in my hand. The ghostly thing moved lithely to the edge, peering at the oil slick on the water's surface. I noticed something different about its face—the shape of its forehead, a smaller nose—and that its sexless model body was bone dry. It was like seeing tiny discrepancies in one-third of identical triplets, and I realized that the creature from my house, the thing at the bottom of the river, and the one standing several feet away were three distinct but eerily similar ice cream creatures. A red line appeared beneath its eye as a bloody tear cut across its snowy cheek. "You killed Beauty," it whispered.

"I didn't . . ."

"You killed *my Beauty!*" it shrieked, and I gagged a little, looking at gray stumps where teeth had been and a tongue as slickly black as the truck. The thing was shaking so violently that the silver ice cream cone at its neck danced across its chest. I looked at another truck parked at the bottom of the bridge—I hadn't heard it approach—and realized that they'd chased me tag-team style throughout the past month, one picking up where another left off. After all, a caravan of speeding black trucks would draw the attention of even the most indifferent Chicago cop.

I also realized that whatever they'd been to one another—siblings, friends, something else—they'd loved one another.

When I looked back, the thing's eyes were glued to mine—I'd already begun to think of it as Teardrop—and what I saw in them was different from its dead partners, who had faced me with the detachment of hunters. On the contrary, Teardrop trembled with malice and revenge. I didn't have time to lift a hand before it deftly sprinted the short length between us and punched me in the face like Mike Tyson at his baddest, sending me onto my butt, scrabbling not to fall through the girders. I got to my feet quickly and carefully, spitting blood and pain, knowing it was too strong and fast for a thing that belonged on a Fashion Week runway; it had to be fueled by insanity, chemicals, or both. Its drowned partner slurped soft serve before trying to run me down, and I wondered only briefly what was in that shit before Teardrop charged me again. I couldn't deploy ghiaccio furioso against it, but the flame leaped nonetheless, and I put it into my left hook. Teardrop caught my fist and squeezed, and it felt like bones being crushed. I swayed, enervated and limp as cold fury jumped to my chest, needled into my brain, and I saw my own worst fear.

It was my parents and Lou alone in an empty room, throats cut and eyes wide open staring at the end of the world.

Reality and fear melded into one dark thing and I had no ability to convince myself the image was anything but true. They were dead. The creatures had murdered them, and I was suddenly vibrating with a hellish desire to kill Teardrop because I owed it to my family—and because I was wired to kill things just like it. My left hook failed but I still had my right, and I connected to its face with what felt like a thousand deadly volts as it went into the air and skidded onto its back. I was determined to crush its bleached face like a rotten egg, and I brought my heel down against its cheekbone, hearing it splinter and crack, filling me with morbid pleasure. I lifted my foot, ready to do it again, when that inner electricity buzzed, faded, and I thought, *What am I doing?*

An answer came just as quickly—*I'm about to commit murder.*

The need for self-preservation came flooding back, washing me away from the limp form at my feet as I sprinted to the Lincoln and gunned the engine. A single thought pushed through the surface of my roiling mind—how the creepiest things lurk beneath a veneer of sweetness, like leering clowns and possessed baby dolls.

"Like ice cream creatures," I whispered, racing toward the safest place I knew.

2

CHICAGO PASSED BY IN A WHISTLING SMEAR
of shapes and colors as I sped through the streets. Images
leaped from the jumble—a giant little girl with an umbrella
and rain boots on the Morton Salt warehouse on Elston Avenue; an old man's lonely face as he stood on the corner of
State and Randolph; the flag of Chicago with its red stars and
bands of blue, snapping above the Damen Avenue firehouse—
and then disappeared as I left them in my dust. Gripping the
wheel with both hands, I thought obsessively about the electricity that had taken over my brain, body, and—deeper—the
edges of my soul. It wasn't so much that I'd decided to kill
Teardrop but that I *needed* to kill it, *hungered* to kill it, couldn't
not kill it, and now couldn't stop thinking about it.

An angry horn screamed as I veered into its lane.

Escape demands concentration, and I shook my head, ridding my mind of the creature's bloodred eyes.

I changed directions and doubled back in case another
phantom truck appeared, and raced south on Lake Shore

Drive. Venerable apartment buildings on one side of the drive and the gray lake on the other were momentary streaks, the park a green flash, Buckingham Fountain a burbling blink of the eye. I exited at Roosevelt Road at the last minute, cutting lanes and pissing off drivers, and sped past college campuses, belching factories, and blocks of storefront businesses with Italian names. Finally, I crunched past the limestone tower guarding the entrance to Mount Carmel Catholic Cemetery. It's a short drive to the Rispoli family mausoleum—right at Al Capone's grave, past the Genna brothers' tombstones, left at Frank Nitti's monument—and there was the small, moss-covered building. A molasses barrel carved from marble perched on its roof, our name was etched above the door, and a small stand of poplar trees (planted by Great-Grandma Ottorina after Great-Grandpa Nunzio's death) grew behind it, leafy enough to conceal the Lincoln. I cut the engine and went to the trunk. Ever since I can remember, my dad has kept a blanket, first-aid kit, flashlight, and bottled water in the car, just in case. I've kept up the practice since my life has become an unending series of just in cases.

Stretching to grab water, my fingers felt the edges of a book.

It was this one, the one I'm writing in now, my Fep Prep journal.

It had been there, gathering dust in the trunk, since school let out for the summer.

As I stood reading, the sun cast its last pink rays of the day over fields of slumbering dead. I could not believe the naïve, innocent girl who wrote those words was me; for a person so young, death as a possibility had occurred too often. My family's duplicity and the violent consequences of their decisions had worn away parts of the old me, and again I asked myself a persistent question, *Who am I becoming?* I shot at the first creature through the convertible top without the slightest hesitation. It was an act of self-preservation, as was helping the second one drown instead of being crushed by its truck. But nearly murdering Teardrop was not about survival; on the contrary, it was guided by an undeniable urge to kill.

It was clear now that whether or not I'd gone through with it, I'd failed my family terribly. A basic Outfit rule (which I obviously hadn't learned) is that sometimes an enemy can be much more valuable alive than dead. I badly needed a creature to lead me to the Mister Kreamy Kone headquarters, which would've been impossible if it had a crushed skull. On the other hand, running away and leaving it lying there was almost as bad. I was too beat up to consider it further. I sighed, lifted the briefcase, and moved carefully to the mausoleum entrance. There were no graveside mourners nearby, so I pulled a false stone from the wall and removed a cobwebbed skeleton key. The door unlocked easily. I ducked inside and locked it behind me.

A shaft of twilight streamed through a stained-glass window, while dust motes danced toward four caskets holding my great-grandparents and grandparents. It may not have filled me with inner strength or cosmic peace, but it calmed me down a bit, being with other Rispolis. I'd taken cover in the mausoleum for the simple reason that I couldn't risk being followed to my hideout at the Bird Cage Club, where Doug Stuffins, my loyal friend, and Harry, my somewhat loyal dog, lived as well. So far, I'd managed to avoid being tailed to the forgotten Loop high-rise, the Currency Exchange Building, where an old speakeasy occupied the penthouse. But that was when I thought only a single truck was pursuing me. Now I knew there were more and that they'd doubled their efforts to trap me.

The mausoleum was cold and damp, and I spread out the blankets, treated the wounds on my neck and face with the first-aid kit, flicked on the flashlight, and opened the briefcase. I set aside the stack of cash that was thirty-two thousand dollars lighter than its original ninety-six (bills, bribes), AmEx Black Card (unused; scared I'll be tracked), and Sig Sauer .45 (warm from recent use) and lifted the notebook.

Its final chapter, *"Volta,"* is the source of my frustration.

I believe it contains what I want and need more than anything else—the secret to "ultimate power," a mysterious force that could be the solution to finding my family. The notebook was assembled and written by my great-grandfather Nunzio, and added to by my grandpa Enzo and dad, as an instruction manual for each generation of Rispolis to navigate and operate within the Outfit. It's educational, yes, but as much as anything the notebook was created to protect ourselves from the violent, double-crossing organization that we serve as counselor-at-large. I don't know what "ultimate power" is, but of all the Outfit secrets revealed by the notebook, it's the one that seems to have been purposely obscured and hidden. The effort put into concealing that secret in particular by my great-grandfather Nunzio convinced me not only of its extreme value, but that it could be used as some sort of deadly weapon, as well. I'm aware that putting blind trust into such an unknown quantity is desperate, even foolhardy, but in this life of despair, I had to pin my hope on something.

The problem is, the entire chapter of *"Volta"* is indecipherable and incomprehensible, a jumble of senseless sentences. The term *volta* (which means "vault"), the brass key taped to the back cover of the notebook (with the mysterious inscription *U.N.B. 001*), and my trustworthy gut led me to conclude that ultimate power is buried within its pages—but I simply can't understand the words. Throughout the summer, I've sat late into the night with an Italian-English dictionary trying to comprehend the carefully hand-printed paragraphs, the phrases inscribed so closely together that the whole thing seems like a ten-page-long sentence. For example, one passage is so tightly written it looks like this:

ciavissijutusitum'avissidittunniestie'siccomuancoraèn'amicu viracifarivagnariupizzupicciotto.

Smaller verbs reveal themselves, as well as some blunt nouns, but the majority of it doesn't translate—it's mostly written in some other language than Italian, flowing together like a rushing river of letters. Also, maddeningly, nothing is capitalized. I can discern where a sentence ends based on punctuation, but have no idea where individual words begin. It was during one of these hair-pulling sessions that Doug looked over my shoulder at the notebook, massaged his chubby chin, and said, "Hmm. I wonder . . ."

"You wonder what?" I said.

"Remember the movie we watched, the noir flick from the 1950s set in New Orleans? *Blood on the Bayou,* with Richard Widmark and Ida Lupino."

"Yeah, so?"

"So, he spoke French, but when he tracked the murderer into the swamp, he barely understood a word anyone said. Even though it was still sort of French. That's why he needed her to go with him."

"She spoke Cajun, right?"

Doug nodded and flipped open his laptop. "Cajun is a dialect, like Sicilian," he said, tapping the keys like a concert pianist.

"Sicily . . . where my family is from."

Doug looked at the screen and said, "It says here that there are a lot of different Sicilian dialects."

"How many?"

"So many that most are understood only by people in the remote villages where they're used." Doug read aloud how Sicily's century-upon-century history of being conquered by one punishing invader after another taught its native people the value of speaking and writing a language that their occupiers couldn't understand. The problem was that Sicilians themselves sometimes couldn't understand other Sicilians— the dialect of one region differed from another to begin with, plus generous helpings of old Roman, Greek, Arabic, Spanish, and French, and pretty soon it was impossible to comprehend what someone was chattering about only a few miles away. The unification of Italy established a common language, which only encouraged always-suspicious Sicilians to determinedly preserve and practice their dialects. Unification or not, Italy was just one more occupying country. Sicily was forever.

"What's the name of the village your family came from?"

"Buondiavolo," I said. "All I know is that it's as far south on the island as you can go before falling into the Mediterranean."

Doug's fingers flew over the keyboard. A moment later he stared at the screen and said, "Um . . . was."

"Was what?"

"Was as far south on the island as you can go." He looked up and said, "It did fall into the Mediterranean."

"What are you talking about?" I said, staring at the screen, reading how little Buondiavolo sat at the base of simmering Monte d'Peccato for a thousand years, looking nervously over its shoulder until the volcano finally erupted with fury in 1956. Billowing clouds of smoke and ash suffocated the village, and then a merciless lava flow swept it up and dumped it into the sea.

"Holy shit" was all I could think to say.

Doug nodded in agreement, sighed, and said, "If that chapter is written in—what would you call it . . . Buondiavolese?—well, good luck finding anyone to translate it."

He was sadly correct in two ways. It wasn't just that the entire population of Buondiavolo had been wiped out decades ago, but that if someone actually understood the dialect, I couldn't ask for help without revealing the existence of the notebook. Whoever wrote the chapter—my great-grandpa or grandpa—intended for ultimate power to be discovered only by someone who understood Buondiavolese. So far all I'd discovered was that the language, or at least anyone who spoke it, was long dead.

One night, at a loss of what to do next, I read the words aloud, phonetically.

When the polyglot left my lips and reached my ears, a blip of memory appeared. It was a typical Sunday afternoon at our house—my grandparents and Uncle Buddy had come for lunch, which segued into dinner. It was the first time my uncle brought his girlfriend, Greta Kushchenko, who would become his harpy wife and my nightmare "aunt." During the lunch-to-dinner break, Lou convinced me to play hide-and-seek. At age fifteen, I was too old for the game, but my brother (a science whiz) was formulating a theory of telepathic tracking— locating a person by honing in on brain energy—and I was intrigued. While he counted, I slipped into the pantry, leaving the door open a crack. Soon after, my dad and grandpa came into the kitchen. They spoke in Italian, something about the bakery, something that sounded like business, and then Uncle Buddy and Greta entered. My dad and grandpa paused as Uncle Buddy rummaged through the fridge, and then began speaking again, but differently.

I heard it in my memory—Buondiavolese.

It was lyrical and incomprehensible.

Uncle Buddy slammed the refrigerator door and said, "Knock it off, wouldja?"

Greta asked why he was upset. Uncle Buddy glared at my dad and grandpa and said, "Every time those two don't want me to know what they're talking about, they switch to that mumbo jumbo! It's their personal pig Latin or something, because old Buddy's just *too* stupid to understand business stuff! Right, Pop? Right, Anthony?"

"Benito . . . ," my grandpa said softly, trying to comfort him.

"Buddy . . . ," my dad said gently.

"Aw, screw it!" Uncle Buddy said, leaving the kitchen with Greta in tow. As the door swung shut, his voice faded, saying, "You'll see! I'm not as dumb as you think!"

I thought about my unfortunate uncle, how he assumed that his own father and brother were excluding him from the Outfit when they were actually trying to protect him from it. He didn't possess ghiaccio furioso (which would've made him valuable and therefore untouchable), and without it he was just another schlub with a gun. They were sure he would get hurt or worse, and of course "worse" happened to Uncle Buddy after all—the price he paid for pursuing ultimate power was the loss of his life. I realized then that the more time I burned trying and failing to translate *"Volta,"* the greater the chance that I would lose my family too. I was getting used to bitter, continuous loss. My brother had been standing in front of me at the Ferris wheel and he disappeared before my eyes.

Every new day felt like my family disappeared all over again.

I looked down at the notebook turned to *"Volta,"* its words scrabbling away from my comprehension like tiny black spiders. And then I glanced at the other book, my journal, and flipped it randomly toward the end, reading my own handwriting:

Somewhere in that collection of tattered and worn pages stuffed between old leather is a secret that tops all others—ultimate power that I hope will help me find and free my family.

And that's all it took, one short paragraph written by yours truly to spark a revelation. *Somewhere in that collection of tattered and worn pages*—I thought the secret to ultimate power would pop from *"Volta,"* screaming to be found, but now I knew that nothing so valuable would be so obvious; it would be disguised and camouflaged, just like Capone Doors, those secret entrances and exits hidden by the Outfit all over Chicago. Even more important, it would be concealed in such a way that a Rispoli, and only a Rispoli, could find it. The key to unearthing that crucial nugget, I now believed, was spread throughout the notebook, scattered like golden puzzle pieces among its chapters and verse. I could never decode Buondiavolese on my own, but I was sure there were vital clues concealed in the pages, between the words, that would help me do it. I turned back to *"Volta"* and yawned, fighting to keep my eyes open as my chin touched my chest and consciousness receded.

Seconds later, I opened an eye to a puff of cool outside air. It grazed my face like baby's breath.

I opened the other eye as a scratch of footsteps moved across the floor.

The creatures had come for me, I was sure of it, and I leaped to my feet wildly, swinging the flashlight as the squeal of tiny voices filled the air and the ground moved in an undulating mass. I stood against the wall and looked down at hundreds of Great-Grandpa Nunzio's rats, those loyal descendants of Antonio and Cleopatra, blanketing the floor. To other people with other sensibilities, a flash mob of rodents would be terrifying and repulsive; to me they were welcome family friends. Sensing a Rispoli in need of aid and comfort, they'd converged on the mausoleum to form a protective snuffling circle—but how, and from where? The limestone tomb was sealed tight to keep out moisture and nature, but here was nature in full bloom, with worm tails and glowing eyes. And then I felt the wind again, chilled and musty, and followed it across the room. The rats parted, and I stopped at a heavy marble panel on the far wall inscribed with a Latin phrase—

SILEO IN PACIS

—which translates as "Rest in Peace." I traced a finger down the cool rock, stopped at the raised *C* in *pacis,* and gave it a push. It was slightly ajar from the rats, and now it opened fully, revealing a flight of stairs dropping into darkness. The reason for a Capone Door in the family crypt was easy to understand; it would've been a great place to hide booze during Prohibition or for a counselor-at-large to conduct a sit-down. The irony was that my great-grandparents and grandparents had an escape hatch at their fingertips but they weren't going anywhere, ever. My instinct was to investigate what lurked beyond, wondering always if the next secret passageway would bring me closer to my family. I moved toward it, ready to descend, when the rats squeaked insistently, drawing my attention to their snuffling circle around the blanket.

Like concerned relatives, they were urging me to rest. Flushed with weariness, I knew that what lay beyond the stairs would have to wait until another day; exhaustion and unexplored dark tunnels were a lethal combination. I shut the door tightly against the possibility of anyone or anything opening it from the other side, comforted by my newfound willingness to use the .45.

I sighed, crossed the room, and lay down, allowing myself to be surrounded by hundreds of warm, breathing bodies.

I came to the mausoleum to be near loved ones, and they'd found me.

MY Cs LOOK LIKE CROOKED Gs.

Most of the Ts seem like rejected Fs.

My own name is so poorly written that it reads like some kind of disgusting special of the day on an Olive Garden menu.

This is the long way of saying that after writing in my Fep Prep journal this morning (one of the bleariest Sundays ever), it's impossible to ignore that my right hand jumps like a Richter scale needle all over the page. I held it out, comparing it to the other, which trembled even worse—not a good thing for a boxer who depends on her left hook. My eyes involuntarily wink and twitch, and a rumbling nausea with the threat of projectile puking made it impossible to eat. Also, if my fingernails could feel fear, mine lived in constant terror of my tense, gnawing teeth. After my terrifying run-in with the creatures on Friday and then spending that long, achy night in the mausoleum, I'd returned to the Bird Cage Club early Saturday morning, pulled the shades, crawled beneath a blanket, and stayed put. When I wasn't writing, I was sleeping (flailing-twisting-muttering), and when I wasn't asleep, I was sweating like a sumo wrestler in a sauna. At first I thought it was an emotional reaction to being attacked by gender-neutral, cherry-eyed mutants.

And then the electrical crackling began, subtly, like joy buzzers grazing my skin.

The pen jumped from my hand when rogue electrical storms broke out over my shoulders and snapped through my bones. I lay back with an arm over my face as the current zigzagged inside my body, into my brain, and settled behind my eyes, humming. There was a knock at the door as Doug entered late Sunday morning, took one look, and bit his lip. Harry backed away with his ears on his head and tail between his legs, whining.

"What?" I said weakly.

"Nothing." He shifted uneasily. "It's just that you look, well . . ."

"Extremely exhausted?" I croaked.

"Completely insane," he said. "Like you're taking a break from the straitjacket for a few minutes before you return to the padded cell."

I sat back, wiped my forehead, and told him about my house and the bridge—how the first creature was there to snatch me, the second drowned trying to run me down, and that Teardrop turned murderous after I "killed Beauty." And then I explained the electrical current that had possessed me, how it overrode the frozen logic of ghiaccio furioso. Each Rispoli counselor-at-large used the power of cold fury as a business tool—to resolve disputes, broker peace, and force thugs to work together—in other words, to keep the money flowing. Admittedly, there have been times while using it on a depraved mobster that I've been tempted to inflict some well-deserved pain. Except that it's tough for a depraved mobster to earn enough to make his monthly Outfit payment if his arms are broken. Logic dictates that as long as he's earning money and it's business as usual, the Outfit will leave me—and the question of my absent father—alone.

On the bridge, all-encompassing voltage had nullified good judgment.

Cold fury should've reminded me that the creature was more valuable alive than dead. But the electricity radiated its own logic, the inhuman rationality of murder, and caving in Teardrop's face felt natural. Anyone else would've interrupted as soon as I'd uttered "ice cream creature" and "electricity in my brain," but Doug was formed by thousands of movies that made the unbelievable completely believable. Throughout the summer, as we tried to unlock *"Volta,"* I schooled him in all things Outfit—its corporate structure, virtual invisibility while remaining integrated in every aspect of Chicago where there's a buck to be made, and my expanding role as counselor-at-large. For his part, Doug explained how cruddy his home life was, with a mom more concerned with vodka and his lawyer stepfather than Doug, and a dad who basically smoked dope and ignored him; he moved into the Bird Cage Club with no protest from anyone. He also confessed that helping me had sparked a sense of self-worth, and that the quest to find my family had become his own. "That means everything to me,"

I told him. "But eventually you'll have to find something or someone that's all your own."

"Someone?" he said, opening his arms, displaying a XXL chunkiness. His face was a series of concentric circles, from tiny, round eyes to a pudgy piglet nose to multiple chins, while his hair had a fuzzy mushroom quality to it. He snorted and said, "Who the hell would want me, besides the manufacturers of big-boy jeans?"

Doug is impossible to BS and harder on himself than any bully or best friend could be. He eats right and exercises for a few weeks, but then he faces yet another existential crisis that seizes his attention, derails his diet, and sends him back to Munchitos. Is he gay or not gay? Does he hate his boozy mom or love her? Is *The Godfather* the greatest film ever or is it *Citizen Kane*? Ironically, the fact that he's so obsessive is why he's devoted to my cause. As I've learned, he's precisely the person to have on my side—smart, loyal, and thoroughly courageous. That's why he could listen analytically, steeple his fingers, and say, "You were flooded with electricity after believing your family was dead. But in reality, you don't know if they're dead or not."

"No," I said. "But there was a moment when I was sure they were, and that the creatures were responsible. Right before cold fury kicks in, I feel scared or threatened, but this was different. It wasn't a terrible thing that *might* happen to my family . . . it absolutely *had* happened. My love for them morphed into something murderous. It was like, if I loved my dad, mom, and Lou, then I owed it to them to kill the creature."

"The subconscious is quite a little taskmaster. It can really drive you nuts."

"That's the second time you've mentioned mental instability . . ."

"Relax. I don't think you're crazy. I think you're going to the next level."

"Next level? Doug, look at me," I said with shaking hands and a twitchy gaze, perspiring like a melting ice cube. I peeled hair from my face and said, "Does this look like the next level of anything other than pneumonia? I feel like I'm shorting out."

"Or maybe you're coming online," he said. "Like, say this is a by-product or even an evolution of cold fury. It feels related, doesn't it?"

"Yeah. It does." Instinctively I knew cold fury had to be activated for the electricity to flow. The scary part was that in the grip of the raging ions, I *needed* to kill Teardrop; I'd savored the sensation and felt diminished when it faded. Recalling it now, I licked my lips, wanting to experience it again, while Doug's mouth moved silently.

"What . . . what did you say?" I asked, blinking through the haze.

"I said for your own safety, we should try to understand whatever the hell's bouncing around inside you. Let's try an experiment. See if we can kick-start it."

"I don't know," I said. "I'm not sure it's safe."

"Who said science was safe?" He smiled.

Ten minutes later, I sat in a chair in the middle of the Bird Cage Club's main room—a round, high-ceiling space encircled by floor-to-ceiling windows that make up the twenty-seventh floor dome of the Currency Exchange Building. When it was a speakeasy long ago, it had been furnished with a bandstand and bar, cocktail tables, roulette tables, and other games of chance. Now the vast room was mostly empty except for a heavy bag I punish daily, a couch where Doug sleeps (with Harry wrapped at his feet), and a large, round platform that looks like the part of a lamp into which a light bulb is screwed—which is exactly what it is, on an oversized scale. During Prohibition, the club signaled to its clientele that it was open for business by flashing a beacon across Chicago. Doug found a bulb at a theatrical prop store that actually fit, but the old fixture still didn't work.

Also, there's the control center.

It began with a scarred dining room table rescued from a Dumpster. Doug covered it with computers humming with every conceivable tracking software, every accoutrement to aid in the collection and dissemination of information. I added reference books on Chicago history, crime, and architecture. The wall-sized city map with its mysterious stickpins had come from Club Molasses, my family's other speakeasy located deep below Rispoli & Sons Fancy Pastries, and now hung behind the control center, showing the city as a long, thin jigsaw puzzle of neighborhoods. It was there, high above the city, where Doug and I stared at screens, books, and maps, hoping that secrets would reveal themselves and help lead to my family.

The Bird Cage Club had once been a secret itself, known only to a select few.

It was hard to believe that I lived there.

Sometimes I awoke not knowing where I was and had to remind myself I'd been hiding out in the old club for months. The small, mahogany-paneled room where I slept revealed itself during the first week without my family, when I'd tried to fix a loose sconce. I gave the lamp a tug and a wall moved, revealing a hidden room complete with a dusty rolltop desk, cracked leather chair, and a tall floor safe. Every speakeasy had a secret office where the owners could skim cash in peace; this one, with walls of bulletproof steel and a private bathroom outfitted in gold fixtures, is where I dropped a mattress.

Now and then I try to picture what the Bird Cage Club was like ninety years ago.

I see tough guys in tuxedos, flappers in shiny dresses and glassy beads.

I hear the squeal and bop of a jazz band punctuated by the jingle of slot machines.

It was Tyler Strozzini, the Outfit's VP of Money and owner of the Currency Exchange Building, who told me that, in addition to the Bird Cage Club (our family has a hundred-year lease on the twenty-seventh floor) and Club Molasses, there had been hundreds of other speakeasies all over Chicago owned by all types of Outfit members. Tyler's eighteen and about to start college. As VP of Money, and with me serving as counselor-at-large, we work-flirt, flirt-work on a regular basis. I know about his revolving door of girlfriends (he makes a point to tell me) and he knows about my boyfriend, Max Kissberg—especially how Max spent the summer in California. Every time we meet to resolve Outfit disputes, Tyler flashes a perfect smile, leans over, and whispers, "What guy would leave his girlfriend, especially one who looks like you, alone and lonely for the entire summer?"

I always answer with a slow smile that (as I've learned) melts Tyler's natural cool, if only for a split second. "A guy who knows that his girlfriend loves him."

"Love?" Tyler chuckled. "Okay, but remember, love makes you weak." It was during our most recent sit-down that he looked around the Bird Cage Club and said, "Nunzio had a real talent for speakeasies, I'll give him that."

"Yeah, this place and Club Molasses must've been awesome back in the day," I said, scribbling the Outfit decision in the ledger. I'd resolved an issue between Muscle and Money, in favor of Muscle. Old Knuckles Battuta, VP of Muscle, buzzed away victorious in his Scamp, chortling with crusty teeth at Tyler; there was no love lost between them. Tyler was resentful, which put him in a needling, know-it-all mood. Outfit guys always try to show how "inside" the organization they are by demonstrating superior knowledge of its secrets and history (somehow they all had a grandfather who'd been best buds with their god, Al Capone), and Tyler was no exception.

"Most of the other speaks weren't so high class," he said, pinning his green eyes on mine. "Pretty creepy stuff went down in some of them. But of course, you're aware of that."

"Oh . . . sure," I said, always careful to pretend I knew just as much as he did.

"Like for instance . . . ," he said slyly, pausing a beat too long so that it was impossible for me to look away from his chiseled face, his smooth, copper colored skin, "the Catacomb Club."

"Uh . . . right. The Catacomb Club."

"We all know what happened there. What your grandpa Enzo did," he said with a wink, raising an eyebrow and adding, "allegedly."

"Uh . . . right," I said, keeping my eyes pinned to the ledger.

Tyler stood and looked over my shoulder, a whisper of lemony cologne reaching my nose. "You're pretty busy, huh? That's good . . . hard work keeps a girl honest," he said, slipping a perfectly tailored jacket over his broad shoulders. "But listen, when you get tired of waiting for Mike . . . Mark . . . ?"

"Max."

"Give me a call. I'll take you somewhere nice. Ever been to Paris?"

"Not recently," I murmured as he left. I made a note in the margin of the ledger (*Catacomb Club???*) and resolved to track it down in the notebook.

Sitting in the chair now, waiting for Doug, my mind went back to it—the notebook!

As Doug entered the room, I remembered the revelation I'd had in the mausoleum about the tattered collection of old secrets. "Hey," I said excitedly, "I think I know how to figure out 'Volta'! I've been trying to translate it when I should've been looking deeper into . . ." Doug spun around with an odd grin, and with speed I didn't know he possessed, he snapped handcuffs around my wrist and the arm of the chair, binding me tightly. Before I could react, he cuffed my other wrist. "Notebook?" I muttered, but he was snapping a third pair of handcuffs around my ankles to the chair legs. "What are you doing?"

He took a step back. "Applying restraint. Just in case."

"In case of what?"

"In case," he said, stepping back, "you think you're some kind of hard-ass."

"Huh?"

"Sugar Ray Rispoli and her killer left hook." He chuckled mockingly.

"What does this have to do with an experiment? What are you doing?"

"Holding up a mirror. Showing you who you really are, you big . . . nosed . . . geek."

"Doug . . ."

"You breathe out of that thing or sniff for truffles? I'm lucky I don't suffocate, the way you *bogart* all the oxygen with that honker!"

"Bogart?" I said, gritting my teeth. "What the hell are you talking about?"

"At least I *can* talk!" he shrieked. "You know why that nightmare on your teeth is called braces? Because I have to *brace* myself every time you open your mouth!"

"Doug, you'd better . . ."

"I'd better what? Do whatever you tell me to do and like it? Or you're going to stare me into submission with that *cra-aazy* cold fury?" He popped a fist against his palm and said, "Maybe it's your turn to have your butt kicked. I took a beating for you from that ski-masked freak, Poor Kevin. That was *months* ago and did you even thank me?" I was quiet then, my whole being aflame, and I yanked at the handcuffs as the metal bit into my wrists. "Did you?" he screamed, throwing a punch, holding it inches from my nose. When I opened my eyes, he grinned again. "Made you blink, hard-ass." Before I could grab his eyes, he turned away, saying, "Nuh-uh-uh. Dougie no lookie."

"Free me now," I said. "Whatever this is, it's over."

Doug shook his head, strolling the room with his arms behind his back. "It's over when I say it's over. By the way, it's not really an experiment. It's revenge."

"What are you talking about? Revenge for what?"

"For not *appreciating* me!" he screamed, punching the air. "For making me your chubby little *sidekick,* always doing the grit work, the endless research, and for what? O-o-oh, lucky me, I get to be Sara Jane Rispoli's *friend!* I guess I should just whistle Dixie out of my butt cheeks every time you throw me a *scrap* of appreciation, right?"

"Doug!"

"*I* want to be the tragic hero! *I* want to have scary eye-power! When is it *Doug Stuffins's* turn to drive the boat?"

"Listen . . ."

"No, *you* listen! Maybe I can't hurt you physically . . . maybe you're too tough. But there are other ways," he said confidently. He looked out the window at the tops of buildings extending like a checkerboard to Lake Michigan. "You've had an exciting couple of days, I know, but it's not possible you've forgotten that school starts tomorrow? Our junior year, day one?" I'd forgotten, all right. Who wouldn't, after being attacked by red-eyed zombies? I started to reply when he said, "Start of the school year means Max is back. Have you spoken to your *boyfriend* since he got into town? Actually, the question is, has Gina spoken to you *about* your boyfriend's *adventure* in La-La Land?"

That stopped me.

Gina Pettagola, my semi-friend, was the unquestioned gossip queen of Fep Prep. Although school had been out for the summer, she kept her finger on the pulse of everything about everyone that was none of her business. Besides movies, Doug loved nothing more than a scandal; if Gina knew of one, he would've heard about it. Now he pumped a fist, saying, "Boom, gotcha! Okay, so there's a rumor flying around . . . really, I shouldn't call it that since it's true . . . about how your loyal, honest Max had a fling in sun-kissed California. Wait, *fling* implies something transitory. This was a romance."

"It's not true," I hissed. I'd always had a sneaking suspicion that Max wouldn't stay with me, and it whispered again now as the blue flame leaped in my gut.

"I didn't catch her name, but Gina heard she was tall and blond with two big . . . brown eyes," Doug said. "And apparently, just the cutest little nose you ever saw. Of course she's back in California and Max is here, but Gina said . . ."

His voice was smothered by pounding in my ears as my heart exploded, because I'd lost Max. My brain bulged with that repressed fear as I watched the back of his brown curly head pull away from a laughing blond girl's face after he'd kissed her—he didn't turn, but I knew it was Max. The love I had for him was so strong that it made me weak, and my cold fury weakened too, until something danced and crackled through my bones, into my brain. When I looked up, I saw a different Doug than my friend and confidant; instead, he was a bloated bearer of bad news who made it come true simply by delivering it. I tried to free my arms but was cuffed too tightly, so I put all of the murderous voltage behind my eyes. Doug turned and froze, his face a combination of triumph and horror. He'd succeeded in activating the electricity but now his own deep, dark fear stared back, causing a wet spot at the crotch of his pants. I looked into his mind, seeing a film clip of him aimlessly roaming the Bird Cage Club calling out my name and feeling his terror—his only friend had abandoned him. "No," he said quietly. "Please . . . oh no . . ."

"Oh yes . . . ," I said with gleeful hatred, nailing my eyes to his with the need to slit his throat pulsating outward in waves, matching my heartbeat.

My body jerked against the handcuffs, a loud rattling began, wooden at first and then glassy, and then the universe split and cracked as the wall of windows exploded.

The shock broke my gaze from Doug's and he dove beneath the control center, sending books and computers flying. Bound to the chair, all I could do was wait to be cut to pieces, but instead the force blew the glass outward. I watched translucent shards spiral through the air like icy razors, glinting in the moonlight before falling onto the El tracks and surrounding roofs. The Currency Exchange Building was an ancient skyscraper occupying an odd slice of real estate that, throughout the century, had been boxed in by other buildings and the train several stories below; very little glass would reach the empty nighttime sidewalk and whatever did would be blamed on myriad urban accidents. I inhaled deeply, feeling the cold fresh air scrape at my lungs, overcome by an exhaustion that was like being filled with cement. Slowly, Doug climbed out from under the control center and said, "Remind me not to mess with you about Max."

I looked at the debris covering the floor and used every ounce of energy I had to say, "What the hell . . . just happened?"

"You generated a tsunami of electrical current," Doug answered, looking around in awe. He knelt down, unlocked the handcuffs with clumsy hands, and said, "Which you then used to try and slice me into meatloaf with your crazy eyes."

"For the last time, stop calling me crazy."

"I wasn't. I really meant your eyes. They were glowing."

"Please don't say red," I said, staggering to my feet.

Doug shook his head. "Blue, like your normal color but with light behind them. It was pretty terrifying, but damn . . . it was *awesome.*"

"Great. My evolution as a circus freak continues. I was perfectly aware of what I was doing, by the way."

"Which was what, exactly?"

"To put it bluntly," I said, as teensy pops of enervating voltage jumped along my spine and faded away, "I was killing you because you deserved to die."

Doug, always analytical, even with peed-in jeans, asked, "Why?"

"What you told me about Max. Part of me is sure he'll dump me someday, and you tapped into it and made it real. And then, when I was sure it was over between Max and me—like I'd been sure my family was dead—all of the love I had for him was turned into murderous hatred for you," I said with a shrug. "You deserved to die."

"You know I made it all up, right? To get the electricity flowing?" he said. "The stuff about Max and some girl in California? It was all nonsense."

"Yeah, I know now. Good job with that."

"Ugh, thanks," he said with a ripple of fatigue, drawing a hand over his face and sighing. "God, listen . . . all of that shit I talked was to activate cold fury. It definitely has to be rolling before the electrical part kicks in."

"Like 'big-nosed geek'?"

"Right," he said sheepishly. "It wouldn't have occurred to me if you weren't always bringing it up. Your braces too. I never notice them unless you're eating, like, corn or something." He sighed and said, "You know I . . . well, what I mean is, I love being your partner in this thing . . ."

"I know. I love you, too, Doug."

He blushed, looking at his shoes, and then kicked away some books and papers. "What's this?" he said, lifting the silver ice cream cone dropped by the creature. I'd placed it on the control center for his analysis, and explained how the thing had slurped at it before trying to run me down. Doug held it to the light, reading, *"Soy belleza . . ."*

"And beauty is me," I said.

He rolled it between two fingers. "Reminds me of a one-hitter . . . the little metal pipe thingies used to smoke dope? My dad used to leave them all over the house." He looked inside it at the pink, sticky residue and sniffed. "It smells like a chemical."

"It was soft serve."

"There are tons of chemicals in Mister Kreamy Kone concoctions," he sighed. "Delicious ones."

"Track it down online, figure out what it is. It could lead somewhere."

"Give me twenty-four hours," he said. "By the way, your eyes aren't glowing anymore. But when the electricity was flowing, man, you should have seen them. They were also projecting these little beams of gold light."

Watching Doug push a broom, cleaning up glass, I realized how correct he'd been to try and discover the source of the electricity. If I was forced to shuttle between the remnants of the former Sara Jane, ignorant but happy daughter and sister, and the emerging Sara Jane, counselor-at-large, it was vital to understand what was contained in my brain. Everything nudged me back to the notebook, and now so did that word Doug had uttered—*gold*. Chapter one (*"Nostro"*—Us) refers to the Outfit in general and the Rispoli clan in particular, especially an ancient ancestor, an Egyptian tribal leader with gold-flecked eyes.

I understood then that the notebook was not just a repository of old secrets.

It was also a living document where I'd find traces of me.

4

I ONCE WATCHED A NATIONAL GEOGRAPHIC program with my brother, Lou, when he was in his large-animals-that-eat-other-large-animals phase.

With a combination of awe and horror, I witnessed an anaconda swallowing a deer, and then a seventeen-foot python gag down a startled antelope. In both cases, their respective dinners were enough to satisfy each reptile for days. And then came *Carcharodon carcharias,* or as generations of terrified beachgoers and moviegoers know it, the great white shark. As the segment began, Lou elbowed me and said, "Pay attention. This monster is *never* satisfied." And he was right. The twenty-foot-long floating predator ate tunas, seals, porpoises, manta rays, charming dolphins, inattentive dogs, paddling people, other sharks, surfboards, and then, following a quick nap, started all over again.

After blowing out the windows earlier in the day (it would be open-air living until they were replaced), I locked myself in the office/bedroom with the notebook on Sunday evening.

Hours and chapters later, I put it aside, thinking of the Outfit as a great white shark.

First, there will never be enough money to satisfy its greed.

Second, it's a monster that, through a chilling combination of bland anonymity and appalling brutality, is more terrifying than any red-eyed ice cream creature.

Its hunger for cash means there will never be enough things to steal and fence, never enough businesses to defraud and extort, and never enough people to betray, exploit, beat, and kill. I read about schemes and tactics great and small, mundane and murderous. One was the "Wedding Party": Outfit thugs consult the newspaper, pick a wedding reception in a ritzy neighborhood, and hold it up at gunpoint, making off with cash and gifts. There was the "Brick Job," an act of brutal, simple extortion where, unless a certain amount was paid, a victim is put into the trunk of a car loaded with bricks and driven wildly around a parking lot, being crushed, battered, and cut to pieces by the heavy, sharp stones. Consistent Outfit income was supplied by juice loans (desperate suckers pay astronomical weekly percentage rates on cash loans), street tax (a huge monthly fee paid in order to run a business without interferences such as arson or death), bleeding a business (the Outfit forces itself in as a partner and then slowly liquidates the business for cash until there's nothing left), and the old standbys of drugs, hijacking, gambling, car theft, and prostitution. I learned that the Outfit financed casinos in Las Vegas and Atlantic City, but over the decades had invested much more into the ownership of politicians and law enforcement (I can't believe the names I read—mayors, governors, cops and

FBI agents, senators, congressmen, foreign heads of state, two former U.S. presidents) in order to protect its businesses.

The Outfit's monstrosity is very good for business.

It's rooted in the pathological ease with which it kills.

It will kill to eliminate competition, kill non-payers and underperformers, and, like the great white shark, kill its own out of insatiable hunger.

The Outfit places no value on people other than as potential, disposable ATMs. It follows no code of moral conduct, has no sympathy or empathy, and is loyal only to self-enrichment; if its members ever had souls, they sold them long ago, stole them back, and fenced them again. I paused at this conclusion, uncomfortably recalling the thrill of inhuman power I possessed (or which possessed me) while in the grip of the electricity, opened to the chapter entitled *"Nostro"* ("Us") and flipped to a section that discussed the Sicilian village of Buondiavolo, where my family had come from. In 1906, a team of researchers traveled there to investigate a legend: the remote village was inhabited by ancestors of an ancient, blue-eyed Egyptian tribe that had once been the preeminent fighting unit of Alexander the Great's army. According to folklore, the tribe's chief claimed that his people's power came from eating gold—that over the centuries, the rare salts contained in the precious metal had infiltrated their blood and brains, endowing successive generations with otherworldly powers. I moved on, reading:

There was a rumor of an even more mysterious property to the phenomenon (ghiaccio furioso). Supposedly, there was one family in particular known for its blue eyes flecked with the same gold as their Egyptian ancestor. These people were capable, in times of extreme pain or passion, of emitting a charge or spark from that fearful gaze, with the gold serving as an emotional-electrical conductor. While the research team did not witness this attribute, it did note several volatile electrical storms happening in Buondiavolo. It was also noted that every home, without exception, bore a lightning-scarred weather vane.

I lowered the notebook, thinking of the weather vane atop our house on Balmoral Avenue.

The night Grandpa Enzo died, I came home to the news in a swirl of wind and rain. My dad, clearly traumatized, opened the door just as a bolt of lightning destroyed a tree. The rest of the evening, while the household mourned and an emotional storm churned within my father, lightning repeatedly struck the old weather vane. Now I wondered, *Was it the storm or my dad?* Also, the sentence that read "a rumor of an even more mysterious property to the phenomenon" confirmed that cold fury and electricity were interrelated. Those who bore gold flecks in their eyes conducted electricity "in times of extreme pain or passion," meaning *after* cold fury had kicked in.

So now I knew how it appeared. I wondered, then, if its purpose was anything other than lethal.

Rereading the page, I found the thread of an answer in the first paragraph. "Alexander . . . absorbed the tribe into his army, making it an elite unit, the first to engage difficult enemies."

I flipped to the chapter entitled *"Metodi"* ("Methods"),

and traced the page with a finger until I found frighteningly similar words. A note scribbled in the margin read, "Daggers is the first line of defense against our difficult problems." The chapter discussed notorious Outfit guys with names like Harry "The Hook," Jimmy "The Bomber," and Eddie "The Axe," all of them small potatoes compared to Nicky "Daggers" Fratelli. The others' nicknames were self-explanatory, and while it seemed as if Fratelli's was too, it actually had nothing to do with his use of knives; it referenced the fearsome gaze he affixed to his victims, as in "shooting daggers." The chapter explained how he would start an argument, escalate it to a confrontation, and, when he was nice and pissed off, immobilize the poor mope with his terrifying glare and then coolly murder him.

Funny, I thought with horror, *Uncle Nicky seemed like such a sweet old man.*

He'd been Grandpa Enzo's second cousin, a frail, elderly, soft-spoken presence at holidays and birthday parties when I was little. Even now I can see his watery blue eyes dotted with fading flecks of gold as he patted my head and slipped me a twenty-dollar bill. He was an old man by that time, an Outfit veteran past his prime and, as I learned from the notebook, known far and wide for his infamous "Look," which froze adversaries like rats in a headlight. Of course I realized he was using cold fury—the ancient *ghiaccio furioso* of our ancestors. The notebook explained how from 1959 through 1983, on Outfit orders, Uncle Nicky murdered four hundred and thirty-three people in eight states and four countries—a gag-inducing average of twenty-four corpses a year. It was enough to dry out my tongue, but the next passage made me feel as if I'd mainlined Novocain:

And although Daggers never revealed his precise method for pushing a button, it was clear Ben Franklin had nothing on him: every one of his "clients" met their maker through the tried and true procedure of electrocution. In fact, most of them were found with their eyes burnt out of their skulls and . . .

I lowered the notebook. The Outfit had used violent death for punishment or profit, or both, for a hundred years. Sometimes killings were secret (bodies dumped into the Sanitary Canal), other times they were staged as grisly spectacles to maximize public shock (victims riddled with bullets in barber chairs). However, despite the existence of every possible depravity in the Outfit, it still wasn't easy to find members willing to kill. It required a rare individual for whom murder was abnormally easy—guys like Uncle Nicky. Thinking of it now reminded me of my English lit teacher, Ms. Ishikawa, mesmerizing us with tales of ancient rulers who dealt with their most problematic enemies by deploying select groups of killers to wipe them out. Was it possible all of those rulers located their own personal Uncle Nicky, or battalions of Uncle Nickys, through sheer coincidence? Or was there a connection?

My suspicion was grounded in the past, but the answer existed in the present, online.

I flipped open Doug's laptop and tapped tentatively, reading about the Macedonian Empire where it all began with Alexander the Great recruiting my Egyptian ancestors as his specialized corps of killers. I searched forward in time, using keywords—blue eyes, gold flecks, family of assassins—and tracked them through the ages. The Ptolemaic Dynasty (305 BC–30 BC), led by calculating Cleopatra, left behind proof of my family that made me gasp. I looked at a hieroglyphic image of a cunning assassin wielding neither spear nor knife, but a deadly pair of gleaming blue eyes. The same held true with a rice paper scroll from the Yuan Dynasty (1271–1368), where a platoon of soldiers stood cowering before just one of Kublai Khan's men; he stared them into submission with a gaze as cold and blue as a frozen lake. I moved on to recent history, pausing at the Battle of Stalingrad (1943) between the Russian and German armies. The Russian premier, Joseph Stalin, sent in a select corps of soldiers called the Синяя Молния, which swiftly and brutally ended the conflict. I pasted the term into a translator, and when the words popped onto the screen—Blue Lightning—I'd finally read enough.

Cold fury ignited the electricity.

The voltage powered an inhuman ability to kill without remorse.

Taken as a whole, my ancestors were history's hit men.

I opened my tiny office window and let the midnight air whisper over my prickly skin. Nunzio staked his (and our) claim in Chicago as counselor-at-large, but it was obvious that, like the great white shark, we served a deadlier purpose. The term came to me from a movie—*Natural Born Killers*—and I shuddered. I understood genetic predisposition (thanks, health sciences class) and imagined an ominous cluster of cells floating through my body, searching for a place to fester.

Just thinking about it felt like I'd stepped from a cliff in total darkness. The intense crying jags I used to experience had long since dried up, displaced by a dry sense of doom. What I'd discovered made me plummet again and fantasize about falling forever. I crossed the shadowy dance floor and stepped outside to the terrace. Looking at buildings that stretched away like tombstones, I wondered how Nunzio, Enzo, and my dad had resisted the urge to kill.

And then it occurred to me—maybe they couldn't stop themselves.

Using cold fury to unwillingly preside as counselor-at-large was one thing, but electrically shape-shifting into a ruthless hit man was another, and I wondered then how long it would take until *I* morphed into a teenage version of Nicky "Daggers" Fratelli?

"What are you doing out here?"

I turned slowly, the breeze whipping hair at my face. "I'm a murderer, Doug," I said softly, hearing my words blow away.

He looked around. "Where's the body?"

"I mean it. I'm a murderer. It's there, in the notebook."

"I think someone's read enough scary secrets for tonight," he said, extending a hand. "Come on, back to bed for you."

"No, goddamn it . . . it's too much! It's too goddamn . . ." I screamed, shaking violently, punching at the air. There were no tears, but none were necessary; I was choking on rage, babbling with frustration. It rattled Doug worse than when I'd blown out the windows, and he eased me to the terrace floor with an arm around my quivering shoulders. It wasn't just the threat of being a natural born killer but also my constant sense of loss or loneliness, with loneliness being the sadder and grayer of the two. Loss means that someone beloved is irretrievable, and as bad as that is, a person can eventually accept the fact of permanent absence. But loneliness is terrible because it's specific, open-ended, and alive. You want precisely whom you want, no one else, and it's torturous because they're out there somewhere but you can't be with them—you can't even *find* them—and that's when you realize that the hollow isolation in your gut will never go away. Of course, it's only made worse by the never-ending paranoia of being just about to have your brain pulled from your skull by an ice cream creature. As hard as I run, they're always waiting around the corner.

"Sara Jane," Doug said quietly, "it's okay."

But now all of those things felt remote and even childish compared to my genetic destiny of furious Jekyll and electrical Hyde awakening inside my cells, body, and brain, and I couldn't see any way to avoid it or any reason to—

"Come here," Doug said, pulling me close, holding me like a panda bear embracing a kitten. "Calm down," he whispered. I sat back, wiped my face, and told him everything—Uncle Nicky, my ancestors, my own DNA predisposition toward murder. Instead of the usual Doug Stuffins's analysis of unbelievable facts, he said softly, "That's complete bullshit."

"What?" I snuffled.

"This isn't some crappy movie, Sara Jane. Some fantasy about kids who are witches or magical douchebags shooting lightning bolts from their fingertips," he said. "This is real life, your life. You don't have to be anything you don't want to be."

"But Uncle Nicky . . ."

"Uncle Nicky was a psycho for hire. You're not."

"The electricity. You saw the windows!"

"I don't know about that. I got a C minus in science, so don't ask me," he said. "Listen, after my dickweed father deserted my mom and me, she came out of her vodka stupor just long enough to see that I was eating my anxiety. You think I'm fat now?" He shook his head and said, "She sent me to a shrink. I lasted a session and a half and then quit because the guy said something so true, it scared the shit out of me."

"What's that?"

"The dude looked at me and said, and I quote, 'Douglas, in the end, it doesn't matter who your family is or what they've done or not done for you. As you become an adult, *only you* are responsible for who you become.'" He shook his head, saying, "I couldn't handle it. Still can't. But I know it's true. No one but me chooses Munchitos over a Stairmaster. It's not my fate to be overweight and alone. It's a choice."

"Then why do you do it?" I asked quietly.

"Because it's easy and I'm weak," he said, holding my gaze. "But you're not."

I bit my lip, shaking my head. "A couple of days ago. On the bridge, I almost . . . I thought about . . ." I felt tears inching down my cheek like cold snails. I was so ashamed of myself that the words wouldn't come. "I'm just so tired."

"It's late."

"I don't mean that kind of tired."

"I know," he said. "Look, I can't make you feel any other way than how you feel. I can only tell you two things. First,

53

you don't know what's true about your family and what's not because they're not here to ask. It's the same with *'Volta.'* Wherever that vault is, whatever the inscription on the brass key means, there's no one to ask, so we're going to have to figure it out ourselves. Second, if you kill yourself, I will too."

"What? Doug, that's crazy."

"I mean it. Just like I can't make you feel differently, I also can't make you *not* do it," he said. "But I can do for you what you did for me, which is make you think before you do something stupid. And what I want you to think about is, if you kill yourself, you'll kill me too, because I'll follow you. You're all I have. If I lose you, I lose everything, so I might as well die."

"No."

He grabbed my hand and squeezed. "There. We just made a suicide pact. So think hard, Sara Jane."

I tried to remove my hand, but he held tight. And I looked at him, seeing the truth in his eyes. "Okay, Doug," I whispered. "Okay."

Harry gave a tentative bark from the terrace door and segued into a walking whine, circling before sitting between us. Doug scratched the little greyhound's ears, and I extended a hand. Harry looked at me intently, like trying to read my mind, and then his gaze softened and he placed a paw in my palm, just once, a brief touch, and turned back to his darling Doug. As he massaged Harry's bony spine, he said, "*Gone with the Wind*? Scarlett O'Hara lost her home, family, that goofy nerd she loved, Ashley. And then she sort of gets it all back when she marries the guy with the mustache . . ."

"Rhett Butler," I murmured.

"But then he realizes what a bitch she is and leaves her. It's that 'Frankly, my dear, I don't give a damn' scene. First Scarlett's weeping and falling apart, and then boom, she's made of iron. She's going to keep rolling until everything works out. Her last line, remember? 'Tomorrow is another day.'"

"Yeah. Right."

"I don't really like the movie. The glorification of the Confederacy is actually pretty creepy," Doug said, rising and carrying Harry toward the door. "But Scarlett had a point. In fact, second heads-up . . . tomorrow's the first day of school."

"I know, I know," I said, my stomach flipping as I thought of Max. It would be the first time we'd seen each other all summer. Of course we'd spoken on the phone. But to be safe, I never kept a cell for long, ditching the disposables in Lake Michigan at regular intervals and then activating a new one and blaming my lousy carrier. The fact that he'd been in Chicago for a day or two and we hadn't spoken yet wasn't unusual; actually, it made the anticipation of seeing him even greater. I sat up straight, feeling the encouraging nudge of something like hope, and said, "I can't wait."

"No jumping," Doug said with a yawn. "I'm too tired to follow."

Watching him shuffle away, I realized that he picked the wrong movie analogy. Instead of *Gone with the Wind,* my life was *Jaws,* dominated by the frenetic intensity of a great white shark.

Then again, tomorrow really was another day, and at least I'd be there to see it.

5

THE LESSON DRILLED INTO MY HEAD SINCE THE day I was born—gently by my mom, urgently by my dad, in a singsong voice by Grandma Ottorina, with a raised eyebrow by Grandpa Enzo—was that a Rispoli never, ever draws attention to herself.

I know now that it came from our place in the Outfit; anyone who wasn't on guard was, in the words of Grandpa Enzo, *una testa di nocca*—a knucklehead. We were demonstrative at home (no one can hug and kiss like a Rispoli) but retained poker faces in public. Holding our feelings close to the vest was an ingrained defensive tactic, and as my parents and Lou have drifted further away and sinister elements have crowded in, I've become even more insular and withdrawn. Any expression of emotion, especially on the street, feels like I'm begging to be attacked, which is how I was able to refrain from making a spectacle of myself on the first day of school.

I didn't want to hold back. I wanted to explode but held my emotions in check.

I saw Max in front of his locker at the end of the jostling hallway and gritted my teeth trying not to spin into a running-screaming-hugging whirlwind.

He was California tan, brown hair a sun-bleached blond, and he seemed taller. And then he turned toward me with a smile that made me forget the last electrical, suicidal twenty-four hours. He eased through the crowd, and when he embraced me and didn't let go, I wanted to cry. For an instant it felt like my family was at home and ice cream creatures were a silly nightmare. He looked down with his trademark grin, and before I could say anything, he leaned in and kissed me. The public display of affection set off internal alarm bells as a thought emerged—*This is probably as dangerous for him as it is for me*—but quickly faded as he wrapped his arms around me. "I've been waiting for two months to do that," he said.

"Me too, for that to be done to me," I said. "For you to do that. You know what I mean, right?"

"I always know what you mean," he said with a smile, reminding me of the talk we had the evening before he left for L.A.

It had been a balmy night in June, just before dusk, and we'd ridden his motorcycle to Hollywood Avenue beach. Initially, we'd both been hesitant to start a real relationship. Max's reason had to do with his parents' divorce, which made him feel unsettled. And me? I was bottled up with dangerous secrets about my family and the Outfit; I couldn't tell him anything for fear of putting him in danger. But then a couple of months passed and we kept talking, kept finding opportunities to be together, and soon we were a couple. Now he was leaving for the summer, and it was such an odd time for me, having endured the attacks of Elzy and Poor Kevin and then losing a connection to my family when Lou disappeared from the Ferris wheel. With Max about to leave, I'd never felt so alone. We sat on a blanket watching Lake Michigan turn gold from the setting sun, me hugging my knees, him with an arm around my shoulders. My feelings must've been etched on my face, because he glanced over and said, "Yeah. Me too."

I put on a smile. "It's only a couple months. You'll be back really soon."

He nodded silently, and said, "Hey . . . I stopped on Argyle Street and got a banh mi. I left it in the carrier on my motor-cycle. We can dine by sunset." He stood, touched my head, and walked away. As he did, the blanket buzzed. I moved it aside and saw his phone, which had slipped from his pocket. Against my better judgment, I lifted it and looked at a floating text box from someone named Chloe that read:

Still can't believe ur going to Cali . . . so sad . . .

My gut felt like it was flooded with ice water, and the phone trembled in my hand. The suspicion I'd always had—that Max would dump me—made my index finger scroll up to the previous text, from Max to Chloe.

This has got to stop, Chloe. Not good for me or u.

And the previous one from Chloe to him:

Remember the lake? Remember the private beach we found? Just the 2 of us . . .

And I was about to look at the one before that when Max said, "Uh . . . are you reading my messages?" He stood over me, holding a paper bag, his brow crinkled.

I looked from the phone to him and offered it up. "Chloe can't believe you're going to California," I said, trying to keep my voice steady. "She's taking it pretty hard."

"Oh . . . shit," he said, reading the text and rolling his eyes. He dropped to his knees on the blanket, stared at the ground, and then wearily moved a lock of brown curly hair from his eyes. "Okay, look," he said. "So . . . um . . . I cheated." I nodded slowly and began to rise without a word because I'd cry if I spoke, and I refused to do that in front of him. Max grabbed my arm, but I pulled away. Then he did it again, harder, and I sat back as he said, "Not with her! I cheated with *you,* Sara Jane! I cheated *on* Chloe." I thumbed away tears and looked into his face, pinched and troubled, as he said, "When you and I first met, I said I needed some time before we really started dating because of my parents breaking up. That was true . . . but not the whole truth."

The other part was that he was still seeing Chloe, his girlfriend in the suburbs.

Even before he'd moved back to Chicago with his mom, his feelings for Chloe were changing—"fading," as Max said— and then he met me again. "And that was it," he said. "The whole 'love at first sight' thing . . . what does Doug call it in movies, the 'world slows down' moment? It wasn't like that."

He shrugged. "But there was love in it, right from the start." He held my gaze even as the hint of a blush touched at his neck. "And then there was more and more, and here we are."

About a month after we met, he tried to end it with Chloe, but she'd gotten upset, made disturbing noises about hurting herself, and he backed off. "I should've gotten it over with, but to be honest, it was easier to let it linger," he said. "The divorce, getting used to Chicago and a new school . . . Chloe was one more thing to deal with, and I didn't. Instead I got closer to you and called her less and less. And then she ate a bunch of pills. I just . . . I didn't think she was serious." Luckily she recovered, and when the crisis was over, Max told her about me. Therapy helped Chloe move on, but now and then she started a text conversation, asking about Max's life, talking about the past. He held the phone out. "Here, read the whole conversation. Call her if you want and ask about it. She's sort of stalkerish but Chloe's a good person. She won't lie."

I pushed it back. "Would you have told me if I hadn't seen the text?"

He was quiet a moment. "No. Probably not."

It was a disturbingly honest answer that made me sad and a little angry, but mostly curious. "Why?" I asked.

"Because I didn't want you to think I was an asshole for stringing her along. I mean, I was, I admit that." He sighed. "But not telling you about it doesn't make it less true. Some things are just over, you know? They don't have anything to do with now."

I couldn't have agreed less.

I'd learned the hard way that events of the past led directly to the present, and I was about to say so when Max spoke first. He touched my hand and I let him. "If anything existed between me and Chloe, if I was holding back or hiding something about right now, the present, then you'd have every right to hate me and not trust me. Because I wouldn't be the person you thought I was. But that's not what this is."

That's exactly what it was, but it wasn't his fault.

My whole relationship with Max was based on one long lie by omission—how could I not expect him to have secrets of his own? It was the ultimate moment to tell him everything in a way that might save him from hating me, but I paused. Max must've interpreted my silence as deliberation, when in fact it was cowardice. Again, he spoke first, saying, "I'm a normal person, Sara Jane, with faults like anyone else. What I did to Chloe was wrong, but it had one good effect—it made me resolve never to lie to you. I promise."

"I . . . I don't know what to say," I mumbled honestly, since I was the one who felt like a fraud. So I spoke about myself instead, adding, "Except . . . except it would be great if everything could always be up front and perfect, but it can't be, because . . . because . . ."

"Because we're not little kids. And this is real life," he said.

I nodded slowly and stared across the lake as Max put his arm around me again. "So," he asked, "are we okay?"

"Yeah. We are," I said, happy to answer in the affirmative but aware that it was more than partly wishful thinking.

"You know I'm all in, right?" he said. "There's no one else I want to be with. In some ways I know you better than any person in the world, and in others, there's so much about you I don't. It's cool that we still have so much to learn about each other."

"Yeah. So much . . ."

"Just promise me one thing while I'm gone, okay?"

I turned to him, resting my head on my knee. "What?"

"Have a really boring summer." He grinned, placing a hand gently on my face and kissing me.

And now he was kissing me again, holding me tightly as kids streamed past on their way to first period, when a deep voice said, "Break it up, Romeo and Juliet. Get to class, now." We turned to a large, stone-faced security guard, smiled weakly, and walked away holding hands. With cameras and metal detectors at every entrance, Fep Prep is run like a scholarly penitentiary. It was a Chicago thing, a big-city, urban thing after guns began popping up in lockers in the 1990s in even the best schools. The threat of random violence was regarded as inevitable, even if nothing ever happened, and at Fep Prep it hadn't. Still, that didn't affect the security rhythm of the school, which was basically locked down at all times. Beginning today, for almost a whole year, I'd be sheltered, watched, and protected seven hours a day.

Even better, Max and I would be together in that bubble of safety every day.

For the entire first week of school, I was the supportive, affectionate girlfriend he deserved. We met each morning at Bump 'N' Grind for espresso, ate lunch together, and hung out after class, and I even managed to have dinner with him in Greektown without looking over my shoulder every five seconds.

Most of all, I listened.

I'd been consumed by my secret life before he left for California, but now I gave him undivided attention. That's how I learned his summer was spent splashing around a pool with his dad's new stepsons (ten-year-old twins), and that after a couple of weeks he was thoroughly depressed. He'd left me behind to reconnect with his dad, but instead became a de facto babysitter. His dad left early for work each day and then, at around ten a.m., his stepmom slid on huge sunglasses and asked Max if he minded watching the boys. All he could say was okay, and she waved as she backed out in a Mercedes convertible and didn't return for hours. She and his dad were good together; in fact, his father seemed so happy in a new life with a new family that Max felt like an interloper, and wondered what the hell he was doing there. Max being Max, he asked his dad using those very same words.

To his surprise, his dad apologized profusely.

It turned out that he and his wife hoped that time alone would help Max bond with his stepbrothers, and that she was actually a little intimidated by him. She'd stayed away each day longer than intended, nervous about being compared to his mom. In fact, she and the twins liked Max a lot, and he liked them, and once it was all out in the open they came together as a patchwork family. Max had important, overdue talks with his dad about the divorce, about his dad's abrupt departure from Chicago, and about feeling deserted by him.

As Max told me, they still had a few miles to go before things were okay, but by the time summer ended, it was actually tough for him to leave.

"Then I thought of you," Max said, squeezing my hand, "and it was easy."

I smiled, unable to repress a twinge of jealousy at Max having two families, or at least one and a half, while I had none. And then he asked me what I'd done all summer. At first I bobbed and weaved around the question like the boxer I am, explaining how the details would bore him, and that all I wanted was to spend time together. During that first week of school, I'd enjoyed healthy doses of peace and affection, and even the creatures receded (which should've set off alarm bells). I was lulled into thinking that maybe I could enjoy a semi-normal existence. So when Max asked again what I'd been up to while he was gone, I decided to tell the truth as well as I could. "I ran a lot," I said, omitting that it had been from creatures, and added, "and I read a ton," thinking of the countless times I combed the notebook. "Also, I hung out with Doug almost every day."

Max nodded and asked, "What about your family?"

"Um, well, you know how summer is. People get busy," I said with a shrug. "It's like I didn't see them at all." He looked at me suspiciously, since it sounded like I was holding back information. I ran, read, hung out with Doug, and didn't see my family? That's it? The doubt in Max's eyes, the idea that he had even the slightest negative thought toward me, was scary. I stumbled past it, asking too loudly if Doug told him what the theme was this week in Classic Movie Club.

"He didn't mention it," Max said, avoiding my gaze.

I took his hand and squeezed it like he does to mine. "It doesn't matter," I said. "Whatever it is, as long as we're watching together, it will be great."

"Yeah. You're right," he said, looking at me with a grin in place. "Or if not great, then at least interesting," he added, "since Roger Ebert Jr. is in charge." I'd handed leadership of the Classic Movie Club to Doug this year (Doug, Max, and I were still, pathetically, its only members), and he'd proclaimed that we would view films based on themes of his choice, instituted at his whim. In the past, his obsessions shifted between actors, genres, and directors, but now they were based solely on finding my family—basically, everything we watched was research. Of course, Max didn't know this, and Doug would never give it away. Instead, he framed the series of three movies (the club normally met Monday, Wednesday and Friday) by theme. For the first week of school, it was "Disappearance." We watched *The Lady Vanishes* from 1938, *Frantic* from 1988, and finally *L'Avventura* from 1960.

The last one gave me pause, since it felt like real life.

Afterward, I looked in Doug's book, *The Great Movies,* and read Roger Ebert's quote about the film *L'Avventura,* in which a woman vanishes during a trip to an island, never to be seen again: "What we saw was a search without a conclusion, a disappearance without a solution."

Thinking about it caused a pang of anxiety, but it didn't affect me nearly as much as the Sausage King of Chicago.

The second week's theme was closer to home—"Chicago-centric." The first two were *Angels with Dirty Faces* and *The*

Untouchables, but it wasn't until Friday that I saw and heard something that rattled me. For years, when my family couldn't agree on a movie to watch, we would default to *Ferris Bueller's Day Off* since there are things in the film that appeal to each of us.

Lou's favorite part of the movie takes place in a fancy restaurant.

Ferris is trying to BS a maître d' into giving him a table by claiming to be someone he's not. The maître d', with his weasel mustache and puffy pompadour, looks at the reservation book, then at fresh-faced, teenaged Ferris, and the scene goes like this:

> MAÎTRE D': You're Abe Froman?
> FERRIS: That's right, I'm Abe Froman.
> MAÎTRE D': The Sausage King of Chicago?
> FERRIS: Uh, yeah, that's me.

I would ask Lou, but isn't it just lying—isn't he just a con man? My brother would shrug and say that a con man is a glorified thief, and Ferris doesn't steal anything; he borrows the alternate identity of Abe Froman, gets a great table, and pays for a delightful meal. It's all about having the self-confidence to take a risk and seize an opportunity. Afterward, whenever Lou encountered an act of bravado—a Cubs player committing a daring base steal or one of those stories where someone leaps onto the subway tracks to save a life—he'd murmur, "Abe Froman," and I'd know exactly what he meant. Sometimes, whether a chance pays off or not, it has to be taken, since the "taking" part is the whole transformative point.

My parents' favorite scene in the film couldn't be more different than Lou's.

It's a sappy song that makes them exchange a look as my dad caresses my mom's lovely long fingers.

The first time they met, my mom was working as a hand model at Marshall Field's, an improbable gig if there ever was one, but her natural beauty really did extend to her fingertips. It's an often-told story in my family—my mom displaying a diamond ring, my dad removing it from her hand, inspecting it, putting back on her finger and asking her to marry him. There are so many little details—what they wore, what they discussed, but the one that stuck with me was the song playing over the tinny department-store sound system. It was a pop tune from 1963 sung in a falsetto that I'd later be surprised to learn was sung by a man, and famously lip-synched by Ferris Bueller on a parade float.

The song is "Danke Schoen."

It means "thank you" in German.

When the scene appeared, my parents gazed at each other and sang along, while I tried to pretend that their nostalgia fest wasn't happening on the same couch. I didn't think much of it when Doug announced that we would be watching the film in Classic Movie Club. But first came Abe Froman and then "Danke Schoen," and I was overcome by that plummeting feeling, pulled over the edge by helpless sentiment and desperate love. And then anger took root and mushroomed in the muck, an organic wrath spreading through my brain and body. I thought about what Lou had told me at the Ferris wheel about my dad's brain being invaded by merciless captors, pictured my family being violated like lab rats, and the blue flame flickered. I was filled with the same preternatural calmness that stills the sky before lightning strikes, and when I blinked, blips of blue light from my eyes reflected in the dark. I gritted my teeth, trying to hold it back, and turned away so Max wouldn't see me, but it was impossible to stop thinking about my family. I was peppered with tiny sharp volts, and it was even more impossible not to picture my dad caressing my mom's hand as Max tenderly took mine in the dark.

I thought, *All of the love my family had for me is dead, while he has both of his parents plus a whole new family?* Showers of sparks turned the room orange and gold as I squeezed his hand as hard as I could and didn't let go, even after he stopped screaming. And then I was on the ground being smothered by Doug, shaking my shoulders so hard that my head danced on my neck. I wasn't sure where I was or what had happened until he shrieked, "Are you done now? Is it you again?"

"Doug . . . what . . . ? Where's Max?" I said, trying to sit up, feeling little electrical *clicks* and *zips* draining from my fingertips.

"There, on the floor!"

He was crumpled on his side, unconscious, with his hand raw and purple where I'd touched it. It was burned, not seriously but sure to be painful. I felt his pulse—it was steady—then lifted his head, touched his face, and whispered, "Max. Oh, Max . . ."

"What did he do to piss you off?" Doug hissed.

"Nothing!" I said, staring at Max's eyes, willing him to wake up. "It wasn't like with Teardrop when the thing was *trying* to kill me, or you when you were *trying* to make me mad! Something about the movie ignited cold fury, and then the electricity kicked in, and Max was just sort of there."

"You mean like a convenient target? You attacked him because he was nearby?" Doug said, gaping at me with awe and dread, shaking his head. "This is getting too dangerous. You could've hurt him a lot worse than a simple burn. You could've . . ."

"Don't say it," I muttered, as Max emitted a faraway groan.

"It's time you told him."

"Told him what?" I said, as Max's eyelids fluttered and he groaned again.

"Everything," Doug said. "Not just this electrical crap, but all of it, every detail. You can't be with him and not tell him. It's not fair. I mean, Christ, you just blew the guy out of a chair!"

"If he knew, he'd want to get involved," I said. "Or else he might . . ."

"Not want to be with you anymore?" He held my gaze, saying softly, "Sara Jane, did it ever occur to you that that might be the best thing for him?"

Once Doug said it aloud, I realized that the idea of Max being safer without me had been in my mind all along. The threats posed by my Outfit connections, ice cream creatures, and now this internal lightning storm easily made me the most dangerous girlfriend at Fep Prep. I'd missed him every second he was gone, but now it was undeniable that he'd been safer in California. Something whispered of sacrifice and responsibility—that the best thing would be to drive him away so none of the collateral damage that followed me like a shadow could ever harm him.

"Tell him!" Doug whispered.

"Shut up!" I hissed as Max muttered a few words, blinked his eyes, and stared around with huge, disoriented pupils.

"What . . . the hell . . . ?" he said, trying to stand up, stumbling backward and flexing his hand. "Ow! That stings."

We helped him into a chair as I said, "You probably don't remember what—"

"Yeah, I do. You shocked me. Sorry, you shocked the living shit out of me."

"It must have been some kind of electrical surge," Doug said, fake-fumbling with his laptop until the movie reappeared on the screen. "Yep, that's what it was. Crazy, huh? Max, are you okay? You need anything for your hand?"

"It looks worse than it feels," he said. "Maybe some water . . ."

"Water, right, I'm on it," Doug said, going for the door, looking back and mouthing the words "Tell him!" as he left.

He inspected my face, searching my eyes. "Are you okay?"

"Oh, yeah. Yeah, I got shocked a little bit but I'm fine."

Max was quiet a moment and then said, "I guess I don't mean from the surge or whatever it was. I mean, is everything okay between us? You sort of explained what you did all summer, but it feels like there's a lot more that you didn't. Did something happen while I was gone that you're not telling me?"

Ferris Bueller set off a tidal wave of loneliness and anger, which ignited cold fury, which somehow turned me into an electrical killing machine, which is not the sort of thing you tell someone you love and are terrified of scaring away. On the other hand, looking into Max's concerned eyes, knowing how smart and cool he was, I thought maybe Doug was right; maybe it was time to tell him the truth. I sighed, bit my lip, and said, "I'm not sure how to start, but it's basically a family issue."

"I knew it." He sighed.

"You did?"

"Look, I shouldn't have put them before you. I mean, going to California for the entire summer to be with my dad's family wasn't fair . . ."

"Oh. Well," I said, his misinterpretation a perfect excuse not to tell the truth. "I mean, yeah. I really missed you."

"So, look, you can tell me if . . .," he said, and paused. "Did you meet someone?"

"What? Max . . . ," I said, but I held back as it occurred to me that loneliness while he was in L.A. combined with a phantom "other guy" could serve as the perfect reason-excuse why I'd withheld information. In fact, it could explain much of my behavior—instead of a freakish organized-crime girl, I was just neglected, conflicted, and confused! Besides, people met other people every day and were attracted to other people all the time—surely Max and I could work through it, even though *it* was a fabrication. Something possessed me then, which seemed inspired at the moment but in retrospect was one of the stupidest things I've ever done. Before I could stop myself, I blurted, "His name is Tyler. He's older than we are. About to start college."

"Tyler," he said, trying out the name, and I could see that it hurt him to say it.

"It was just a flirtation, Max. He and I are . . ."

"Let me guess. Friends?"

"Something like that," I said, and the disappointment in his face scraped against my heart. I couldn't go back and tell the truth—with just a few idiotic sentences I'd taken it too far—and I fumbled, saying, "Our dads work together, so I see him now and then because of, you know, business. But it's nothing."

He nodded, looking at the ground. "No, you're wrong. It's something. I just have to figure out what," he said, running a hand through his hair. "Wait . . . is this payback for the Chloe thing?"

"What? Chloe . . . no. Can we just talk about it?"

"No, not now."

I touched his shoulder gently and said, "I know you want to talk to me."

"No . . . I . . . *don't!*" he barked, shaking me off, startling me with his tone. He shook his head and said, "Jesus . . . first you keep this thing from me, then I have to coax it out of you, and now you won't even let me think? Don't you see how effed up that is?"

I was quiet because he was right, it was, and I was. My mind was so twisted by habitually keeping secrets that I'd made one up that didn't even exist. There was no way to take it back without revealing I'd lied—that I was a liar—and so I awkwardly tried to hug him, but he pulled back and I banged into his hand. It was impossible to tell if his pained expression was from the burn or me. "Max," I said, "are you okay?"

He nodded slightly, dipped his head, and turned to leave.

I wanted to ask if he and I would be okay too, but I was scared of the answer.

He disappeared down the hallway then, opening and closing his hand slowly like a boxer headed toward the ring.

6

THE IDIOTIC COMMENTS I'D MADE ABOUT TYLER
were like bitter ashes in my mouth.

Even more disgusting was the frozen "treat" I consumed
(gagged on) hours later.

It was at the end of one of the longest and worst Fridays in
recent memory, when I'd electrocuted my boyfriend and possibly sabotaged our entire relationship. Max avoided me the rest
of the afternoon; within the crowded hallways full of chattering kids and their friends, being disconnected from him made
me feel like the walking dead. When the bell rang at three fifteen, I hurried out of Fep Prep to get to the El stop at Diversey
Avenue and back to the Bird Cage Club, failing to pay as close
attention to my surroundings as usual. If there was nothing I
could do about Max at the moment, at least I could dive back
into the notebook. Over the past several nights, I'd plowed
through the second half of it, searching *"Volta"* for clues, but
all it yielded was late-night despair. Each time a dark thought
crept into my head, it was accompanied by an image of Doug

plummeting after me, which was enough to make me sigh and turn back to the stubborn notebook.

"Sara *Jane*! For the *third* time!"

I'd been hustling toward the sidewalk in a fog; when I turned, Gina Pettagola was looking at me in her particular Gina way—arms (toned and tanned) crossed, eyebrows (precisely plucked) arched, head (showing off hair that shines in a way mine never will) tilted, with a bemused look on her face. Gina is always perfectly put together, a curvaceous little beauty barely five feet tall who, as Fep Prep's unequivocal queen of gossip, wields the power of an Amazon over the student body. We were best friends when we were little, and then semi-friends, and now just friendly. It's weird how you can have a history with someone and even like the person, but never think of her unless you need something. She needed something now and it could only be information. Her method of data extraction was never directly asking what she hoped to learn; instead, she started a benign conversation with the sort of opener that forced the other person to talk.

I didn't even have a chance to say hi before she said, "What's with your nose?"

I touched it, scared something was leaking. "What do you mean?"

"Forget it. I haven't seen you all summer. It's just . . ." She made a motion with her hands that seemed to indicate a balloon filling with air.

"Bigger?" I said weakly.

"More ethnic," she said with a wink. "Personally, I think an Italian nose is a beautiful thing."

"Yeah?" I said. "Then why did you have yours done?"

She moved closer quickly and whispered, "That was *only* to correct my sinuses! Besides, my sister had hers done at the same time. We got a deal. And that's *not* for public discussion."

"What do you want, Gina?"

"Nothing. Just a little girl talk."

"You know I suck at girl talk. What do you *really* want?"

"I was just curious . . . about Max."

"What about him?" I asked suspiciously, wondering if she'd somehow found out about our little electrical incident.

"Just . . . does he realize he's with someone so naturally gorgeous that she could get a crew cut and wear overalls and still turn heads?"

"I'm not gorgeous," I said, feeling a blush on my neck.

"Okay, you're not," Gina said, rolling her eyes. "Except that you are and somehow, magically, it manages to shine through a truly horrific wardrobe."

"You mean this?" I said, suddenly acutely aware of my ratty Cubs T-shirt, faded jeans from last year, and shredded Chuck Taylors. "It's comfortable, so . . ."

"Anyway, I was wondering about Max's opinion of what constitutes attractiveness and hotness, since you're so different from the women in his family."

"What are you talking about?" I said, confused, until it clicked. "Or should I ask, *who* are you talking about? You mean his cousin, Mandi Fishbaum, right?"

"What about her?" Gina said innocently, sliding on a pair of sunglasses.

"What do you mean, what about her?"

"I don't know, Sara Jane. You brought her up," she said, looking over my shoulder. As she did, a tinkling reached my ears along with Frank Sinatra's voice, and I turned slowly as Gina said, "Oh, yum! Mister Kreamy Kone!"

"No. No, Gina . . . ," I said, seeing the black truck creak to a stop at the curb.

As always there were kids everywhere after school, chattering in clusters, texting and hanging out, but I was the only one rigid with terror. That's because Mister Kreamy Kone trucks—or at least ice cream trucks in general—had been around forever. No one noticed them the way I did, but then, they were simply selling other kids ice cream; it was only *me* they were intent on capturing. Kids gathered around, feeding dollar bills into its side, making selections. It was like a sucker punch seeing it parked there, knowing something inside was staring at me with red eyes through darkened windows. "I . . . I have to go," I muttered, turning away.

"Oh, come on," she said, yanking me back. "I'm buying. We'll have a little ice cream and you can confirm or deny whether Mandi really had an abortion this summer, and if Walter J. Thurber was the donor."

"What? I don't know anything about that," I said as she dragged me down the steps. The truck revved its engine while kids ate and joked and howled with sticky crap smeared on their faces, and "Chicago" plunked loudly through the speakers. I planted my feet, Gina skidded to a stop, and I said, "Listen, really, I *have* to go."

"Okay, fine. But in my book, that's a confirm."

"No, look, I barely spoke to Max this summer," I said, instantly regretting my choice of words, knowing how scandalous it sounded to Gina's gossip-honed ears. Before she could reply, I said, "He was in California with his dad and now he's back. We're together and we're fine."

"Oh?" she said with a catlike grin. "You were in one state, he was in another, and you both remained completely loyal? Seems unbelievable and even a little unnatural, but maybe you can convince me with ice cream and some Mandi talk. Then again, if you *really* have to go, I can always ask around about you and Max." I knew what that meant. Even though Gina felt a certain loyalty toward me (I stepped in front of a bully and saved her from an epic ass-kicking when we were ten), she would still send out probing test balloons about me and Max—not lies or rumors, but loaded questions—to see what came floating back. Nothing would, but people talk (people *always* talk), some of it would reach Max, and hadn't I just stupidly planted the idea of Tyler? Of course, he would assume that Gina's speculation was partly legitimate. The truth was that he and I weren't fine, we were fragile, and I couldn't afford to further endanger our relationship.

"Okay," I said, reluctantly following her to the truck, knowing that there were too many witnesses around for whatever was behind the wheel to make a move. "But I have only a few minutes, and I really don't know anything."

"Everyone always thinks they don't know anything," Gina said, "until I get them talking. And then, magically, it turns out that they know *something*."

I can't tell you exactly what we discussed.

I know it had to do with Mandi and Walter and that I mainly listened and nodded.

My mind was on the truck, knowing it was there for me, my every move being tracked, and that it was biding its time.

Somehow half an hour passed as an ice cream treat Gina insisted on buying for me (optimistically called an Artesian Velvet Delight) melted in my hand. The truck didn't sell the pink-and-white soft serve; my guess was that the terrifying concoction was reserved exclusively for creatures. Still, the thing that slid out of the Mister Kreamy Kone truck looked like poison on a stick. I licked once, did the gagging-baby-bird thing as my puke reflex kicked in, and then held it politely while Gina prattled on. Her stream of insinuations and innuendo was limitless and hypnotic. When I looked around, the other kids had dispersed and it was only the two of us. Finally she dabbed at her lips, threw away the remnants of something gooey, and said, "You weren't kidding. You really don't know anything, do you?" Before I could answer, a car horn sounded, and she turned and waved at her mother. "Don't sweat it, by the way, about you and Max," she said. "I'm only interested in juicy stuff and you two are, well . . . you're juice-less."

"You mean we're normal."

"I mean you're boring," she said with a smile. "Do you need a ride home?"

I thought about it, how easy it would be to get in the car with Gina and her mom and make my escape. But then I remembered how deserted our house looked, and I couldn't ask for a ride into the Loop to the Currency Exchange Building—each of those things was fodder for major gossip. The prospect of remaining behind with the little black truck was terrifying, but when I turned, it was gone. I told Gina thanks but no thanks, she waved once and drove off, and then I was alone in front of Fep Prep. I wadded up the melted gunk in paper napkins and sprinted to the train. There was a garbage can outside the station door, and as I flung the mess into it, the ice cream's little wooden stick came loose and fell on the ground.

It was when I bent to pick it up that I saw the feet.

Unconsciously I slid the stick in my pocket, staring at glossy black boots.

Dark-blue pants rose above them and then a light-blue shirt beneath a thick bulletproof vest, and then a head framed by a perfectly fitted beard and police hat.

The face was smudged with flesh-colored makeup, covering its bleached skin and the cheekbone I'd crushed with a volt of inhuman power, while its bunchy clothing revealed only a thin edge of black uniform. Nothing could completely hide Teardrop's red eyes, but the cop sunglasses obscured them just enough from passersby. Stalking me outside Fep Prep, my sanctuary, had been alarming enough, but this was so much worse. It had disguised itself to confront me in broad daylight, aware of the attention it would draw, and equally aware that I wouldn't make a scene. The worst kind of fear coursed through my veins—daytime, out-in-the-open, nowhere-to-hide fear. The world honked, walked, and sped past, while I rose slowly, cursing myself for thinking the creatures' disappearance was anything but temporary.

It was obvious now that they'd pulled back in order to change their strategy.

Instead of chasing me through the city, they'd gone from macro pursuit to micro and added the element of disguise. To top it off, the pistol on Teardrop's hip looked as real to me as the murderous hatred radiating behind its sunglasses. It was the first time I'd been cornered without being encased in two tons of Lincoln Continental, with the steel briefcase and .45 on the seat beside me. I knew cold fury alone couldn't penetrate its eyes. Whether or not I was in control of the electricity, at least it was a weapon that could save my life, except that I had no idea how to summon it. As I rose, Teardrop laid a hand on the gun and said, "You will walk slowly. You will get into the truck."

I glanced past it at the vehicle parked down the block, looking to the world like an innocent ice cream truck, but to me, a one-way ticket to brain invasion. Stomp me, shoot me, twist my neck, whatever, but there was no damn way I was getting in there, and I said it. "There's no damn way."

"I thought so. That's why I brought you an incentive," Teardrop said, opening its hand to reveal something familiar, slender, and ghostly white against its black glove.

I touched at my neck, feeling the chain that hung there, searching for my mom's gold signet ring bearing the Rispoli *R* in diamonds that was attached to it. Words caught in my throat and I swallowed thickly. "It's not . . . you didn't cut off her . . ."

"Oh, how she screamed," it said. "And what lovely hands she has, or had, I should say. It doesn't count as a complete hand if it's missing a ring finger, does it?"

I tasted horror, inhaled violence, bit down hard on vengeance and revenge, but still the blue flame did not flicker, and I knew that for the moment, cold fury had been extinguished by hard truth. The idea that terrible harm loomed over my family had been a wildly motivational idea, spurring me on to constant, frenzied action, but also an abstract one—things *could* happen or *might* happen, but surely I'd prevail in time to stop them. Seeing a living part of my mother dead in the creature's hand was confirmation that terrible things *had* happened and were happening still. It was appalling and hideous, but far, far worse, it was real. In a blink of tortured silence, the creature took another step, and stood so close I could smell its vomit-sweet breath. "If you want to see the rest of her, all you have to do is get into the truck. She's waiting for you. Your whole family is waiting." Teardrop leered, showing rotten stumps and a slick, black tongue. *"En pedazos, pero a la espera* . . . in pieces, but waiting." I was frozen by the prospect, and Teardrop, seeing my defenselessness, extended a hand toward my arm.

I was not percolating with cold fury.

I was not humming with electricity.

All I possessed were the secrets of the notebook, and I remembered two of them now, one strapped to my ankle, the other around the corner.

I'd come across the first in the chapter titled *"Metodi"* ("Methods"), in a section that described in great detail the many varied ways to collect money from people who don't want to pay, or how to force them to give up secrets they won't confess. There are several terms for it—blackjack, slapjack—but my favorite was "sap," since a person had to be one to get to the point where someone else was about to hit him with a cylinder of heavy lead encased in leather. Mine was small, dangerous, and fit into the palm of my hand, and I'd taken to wearing it strapped to my ankle in case, well—just in case. In fact, I wore it so often I'd nearly forgotten it was there. "Wait!" I said loud enough for Teardrop to pause, "I want to tie my shoe," and dropped to one knee. It lunged for me, and I came up swinging the sap by its leather strap, cracking Teardrop across the hand. When the thing gasped in shock, I swung it again just as the notebook had instructed, directly on the elbow joint, hearing it slap and crunch in one fluid motion.

And then I was running for the second secret.

It was around the corner from the Diversey El stop, on Wolfram Street.

It was a place for dead people, and I couldn't get there fast enough.

Chapter five of the notebook is *"Sfuggire"* ("Escape"), which contains a list of all known Capone Doors in Chicago; I'd taken the precaution of memorizing locations close to Fep Prep. Strozcak's Bohemian Funeral Parlor on Wolfram Street, housed in a castlelike brownstone, had been an Outfit front business for decades. I sprinted through the station, out the back door, and jumped a fence as Teardrop galloped after me. I had a head start but knew it wouldn't last. The creature was determined to mete out punishment for drowning its friend before delivering me up to have my skull unscrewed. The funeral parlor was only a block from the El, with its peaked slate roof usually visible from the street—except today I saw no slate and no roof. Instead, a sign stood in front of the rubble of a building in the process of being torn down. It read COMING SOON, WOLFRAM MANOR LUXURY CONDOS! I knew that the Capone Door had been located in the basement, and I turned to see Teardrop flying up the sidewalk. Without hesitation I scrambled over the construction fence. The old brownstone looked like it had been hit by a tornado—the facade stood, and parts of the walls, but the roof was gone and mounds of bricks had been clawed free. I ripped away yellow warning tape, kicked open the front door, and ran into the shell of a building as warped wooden slats groaned ominously beneath me.

"Stop!" Teardrop shouted, and I turned to see it pointing the gun at me.

It took a step, the old floor creaked painfully, and the creature screeched as it disappeared before my eyes.

I turned for the door but the world splintered, and all that was beneath me was air as I fell into the basement.

When I blinked my eyes, everything was quiet and dark. I was bleeding on my back where shards of wood and rusty nails had torn at my flesh as I fell through the floor. In blazing pain, feeling like I'd been hit by a tractor, I pulled myself to one knee, squinting into the gloom, overcome by an alcoholic odor that felt gluey on the inside of my nose. I tried to stand but my ankle gave way, and I grabbed the edge of something cold and metallic to stop from falling. And then my eyes adjusted to the darkness and I saw that I was leaning on a steel table. There were drains at both ends from which yellowed hoses hung, stained by brown gunk. I'd kicked over a large jar of something milky that was pooling beneath my feet. I looked down at the label.

Formaldehyde.

It was the stuff used to embalm dead people.

I lifted my hand from the table, realizing it was where corpses were drained of bodily fluids and refilled with the preservative ooze.

I shuddered because it was so gross, and because it made perfect sense according to Outfit logic. An embalming room is the creepiest place in a funeral home (perhaps in the world) and the last place anyone chooses to go (except an embalmer), which made it the ideal place to hide a Capone Door. Disgusting junk is always left behind in old, abandoned buildings—worn-out couches, stained mattresses—but this was unusual, and unusually nauseating, and it was when I bent to puke that I saw the zephyr. It appeared in a tiny, swirling tornado made of dust from a hairline crack in the wall that was leaking air. I knew Teardrop was down here somewhere, and on cue, it groaned and thrashed violently, kicking over something heavy trying to get to its feet. I hobbled to the wall and scanned it desperately, seeing empty shelves, a corroded sink, and a crusty, peeling anatomical wall chart. Looking closer, I saw the outline of a human body crisscrossed by bloody red lines, showing how formaldehyde flowed through the circulatory system.

Each part was titled—heart, aorta, superior vena cava—

and it was when I saw the raised, metallic *C* in *cava* that my own heart leapt.

My finger was moving for it when a glass jar exploded above my head. I was covered in slime, and another just missed me when I ducked out of the way of Teardrop's missile. It was on the move, trying to brain me. The only thing slowing it were overturned tables and boxes of who knows what, and I jammed my finger against the *C*. The wall coughed and lifted, and I leaped into darkness, expecting to touch a platform or the top step of a staircase, but there was nothing. My fall through the floor had been painful but short, while this was a genuine plummet, a head-over-heels free fall, and I screamed, smelling the sewage below. I managed to shut my mouth and land on my back, hearing the sticky *splock!* as warm sludge washed over me. I got to my feet, hacking and spitting, and spotted the bones of an old, collapsed stairway. It had once connected to a walkway along the edge of the sewer, safely above the crud.

I looked up, seeing Teardrop looking down, trying to decide what to do.

I had no trouble deciding and clambered up to the walkway.

When I heard the *splock!* behind me, I knew the creature had made up its mind.

The walkway twisted, I felt my way around a corner, and a narrow, shadowy doorway appeared out of nowhere. It was just an indentation in the wall, easy to miss, and I stepped into it, hugging the wall. It was then that I noticed faded red letters stenciled in curlicues higher up on the brick:

The Catacomb Club
Buzz twice
Gents, kindly check your gats

There was no door below it, or at least I thought there wasn't
until I touched the wall and felt a wooden frame painted over
to blend in with the brick. Seconds later, Teardrop charged past
without seeing me. I glanced around the corner, scanning the
smooth, wet walls, seeing narrow catwalks leading to large,
screened air vents but no other way out. The disguised door
was my only chance. Carefully, trying to mute any noise, I
pushed a shoulder against it. There was a complaint of warped
wood, so I did it again and something splintered. I leaned with
all of my strength, sure it wouldn't open, but then by stubborn,
scraping inches it did. A sour exhalation blew over me as I
slipped inside. I remembered Tyler hinting at a story about the
Catacomb Club and Grandpa Enzo, which I'd pretended to be
aware of. At the moment, though, all I cared about was that
a speakeasy *always* had a secret exit, and I was determined to
find it. Squinting into grayness, I saw a bar on one side of the
vast room and moved toward it, groping air. My fingers grazed
a table and when I leaned on it for guidance, it rotated beneath
my touch.

Tic-tic-tic . . .

The noise was calibrated and cold, like the spinning chamber of a loaded pistol.

. . . tic-tic-tic-ic-ic-ic.

Until it stopped slowly, and the room was silent again. I bent toward the table, seeing a roulette wheel, the small white ball taking its final leap from black to red.

And then I saw a hand pushing money toward it.

I gasped and drew back, because its flesh was leather.

When I moved, my heels caught at a pile of something on the floor behind me, and I fell onto half of a human torso.

I babbled with terror, a whispered stream of "Oh God! Oh no! Oh please!" as I scuttled away like a crab, crushing something as brittle as kindling, seeing a desiccated leg beneath a sequined skirt. I was on my feet in a flash, stumbling past gambling tables and slot machines, and pressed against a wall, my heart tripping like a jackhammer. I moved my hand across cold plaster until I located a light switch, and with trembling fingers, I flipped it. First one, then another and another light fixture blew its old bulb to bits. Shielding my face with a forearm, I lowered it to see a lone fixture oozing light, turning the room a ghastly yellow, changing the mass of slumped shadows into corpses. I sucked back a scream, covering my mouth with the back of a hand at the sight of the brutal carnage. There were bodies everywhere, shot down where they'd stood or sat. Some, like the one I'd fallen on, had been ripped in two by bullets. Dried black blood pooled on green felt tables and tiled floors, spattering the walls like abstract art. I had no idea how long they'd been here, but with revulsion and sick curiosity, I noted that decomposition was at a point between mummy and skeleton. Generations of spiders had infested the scene, draping it in a stringy cloak of webbing. It was a mix of men and women dressed in the style of the fifties or sixties, and then I noticed something else.

Besides blood, cash was everywhere, in thick piles or scattered like blown leaves.

This was not a robbery gone wrong.

I was looking at the remains of a massacre.

My mind choked on so much murder, with one thought shouldering aside the rest: *Whoever did it left these people down here to rot.* It was a notion I'd pull apart later, but now my ear twitched at the scratch of footsteps. I ducked behind the bar, stifling a scream at coming nose-to-nose with a bartender missing half his skull, and carefully peeked over the top. At the front of the expansive room, near the main entrance, Teardrop's face glowed in murkiness like a beacon of death. He moved warily, looking for me but obviously taken aback by the butchery. From this viewpoint, I discerned the layout of the place—main entrance leading to gaming tables, which led to the bar (where I cowered) and a small stage at the rear of the room. Half the bodies were clustered at the front, but the rest had been cut down toward the back. Some had been trying so desperately to reach the rear of the room that they'd run right out of their shoes.

They were attempting, unsuccessfully, to escape.

There had to be an exit back there.

Nearly hugging the floor so Teardrop couldn't see me, I went down on all fours and crawled madly and silently toward the small stage. I passed by a hallway with no doors or windows, only an ancient cigarette machine; long ago, coins were fed into it and levers yanked as packs of smokes tumbled out. I rose, crouching in shadows, peering at one brand in particular, Carlyle Red, with a tiny raised *C.* I pulled the lever, cringing at the echoing *thunk!* as the machine swung aside, revealing a flight of stairs. Clawing cobwebs from my face, I ran up the steps, hearing Teardrop kicking over chairs and cadavers as he came after me. A door popped open at the top and I found myself on a narrow catwalk leading to a large, whooshing air vent. I lunged for the screen and grunted, ripping it free and lifting myself inside, when a steely hand closed around my ankle.

Teardrop hissed, "Got you, you smug little bi—" but didn't finish since I hammered its festering mouth with my other foot until it gurgled and let go. And then I was crawling rapidly through inches of smelly water. When I reached another round screen, I realized I wasn't inside an air vent but a drainpipe.

Those weren't screens—they were, like, poo filters.

I squinted through the filter in front of me and saw that the pipe on the other side flowed directly toward me, dribbling water. Behind me, I heard a slap and a splash, and I knew Teardrop was on the move. I yanked at the filter but it held tight, and that's when I saw two buttons on the other side of the screen—a red one marked "lock" and a green one marked "unlock." Of course they were on that side, since that's where the utility guys came from, and of course the filters were locked, to keep trespassers out and rats in. I tried to push the unlock button, but it was just out of reach, my fingers straining through the filter as Teardrop called out, *"Es el estremo de la linea, puta . . .* it's the end of the line. Time to meet Mister Kreamy Kone in person."

I thought, *Of course! Mister Kreamy Kone!*

I patted my pockets desperately and fished out the ice cream stick.

Squeezing it between my fingertips, I slid it through the filter and pushed the button. There was a *click* and a *pop,* and Teardrop crawled faster, panting with rage. I slammed my shoulder against the filter, dove through, and kicked it shut just as the red-eyed demon lunged. A quick punch to the lock button and it latched into place.

"No . . . no!" Teardrop howled, grappling at the filter, scraping it with sharp knuckles. It swallowed its rage, hissing, "Just wait. You're mine."

"I'm no one's," I said quietly, backing away.

The wall behind me was fit with metal rungs to climb in and out of the sewer. I went for the rungs as a rumble sounded from the pipe. It was followed by a noxious odor that made my stomach heave, and raw sewage rushed toward us. Teardrop heard it too, face pressed against the filter, gaping. "I'd close that ugly mouth if I were you," I said, climbing quickly away. A stream of stinking goop rolled beneath my feet and I paused to watch it bubble up as high as Teardrop's shoulders before subsiding. Trapped in muck, its eyes blazed up at me, but I was gone, rising toward a manhole cover. I pushed it aside and pulled myself into an alley, seeing the Biograph Theater across the street, which meant I was on

Lincoln Avenue. It was showing a vintage Humphrey Bogart film, its marquee glowing with the title *The Stick-Up*. It reminded me of my savior, the ice cream stick. I looked at it now, seeing words stamped on it that had once been covered by a frozen treat.

It read, *Find Mister Kreamy Kone on Friendbook!*

7

UNTIL YESTERDAY, I COULD ADJUST THE intensity of ghiaccio furioso but was unable to summon it. There had to be a perfect storm of emotion—intense hatred, love, or fear—in order for cold fury to kindle and flicker.

Not anymore.

Now I am its master.

Now I think of what was done to my mom's hand, the horrific pain and shock she must have suffered, and blink my eyes just once. The blue flame leaps at my command as I burn with fury, all the while remaining as cool and calm as a black-jack dealer. I'm possessed by a sense of power that I haven't known before, since cold fury was transitory, rolling in unbidden and blowing away like a hurricane. I lay in bed tingling with the new knowledge, then got up and looked at myself in the mirror. Slowly closing and opening my eyes, there was an internal, audible hum as my pupils went to pinpoints and the blueness deepened to cobalt. I'd never seen what they looked like while deploying cold fury since it normally ended almost as soon as it began, but now I saw what other people saw.

It was all of the loneliness that had ever existed since time began staring back at me.

It was abandonment and torture, humiliation and disease, rejection and death searching for a warm, pulsating place to infiltrate and infect.

My eyes were the nightmare mirrors of other men's souls.

I blinked and was myself again, except that the other Sara Jane—the one who disappeared before my eyes—was also me. Being able to control cold fury added a new dimension to my double life, and I wondered if I'd be able to control the electricity as well. All I knew for sure was that my current evolution had been induced by a trauma so disturbing that it had broken down whatever mental or emotional boundaries had existed and drawn cold fury to my fingertips—and there I was again, thinking about my poor mother's fingers.

And then my phone rang.

The clock on the table next to me glowed 5:03 a.m. I lifted the phone and Max whispered, "Hey, it's me . . ."

"Is everything okay? It's so early."

"I know, I'm sorry," he said, "but I've been thinking about us. And I need to show you something important."

"You mean now?"

"Yeah. If you're not too tired, I mean."

"No!" I said enthusiastically, a little too happy that he'd called me. I really wasn't tired since I'd gone to bed five hours earlier than usual. I'd returned to the Bird Cage Club the day before, stinking like the underbelly of Chicago after my sewer hide-and-seek, and left the Mister Kreamy Kone stick on Doug's laptop where he'd find it. I showered, still stunk, showered again, crawled into bed, and slid into a deep sleep before seven p.m. I was awake and alert as Max told me to meet him at the corner of Hermitage and Cortland in Bucktown. When I asked why, he said he'd answer my questions later and that time was of the essence. It's one of those terms—"time is of the essence"—that spurs people to action. I dressed quickly and tiptoed past Doug and Harry sleeping on the couch. Passing the control center, I saw a note Doug had left for me, scrawled in red pen on the back of a fast-food bag, with an arrow pointing at the ice cream stick:

Wait until you see what I found online!
Mister Kreamy Kone fans are freaks!
A hug from—
Doug

I bristled with curiosity and was tempted to wake him, but Max's admonition to hurry kept me moving; butterflies did backflips in my stomach as I rode down the elevator. Twenty minutes later, I pulled the Lincoln to a curb in Bucktown. Max was on the corner leaning on his motorcycle, his brown hair early-morning messy in a good way. He wore classic biker gear—jeans, boots, and a snug leather jacket; it would be warm by noon, but was chilly in the predawn darkness. I approached cautiously, wondering if he was going to break up with me here, on a deserted street. Instead, his frozen breath preceded his lips when he kissed me lightly.

"How do you feel about going to Italy this morning?" he asked.

"Uh, well . . . we have to be in school, remember?"

"It'll be a quick trip. Short but sweet. As long as you're not scared of angels."

"I have no idea what you're talking about."

"Great, that makes it even better." He grinned. His eyebrows rose in happy anticipation, and he nodded his head across the street, saying, "Follow me." We crossed over to an enormous old redbrick church so huge and imposing that it consumed an entire city block. A tower of scaffolding clung to the wall and rose into the sky. Max looked around and then gave the scaffold a hard shake, making sure it was secure. He grinned again and said, "They're repairing the brick. All the way to the roof."

"How high is the roof?"

Max shrugged. "Fifteen, sixteen stories, maybe. Are you okay with heights?"

I looked up, considering my safe haven on the twenty-seventh floor of the Currency Exchange Building on the one hand, and dangling from a hundred-and-fifty-foot-high Ferris wheel on the other. "Sometimes yes, sometimes no."

"It's completely safe," he said, drawing my gaze back to him. "Trust me."

I looked into his warm, open face, thinking not for the first time that he sometimes seemed too good to be true, but then I shook it off; it was my paranoid gut, trying to jinx me. I smiled back and said, "I do. Always."

And then we were climbing silently from pole to platform until Max said, "Be careful of his feet . . . her feet. Whatever, there's a pair up here." I looked past as he pulled himself onto the roof, and he was right—two large, snow-white feet were at the base of a tall body clad in drapes of alabaster robe, and behind them were a huge pair of folded wings. Max helped me onto the roof and I saw that the angel's arm extended toward me, offering another hand up. "There are twenty-six of them along the wall of the roof."

"Parapet," I mumbled, staring into the face of the giant winged creature.

"Each statue is nine feet tall, made of solid marble," Max said, "and they're all committed to protecting beautiful, dirty old Chicago."

The angel's delicate features transfixed me. It was definitely feminine, with the set of her jaw reflecting a fierce determination. Although my family had been casual when it came to attending mass, I knew the role of certain angels was that of guardian, existing solely to save humans from dangerous situations. Another concept I'd picked up during my (rare) trips to Sunday school was that the sins of a father were sometimes passed on to his children. It was impossible to deny that Great-Grandpa Nunzio's role as counselor-at-large for the bloody Chicago Outfit, passed on to Grandpa Enzo, my dad, and now me, was ultimately why my family was missing. I noticed then how familiar the look carved into the angel's eyes was, seeing it as a beatific reflection of my own in the mirror while deploying cold fury—part serenity, part end-of-days wrath. It seemed appropriate, considering that the angel was specifically created to protect and rescue all those fathers from their sins, and I thought, *Lady, I know how you feel.*

"Sara Jane," Max said, taking my hand, "follow me. It's almost time."

"For what?"

He smiled and took my hand. "Rome," he said, and led me around the massive tile and terra-cotta dome where two lawn chairs sat side by side.

I looked at them, at the thermos and cups between them, and a jelly jar holding a rose. "Max . . . for me?"

"We don't want to miss it," he said. "Sit." We eased into chairs and he poured two espressos. I sipped, watching him blow steam from a cup. He stared straight ahead and said, "Now . . . we wait." It seems like waiting is an element woven into our relationship—waiting to get together because of a divorce and a secret Chloe, because of a missing family and Outfit secrets. We're young and haven't been together long enough, and we both feel (thankfully) that the time isn't yet right to take the next big, scary romantic step, which means more waiting. And here we sat, side by side on a roof in the chilled semi-darkness, and I realized that there was no one in the world I'd rather wait with.

He pointed east. "Ready? Watch."

Far out over the snaking lanes of the Kennedy Expressway, traffic was just beginning to move like distant, tiny beetles, while farther beyond, an orange-pink aura glowed over Lake Michigan. The sun rose by the second, throwing back the blanket of darkness from the suddenly shimmering city and sending a wave of light rolling toward us. When it finally kissed the dew-covered dome, a veil of gold covered Max and me—we looked at each other incandescently—and he said, "It's just like Saint Peter's in Rome. This is the light of Italy, Sara Jane." It was the most beautiful moment of my life—literally a moment, since its luminescence faded almost as soon as it had begun. I closed my eyes, trying to absorb it before it faded—the peacefulness of the early morning roof, the guardian angels, the dome of gold with Max next to me—and I felt his hand pressing mine. This time there was no voltage, only warmth. I looked down at a medallion he'd placed in my palm. It was round steel with a raised blue *T* on one side and *Triumph* on the other, also in blue, the tail of the *R* underlining the word. Max said, "It's the logo from my motorcycle. You know, a Triumph. It's a vintage zipper pull from a biker jacket, like, from the 1950s. People wore them to look cool."

"It is . . . so cool," I said, turning the thick, quarter-sized metal in my hand.

He cleared his throat and moved a lock of hair from his face. "So it's my way of saying that I don't ever want to not . . . be with you." His cheeks colored at the tangle of words. "I mean, us being together is good . . . better than us not being together."

"Max, I totally agree."

He looked into my eyes, smiled a little, and his nerves evaporated. "Things have been so weird between us. And when you told me about the guy, Tyler . . ."

"I shouldn't have mentioned it. It was nothing," I said, regretting the heartache I'd caused. "Less than nothing."

"Really?" he said. "Because with you, Sara Jane, only you . . . the best way to say it is that you make me feel more like myself and less alone. You know what I mean?"

I understood then that he needed me as much as I needed him. Maybe it had to do with both of us feeling the void of our families—his dad in California, his mom dating "Gary the dentist," and Max somewhere in between. For me, it was the fact that since forever, my parents made Lou and me understand that they loved nothing in the world more than us simply because we existed. That love freed me to be who I am; without it, I felt the opposite of free, trapped in aloneness except when I'm with Max.

"I thought you could wear it next to your mom's ring," he said.

I touched at my neck and removed the chain holding the gold signet ring. I'd worn it there since Lou gave it to me on the Ferris wheel before he slipped away, back into the void of Chicago. The medallion felt cold and real in my hand; the *T* on one side and that word on the other, *Triumph,* seemed like a good omen. It was a symbol of feelings that were exclusively between us, just Max and me, and it suddenly seemed important that it stand alone. I removed the ring from the chain, put the medallion in its place, and slipped the ring on my index finger. It was then, hugging Max as hard as I could with my eyes squeezed shut, that I decided to trust him and tell him everything.

When I opened them, we were being watched.

I would have missed it if I'd blinked.

He was on the parapet, standing behind one of the angels, imitating its stance to remain unseen, until he moved an inch to get a better look.

I continued holding Max tight in order to watch who was watching us. It was a guy in filthy jeans, shredded hoodie, and beater boots, and when he moved again, I saw his face and stifled a gasp; it was nearly the same bleached tone as Teardrop's. His head had been violently shaved in a manner similar to Lou's when I'd seen him at the Ferris wheel, and he was thicker than the creatures—not quite as model-thin, but close. And then he shifted, revealing more of his face.

Even from that distance I could see the shocking contrast of one blue eye and the other glowing ice-cream-creature red.

I turned then, and he saw me move and leaped like a rabbit. Pushing away from Max, I sprinted across the roof, gawking over the edge. The street and sidewalks were empty. Then something moved on the apartment house across the street, where he scrabbled up the drainpipe. Max came up alongside me, saying, "What's wrong?" I kept my eyes on the opposite roof, seeing the guy hop away across building tops, and by the time Max looked in the same direction, he was gone. "Did you see something?"

I had, I just wasn't sure what until my paranoia answered— if the guy had something to do with the ice cream trucks, it was a blip of danger that just barely veered past Max. I swallowed hard, touched the medallion, and forced a smile. "It's just . . . this means so much to me. I was overwhelmed for a second because I feel the same way you do." He took me into his arms, and I looked over his shoulder at empty rooftops, my gut whispering how the guy had been a forewarning of something bad about to happen.

And then it did.

"So," Max said, "does this mean I can finally meet your parents and brother?"

I'd feared it was coming at some point. I may not have dated much before Max (understatement alert) but at least realized that not introducing him to my family meant that I was embarrassed to be with him. The statute of limitations had run out on my original excuse—they would've had to be on the longest cruise in history. For someone who tries to be prepared for every eventuality, I was caught flat-footed, and when I opened my mouth to lie, nothing came out. "I'll stop by your house any night this week that you choose," he said. "I'm inviting myself, and I won't take no for an answer. It's my fault I wasn't around all summer to meet them. It's way overdue."

Nodding dumbly, I realized that there was no realistic way to explain my vacant, locked-up house.

I was as cornered as I had been on the Wilson Avenue Bridge, except this time there was no escape.

8

THE DEEPER I SUBMERGE MYSELF INTO THE Outfit and the more I struggle with whom I'm becoming, the more I doubt that anyone lives one life with only a single identity.

No one is solely who she says she is or does only what she claims to do. In the Outfit, every front business has a back room where the real business is conducted, and a person's name on his driver's license is not the name he goes by on the street. Smiling Bill's Auto Barn, which sells steel-belted radials and snow tires on the showroom floor, also deals heroin out of the back, where Bill is not known to smile—ever—and is referred to by associates as "Willy the Needle." The customers of a beloved Greek diner known for its simple but tasty fare have no idea that Gus, its kind, elderly owner who hands out lollipops to their children, is one of the most notorious bookies in Chicago, "Greasy Thumb" Gus, taking illegal action from addicted gamblers on any sporting event in the world. And it's not just business owners. Police Detective O'Hara, twice decorated for heroism in the line of duty, has made so much money moonlighting as an enforcer for the Outfit that he was able to buy a cozy little weekend getaway in the Wisconsin Dells. His preferred method of enforcement is a lead pipe to the kneecap or elbow joint. Detective O'Hara has worked over so many bones, he's known as "the Chiropractor." It may seem like two-facedness is something to be endured only in high school—think of the super-popular cheerleader, envied by one and all, who suddenly kills herself or the straight-A honor student who deals weed—but the truth is that the potential for duality is alive in each human being.

I'm the perfect example.

From 8:15 a.m. until 3:30 p.m., I am Sara Jane Rispoli, Fep Prep junior.

During other more intense hours, I'm Sara Jane Rispoli, counselor-at-large.

Each time I preside over another sit-down between criminals, my brain grows more crowded with filthy, unwanted facts, and the more I become part of the Outfit. It's a line you hear in movies all the time—"She knew too much"—but it's true, I know far too much about far too many dangerous people. As I've progressed in the role, I've sat in judgment over conflicts about neighborhood prostitution borders, squabbles between drug dealers over contaminated cocaine, claims by extortionists, kidnappers, and gun-runners that they weren't paid enough—and then there are the endless altercations between Money, the vital branch of the Outfit run by Tyler Strozzini, and the equally pivotal Muscle, directed by old Knuckles Battuta. They despise one another even more than when I first met them, but neither division can operate without the other; the business model of the Outfit is to generate income by usury, coercion, intimidation, and violence (Muscle), and of course, those brutal enforcers have to be paid for their work (Money). In the end, no one in the Outfit ever wants to concede an inch, or compromise, or make peace, and without ghiaccio furioso, no one would. My use of cold fury in settling disputes is of utmost importance since it gets business back on track, allows tainted profits to keep rolling in, and keeps the Outfit alive. I hate every vile moment of my role, and my loathing of the organization grows with each decision I make.

The problem is, I'm good at it.

I have no idea how my great-grandpa, grandpa, or dad ran a sit-down. But by trial and error, I devised a method based on a combination of movie courtroom scenes, debate club, and the "I'm counting to three" form of discipline used by my parents on me and Lou when we were little, as in "I'm giving you until three to put away your toys. One . . . two . . ." with the third digit holding the threat of punishment. In my case, Outfit goons have come to understand that by "three," I'll have grown angry enough that my blue eyes will start blinking, followed by the swift deployment of cold fury. Sometimes, the risk that they will be emotionally paralyzed into making a concession is enough to start a reasonable dialogue. But more often than not, I have to show them their worst fears, the ones that wake them in the middle of night with the type of dread that feels like drowning in motor oil—lungs clogged, hearts about to detonate—and then I make the decision for them. Certain things in the Outfit are sacred—money, the veneration of Al Capone, money, more money, and the role of counselor-at-large. They don't like that I'm a woman, and sometimes I can feel their hatred of me—but without a Rispoli as counselor-at-large, there's no them, no Outfit. I help those shadow people to live their double lives, secretly and profitably.

As much as I'm convinced of Outfit alternate identities, I believe the phenomenon exists in the general population as well.

How else to explain what Doug discovered on Friend-book? What other explanation could there possibly be for the participants on the Mister Kreamy Kone fan page? It was the same day Max had taken me to Rome. Even as he'd asserted his right to meet my family (how in the world could I weasel my way out of that?), I'd been thinking about the note Doug had left me and what he'd discovered. I'd hurried back to the Bird Cage Club after leaving Max, but the only thing waiting for me was another one written in the same hurried scrawl:

Harry and I ran an errand. No peeking at my computer!

Kisses—

D. Stuffins,

at your service

By the time he and Harry returned, I was a sweaty mess. I'd been so impatient that I'd had to work off pent-up energy on the heavy bag. I was unwinding the wraps from my hands when Doug entered, pulled the silver ice cream cone from his pocket, held it to the light so it glinted, and said proudly, "La

Plata." I looked from his plump grin to Harry's dog smile, complete with little pointed tongue and wagging tail.

"Huh?" I said.

"The sixth-largest city in Argentina. Where this thing was made. It literally means 'silver,'" he said. "I took it down to Jeweler's Row and went store to store until some old guy who specializes in precious metals identified it." He turned it on his palm, showing the inside. "See the letters inscribed below the edge?" I squinted at a tiny L P, AR. "It stands for La Plata, Argentina. The city has a tradition of silversmithing or smithery, or whatever you call it."

I took it from him and inspected it. "So where does that leave us?"

"La Plata," he said with a shrug. "It's an Argentinian connection."

"Vague."

"At best," he said, and grinned. "So let's switch to specifics. How about a weirdo calling herself 'Ice Queen' who loves-loves-*loves* Mister Kreamy Kone!" He led me to his laptop, logged into Friendbook, and pulled up a page bearing a corporate logo—a glossy black ice cream truck with MISTER KREAMY KONE beneath it, and a wall filled with effusive commentary. There was nothing else on the page—no information about the company or its elusive whereabouts, no pictures of the freaky fans, and no further discussion. All it told me was that 1,686 people liked it, followed by lines of oddly glowing pronouncements about their beloved MKK— Mister Kreamy Kone. Reading on, I encountered words like *miraculous, unbelievable,* and *astonishing.*

"A little over the top about ice cream, aren't they?"

"Tell me about it. Check this out," Doug said, scrolling down the page, tracing his finger on words. "There's a phrase here, here, and here . . . it appears in a lot of the comments, right to the end."

I looked at where he was pointing. "'Life-saving'? It sounds more like a support group than a bunch of people who like ice cream."

"No one has to tell me about the commitment a junk-food junkie makes to his favorite shit. Munchitos and I have a very meaningful relationship," he said. "But these people are beyond that . . . the term *fetishistic* comes to mind. They actually get together just to eat ice cream. See?" and he pointed at the screen, which read:

MeltMyHeart: Calling all MKK fans—it's on! S-C Party next Fri. nite!

DoubleDip: It's about time! Ur a lifesaver! I need me some S-C!

SuperScooper: When/where? Can I bring newbies?

MeltMyHeart: All are welcome, especially new MKK recruits! 8:00 p.m. on the North Side, near . . .

"What's S-C?" I said.

Doug shrugged. "Seriously Crazy? These people are freaks, I tell you."

I stared at the address on the screen, knowing there could be a connection that would lead me to the Mister Kreamy Kone headquarters. "I have to go to that party," I murmured.

"Are you nuts? What if that mutant Teardrop is lurking around?" he said. "Nope, I already made up my mind. I'm going."

"I won't let you do that. It could be dangerous."

"Sara Jane," he said, swiveling in his chair, "I *need* to go. It's important that I'm a real part of this thing . . . a genuine help to you rather than the geek behind the screen. No one will even notice me. If these people are as into ice cream as they seem, I'll be just another fatty. And if there's something to learn, I'll pick it up. Trust me."

I looked at the earnestness in his eyes—basically, he was begging to put himself in harm's way for me. There was no way to refuse, and I said, "I do. I trust you, Doug."

"Fine, it's settled," he said. "Yay, I actually have plans for Friday night."

I did too—a sit-down with Knuckles Battuta and a pair of his thugs. The two animals had argued over the best method to beat a gambling debt out of a late-payer—one preferred a Brick Job, while the other insisted that tossing the guy down a flight of stairs would do—and the disagreement grew until guns were drawn. The bad blood between the two enforcers had continued to flow until it was time for me (and cold fury) to intervene. Knuckles demanded peaceful coexistence, which meant productivity, which meant profits—how could he be expected to earn if his own guys were pointing guns at each other instead of at mopes who owed the Outfit money?

The week flew past, and on Friday evening, Doug and I went our separate ways, him to the mysterious S-C Party, and me to the sit-down with Knuckles. He'd suggested Club Molasses as a meeting place, located deep beneath my family's bakery, which filled me with dread. I'd been purposely avoiding the place—seeing it so empty of life kick-started the type of depression I'd learned to avoid for my own mental well-being. In fact, I'd been careful to regularly update Knuckles on my dad's illness, telling him that it was even more serious than we'd known, and that the bakery would be closed indefinitely. I made sure to include relevant details—how my dad couldn't have visitors, how my mom was his sole caretaker, which was why she was never around, and how, besides school, Lou was always at my dad's bedside—weaving the kind of tale that would deflect suspicion.

Except it had the opposite effect.

Knuckles could not have succeeded to a ripe old age in the Outfit without being skeptical of everyone and everything, and I knew he harbored doubts about my story. My saving grace so far was that I'd done well as counselor-at-large. Business was booming, and it was strictly against generations of Outfit protocol to make problems when the money was flowing. Still, it was a myth that everyone in the Outfit watched one another's backs, like some kind of fraternal organization. The truth was that each hoodlum was loyal only to himself and his bank account. I wondered if he was testing me by insisting on Club Molasses for the sit-down. My own suspicion was a defensive skill that I, too, was developing as a member of the Outfit. Knuckles was teaching me by example that every crook had more than one motive.

And then he taught me something else.

I was waiting in the alley, dressed as usual for a sit-down in an outfit put together by Doug—black skirt and boots, white top, my dark hair pulled back. Doug's inspiration was Loretta from the film *Moonstruck,* who, as he reminded me, was "An Italian-American bookkeeper, beautiful but all about business, emotionally stunted by loss, with no time for love." I was thinking about that term *emotionally stunted* when I remembered Knuckles's Scamp—there was no way the huge old man would be able to fold himself and his motorized wheelchair into the Vulcan. When I discovered the small elevator hidden inside the bakery's industrial oven, even I had trouble fitting inside. Just then, his pink-and-blue van with BABYLAND—FOR YOUR PRECIOUS BUNDLE, WITHOUT SPENDING A BUNDLE emblazoned on the side rumbled to a stop. Knuckles unloaded himself, snapped a lighter, and put fire to a crusty cigar. "Let's get this show on the road," he said, and buzzed straight for the bakery's alley wall. For as long as I could remember, a metal box had been attached there, stamped with the ominous warning DANGER—LIVE ELECTRICAL CONNECTION—DO NOT TOUCH!, along with an image of a tiny person getting zapped. It was held fast by a rusty padlock. "Well?" he said. "Got the key?"

"Um . . . ," I said, pulling my dad's key ring from my pocket. It held keys to our house, the Lincoln, and the bakery—I'd never really looked at them all. Holding the ring now, I saw a small red one. "I think so."

"She thinks so," Knuckles said, shaking his massive head.

My grandpa and dad had warned me never to go near the metal box for fear of electrocution, and my hand shook as I inserted the key. Instead of a *flash-buzz,* it opened without incident. Inside was a button, which I pushed. A low rumble and squealing of chains sounded far away as a door-sized section of the wall began to rise, the bricks rolling back on themselves like the tracks of an army tank. Inside was an elevator car. A small chandelier made of crystal teardrops hung from the ceiling. The car was lined in tarnished brass and trimmed in the same cracked green leather as the club's bar. The wall bore a sign in golden script that read:

Club Molasses — One Story Down — Password Required

"Whoa . . . ," I murmured, and immediately regretted the amazed tone, as if seeing it for the first time, which I was. I tried to cover, adding, "That thing *really* needs oil! Squeaky!" but Knuckles looked at me with slits for eyes. He rolled inside and I followed, trying to act as if I rode concealed alley-vators every day.

"The box," he said, smoke leaking from his nostrils as he lifted bushy white eyebrows. "Maybe you should lock it?"

"Oh . . . right," I said, hurrying out and turning the key. When I stepped back inside, Knuckles inspected me suspiciously. I looked away, pushing the single button, and down we slid. The chandelier tinkled, flashing as we fell, and then the car shuddered to a stop, doors parted, and we stepped into a foyer. It was pure faded glory, from flocked, peeling wallpaper and worn, fancily patterned carpets to a velvet chair and couch covered in dust. Wall sconces were dark and cobwebbed from age. To the left was a hat-check stand, its sign tersely informing patrons that surrendering "Fedoras and Hardware" was strictly required by management. I looked past the sign to a long metal box sitting on the floor, the size of a small coffin, held tight by a huge padlock. Knuckles buzzed close in his Scamp and grinned with teeth as yellow as a corncob. "That's where the bouncer stored the Chicago Typewriters," he said. "But you knew that, yeah? Or maybe your old man never told you about it."

"Maybe," I said, trying to get past it. "Come on, let's get started with the—"

"Chicago Typewriters," he interrupted, "were the nickname for Thompson submachine guns . . . tommy guns, the weapon of choice for the Outfit in the good old days, when we blasted off thirty rounds to show who was boss. That's where the typewriter thing came from . . . the *clackety-clack* of bullets being the last noise some mope heard before he met his maker."

"Right. Now I remember."

"It's all coming back to you, huh? Everything your pop taught you before he got . . . sick?" Before I could respond, he nodded at a metal door leading into Club Molasses, with a slot just large enough to peer inside. In days gone by, a pair of suspicious eyes looked out at anyone who approached, waiting to hear a secret term that allowed entry. Knuckles grinned again, jack-o'-lantern style. "You know the password?" His tone was flatly disrespectful, and that was it, I'd had enough.

"Yeah, I know it. *Un stupido vecchio non può riconoscere la morte, ancho quando fissa lui nel fronte,*" I said, blinking once as the cold blue flame leaped furiously and I locked onto Knuckles's gaze. His face collapsed, and I saw his implacable fear of being cold, dead, and alone. On Doug's advice, I'd continued studying Italian—it was a solid emotional link to my parents, who'd promised me a trip to Italy if I graduated from Fep Prep with honors. Recently I'd delved into Italian proverbs, and that one had popped into my brain—"An old fool doesn't recognize death, even when it stares him in the face." I was staring at Knuckles now, and maybe he wasn't a complete fool, since he definitely recognized what we were both seeing. I said, "Old man, you will *never* ask me about my dad again. Do you understand?"

"Yes," he whispered, tears clouding his eyes.

"When you talk to anyone about him, me, or my family, it will be only in businesslike terms and respectful of the office of counselor-at-large. Understand?"

"Yes," he said in a desolate tone. "Oh God, yes! Please kid . . . *please* . . . !"

I blinked again, the flame subsided, and I recalled another proverb, *"Burrasca furiosa presto passa"* ("A furious storm passes quickly"). My command of cold fury—how fast I could make it come and go—amazed even me, and I prayed that I'd gain the same authority over the murderous electricity. When Knuckles gained control of himself, we pushed through the door into the club. The entrance was hidden inside the pyramid of molasses barrels stacked along the interior wall. My guess was that it had been the club's main entrance. The Vulcan was probably for Rispolis only.

Entering and exiting the club reminded me of Harry.

Only months earlier, the Italian greyhound blasted out of the Club Molasses gloom and attached his teeth to Poor Kevin's butt, saving me for the second time. I'd always wondered how he made his way down here. Besides the Vulcan and garage Capone Door, which accommodated the Ferrari, I'd suspected other secret ways in and out of the bakery existed, and now the alley-vator confirmed it. Still, as smart as Harry was, it wasn't possible the dog could've turned a key and pushed a button. There must've been yet another entrance, which led me to a further conclusion—Harry had to have been *shown* the way down here, and there was only person who would've done that.

My missing brother, Lou.

Had he known about Club Molasses?

As the only male Rispoli of our generation, was he told about my family's place in the Outfit? Did even Lou himself keep me in the dark?

The troubling thought that my little brother had a secret life and dual identity of his own was interrupted by a sharp *buzz!*—once, twice, and then a third time, the last a tiny *bz!*—as a red light flashed behind the bar. The brass beer taps were still in place, the top of one glowing crimson. Knuckles cleared his throat and looked at me cautiously. "Two long and one short . . . that's my guys buzzing from the alley to be let in. You . . . you gotta pull the beer tap handle to send the elevator.

But I'm *sure* you knew that," he said in a tone so deferential it was almost an apology. I looked at the flashing tap handle emblazoned with the words *Club Molasses Special.* A wire connected to it ran under the floorboards, and I thought, *So that's how customers entered the club. Of course they wouldn't have keys of their own.* I gave the tap handle a pull, the light stopped flashing, and soon afterward a pair of bent-nose guys entered the club, clearly despising each other.

What happened next was typical of that type of sit-down.

I perched on a tall stool, judge style, higher than those I presided over (borrowed from *A Few Good Men*), while each thug stated his respective grievance. After they'd fouled the air with every combination of expletive in regard to each other and the other's mother and pets, I called on Knuckles. The old man jabbed his smoking turd-cigar and barked how the *stupidaggine* was costing everyone money. And then I sighed, blinked once, and informed them in a cold and furious manner that their feud had come to an end. They shook and wept while hugging, pledging undying loyalty, courtesy, and every other genial thing I'd ordered into their psyches. Knuckles lingered after his guys had gone, saying, "I gotta talk to you about something, kid. Something serious. You're being whistled in."

I paused, wondering if I was being tested again, but I knew our little cold fury session had made a lasting impression. "What does that mean?"

Knuckles cleared his phlegmy throat. "You're being summoned by Lucky. He wants to talk to you. In person."

Lucky, the Boss of the Chicago Outfit, whose predecessors included "Scarface" Al Capone, Paul "the Waiter" Ricca, and Tony "Batters" Accardo, and who had to be as sly and deadly as those killers to hold the position. I had no idea what he looked like, how old he was, or where he lived, and that was all by design. After Capone went to prison in 1932, his successor, Frank "the Enforcer" Nitti, streamlined the Outfit along corporate lines, creating divisions (like Money and Muscle) and titled roles (like, of course, counselor-at-large) that helped it evolve into the efficient underworld entity it was today. More important, he devised a way to isolate the Boss (i.e., the CEO) within the dense, multilayered organization, protecting him from the prying eyes of the outside world and the jealous ambitions of the Outfit itself. The Boss is like a spider sitting unseen at the center of a massive web; by the time you figure out where he's hiding, he's off spinning new plans. As Boss, Lucky is impossible to find and even more impossible to refuse.

"Why does he want to talk to me?" I asked cautiously.

Knuckles shrugged his massive shoulders. "None of my business. It came down from on high is all I know." He narrowed his eyes and dropped his voice. "Your dad will tell you, but I'm gonna make the point too . . . *do not* use that Rispoli mumbo jumbo on Lucky. I've been around long enough to know he hates if someone tries to intimidate *him*. You stay on his good side because you need him on your side. If not, he'll give the order for my guys to take care of you."

I heard myself swallow hard. "Thanks for the warning."

"It ain't because I like you. It's because I need you," Knuckles said, handing over a sealed envelope addressed to me. With that, he touched his cap and buzzed for the exit. I opened it and removed a typewritten message (no incriminating handwriting samples), providing a date, time, and address. At the bottom, I noticed an additional line:

P.S. Bring three dozen molasses cookies.

I sighed, staring at the note. The Boss of the Outfit had not only whistled me in to an ominous sit-down, but also demanded a type of cookie I'd eaten thousands of times but never learned to bake. Sitting alone, deep beneath the bakery, I realized that what I required most at the moment was precisely what I'd needed since this whole tragedy-on-the-run began—my mom, dad, and brother.

And then, out of thin air, my family appeared.

9

I RAN FROM ICE CREAM CREATURES AND THEIR red, dead eyes.

I'd actively avoided the ghosts of the bakery.

But there was just no way I could've anticipated the living dead.

After the sit-down with Knuckles on Friday evening, I entered the darkened bakery to find the molasses cookie recipe. Showing up empty-handed would be suspicious; even if my dad were actually sick, he'd at least be able to tell someone how to make cookies. I folded myself into the Vulcan and whooshed earthward, the light flickering as I rose. I stepped into the white-tiled kitchen filled with shadows shifting through the skylight. The long baking tables stretched like empty runways while the round, three-legged mixing machine squatted in the corner, clean and quiet. The only noise was the low growl of the stainless steel refrigerator. I turned on a counter light and my eyes ran across rows of spiral-bound folders and age-creased cookbooks until I came to a spine with the hand-printed word *Biscotti*. I removed it, sat on a stool, and flipped the pages until I came to one that read:

Biscotti di Melassa—Molasses Cookies

Una ricetta di Ottorina Rispoli—A recipe by Ottorina Rispoli

The recipe was my great-grandmother's, but the molasses had come from Nunzio. He imported it into Chicago during Prohibition, to be distilled into illegal alcohol, with Ottorina appropriating enough to make amazing cookies. The Rispoli *biscotto melassa* was known throughout the neighborhood and beyond as one of the finest pastries in town. In the solitude of the kitchen, I traced my finger down the instructions, reading:

In a large bowl, cream together shortening and sugar until smooth, and . . .

Somewhere, metal rattled against glass.

Beat in eggs one at a time, and then stir in molasses. Next . . .

It was more insistent now, violating the refrigerator's hum.

Combine cinnamon, allspice, and ginger into the molasses mixture until . . .

I heard muttering voices, closed the book slowly, and rose without breathing. The rattle sounded again, followed by muffled words, and I peeked into the front of the bakery. The display cases crouched in nighttime gloom, the brass cash register yawned with its drawer open. A section of the paper I'd used to block out the windows had come loose and folded back on itself, but the front door was covered, and behind it was the silhouette of a person on the sidewalk—no, three people. It was nine p.m., the bakery was obviously closed, but they wanted inside, and my gut told me to find something blunt to persuade them otherwise. I reached for a rolling pin,

feeling its heft, and then thought of one of my favorite movies, *Pulp Fiction,* remembering how Butch prepared to descend
into the freak-infested basement. I put it down and lifted a
large pot by its handle, the thing heavy enough to crush a
skull. And then it occurred to me that three against one required something more lethal. I grabbed the biggest knife in
the kitchen, one that could split a melon with a single whack,
and slid around the corner.

The handle of the locked door rattled again.

A human outline moved to the window where the paper
fell open and a shaft of street light shined inside the bakery.

My dead grandpa Enzo peered inside, waving when he saw
my startled face, and I dropped the knife, nearly losing a toe.

It couldn't be—it wasn't possible. Yet there he stood, smiling now, tapping the glass—and I realized that unless tou-
pees were being handed out in heaven, it wasn't him. My
grandpa had a fringe of fuzz that encircled his tan, bald skull
while the alternate-universe grandpa had a full head of wavy
white hair as thick as shag carpeting. And even from across
the dim room I could see he was missing Grandpa Enzo's
most distinctive feature—piercing, Rispoli-blue eyes. This
little old man blinked at me with a pair that was decidedly
brown. My gut blared with warning sirens but I couldn't ignore him—he looked too much like my grandpa. I crossed
the floor, unlocked the door, and stood back as he entered,
looking around in wonderment as if entering the Sistine
Chapel. His gaze moved to mine, his face stretched in a sad
smile, and tears filled his eyes as he said, "I'm home." And
then he was hugging me. His little body felt like Grandpa

Enzo's. It had been so long since I'd embraced anyone in my family that I couldn't help myself—I hugged back, trying not to cry at the deep, needful sensation of it. We separated, but he held my arms and sniffled, saying, "Who are you?"

"I . . . I'm Sara Jane . . . Rispoli."

His eyes searched mine, pleased but confused. He turned toward the people behind him and I did a double-take at the one nearest us. As much as the old man looked like my grandpa, the middle-aged woman bore a haunting resemblance to Uncle Buddy. She was as short and thick, and her eyes, also brown, glowed with the same warmth that had animated my uncle's before he became obsessed with the notebook and its promise of ultimate power. She wore a scarf around her neck, almost to her chin, and turned to the old man, moving her fingers nimbly, communicating in sign language. When she finished, he looked at me and said, "Of course. Anthony's daughter . . . my brother's granddaughter." He drew me into another hug, where I stood limp and confused. "I'm your great-uncle, my dear. I'm Uncle Jack."

My mind reeled backward, mentally flipping through pages of the notebook until I arrived at the chapter entitled *"Nostro"* ("Us"). Inside is a section called *"La storia della famiglia Rispoli è la storia del Outfit a Chicago"* ("The story of the Rispoli family is the story of the Outfit in Chicago"). I remembered an obscure footnote, how Great-Grandpa Nunzio named the bakery Rispoli & Sons, plural, because Grandpa Enzo had a younger brother whose name and fate weren't recorded. And who, obviously, was hugging me now. He thumbed at his eyes, gestured at the Uncle Buddy look-alike, and said, "My daughter, Annabelle." She moved forward without hesitation and I was engulfed in her embrace, actually delighting in it since she smelled like tart lemon meringue and a fresh tray of brownies. Annabelle let me go with a cheek-pinch, and then tapped Uncle Jack's shoulder. "Of course," he said, sweeping his arm theatrically at the third person, saying, "Sara Jane, meet Annabelle's daughter, my granddaughter, and your cousin . . . Heather."

She stepped forward, extended a hand as gracefully as a deer, and said, "Hey."

I took it, feeling incredibly homely, and said, "Hey."

Even an entirely new word, some hybrid of *beautiful, blonde, bronzed,* and *booby* (*booblonzooby?*) couldn't adequately describe her appearance. Her face was perfectly smooth, proportional, and shimmering, as if it had been freshly clipped from *Vogue* magazine. She was tall, thin, *and* curvy, with a spray of freckles like a field of daisies decorating a nose so buttonlike, you wanted to push it and say "boop." Her large, wide-set eyes were the type of deep green seen at a Caribbean seashore on a sunny day; it required a force of will not to swoon while gazing into them. All in all, Heather looked as if she were composed of all of the best parts of the thousands of models and starlets that populate the public's collective consciousness.

There's a phenomenon among girls where we can be in awe of another girl's gorgeousness without it being sexual; instead, it's a deep understanding that in this world, largely ruled by the politics of physical beauty, she is a powerful being. It's unfair but true, and in general, society does little to discourage it. Hair must be highlighted, lips must be glossed, jeans must be tight, all of which, to me, seems like it should be optional and personal rather than mandatory. I'd just met Heather; I didn't know anything about her other than what I could see. But after months of searching every strange face for even the flicker of a threat, my ability to take the measure of a person was razor-sharp. What I saw looking back was some-one who was aware of the power she possessed. It didn't make her good or bad, but it did arm her with a strong weapon, which put me on guard. And then there was the fact that she was at least partly Rispoli. I wondered what she knew—what *all* of them knew—especially the man who'd grown up with Nunzio "Blue Eyes" for a father and Enzo "the Baker" as a brother.

That's when Uncle Jack started talking.

A half hour later we moved to the kitchen, where I made coffee.

When he finished at midnight, it was clear that he'd forgot-ten more than he knew, and he was forgetting more each day.

For example, he recalled that he was eighty-one years old and had been born Giaccomo Rispoli, but he had forgotten his own mother's maiden name. He realized that he was in the secondary stage of Alzheimer's disease and took his medica-tion (something called Remembra) regularly, trying to hold it off as long as possible, but he was aware that it was growing rapidly worse. What he hadn't known, and what I broke to him gently, was that Grandpa Enzo had died, the surprise on his face shifting to grief. "We used to write regularly. I think I received a letter from him only last year. Or maybe the year before," he said. "There are so many things I haven't thought of in such a long time." He described the function of his mind as a TV constantly changing channels; while his awareness of the present was fairly stable, words and images from the past appeared with crystal clarity for only minutes before flipping away, replaced by other distant scenes. Sometimes, even worse, it was all replaced by nothing but static.

Memories of his long career in show business were more intact than the rest.

He explained how he'd gone to Hollywood in 1956, trading his identity of Giaccomo Rispoli for Jack Richards.

His specialty was TV, where he was known as "the A Plus of B-List Actors."

Over the years, in hundreds of shows, he played lawyers who lost the case, doctors who broke the bad news, and ex-husbands who saw the kids only on weekends. His were never the starring roles, but the smaller, forgettable ones necessary to a story. His big break came in the seventies on a show called *City on the Make.* It was set in an unnamed metropolis where a tough, squeaky-clean police lieutenant was dedicated to ridding the town of a criminal group called the Organization.

Uncle Jack didn't play the lieutenant.

Instead, he played the lieutenant's sidekick, Detective Ned Keegan, an alcoholic bookworm-cop with all the relevant data at his fingertips, along with a glass of whiskey. He supplied the facts, usually drunkenly, while the hero lieutenant kicked down doors. The old man scratched his lustrous head and said, "It's all mixed up now. I can't remember what's real and what got stuck in my brain from that damn TV show." I waited for him to at least hint at our family's place in the Outfit, but instead he just sighed. "That's why I came back to Chicago. I wanted to see Enzo once more before I'm completely unable to . . ." He paused as his eyes grew wet. "Most of my childhood memories are gone, wiped away by time and disease. Only my brother remained. It was Annabelle's idea—my dear daughter, without whom I'd be lost—to make the trek from L.A. to see Enzo. I wanted to surprise him." Annabelle drew his attention, speaking with her hands, and I could see he was having trouble following her.

"My mom's wondering why the bakery is closed," Heather said. She was sitting on a metal table, sipping coffee, and smiled brightly when I turned to her. "He's starting to forget sign language. I'm the communication conduit between them sometimes. After all . . . being useful and engaged is vital to sustained inner strength," she said, as if reciting a mantra. "It's a rehab theory. And rehab is *very* L.A."

Before I could ask what she meant, Uncle Jack massaged his forehead and said, "The oven there. I'd swear Enzo and I played inside it when we were boys. But who would play inside an oven? It must be from a TV show. I can't recall . . ."

Annabelle moved her hands and then put her arm around him as Heather said, "Mom's right, Grandpa. Don't worry about it. It's been a long day." She lifted the coffee mug toward me. "So . . . fill us in on your family."

They didn't seem to know any more about my parents, Lou, and me than what Grandpa Enzo must've related in letters—generalities and anecdotes, but nothing about the Outfit. I wondered then if my dad had known that Uncle Jack and his family existed. Grandpa Enzo's brother was mentioned in the notebook but maybe my dad never noticed it. Or maybe my grandpa brushed it off like one of those past-generation things, where people didn't discuss sensitive matters; after all, burying secrets was a congenital trait in my family. I didn't see the risk in telling the same old lie, but with a twist to explain my dad's prolonged absence. I said he was ill but stable and that my mom had taken him to New York to be treated by specialists. After satisfying their concerned questions about him with a stream of bold-faced whoppers (my easy ability to BS amazed even me), I finished by saying that Lou was at boarding school and I was here, attending Fep Prep.

"Sixteen and home alone?" Heather asked, arching a perfect eyebrow.

"Mature for my age and staying with friends. We locked up our house and closed down the bakery until my parents return," I said, telling the semi-truth.

"Wow," Heather said dreamily. "I can't even describe the party that would've happened if I'd ever been left alone for a month. Kids from the valley to the hills would *still* be wasted and *still* be talking about me." Annabelle's eyes narrowed and her fingers danced as Heather raised her hands. "Relax, Mom. I was talking about the past, not the sober present. No worries, no parties, okay?" She glanced at the wall clock. "By the way, Grandpa's Remembra is overdue." Annabelle made an "uh-oh" face, rummaging through a purse and coming up with a prescription bottle. Heather nodded at the back door. "Alley?"

"Yeah."

"Smoke break," she said. "He has to take three ginormous pills, baby-bird style. Gagging, snorting . . . it's not pretty. Join me?"

I looked at Annabelle shaking out marble-sized capsules, at Uncle Jack's fretful expression, and said, "Sure." We pushed into the cool night air, the streetlights dropping puddles of illumination. The Lincoln was where I'd left it, and I said, "That's mine."

"Cool. When did you get your license?"

"Um, well, I've been driving for a while," I said, wondering if I'd ever get one.

"Vintage '65 Continental ragtop with those cool old doors that open out, like a barn . . . what are they called?"

"Suicide doors," I said.

"Right, suicide," she said, tapping a cigarette from a pack. "*Very* L.A." She lit it, looking at the shredded top, at the bumps and dents I'd accumulated while chasing or being chased, and exhaled smoke. "DUI?" she asked.

"Who, me? No, I don't drink. It was just, you know, an accident here and there."

"Looks like my handiwork."

"You've had one? A DUI?"

"I wish it were just one," she said with a smirk. "I have what is known as a 'chemical reliance issue.' 'Alcoholic' or 'junkie' is probably more accurate, but negative terminology was prohibited at Rancho Salud." She tapped an ash from the cigarette. "You want one?"

"I don't smoke either," I said, knowing it could kill me, but still feeling like a total geek seeing how sultry she looked as a feathery plume leaked from her nostrils.

"Good for you. I'll quit someday, and then I'll never have another bad habit . . . well, never say never." She winked and told me about her latest stint in rehab dealing with a coke habit that had gotten her arrested three times in three years. "DUIs—deweys—are *very* L.A. Angelenos live in their cars." She'd missed the end of her senior year of high school and would have to re-enroll or get a GED, but it was worth it— at age seventeen, she was clean for the first time in years. When she was released from rehab, her mom and grandpa announced they were traveling to Chicago; Annabelle was determined to keep a constant eye on her. "My mom blames herself for my problems," she said. "But really, it started with *Two Cool for School.*"

"You mean the TV show?"

"Yeah," she said, flashing a smile that was both sweet and seductive. "I was the original Becky."

"I knew I'd seen you somewhere!" I said, thinking of the show that had been a mainstay of my tween years. It chronicled the romantic middle school adventures of bubbly fraternal twins (the "two" in the title) Justin and Justine. The cast included every TV stereotype—skinny nerd, Asian brainiac, black rapper, cynic in a wheelchair, and of course, Becky, the evil blond temptress who constantly got between Justin and his girlfriend, or Justine and her boyfriend. Heather's dad had been the ultimate stage parent, ushering her into commercials when she was tiny, accompanying her to auditions as she grew, with her mom reluctantly going along. "She was against show business?" I asked.

Heather nodded. "She grew up in it, with my grandpa playing Detective Keegan, and despised it. Her opinion is that being an actor gives a person free rein to slip inside other personalities and behave badly. But my dad won the argument because he was, like, super domineering. To quote the Rancho Salud handbook, he's a 'Self-First' personality. Supposedly he was building my career, but really it was all about him," she said with a weary grin. "Oh God, we just met . . . is this TMI?"

"What?" I said, fascinated. "Uh, no. Unless you don't want to talk about it."

"Addicts *love* to talk about themselves. Especially celebrity addicts. Daytime TV couldn't exist without us," she said, and she told me how her dad wrangled an audition that landed her the role of Becky. "The problem is that there's no such thing as being a kid in show biz. You grow up too fast, learning stuff you shouldn't."

"Yeah. I know what you mean."

"The more successful you are, the more you're treated like an adult. But you're not." She sighed. "So anyway, there was this producer on the show, smart, good looking, in his twenties. And so nice to me in a way my dad wasn't . . . complimentary, a little conspiratorial. We'd whisper together, making fun of the other actors. You can probably guess where this is going."

"Um . . . I think so," I said carefully.

"And it almost did . . . *happen,* I mean. I was terrified, with no idea what he was trying to do until the last minute, and then I screamed bloody murder. Seriously, I rattled the Hollywood sign. He ran in one direction, and I ran in the other. The perv quit the show a few days later, with no repercussions."

"What did your parents do?"

"Parent, singular . . . of course I told my dad first, he was my manager. In typical father-of-the-year fashion, he responded with three commands. First, don't rock the boat by making a big deal out of something that didn't *quite* happen." She smirked. "By that time, the show was huge, and I was its rising star . . . magazine covers, websites devoted to Becky's bitchdom, amazing money. The second command . . . do not tell my mom because it would upset her, and if I did, he'd be super angry with me."

"That sucks."

"I know it now, but then?" she said, looking past me. "Then, I would do almost anything not to disappoint my dad. It wasn't fear as much as, like, lowering my value in his eyes. It's hard to describe. It seems like a long time ago."

"What was the third thing?"

"Hmm?" Heather said, almost surprised to see me. "Oh. The third command was the worst. He told me, a fourteen-year-old, that instead of whining about what happened, I needed to find a way to deal with it. And, oh baby, did I. All the fan, media, and network attention lavished on a kid in a number one show . . . I dove into it headfirst. Adulation was my first, best drug. It's pure freedom. You can do anything, and I did, drinking and smoking weed on the set because I could. So I went on this awards show completely loaded, barely able to stand, and as I was about to receive the best-little-bitch-on-TV trophy, I vomited on the entire front row of the audience. Until then, the network brushed off the drug gossip about me—the show biz rule is deny, deny, deny—but my puke-a-thon happened on live television. So that was it. Career over."

"Do you miss it?"

"Any former star who says she doesn't is a liar." She blew smoke in the air and said, "It wasn't losing my job that caused me to crash and burn, though. After I got fired, my dad totally lost interest in me. He said that from an industry standpoint, not only was I damaged goods but I was also past my prime." She chuckled bitterly. "I'd just turned fifteen."

It was beyond the realm of imagination that my own dad would ever do anything so hurtful and twisted, and before I could stop myself, I said, "He sounds like a total dick."

"That's an understatement. It wasn't just me, either . . . he did a number on my mom too. The more he ignored me and the more I got wasted, the more she defended me. We're very democratic about guilt in my family—we all blame each other for everything. That's exactly what my parents did until it became a divorce. It was so sudden, like, one day he's my manager and dad, and the next it was 'See ya . . . marrying someone else, starting a new family . . . later!' I'm sure he's got big plans for my little half sister. She's pretty and blond, perfect for TV. I should know." She shrugged gorgeously and said, "Oh well. He'll screw her life up too. Anyway, if I was a runaway drug train before the divorce, afterward I was a tornado of self-medicating destruction. If my mom hadn't tossed me into rehab, I would've been a dead fifteen-year-old. Not that I didn't try my best at sixteen and seventeen too."

"All of a sudden a new Becky appeared on the show," I said. "There was something in the news about the old Becky suffering from exhaustion."

Heather snorted, shaking her head. "They didn't even change the name. Just stuck in a new blond girl. Makes sense, I guess. There are millions of pretty little actresses in Hollywood programmed to be the new Becky. The producers picked one from the crowd, gave her my dressing room, and kicked me out the door. Oh well . . . if there's one thing adults are good at, it's screwing over kids." She flicked away the cigarette, put on a diamondlike smile, and said, "So. What's your tragedy?"

It was a small, amazing moment, as her chin tilted and her eyes scrunched, and I saw that within her blond sumptuousness, she really was a Rispoli. There was humor in her question, but also the empathy of a person who had endured trauma. Our life experiences could not have been more different, but Heather and I seemed to share a strong family trait—we were survivors—and I felt the tendrils of bond sprout between us. Quietly, I said, "It's almost impossible to describe."

"So you do have one, huh? I knew it. Not that you're tragic by any means, but after being in and out of rehab"—she shrugged—"I can sense a vibe."

"As stories go, mine's pretty complicated."

"The ones worth telling usually are."

"Some other time."

"Anytime." She grinned. "I might seem like a talker, but I'm a better listener. Plus, it's like my mom always says—sorry, signs—there's nothing in the world that hasn't happened to someone."

I thought for a moment and then heard myself say, "Why can't she speak?"

"My mom? It happened when she was a kid. Boring family anecdote." Her tone thickened a little with regret. "I've caused her a lot of grief. She's never been as happy as she deserves to be. As they say at Rancho Salud, it's time to make a deposit in the old love bank, rather than a withdrawal."

"She seems really sweet."

"That's the perfect word for her, for a lot of reasons," she said. "Like, for example, she possesses a trait that must be in Rispoli DNA."

"She does?" I said warily.

Heather nodded. "She's in the family business."

"She is?"

"And she's good at it too. She's been a pastry chef for years. Weird, huh?"

"Weird," I murmured, relieved but suspicious. "Can I ask you a question?"

"Okay."

"Speaking of the family business, did you ever hear your grandpa talk about it? Before he got sick, I mean. What the bakery was like when he was young?"

She shook her head. "If he did, I wasn't listening. Old stuff has never interested me very much. It doesn't have a lot to do with the here and now, you know?"

"How about your mom? Did he ever talk to her about it?"

Heather arched her eyebrow again. "Why?"

"History," I said. "I'm into it. Especially family history."

Heather leaned in, speaking quietly. "Don't tell her I told you because she's embarrassed by it, but Detective Keegan's alcoholism wasn't all TV fiction. Back in the day, my grandpa had a substance abuse problem of his own . . . another family trait, I guess. She told me once that whenever she'd ask about the past, he'd refuse to discuss it and immediately start drinking. All he ever told her was about a brother in Chicago who ran the family bakery with a family of his own."

On cue, the back door opened and Annabelle gestured us inside. She was excited about something, and while Heather watched her hands, Uncle Jack approached looking tired and old but hopeful. "We have a proposal, my dear," he said.

Heather said, "Absolutely not," and when I turned, she didn't look hopeful in the least. Her brow was lined and her arms crossed, and even pouting she was sexy. "No," she said to Annabelle, "I don't want to." Her mom's hands moved, and Heather issued an Oscar-worthy sigh. "I know. Rancho Salud lesson number one . . . everything's not about *me*." She flicked her gaze in my direction. "They want to stay."

I looked past her at a wall clock. "Uh, well . . . it's pretty late."

"I mean here, in Chicago. They want to work in the bakery."

"I don't understand . . ."

"My grandpa thinks if he's here while the place is up and running, it'll help him remember his childhood. My mom will do the baking . . . cookies and simple stuff. They won't open it, like for customers. It'll be only us, the family, like therapy." Annabelle's hands moved but Heather shook her head before her mom even stopped signing.

"That's all she said?" I asked.

"She also wants me to enroll in school so I can graduate. Your high school, what's it called . . . Fep Prep?" She inspected a cuticle and said, "Not gonna happen."

"I'm desperate, my dear," Uncle Jack said, drawing my attention. "I have an overwhelming sense that there are things I need to remember about my family . . . *important* things, and that they're here in the bakery, buried beneath the years."

"I . . . I don't know," I said, my mind clicking with negative possibilities. What if they accidentally discovered Club Molasses? What if someone spotted them through the windows and asked unanswerable questions about my family? And then there was the Outfit—what if some thug noticed the bakery was operational, and that Anthony Rispoli was *still* nowhere to be seen? The risk was too great, and I said, "I'm sorry, but . . ."

"Uh-uh. I know that you have to talk to your parents. You call me tomorrow," he said, scribbling on a scrap of paper and handing it to me. "I'm proud to say that I can still remember my cell phone number. I put down the name of our hotel as well."

"Really, there's just no way . . . ," I said, glancing at the paper, which read:

thedaleyhotelonoakstreetunclejackscellphonenumberis . . .

In the same scrunched-together scrawl as *"Volta."* It was in English, of course, but the handwriting was identical; I'd puzzled over those maddening letters so often that I could identify them in my sleep. With a combination of shock and excitement, I realized that in the distant past, Uncle Jack—young Giaccomo Rispoli—had written the final and most crucially important chapter of the notebook. I don't know how he did it or why, but it was doubtless that he'd hidden the secret of *potenza ultima*—ultimate power—deep inside *"Volta,"* weaving it within strands and layers of undecipherable Sicilian dialect.

I looked from the paper to his waiting gaze and said, "Buondiavolo."

Small bonfires of clarity jumped in his eyes. His mind grasped for an elusive memory, touching it with mental fingertips. "It's a . . . village," he whispered. "Something to do with . . . with my father?"

"Do you remember Buondiavolese?" I asked carefully, scared of his answer.

I watched the light in his eyes flicker and fade. "I don't know," he said.

Annabelle's hands were moving as Heather said, "My mom wants to know what that is. Buon . . . Buondiavo . . . whatever that was."

Uncle Jack and I stared at each other, my face taut with hope, his lined by confusion. Quietly, I said, "Buondiavolese. It's a form of Sicilian that our family used to speak and write a long time ago. Uncle Jack may have known it once." The old man remained silent, lost but searching, and I looked at

Annabelle and lied as well as I could off the top of my head. "I'm doing a school project on it, for extra credit. I found a story written in the dialect . . . sort of a modern fairy tale, but I haven't had any luck translating it." Turning back to Uncle Jack, I said, "Maybe you can help me."

"I wish I could," he said, rubbing his forehead. "But I don't remember."

"Perhaps you will, if you just look at it."

"I don't know. Perhaps . . ."

I thought about the risk again, about exposing myself to scrutiny, and then shoved it aside, knowing that if I'd ever have a chance of comprehending *"Volta"*—of finding the vault and using the brass key to open it—I'd have to roll the dice. "Tell you what," I said. "If we reopen the bakery and you start to feel better, will you at least try? I'll give you a copy of the story to go over, line by line. It will be good therapy."

Annabelle's fingers moved slowly, reassuringly, while Uncle Jack nodded his head. "Yes, it's a very generous offer," he said, and he turned to me. "Thank you, my dear. Of course I'll try to help you. I can't guarantee anything, but I'll do my best."

"Wait . . . we're *staying*?" Heather said, as if Chicago were a lunar outpost. Annabelle responded efficiently and then, to my surprise, did the Rispoli patting-hands-together thing that signaled the conversation was over. Heather crossed her arms again. "Fine. I'll go to school. But don't expect me to do extra credit like her." She looked at me and said, "I'm sure your little project-doohickey is important. No offense."

None was taken for the simple reason that I liked her.

Out of nowhere, what felt like an (supremely beautiful) ally had materialized.

I smiled politely as my brain raced with danger and possibility.

At least I had an excuse why Max couldn't meet my family—relatives had dropped in unexpectedly. And I wouldn't show up at Lucky's dreaded sit-down without molasses cookies—Annabelle agreed to bake three dozen and was already excitedly perusing the cookbook. It was the first time in months that hope did not seem intangible, because Uncle Jack was real and had written *"Volta."* Ultimate power was hidden inside it, just like Buondiavolese was concealed within his tangled mind.

If I could help him find the language, maybe he could help find my family.

10

ALL DAY SATURDAY FOLLOWING THE SURPRISE appearance of my relatives, the exterior and interior forces threatening to tear me apart—ice cream creatures and my homicidal electricity, respectively—backed off and left me alone.

Things were so placid that it scared me to death.

I cautiously entered the Damen Avenue public library early Saturday morning, prepared as usual to fight or flee from whatever lurked around the very next corner.

It was an elderly librarian at a desk.

She looked up and smiled. I smiled back weakly, and she returned to the open book before her. Gripping the steel briefcase, I hurried to the copying machines, removed the notebook, and prepared to Xerox the ten pages that comprise *"Volta."* I was desperate for Uncle Jack to see and, with luck, translate them, knowing it was a delicate balance. My hope was that exposure to Buondiavolese, written in his own hand, would spur his memory of it; at the same time, I prayed that what he read—whatever was contained in those mysterious pages—would not seem real to him. I needed his knowledge of the language but not his recollection (if he had one) of the content; despite the fact that he was flesh and blood, despite his failing memory, there was still no one I could trust with the secret of my missing family. Allowing him to read it was as much of a risk as allowing the bakery to open, but I had no choice. There was an unforgiving hourglass dripping sand somewhere in the cosmos; dissecting my mom's finger was chilling proof that my family's value was running out. If ever there were ever a time to gamble that an octogenarian Alzheimer's patient could translate a forgotten language, this was it.

I opened the notebook and placed it on the machine.

Quarters clunked, I pushed a button, and a flash of light rolled beneath the pages.

The solitude of the past two days, amplified by the quiet around me, made my tiny neck hairs stand on end.

Disturbingly, the red-eyed freaks had disappeared once before, only for Teardrop to shape-shift out of nowhere as a Chicago police officer—who knew what they were plotting now? As for the electricity, it may've gone dormant, but it was still there, a half step behind cold fury. Knowing that it was inherent and uncontrollable made me feel as much like a mutant as the creatures. I worried constantly during that dead calm, sure that shattered glass, broken laws, and busted bones would explode around me at any moment.

Instead, horror snuck up on muffled monster tiptoes in a silent library.

There were no screeching brakes or squealing mutants but only the sedate *whirr* of the copy machine. I yawned as the first reproduced page of *"Volta"* slid onto the tray. I lifted and glanced at it, and the yawn became a gasp. Streams of words in Uncle Jack's handwriting, in English, appeared around, beneath, and on top of his Buondiovolese text. My eyes skipped across the sheet of paper from the words *tommy gun* to *massacre* to *Rispoli*. For months, poring fruitlessly over *"Volta,"* I assumed its ten pages were warped and rippled from age. But the copier had served as an x-ray machine, revealing other hidden pages *inside* the notebook pages. The concealed English text of those secret sheets was printed right on top of the Buondiavolese text, creating a mishmash of words.

Enough was legible to see that it hinted at a tale of murder.

I shoved everything in the briefcase and bolted from the library, not even bothering to answer the librarian's hushed "Have a nice day." Speeding back to the Bird Cage Club, my eyes darted into the rearview mirror at the street behind me, empty of ice cream trucks. I parked beneath the Currency Exchange Building, rose quickly in the private elevator, and paused only to note that Doug's usual spots on the couch or at the control center were unoccupied. Harry whined insistently, demanding to know where his BFF was. I'd returned late the previous evening after spending hours at the bakery with Uncle Jack and his family, expecting Doug to be awake and waiting to dish on the Mister Kreamy Kone S-C Party; instead, it had been only Harry asleep on the couch, twitching with loneliness and the need to pee. After cautiously walking the little dog, I texted Doug several times to make sure he was okay, received oddly cheerful replies, and then went to bed. He wasn't there in the morning either, but copying *"Volta"* was my priority, and I'd rushed out the door. Now I was back and he still hadn't returned, but his absence barely registered as I hurried into my office/bedroom. Harry followed, ears in the air, as I rummaged through a small but effective collection of weapons—palm-sized can of mace, brass knuckles, rolls of quarters wrapped in masking tape—until I found a switchblade.

Carefully, like doing surgery on envelopes, I slit open the tops of each page of *"Volta"* and withdrew five rice-paper-thin sheets of handwriting.

They were delicate with age and some of the phrases ended abruptly where the ink had faded, but Uncle Jack's run-on sentences still told an old, brutal narrative of Outfit retribution against one of its own.

Irving Cohen was a former bootlegger who, at the end of Prohibition, turned his speakeasy into a full-service gambling den. He possessed ambition and an education—not to mention fashion sense—which set him apart from his criminal colleagues. Thin and dapper, perfectly attired in Savile Row suits (his catchphrase: "Speak Yiddish, Dress British"), Cohen was rarely seen without a fresh yellow rose in his lapel. As a young man, he'd earned a degree in chemistry, which helped him greatly in the 1930s when he was making illegal liquor, and again in 1956, when he had what he described as a "million-dollar idea." That same year, he also made the biggest mistake of his life—he stole money from the Outfit.

In particular, he stole from my family.

Cohen's gambling den was designed for people who enjoyed betting and losing compulsively. There was roulette, slot machines, broadcast sports events, booze to loosen their wallets, and a stage show featuring a stripper who, since it was 1956, barely stripped. In turn, Cohen sunk every illegal dime he made into his front business, convinced that his million-dollar idea would earn the kind of fortune that would eclipse his gambling operation. Using his chemistry skills, he formulated sugary recipes in a South Side neighborhood called Back of the Yards, home to Chicago's famous slaughterhouses. No address was given for his factory, only that it was near Bubbly Creek, named for the methane gas that rose from animal carcasses decomposing beneath its stagnant waters. It was there, in a former rendering plant, that Cohen's idea became a reality. Using lard—pig fat—as its chief ingredient and coagulant, his ironically named "Pure Dairy Confection Company" created a formula for yummy frozen treats that miraculously melted six times slower than normal frosty desserts, even under the most blazing summer sun. It was a revolution in lickability.

The pages mentioned his nickname, and a bitter lump rose in my throat.

Irving "Ice Cream" Cohen.

He intended to sell his delicious toxic products directly to children through a fleet of little tinkling trucks.

To do it, he needed cash to buy them and hire drivers, but he was nearly broke from developing slow-melting lard ice cream. That's when he thought of Nunzio Rispoli. The power behind the old counselor's eyes was capable of forcing the strongest-willed thug to do whatever he commanded; if it worked on murderers, certainly it would work on a quarterback. In 1956, the Chicago Bears were on track to win the NFL championship. Only a moron would bet against them in an upcoming game versus the truly terrible Los Angeles Rams—unless the game was fixed for the Bears to *lose*. Cohen's plan was simple. He'd bet on the Rams while Nunzio used ghiaccio furioso to force the Bears' quarterback to blow the game, winning enough to purchase trucks plus a tidy sum left over to split. Nunzio listened politely and then explained how he'd been approached many times to participate in every type of scheme but always declined; as counselor-at-large, he couldn't show favoritism to one hoodlum over another.

That's when Cohen robbed the Bird Cage Club.

When Prohibition ended, Nunzio's illegal income dried up; bootleggers stopped making black-market alcohol, which killed the demand for molasses. However, his personal value as counselor-at-large had grown immeasurably, as the Outfit leadership realized it could not function without his coldly furious peacemaking abilities. It was decided, therefore, that an annual income of two million dollars would be paid to my family for as long as a Rispoli with cold fury acted as counselor -at-large (I'd wondered how our little bakery supported us all; now I knew). It was delivered on a monthly basis in greasy wads of illicit cash, which meant a good laundering was in order. So Nunzio exercised his hundred-year lease on the Bird Cage Club, which he'd shut down after Prohibition, and reopened it as a supper club. Of course, it was actually a place to exchange soiled Outfit money for clean civilian dollars, but that didn't stop him from making it a first-rate spot with fine dining and dancing, and the best views in Chicago.

Grandpa Enzo's day job was working at the bakery (and as understudy to Nunzio until it was his time to serve as counselor) but he ran the Bird Cage Club at night. He was in his twenties then, so perhaps he wasn't in full command of cold fury, or maybe he was caught off guard; in any event, two masked men stormed his office (my current bedroom) after hours, blindfolded him so he couldn't see (or use cold fury), bound him to a chair, and emptied the safe of thousands of dollars. Holdups like that happened often in Chicago, including Outfit-on-Outfit crime, so there was no reason to immediately suspect Cohen. Even his tantrum after being rebuffed by Nunzio wasn't enough to cast suspicion; he wasn't a stickup man by trade, and only an idiot would hijack a Rispoli. After the thieves fled and Grandpa Enzo freed himself, however, he noticed something on the floor—a fresh-cut yellow rose, the lapel pin still piercing its stem. Cohen's reasoning isn't revealed, but witnessing the lowest forms of human behavior as counselor-at-large has made me aware of the stupidest of all motivations—revenge. He needed money, Nunzio refused to help, and that's all it took to blind him to his own stupid action.

My family's reaction was not blind in the least.

It was clear-eyed, cold-blooded, and calculated.

Through faded ink, the pages whispered of Grandpa Enzo shooting a room full of innocent people to bloody shreds.

It was a few days after the robbery when he entered Cohen's gambling den, his face masked with only his eyes visible, and produced a tommy gun from beneath his overcoat. He ordered everyone in the room to meet his gaze, and then cut them to pieces in a barrage of bullets. Ironically, Cohen himself survived the shooting—he hadn't been there. When word of the massacre reached him, he gathered up his wife and infant son (and presumably the money from the Bird Cage Club heist, which was not recovered) and escaped the United States, never to return. Afterward, the Outfit bricked up Cohen's place, sealing away the gruesome evidence. He was dead to the organization (he would've been deader if he'd showed his face in Chicago again) while the Rispoli family was protected at all costs. My eyes moved to the name of Cohen's gambling den— the Catacomb Club—and then the country to where he fled— Argentina—and I slowly lowered the delicate pages.

The Catacomb Club and its mummified massacre I'd stumbled upon, about which Tyler had smirked, saying, *We all know what Enzo did there . . . allegedly.*

Argentina, where Doug discovered the creatures' silver cones had been made.

My mind sped like Uncle Jack's handwriting—*catacombclubmassacreicecreamtrucksargentina*—as a tiny electrical volt danced across my shoulders.

A phantom mystery from the past had kicked open a virtual Capone Door into the present, showed itself for a split second, and escaped through another, and I suddenly suspected where it was hiding: every electrical fiber of my being told me that my family was being held within the crumbling walls of the Pure Dairy Confection Company, wherever it was.

Too many of those old, dead secrets were roaming the

streets of Chicago for it to be a coincidence, right down to the fleet of Mister Kreamy Kone trucks. I wondered then if my family's disappearance was payback for Nunzio's refusal to conspire with Ice Cream Cohen all of those years ago? No decision is made in a void; each has consequences that ripple outward in time, forever touching those who loved, hated, or were even tangentially connected to the decision maker. Was this whole thing an act of revenge orchestrated by Cohen himself? But no—he'd be far too old and was likely dead and buried in Argentina. Still, *someone* knew about Cohen and his ambitions, and what happened between him and the Rispolis—and that's when I remembered the mention of someone he'd recruited to help rob the Bird Cage Club.

I found it at the bottom of a page in Uncle Jack's scrunched hand.

A stream of legible words followed by dead space where other words had faded away forever, and then the important one—*partner*—followed by a name.

cohenfledbirdcageclubtohisfactorywithpartnerwestonskarlov . . .

I said it aloud, "Weston Skarlov."

Nothing was recorded about his fate, which meant the Outfit had caught and killed him or—or maybe the mask he'd worn during the holdup had been enough and he'd escaped into a world of double or even triple identities. If so, maybe over the years he'd mentioned to someone where the Pure Dairy Confection Company was located. That's what I cared about now—the factory's address and busting its doors down—and I resolved to discover all I could about Weston Skarlov.

What I could not set aside was the massacre of innocents.

I could not ignore that Grandpa Enzo had been a merciless killer. Nunzio had to have known about it—the entire Outfit knew—which made my great-grandfather an accessory. I stared at the date again, 1956, the year Uncle Jack abandoned Chicago and his real identity forever. Like Uncle Buddy, Jack's lack of ghiaccio furioso rendered him useless as a counselor-at-large, and thus of little value to the Outfit. His father had probably forbidden him to hold any other Outfit role in order to keep him safe, just like my grandpa had done for Uncle Buddy. My guess was that after recording the tale of his brother as a murderer and his father as complicit—seeing his family for what it really was and the horror it caused—he fled.

To my dismay, I experienced that sensation less and less each day.

Horror, and its attendant emotions, shock and revulsion, were like the classic boxing combination of two left jabs followed by a right—the more I got hit with it, the less it hurt. That didn't mean it reduced the damage; on the contrary, one of the worst things that can happen to a fighter is the development of scar tissue, which deadens pain but also numbs comprehension of how severely she's injured. What my grandpa did to those poor people at the Catacomb Club was burrowing into my subconscious like an infection; I just couldn't feel it. That didn't mean I welcomed it or, in the long run, would allow it to exist.

Being a natural-born killer, I thought, bristling with electricity, *is no way to live.*

11

THERE ARE FEW THINGS AS SUSPICIOUS IN THE
Outfit as superlative statements.

When a gangster refers to anything—a restaurant, limo
company, another hoodlum—in terms of perfection, it means
something bad is brewing. In the Outfit, where yes is no and
up is down, where the most mundane action such as buying
a cup of coffee or reading a book causes others to doubt your
motives and smell treachery, listening to unqualified praise
puts everyone on alert. It signifies that the restaurant is about
to be firebombed, the limo company has been infiltrated by
the FBI, the praiser in question is a rat informant, and that
other hoodlum, the one who is just so damn wonderful? He's
a dead man. That's why, when Doug burst into the Bird Cage
Club Saturday night bellowing, "I just had the greatest night
of my *life*," his superlative jubilance bouncing off the walls before the elevator arrived, my antennae went up. Harry leaped
from the mattress where I'd been reading the secret pages and
sprinted for the main room. I followed, feeling like a huffy

parent. The only contact we'd had since Friday night were his annoyingly cheery replies to my texts (Awesome-sauce! This party rocks! Woo-hoo!). Now I watched as he stepped from the elevator—to use an old movie term, he *swept off*—saying, "Well hello-o-o, gorgeous! And I'm talking to *me*!"

I stared at Doug's face, which was—there's no other word for it—radiant. Only his eyes, pink at the edges, showed evidence of having been awake for a long time, and I said, "Are you . . . okay?"

He actually did a jig, a joyfully awkward shuffling thing, and lifted Harry to his face, rubbing noses. "Better than okay! I ate and talked and danced . . . Can you believe it? Me, dancing! . . . And talked and ate and talked, but most of all I made *friends,* Sara Jane! All kinds of friends! And everyone was just like me!"

"You mean . . . ?" I said, trying to communicate with my hands instead of saying it.

"No, no." He grinned with rubbery cheeks. "I don't mean overweight! Some were, but no, I mean they were on the fringe, so to speak. Loners, geeks, outliers, whatever . . . we had such similar stories! It was weird and amazing at the same time, and definitely a bonding thing! And the one trait we all *completely* shared? Addiction!"

"You mean drugs?"

"Drugs, alcohol, food, sex, whatever! There were even some homeless people there, like, the type that get blitzed on super-cheap wine! They were *awesome*!" He swooned. "Seriously, it's almost unbelievable, isn't it? Me, making friends, and you know what?" He held up Harry like a trophy. "They *like* me! They really, really like me! Remember? Sally Field, when she won an Oscar for *Places in the Heart*."

"Uh . . . who?"

"Guess what else? They invited me to a big get-together at a Cubs game next weekend! Mister Kreamy Kone has a party suite at Wrigley Field where they entertain VIPs!" he said, dancing with Harry and singing, "Take me out to the ball game . . ."

I stood back, inspecting him. "Doug . . . are you high?"

"You mean stoned? Wasted? Zonked? No, but I'll tell you how I feel," he said, smiling like an electric clown-plug was attached to his butt. Slowly, articulating for effect, he opened his mouth and the word came out.

I paused, making sure I'd heard correctly, and then said, "Don't be offended, but . . . it sounded like you said sexy?"

"I know, right? Well, yeah, it makes me *feel* that way, but it's s-e-c-c . . . Sec-C. That's what Mister Kreamy Kone fans meant about an S-C party."

"What the hell is it?"

"Oh so delicious and like it says online . . . *miraculous! Life-changing!*" he cooed, licking his lips and hugging himself. "It's a completely organic, all-natural, appetite-suppressant ice cream that Mister Kreamy Kone is test marketing!"

"They're going to sell an appetite suppressant out of trucks?"

"No, no . . . the trucks sell regular ice cream. Sec-C will be sold in, like, gourmet grocery stores or somewhere . . . I'm not really sure. All I know is that right now, it's available only to a select few, like yours truly! The incredible thing is that Sec-C isn't *just* for food appetites. According to a Konnoisseur . . ."

"Wait," I said, thinking and then sounding it out. "You mean like 'connoisseur'? Like some kind of expert, except with a 'Kone'? That's really nerdy."

"Trust me, everyone there was a total nerd and outcast, in the very best way. Anyway, the Konnoisseurs host the parties, and according to them, Sec-C also suppresses overactive appetites for drugs and alcohol and obsessive habits, with *tah-dah* . . . no harmful side effects! So it was all of these dependent people licking and talking, and I swear I could feel it working in my brain. The more I ate, the less I thought about Munchitos, and the better I felt about *me*. It must be real, because the Konnoisseurs are all ex-addicts and healthy and *hot*."

"Okay, great . . . but what did you learn about Mister Kreamy Kone headquarters?" I said, unable to hide my irritation. I was choking on Uncle-Jack-and-secret-pages information, not to mention the fact that I'd been whistled in by Lucky, while Doug babbled on about miracle ice cream and seductive junkies. "The trucks hunting me down, remember? The creatures attempting to steal my brain? You begged me to let you go that party . . . did you learn *anything*?"

"Oh, well, not this time, but . . ." And he paused, wincing at my gaze, really *seeing* me for the first time through his happiness cloud. His smile faded and he swallowed thickly, sweat flecking his brow. "Did . . . something happen?"

Trying for restraint and failing, I blurted out how I'd been whistled in by Lucky, the boss of bosses, and what it could possibly mean. Was he aware that my family had disappeared? Did he think my dad was a rat? Did he think *I* was a rat? I shuddered just thinking of it, especially Knuckles's warning not to use cold fury on Lucky, which meant I would be going in there unarmed.

Doug sat slowly. "Wow. You just made my night seem really . . . frivolous."

"Oh wait, there's more," I said. "Two more, in fact—Jack Richards and Weston Skarlov." I recounted the appearance of Uncle Jack, Heather, and Annabelle, and how a slim chance existed that the old man could translate *"Volta."* Doug had questions, all of which I shelved, watching his eyes widen as I explained about Ice Cream Cohen and his jaw drop at the revelation of my grandpa's bloody crime.

"It's connected somehow. From 1956 to the night my family disappeared until today, right up to Sec-C. I have to recopy *'Volta,'* make some pages that Uncle Jack can actually read, and we have to track down that factory immediately. I *know* my family is there. So first . . ."

"Um . . . are *you* okay? I mean, what your grandpa did was brutal. Really . . . terrible," he said cautiously. "I'm surprised you're not more affected by it after, you know, what you've been struggling with."

"You mean never finding the people I love? Becoming something that I hate?" I asked matter-of-factly. "How it makes me consider killing myself before I kill someone else? Is that what you're referring to, Doug?"

"Sara Jane . . ."

"One of the first things I told you about the notebook was that it was my guide to the past. That I couldn't address the present until I understood the history of the Outfit and my family's place in it," I said. "Well, the past has collided with the present. For the moment, everything else—old history, what my grandpa did—is meaningless."

"The death of those people at the Catacomb Club wasn't meaningless," he said.

"I don't mean it that way." I sighed. "Listen, one of your favorite movies, *The Big Sleep* . . ."

"Humphrey Bogart and Lauren Bacall, 1946, directed by Howard Hawks. So?"

"So, Owen Taylor, the chauffeur, dies when his car goes off a pier into the ocean, but it's never revealed whether he was murdered or committed suicide. Why?"

"Because," he said slowly, seeing it, "the only significance of his death is that it propels Bogart's detective character, Philip Marlowe, forward. Why or how it occurred isn't important."

"All that matters for now," I answered, "is whether Uncle Jack can translate that chapter, and how fast we can locate that factory."

Doug nodded thoughtfully. "How do you know that your family is there, besides your gut? I'm sure it knows what it's talking about, but still . . ."

"Teardrop showed me my mom's finger. Why do that if she was really dead? Just show me her corpse and threaten to kill Lou next, or my dad. I believe they're alive more than I don't, and that they're somewhere that's nowhere," I said. "It makes perfect sense it would be Outfit connected, but not *part* of the Outfit."

"It sounds like you're talking about Elzy," Doug said, and thought for a moment, lips pursed. "Could it be her, Sara Jane? She knew a lot about the Outfit and your family. She could've known about Ice Cream Cohen, right?"

"Right," I said, "or wrong. At this point, guessing if it's Elzy is as much of a waste of time as wondering if . . ."

"If Owen Taylor was killed or he killed himself," Doug said.

"Two someones," I repeated. "Jack Richards and Weston Skarlov. They're who we care about now."

We were silent then, with Harry whining contentedly as Doug scratched between his ears. From then on, we reminded each other to stay focused by invoking a mantra—"Remember the chauffeur"—allowing the words to drive us forward.

12

ON FRIDAY EVENING, I MADE THE STARTLING discovery of an unknown great-uncle who was forgetting the past but might remember Buondiavolese; that he had a mute, pastry-chef daughter with an unmistakable (somewhat disturbing) resemblance to Uncle Buddy; and that she had a daughter who made Miss July look misshapen.

Afterward, I used them as an excuse to blow off introducing Max to my family.

I called him Sunday morning, thankfully got his voice mail, and broke the (bad for him, great for me) news. As I left the message, explaining the surprise drop-in by relatives and how their presence would dominate our household for the unforeseeable future, a warning went off in my gut—as considerate as he was, everyone, even a sweet specimen like Max, has limits. It was only natural that he'd be hurt and suspicious, but it couldn't be helped—I was racing that deadly cosmic hourglass. Doug and I decided on a divide-and-conquer strategy to locate the factory; I'd covertly tap my sources for information while he continued on with the Sec-C weirdos. There were eat-and-greets during the week, and the Cubs party the following weekend. He was excited about—as he said—"Going undercover . . . with *friends.*" I made another copy of *"Volta,"* this one without the hidden sheets, and arranged to meet Uncle Jack and his family on Sunday morning, where I'd give him the pages and—I swallowed hard thinking about it—the keys to the bakery.

First, though, I had to puke my guts out.

Afterward, I hid the bloody pinholes on my forehead.

All of it was my own fault for not being observant.

I should've peered over the edge of the balcony twenty-seven floors to the ground before leaving for the bakery on Sunday morning. If so, I would've spotted two ice cream trucks crisscrossing the surrounding streets like a pair of determined black ants. Doug didn't see any creatures at the party, but they must've followed him to the Currency Exchange Building. Other than the underground parking garage (the entrance is so well concealed that sometimes even I miss it), the only way in and out of the Bird Cage Club is a Capone Door hidden in the ground-floor carryout joint, Phun Ho—To Go! They'd probably watched Doug enter and never come out, realizing we were inside the building or nearby. They hadn't followed him into the restaurant, but how could they? Throughout the past several months, the guy in a greasy apron never moved from his place behind the counter where he leaned, staring at a fuzzy TV. The appearance of skinny ghouls in black would've at least caused him to lift an eyebrow.

Instead, they patrolled the blocks, waiting for me to appear.

Normally I would've used high-powered binoculars to scan the blocks below before leaving the Bird Cage Club, but I was preoccupied with secret pages and bakery keys. Now I tugged my hair into a ponytail, pulled on a pair of Fep Prep sweatpants and one of Max's Triumph Motorcycle T-shirts I'd stolen, and hurried for the elevator with the copied pages of *"Volta."* My finger was extended, about to press the button, when I froze. But it wasn't paranoia or even simple caution that stopped me.

It was Heather.

I was sure she'd appear as shiny and fresh as if she'd spent hours prepping for a Cover Girl photo shoot, and even more distressing, she'd have done nothing more than yawned once and rolled out of bed. She was that kind of a chick—deep green eyes, shimmering blond hair, bee-stung lips—so naturally gorgeous that the whole package seemed phony. But it wasn't, and I was suddenly acutely aware of my hair, clothes, and (lack of) makeup. It's that dynamic shared by girls when it comes to judging one another's appearance—a wicked combination of being inspected and categorized based on, say, a pair of shoes, shade of hair color, or a purse, combined with a sort of sisterhood-charitableness that sought out the other person's "positive feature," like slim ankles, or good workout clothes, or the right application of lipstick. This emotional sweet-and-sour can be off-putting for someone like me, who puts almost zero effort into how I look.

Around Heather, however, my self-consciousness flared like a wildfire.

The truth was that I wanted her to like me as much as I liked her.

I walked into the bathroom, stared into the mirror, and didn't even bother sighing. At certain angles, my nose looks like an oversized Mr. Potato Head accessory. The light behind my eyes was dull and my hair was a nest of tangles that even the laziest rat would avoid. I tried doing something to it with a brush, but it fought me, like trying to comb a Venus flytrap, and I gave up and dug out makeup that had sat unused since the spring dance. I had no good idea what I was doing, with the result somewhere between demented raccoon and Cirque du Soleil reject. I looked at the clown-vampire staring back, wiped my face clean, and thought, *Screw it, glamour's not my thing . . . why fool myself? I was built for action. To chase, and to escape.*

Apparently, I was fooling myself about that too.

Only minutes later I was trapped on Lower Wacker Drive.

I'd pulled from the parking garage beneath the Currency Exchange Building onto Wells Street, empty on a weekend morning, with my mind tipping from Uncle Jack to the impending sit-down with Lucky—only four short days away, Thursday at noon! A tremor of unease went through me just thinking about it. It wasn't the fear of the unknown; on the contrary, it was the fear of the known, since, as counselor-at-large, I was acutely aware of what could happen if Lucky believed that my family had fled to the Feds. I drove slowly, considering the death-by-tire-iron-or-blowtorch possibilities as Frank Sinatra came whistling in my ear.

An ice cream truck blasted into me like a heat-seeking missile an instant later.

The Lincoln spun in a smoking circle while I grasped for consciousness, knowing I was done for if I passed out. With all of my strength I yanked the steering wheel and jammed the gas pedal, hopped the sidewalk, blasted a mailbox to kingdom come, and bumped back onto Wells Street. An El train rumbling on tracks overhead interrupted dazzling sunshine as the Lincoln shrieked metallically and I raced away, leaving the ice cream truck in the dust. I was hyperalert for another truck, which, if I hadn't cranked the wheel, would've hit me head-on. It was obvious the creatures had returned to the crush-or-kill strategy of capture. They were behind me now, the one that had attacked, the other I'd avoided, as we hurtled into the concrete guts of Chicago. Lower Wacker Drive descends so deep belowground that city lights dim and noise fades away. Even at noon, when the sun is high, headlights pop on as loading docks and forgotten alleyways fly by.

I was driving fast while the hood spit orange smoke. The rusty stink of burning oil filled the car. I watched the speedometer needle quiver upward, eighty-five, ninety, ninety-five.

The ice cream trucks ignored oncoming traffic, swerving around startled drivers, coming up on both sides like homicidal bookends, and smashing me in the middle. The Lincoln bucked and rocked, metal-on-metal echoing monstrously through the subterranean tunnel as I stomped on the brakes, ripped the car into reverse, and blew backward, away from the tinkling killers. One hand on the wheel, the other arm spread across the seat as I gaped through the back window, I wove wildly away from the cars that came up behind me, horns braying, until the mouth of an alley presented itself. I hit the brakes again, narrowly avoiding a moving van that rocketed past by inches, and flew into a murky dead end. In front of me was a short barrier, not much higher than a speed bump, where the street ended, literally—the other side was a suicidal drop of thirty feet to the next, deeper level of Lower Wacker, or "Lowest Wacker," as the natives called it. But then it didn't matter since the driver's-side window exploded around me. Steely hands clamped around my neck and dragged me from the Lincoln in a jumble of punches to my head; me kicking and connecting, hearing the breath leaving something's body. I dropped to my knees and scrabbled for the Lincoln but was dragged back by an ankle, shoved into the back of one of the trucks and thrown to the floor. It was a pair of them, their hands in constant motion—batting at me, pinning me down—and in the feeble glow of a dome light I saw two things clearly—Teardrop's red eyes brimming with hatred, and the steely point of a hypodermic needle before it bit my arm.

The world grew feathery soft as hot pinpricks peppered my neck and face.

My arms were dense and useless as wet sandbags, and I blinked heavily at four crimson eyes watching and waiting. *"Mi Belleza"* was whispered in my ear, the rotten scent of a decaying tongue finding my nose, drawing me back, and then, *"Te llevaste mi Belleza, y ahora voy a tomar tu cerebro."* My brain, trying to shake itself awake, filtered the words through Fep

Prep Spanish—"You took my Beauty, and now I will take your brain"—as my eyes fluttered and my temples grew feverish. I lifted a sluggish hand, brushing at what felt like a wire, and heard Teardrop warn the other creature, "She's moving."

"She'll be comatose soon," it replied. "Juan said it would take two minutes."

"Just be careful. Juan's not always right. *Él no es Dios,*" Teardrop said coldly.

He's not God, I translated silently. *Juan . . . is not God. Juan is a Spanish name.*

"She's trying to talk," Teardrop said.

"Hallucinating," the creature said, and I heard fingers on a keyboard. "I'll check the electrodes. Blood should be flowing through them by now."

Spanish is the language spoken . . . in Argentina, I thought. The skin at my temples twisted beneath sharp metal pins, warmth oozed across my forehead, and my eyes popped open.

"She's awake!" Teardrop said.

"It's not poss—" the other creature said as I blinked once. The flame in my gut roared into a cold blue conflagration, and with every living ounce of my being, I willed the electricity to find the gold flecks in my eyes. It was instantaneous, the lightning bolt snaking through my body, racing for my brain, and I grabbed and yanked what was nearest to me, the silver ice cream cone dangling from the creature's neck. Its red eyes bulged with shock, my blue eyes radiated a furious calm, and I saw red wires attached to my forehead trailing to a laptop where lines of letters and numerals like hieroglyphics flitted across a screen. In the next second it went blank, my hand began to sizzle, and I turned to see the creature's eyes rolled back in its head, its black tongue flopping like a catfish out of water. Voltage crackled through my body, into my hand, and through the conductive silver cone and chain that hung from the creature's neck, electrocuting it. All I had to do was let go and it might live. But it had tried to infiltrate my brain, and now I wanted to kill it. I'd fooled the other creature on the bridge into drowning itself, but it was different now—I needed to murder this one with my own hands. The muscles in the creature's lean white face rippled, the skin at its neck popped with translucent bubbles, and its body began to vibrate. Gripping the silver cone with all of my strength, I turned my gaze on Teardrop and smiled, just a little, the look on its face not one of horror but surprise. It was obviously aware of ghiaccio furioso and had experienced the electricity firsthand when I nearly crushed its cheekbone, but it must've thought I'd be unconscious before the voltage occurred.

Teardrop pointed its gloved hand at me like a gun and leaped from the truck.

With a shudder, the other creature stopped moving.

A final sour gust of air leaked from between its lips, it wilted and fell forward, and I shoved the thing away from me.

The electricity dissipated, and I hadn't even felt it go. The electrodes were still stuck in my head. I pulled them out, gasping in pain, my fingers warm and sticky. I looked at my hands and realized it wasn't the wires that were red; it was me. They'd been siphoning blood from my head directly into the computer like electronic mosquitos. And then I glanced down at the creature, seeing it for what it was—a dead human being.

Its face was similar to Teardrop's and the others, bleached and angular, absolutely free of extraneous flesh, and young. It was barely twenty, if that, and I was suddenly nauseated. I knew it was from the injection, but it was also because I'd stepped to the other side of a chasm from which I could never return. I'd saved my life but lost something as valuable in the process, and a warning issued by my old boxing trainer, Willy Williams, came to mind. It was when I'd come close to shooting Poor Kevin. Willy cautioned me that murder put a cancer on one's existence. It was precisely how I felt—alive, but as if a deeper part of me had contracted a fatal disease.

A wave of sickly heat washed up my neck and clogged my throat. I barely made it out of the truck before I threw up, gasped, and did it again. Glancing back to where the creature lay motionless, I saw the laptop.

In a queasy blur, I grabbed the computer and jumped into the Lincoln. Quickly, I dropped it into reverse, jammed down the gas, and bumper-shoved the ice cream truck out of the way. Lower Wacker was momentarily empty, and I squealed out backward, stuntman style, just as the side mirror blew to bits. Teardrop was behind me in another ice cream truck, having gone old school with a handgun large enough to shoot a helicopter out of the sky; if it couldn't use electrodes to access my skull, bullets would do. And then the back window shattered, and I sped away, the Lincoln shaking and smoking but still able to fly. Teardrop rammed into my trunk as we wove down a stretch of the drive nicknamed "the Emerald City" for its glowing green warning signals. But the old car was too heavy and the truck too light, and Teardrop actually pushed me forward while bumping itself back dozens of feet. And that's when I saw it—a quivering gray mass pouring out of the drainpipes and up through the sewer grates. Hundreds of beady eyes reflected green light, hundreds of worm tails curled in the air. After I sped past, a wide flowing river of Nunzio's rats rippled across Lower Wacker Drive.

Teardrop never had a chance to brake.

The truck plowed through the undulating rodents, which detonated beneath its wheels like little grenade sacks packed with oily guts and greasy fat. Slip-sliding in the bloody stain, unable to regain control, Teardrop smashed into a concrete pillar and was showered in flickering bits of jade glass. I sat in the middle of the lane as the Lincoln rattled beneath me and offered a silent thank you to the rodent martyrs who had given their lives for a Rispoli, while the remaining survivors scuttled away.

And then a car flew past, blaring its horn, and another, and I proceeded on my way, the very model of a cautious driver.

13

SIX DOLLARS IN QUARTERS WAS THE BEST MONEY I ever spent.

After leaving Lower Wacker and reemerging into sunlight, I showered at a self-serve car wash on Kimball Avenue—first the battered Lincoln and then de-puke-ifying myself. I changed into extra clothes stored in the trunk, fashioned a headband to cover the bloody pinholes at my temple, pulled my hair back, and glanced in the rearview mirror, surprised that showing more of my face looked, well . . . good. And then I paused, staring at my reflection but not recognizing myself.

I'd purposely, physically killed another human being.

It wasn't nearly the same thing as tricking the other creature into driving off the bridge. There had been a chance, however slight, that I could've escaped Lower Wacker Drive without committing murder. Instead, I'd succumbed to the desire for revenge and left a dead body behind. That truth was lodged in my gut, and I knew I'd have to carry it with me. I owned it now.

By the time I arrived at the bakery, I'd mentally removed myself from what had happened—what I'd done—only an hour earlier. I was growing used to burying my sense of self in order to do what the moment demanded. When I pulled to the curb, Uncle Jack and Annabelle were waiting at the front door. I was struck again how similar his appearance was to Grandpa Enzo, but on our second meeting I saw differences too. Uncle Jack was thicker where my grandpa had been wiry. There was also the California tan and graceful way of moving that must've been the result of decades in show business. He kissed my hand while Annabelle went full Italian, pecking, pinching, and patting each of my cheeks. I let them inside and showed them the pantry and how things worked in the kitchen, careful not to dwell on the Vulcan. Annabelle gestured while Uncle Jack concentrated on her hands. "The molasses cookies you asked her to bake," he said. "They'll be ready when you need them."

"Thank you," I said to Annabelle, smiling through the sense of dread at my impending sit-down with Lucky.

She winked and began bustling around the kitchen. When I turned to Uncle Jack, he was staring into empty corners. "This old place whispers to me," he said. "The voices of family and friends, all gone. Besides Enzo, their names are lost. I see faces but then they fade away, like ghosts in my mind. I remember what it felt like to be around them. Sometimes it was wonderful, warm." He paused, his smile draining away. "Other times it was very cold." His eyes looked inward rather than out. My heart ached for him, the old man terribly lost and losing his way more each day. I was learning, however, to smother my emotions, and I cleared my throat while unfolding the copied pages of *"Volta."*

"Remember my school project? Translating it to English from Buondiovolese?"

He accepted the sheets, gazing at them and then at me. "It looks like my handwriting." I didn't reply, just allowed him to drift, until he said, "Of course, that's impossible. It's a story, you said. Fiction?"

"Completely made up," I replied, seeing blank indifference in his eyes.

"It must be this place," he said, "but I have a memory of writing something . . . for my father. His name was . . . what was it? It was . . ."

"Nunzio."

He squinted, focusing all of his strength on the murky past, and began to speak as if I weren't there. "My father's eyes. So blue, and as he grew old, so weak, like electric bulbs on a Christmas tree that burn out. Was he . . . going blind?" he asked. I was unsure, but it made sense since the handwriting changed toward the end of Nunzio's time as the keeper of the notebook; obviously, he'd used his young son as a transcriber. "My father spoke and I wrote . . . letters, I suppose," Uncle Jack continued. He kneaded his forehead as if trying to loosen up memories, and said, "I think . . . I think my father told me Enzo was too busy, so I would have to do it . . . but that writing was *all* I was allowed to do. His voice was very slow and calm, and I put the words to paper," he said, confirming my guess. He stared into the pages and murmured, "Perhaps I wrote this."

"No. It's fiction, remember?" I said carefully. "None of it is real."

He nodded slowly and then his face lit up. "I wrote something. Of that, I'm completely certain! A screenplay," he announced in the confident tone he'd used when recalling his show-business career. "I very badly wanted to make the transition from TV to film, so I wrote it for myself! I tried to sell it but alas, no studio would take a chance on a B-list boob-tube actor. It, too, was fiction, just made-up criminal nonsense. Remind me, my dear, and I'll show it to you."

"I'd like that," I said. "But in the meantime, will you try to translate those pages for me? If you're able to recall Buondiavolese, that is?"

Uncle Jack's gaze was as warm as a little campfire when he said, "For family, anything." After he released me from a hug, I left the bakery and leaned against the front door, pleading silently that he'd succeed—and that Annabelle wouldn't torch the place. When I looked up, Heather was on the sidewalk staring at me.

"Looks like a hangover," she said, lifting her sunglasses to inspect my face.

"What? No, I was just . . . thinking."

"Me too, about killing my mom," she said, lifting a cup filled with icy brown liquid. "Nowadays, whenever I find myself, to quote Rancho Salud, in an 'emotional tornado,' I have to get one of these, stat." She took a sip, staring at me. "I lied to you."

"About what?"

"You know what they say about the earth being, like, seventy percent water? That's about how much of an addict is caffeine. I told you smoking was my last bad habit, but uh-uh . . . without coffee, I'd be screwed. Although a smoke would help."

"Go ahead. I don't mind."

"Here?" she said, glancing through the door and shaking her silken head. "My mom gave me," she paused, furiously signing words with her hands, "*massive* shit for smoking in the alley with you the other day . . . actually for smoking at all, anywhere. I swear to God, her ears jump at the strike of a match or flick of a lighter."

I thought about it then, the times when I was at the bakery and wanted to get away from everyone and be alone. Moving toward the alley, I said, "Follow me."

"I told you, she has the hearing of a bat."

"Just wait," I said, leading her around the corner to a narrow metal ladder attached to the wall. The bakery was four stories high, but Heather followed me up without question, deftly balancing the dripping coffee. We reached the pebbly surface and I led her to the skylight where Annabelle was visible in the kitchen, making cookies, while Uncle Jack sat staring at the pages and slowly scratching his head.

"Can't they hear us? Our footsteps?"

"Nope. Trust me, this old bakery is pure cement and brick, built like a fortress." Heather grinned, produced a cigarette, and lit up. I watched smoke snake into the air and turn invisible. "So . . . why do you want to kill your mom?"

"Because I'm going to Fep Prep after all," she said grimly. "It's not the *going* part. I have to graduate somehow, right? It's the not being asked part . . . just being *told.*" She bit her lip, ashing the cigarette. "I know I haven't exactly been responsible, but having something foisted on you by your parents—sorry, *parent*—sucks. You know?"

Yeah, I knew. There wasn't anything cheery about my existence, and my mom and dad were responsible. I bumped through periods of resentment, always putting it aside, but the feeling ran deep. I said, "It's really . . . annoying."

"Annoying?" She snorted. "That's a nice way of saying it." She flicked away the cigarette and smiled. "I'm celebrating today . . . a month sober. Squee."

"That's great," I said, trying to mean it despite a thorn of anger at my parents.

"It's mostly due to an amazing counselor I had at Rancho Salud. Hey, are you into martial arts at all?"

"Yeah . . . I mean, I box."

"There's this Brazilian thing called capoeira, a very badass mixture of fighting and dancing that . . . well, anyway, my instructor at Rancho Salud was also my therapist, which is *very* L.A. The whole point was that achieving wellness has to be a mind-body experience." She sipped the coffee, set it aside, and faced me. "I want to feel good about my sobriety. I want to be clear of all negative feelings toward my mom. All it takes is some mind-body," she said, extending her hands. "You can help me, SJ."

"I . . . can?" I said, unsure what caught me off guard more—her reaching out to me, or the "SJ," which sounded like something a friend would say. I took her hands tentatively and said, "Um, how?"

"I used to do this thing at Rancho Salud called the 'Trust Test.' You're my mom, and I say everything I feel, and you answer as if you're her. It really flushes out the rage. It's important that we're connected," she said, giving me a light squeeze, "so don't look away, okay?" Before I could respond, she took a breath, closed and opened her eyes, and said, "Why didn't you include me in this school decision, Mother?"

"I . . . I didn't think you . . . would make the right choice?"

"How would you know if you didn't ask?"

"It's just . . . the things you've done in the past . . ."

"But isn't my past partly your fault? Didn't *you* step aside and let Dad use me as his little tween-queen avatar without preparing me for the consequences? *You* never taught me how to make decisions on my own," she said, chewing the words. "Why? Didn't you think I was smart?"

"No, no . . . I know you're smart," I muttered, thinking of how my dad used to tell me I was the smartest girl he knew, yet he didn't prepare me for the consequences of our secret life. A line of sweat crept down my back as I said, "Maybe you're right. Maybe I should have told you."

"Damn right you should've told me!" she hissed. "Having no choice about my own life? It's not *annoying*! It's . . . it's . . ."

"*Bullshit!* A complete bullshit betrayal!" I screamed as the cold blue flame leaped in my gut and a crackle of electricity danced over my shoulders. I threw Heather's hands aside and looked quickly away, panting, knees weak, feeling the fury subside, and then feeling her arms close around me in a hug.

"That was awesome!" she said over my shoulder. "Letting me express myself, seeing my point. Thank you so much, SJ."

She stood back then, pointing at me, and said, "Also? Remind me never to piss you off. You are one intense chick." I couldn't help it, I started laughing because I was empty, all of my anger was gone too, at least for the moment, and then Heather was giggling, and we sat slowly on the roof. "I know you don't smoke," she said, taking out a pack, "but you've earned one."

"Why not?" I shrugged. "First time, and probably last, for everything."

She lit both. I gagged like a beached trout and she exhaled like a sultry dragon, saying, "Here's a weird thing about growing up on TV," she said. "It took TV itself to make me realize how effed up my home life was. There was one commercial in particular that I starred in. I've never forgotten it. Still can't get it out of my head." She smiled shyly, inspecting a cuticle. "It was for this chain of amusement parks. Family Fun Town."

"I think I remember those," I said, vaguely recalling a mom, dad, and smiling little blond girl. "You were the daughter?"

She nodded, cigarette between her lips. "Before the shoot, the director told us to act like a normal family, where the kid is the center of attention, the complete object of affection, and the parents are taking her to this amusement park just to make her happy! I was like, whoa . . . *that's* normal?"

"There was a jingle . . ."

Heather straightened, eyes bright, and sang, "Break away to where the sun shines all day! At Family Fun Town, we wanna be your host! Have fun, fun, fun . . ."

"With the people who love you most!" I joined in, blushing at my croaky voice.

"And then the daughter smiles into the camera while mommy kisses one cheek and daddy kisses the other." She sighed. "So damn cheesy, I know, but when my dad was being his usual dick self or he and my mom were fighting, I used to repeat it like a mantra. I would be, like, I want to live and die in Family Fun Town!"

"Did you ever go?"

"No," she said, stubbing out the smoke, "but that's the commercial that got me *Two Cool for School*. Speaking of, I'm registering tomorrow . . . tomorrow's Monday, right? . . . so yeah maybe we can go together on Tuesday. You can show me around." Her grin, tone of voice, and the fact that she seemed to shimmer made me think she was going to say "you can show me off." Before I could answer, she smiled and said, "You're so pretty, SJ. You know that?"

"I am?" I said, blushing again.

"Are you dating anyone? You have to be. Name, please?"

Somehow through my third blush I told her about Max. It was such a nice but odd sensation to talk about him with someone who really seemed to care. I thought of what she said when we were holding hands—*we're connected*—and it was beginning to feel like we were. I took a breath and asked her the same question.

"Me, dating? Oh, hell no," she said quickly and firmly. "At present, there are few things I trust less, and am less emotionally equipped to handle, than someone telling me he likes or even—ugh—loves me. I'm not kidding, it's something I was working on in therapy. When I was Heather Richards as Becky, I was an attention junkie, couldn't get enough. But as myself, attention feels fake and temporary, and it makes me so nervous I become this sort of mumbling, wisecracking deer in the headlights," she said. "So look, if that happens, you have to tell me that I'm acting like an asshole, okay?"

"Okay."

"Seriously, after a lifetime filled with what you said . . . bullshit? What I need more than anything else is the truth, even if it hurts. You promise? Always?"

"I promise."

Heather's mouth curled at the edges like a show cat. "Anyway, if I have to go to school, I'm glad it's with you. It's cool to have a cousin who's smart *and* good looking."

"Let's don't get into the smart thing again. I can't take it," I said, absently touching my face. "Good looking is another matter. My nose is a real problem."

"Every problem has a plastic solution," she said brightly, making scissor motions with her fingers. "My dad had mine solved when I was thirteen. Custom noses are *very* L.A. No, what I meant was, you look like someone . . . an actress, from old movies. Your eyes are amazing too. They're almost the exact same color as mine."

"Um . . . yours are green."

She blinked once, dramatically. "Colored contacts. I change hues like I change boyfriends. Also *very* L.A."

"You . . . have blue eyes?" I said, feeling the words stick in my throat.

"Yeah, with the same little gold thingies as you. Another family trait, I guess."

"Yeah. I guess," I said, and saying so little already felt like lying to her.

"I better get inside before my mom sends out a therapeutically licensed search party," she said. "Are you coming in?"

"Uh . . . no. I have to go."

"Okay, so I'll see you Tuesday?"

"Tuesday," I said, moving toward the ladder. When we were on the ground, she smiled with sparkling teeth and hugged me again.

"Thanks for talking. I feel like I've known you forever."

"Me too . . . you," I mumbled stupidly as my brain tried to jump out of my skull. Heather possessed Rispoli blood, which carried Rispoli DNA, which created Rispoli eyes (blue with gold thingies!) and I didn't know if that was bad, good, or meant nothing at all. She showed no signs at all of ghiaccio furioso—of experiencing the impossible-to-ignore phenomenon of cold fury—or even an awareness that it existed. Watching her enter the bakery brought to mind one of my cardinal rules. I'd learned it when I first began boxing and, not paying full attention, turned my face into an oncoming fist.

It was a lesson I knew well, considering the upcoming sit-down with Lucky that came out of left field, as well as the sneaky nature of the creatures.

The things you never see coming are the ones you'd better be most prepared for.

14

THAT NIGHT AS I SLEPT, MY SUBCONSCIOUS
worked on the day's events like a curator in a museum of odd-
ities, sifting through black ice cream trucks in green subterranean tunnels, red-eyed kidnappers with silvery hypodermic
needles, hundreds of furry gray martyrs, a blue-eyed beauty
(which seemed the oddest item of all), and finally, a white
face made even whiter by death. Carefully, with a delicate
touch, each curiosity was sorted according to the fear it had
caused, threat it posed, or guilt it created.

In the morning, I awoke with a need to confess.

I'd almost had my brain invaded, so I'd had no choice
but to kill the creature with my own hands. It was done in
self-defense, for survival, but the problem was, well—it had
been undeniably pleasurable. A wave of fear (was I becoming
Nicky "Daggers" Fratelli?) and self-loathing (had I been per-
verted by murder?) washed over me. The idea of telling someone what I'd done seemed like a lifeline back to the world
of non-killers and I rushed into the main room of the Bird

Cage Club looking for Doug, but seeing only Harry lift his drowsy head from the couch. It was Monday, a school day, and I glanced at the control center's bank of clocks, realizing that I'd be late even if I left at that moment.

Doug wasn't at the Bird Cage Club when I'd returned the previous day, either. I'd been in no shape to write down everything that had happened, including Heather's blue-eyed revelation, so I scribbled only a short note, left it and the laptop from the ice cream truck on the control center, and dove into unconsciousness. It had read simply:

Beware: creatures in the neighborhood. Took this from them. Tell you everything tomorrow.

Now I saw another note, this one from him, propped against a bust of Alfred Hitchcock, scrawled in red capital letters so I'd spot it among the avalanche of books and papers. Next to it sat the laptop, wired to a small black box with a row of tiny green lights flashing intermittently. So many notes between us, back and forth—normally Doug was *always* at the Bird Cage Club, and if he wasn't, he was with me. Being separated for only three days felt like a lifetime. I knew that he had attended one of the weekly MKK fan meetings the night before and I was anxious to hear about it, thinking that perhaps he'd mentioned it in his note. I glanced at the first line:

Sara Jane! DO NOT TOUCH computer until you've read this note!

I backed away and sat in his desk chair on wheels, reading.

Sorry I didn't wake you for school but you were talking . . .
actually, screaming (who the hell is Juan?) all night, and
you only got quiet an hour or so ago. Whatever happened
yesterday must have been bad—hope you're okay. Creatures
in the neighborhood? Shit! I'll look over both shoulders.
MKK get-together produced nothing useful re: factory. But
it was fun! And I had some yummy Sec-C ice cream! And
I was urged again by my new friends (yippee-skippee!) to
attend the Cubs thing!

As for the laptop, it is definitely super freaky.

What you're about to watch . . . I think it was created
as a guide to properly getting inside your head, literally.
Besides that, there's nothing else on the hard drive—no
other files, no data of any kind. I scoured it using all
of my computer-nerd genius, but no luck, it's useless.
Anyway, when you're ready, press the Return key. And
then take a mental health day. You've earned it.

Smooches—

Doug "Mr. Popularity" Stuffins

P.S. What's on the computer is a little disturbing
but . . . remember the chauffeur!

I wheeled back and touched the Return button as streams
of numbers filled the screen. Slowly, from the top down, a
3-D image began to form in lines of color, as if created by a

hyperfast Etch A Sketch. It started with a fleshy yellow hue, spherical at the top, cut by ravines and highways of deep lines, anchored in the middle by what looked like the large, curved tail of a whip. While I stared, it began glowing in a cold blue tone, while tiny letters like digital ants skittered next to it. Seconds later the image began rotating, and I saw that it actually contained two parts, a left and right lobe.

Doug had been disturbingly correct.

It was a brain—my brain.

The note quivered slightly in my hand as more letters appeared.

Positive Identification of enzyme GF in subject Sara Jane Rispoli, significant source in production site: limbic system.

Months ago, during our reunion at the Ferris wheel, Lou said he'd seen financial information on a laptop attached to my dad's head, but it was plain now that he'd been mistaken. Staring at the screen, I saw precisely what the blood sucked from my head had yielded—three-dimensional proof that someone was trying to harvest the brains of my family. Knowing it for certain felt like an icy finger drawn along my throat as I reread the blunt sentence. I had no idea what the "limbic system" was—it sounded like a painful exercise program— but "enzyme GF" obviously referred to ghiaccio furioso. As counselor-at-large, holding the gaze of some quivering Outfit thug, I marveled at the otherworldly power of cold fury. Now, considering the word *enzyme*, I was relieved that whatever caused the phenomenon was biological—that I was strictly of *this* world. It made me feel rooted and even guiltier about the death of the creature. No matter what the thing had become, it started life as someone's baby, possibly as loved as I'd been by my parents. It was dead now, having died in a very bad way, and I was responsible. I dialed the phone, knowing what I was doing but unable or unwilling to stop.

"Hello? Sara Jane?" Max answered.

I said yes, weakly, trying to find words.

"Doug said you're not feeling well."

The air in my ear crackled impatiently. "I . . . did something."

He was quiet, then said, "This weekend?"

"Yes."

"When I was supposed to meet your family, but you blew me off by voice mail?"

Emotion clouded his voice—wounded suspicion, sniffing like a dog on the trail of what it already knew was there. I winced, realizing what an idiotic mistake I'd made by calling him, and heard the panic in my throat as I said, "Let's talk later, after . . ."

"Why do you sound so guilty?"

"I want to tell you, but . . . I just can't."

"Was it a guy . . . *that* guy? Can you at least tell me that?"

I sighed and said, "I'm not sure what it was, to be honest."

And then Max made a sound I'd never heard from him before, a snort of derision, before he said, "You don't know *how* to be honest."

It was like a punch in the gut, not only because it had come from him, but also because he was right. I had told him the truth about so little of my life that I had no defense—I couldn't even make one up—and took a deep breath before saying, "Max, maybe we should talk about this in person when—"

He cut me off, saying, "I don't get you, Sara Jane. You say one thing and do another or, like you just said, you want to tell me something but *can't*. Why can't you? Better yet, why won't you meet my mom, and why haven't you introduced me to your family? It's not that I'm dying to meet them, but it's strange that you just won't do it."

No matter how I'd tried to ignore or hide from it, the interim since Max returned from California had been a slow build to that very fact. I loved him, and love meant trust, which meant telling the other person everything. But in my twisted life, *everything* could get him killed, and I had to protect him. I sighed, saying, "I . . ."

"Let me guess. You want to, but you can't."

"Max. Please . . ."

"You know, something happened last year, right before Fep Prep let out for summer. I didn't think much about it at the time, but now it keeps coming back to me," he said, his voice colder and more vacant. "I'd ridden my Triumph to school. After class, when I was starting it up, that guy who dates my cousin Mandi, Walter J. Thurber, came over and started talking about motorcycles. He has an old BMW and . . . anyway, he asked if it was true that you and I were dating. We weren't yet, not really, but . . ."

"But people saw us together," I said, my hands trembling at the thought of being discussed. "And people like to gossip."

"I didn't say anything, just shrugged, which he must've taken as a no. Walter grinned then and said something like, 'I kissed her once, when we were kids.'"

"So?"

"'But that was before she turned into the invisible girl. Besides school, she was nowhere . . . no more parties, no sports, no friends. And you never see her family. It's very weird,'" Max said, finishing Walter's quote. "The thing is, he's right."

"That's . . . a terrible thing to say . . ."

"But I didn't mind at first because you were my kind of weird, and I was your weird, and it was cool. Now it's not." He was silent, and in that place in my mind where I can see what he's doing even when I'm not with him, Max was gnawing a thumb so he didn't utter something he'd regret. A moment later, he said, "Your problem is that you think I'm too good to be true. But you're wrong. I get sick of bullshit just like everyone else."

I pled with him but he cut me off.

"It's not right," he said, "that you ignore me, kick me aside, and don't feel bad about it at all."

"I do . . . ," I said, holding back tears.

"Then tell me what you did this weekend. That's all I'm asking."

I paused with the truth—the whole truth—on my tongue, knowing that right now was the time to tell him everything. "The night you and I went to the dance last spring?" I said slowly. "Something . . . happened."

The line was quiet. "What?" he asked.

"I got home and . . . well . . . ," I said, wanting so badly to finish, to describe the horror of my trashed house and missing family, but it felt suddenly as if danger were a disease, and telling the truth would spread it to Max. "Look, I want to tell you, but . . ."

"You can't, right?" He snorted.

"Max, please, all that matters is that . . ." And the phone went dead when he hung up on me. "I love you," I said to no one. A long moment passed while I stared at the blank display. It went to voice mail when I called back, and I knew he'd turned off his phone; he didn't want to hear any more.

Frankly, it pissed me off.

Max had no idea of the frantic life I endured, while the biggest tragedy in his was a girlfriend who didn't pay him enough attention. I tried to recall what it felt like when the melodrama of being dateless sent me into a tailspin of self-pity—but it seemed surreal and embarrassing, and Max seemed like a pouty high school boy. I threw my phone aside, thinking, *Screw it . . . I was stupid to try and tell him the truth. I don't care if I ever talk to him again,* and I was startled by the feeling. Some internal mechanism had tried to smother my feelings for Max. Maybe it was the cold blue part of my brain or a simple need for survival, but I was shedding traits that tied me to my old life, moving closer to a true Outfit existence. I desperately did not want that to happen—I didn't want to lose the former me—but even my boyfriend was beginning to seem irrelevant, or too much of an extravagance, for the newly evolving Sara Jane.

And then I thought, *Remember the chauffeur.*

I thought, *I have things to do for my family, and I must do them.*

As much as it hurt, I pushed Max aside, and myself too, and flipped through the notebook, looking for unlisted phone numbers. Sometimes the best way to ignore the hard truth of present-day life is to get lost in a cobweb of dead secrets.

15

AFTER SEVERAL MURMURED PHONE CALLS Monday morning, I had three afternoon appointments scheduled with three incredibly different personality types. The goal of speaking to them, however, was precisely the same: information. I twisted my hair into a ponytail and slipped into my uniform of old jeans, Cubs T-shirt, and shredded sneakers. I'd decided to travel by train rather than car—the idea of being pursued by little trucks was unbearable—which meant more exposure. I paused to strap my sap to my ankle. It felt like it might be that kind of day.

Minutes later, I stepped through the Capone Door/urinal (ugh) into the men's room at Phun Ho—To Go! It didn't take long after moving into the Bird Cage Club to figure out that fast food joint was an Outfit front business—it was always open, never had customers, and the counterman's eyes perpetually glued to the TV when I used the restroom like a revolving door. I stepped onto the noontime sidewalk where worker bees hurried to lunch or rushed back with greasy paper bags.

I'd used binoculars before leaving to sweep for ice cream trucks, spotted nothing, and now looked in both directions before running upstairs to the El stop. It was a glaringly hot day, with the scent of pine and asphalt rising from the tracks. A whistle sounded hoarsely as the train appeared, undulating like a steel worm, and eased to a stop. I made sure the car was safe and then rode in silence until a giant infant appeared on top of a block-long building.

Its pacifier was as big as a bathtub.

Beneath it, a pink-and-blue neon sign read BABYLAND.

As far as front businesses went, the one used by Knuckles Battuta, the head of the violently bloody Muscle division, was pretty brilliant.

Minutes later I pushed into a blast of air-conditioning and the soft burble of canned music alternating "B-I-N-G-O" with "Itsy Bitsy Spider." I'd been there before and cut past cribs (traditional, oval, pneumatic), strollers (four wheels, three wheels, running), car seats, clothes, blankets, bottles, and some sort of machine with dual breast pumps (that one made me shudder). I stopped in front of a large framed poster of Charlie Chipmunk in a red sweater (but no pants—why do cartoon animals never wear bottoms?) with a big *C* in the middle. The letter was raised just enough to push. I looked around cautiously and then pressed it, and the framed poster concealing the Capone Door swung open quickly.

It shut even faster behind me.

The space was a deep, dim, cement-block room with a red-stained drain in the middle. Walls were lined with tools of the enforcement trade—clubs, whips, crowbars, knotted rope, cattle prods, bowling pins, lead pipes, acetylene torches, hammers, pliers, baseball bats, electric drills, and mysteriously (although it was one mystery I had no interest in solving), a set of brass cymbals. Something hovered in my peripheral vision, and I looked up into shadows at a hard wooden chair hanging from chains, hooked to a winch. Leather straps with padlocks were attached where wrists and ankles were bound.

It was the legendary Outfit torture device known as "the Highchair."

Fitting, because it was a baby store.

Terrifying, because it was covered in muddy-brown stains of old dried blood.

The first time I met Knuckles here, he'd explained what happened to the unfortunate occupant by saying, "Ever swing at a piñata? It bursts open and out comes . . . well, anyway, out it comes." I tried to ignore the Highchair during previous visits, using as much willpower as it required not to think much about what happened in this room when the door was locked.

Now the sick thing underscored the danger of my upcoming sit-down with Lucky.

Watching it twist, hearing it creak like breaking bones, my role as counselor-at-large came into gut-churning focus—the consequence of decisions I'd made in favor of some people versus others led them into that chair. The Outfit had survived for more than a century based on the brutal treatment applied to members who didn't obey its rules; to remain alive, a thug was wise to toe the line. I wondered how I'd been so foolish. Did I really believe, when I judged someone worthy of punishment, that he received a slap on the wrist? The curtain of willing ignorance had been pulled back, and I saw flaming torches to the soles of feet, beatings with knotted ropes until a body was purple, or worst of all, strapped in and hoisted high while Knuckles and his men reached for baseball bats. There were no guns in the room, or knives, or sticks of dynamite, but I knew my rulings had ended in those methods too, and in the eyes of the law (or anyone with the stomach to look), I was as guilty as any one of Knuckles's guys.

"C'mon, Counselor, what's it about? I'm a busy man," Knuckles rumbled, drawing my attention to his hulking impatience. He sat in his Scamp puffing on a stogie, sausage fingers drumming the wheelchair arms. "I got onesies to sell and knees to crack!"

I'd applied cold fury on him in the past and decided to use it now, needing to get away from this place as quickly as possible. I blinked, and when the old man's fear of solitary death flickered between us, I asked about Weston Skarlov (he knew nothing), the Pure Dairy Confection Company (no idea where it had been located), and Ice Cream Cohen (told me what I already knew). Then, before I broke the connection, Knuckles said, "He changed his name to the way Argentinians pronounced it. Cohen to Kone."

I nodded, wondering who'd added "Mister Kreamy," and asked a final question.

"The old Catacomb Club job?" Knuckles whispered, quivering. "No, none of our guys pulled it. But there was a survivor, some bimbo who had her ear blown off and played dead while the shooter kicked bodies, putting bullets into chests that dared to heave. She identified Enzo as the gunman."

I commanded him to doze off, forget the conversation, and above all to change his adult diaper when he woke. Afterward, I rode the train all the way to Pulaski Avenue, where smokestacks belch brown sugar and the air smells like a cupcake bonfire, and entered the headquarters of one of the largest companies in Chicago. StroBisCo was a gleaming corporate temple to all things fatty. There were no giant babies or elderly enforcers in wheelchairs; it was sleek brushed metal, cool frosted glass, speedy silent elevators, and cold executive stares. The only password required was "Sara Jane Rispoli to see Tyler Strozzini." A receptionist flicked her cool gaze over my informal appearance before hissing into a headset and pointing me to a couch. Instead, I crossed the lobby to a display of captioned photos. It was a visual timeline of the corporation's growth from the humble Strozzini Biscuit Company to the current behemoth pumping out belly-busting junk food for worldwide consumption. Of course, the real function of StroBisCo is as the primary money laundry for the Outfit's filthy cash. Dirty dollars go into its accounts, exchanged for others with different serial numbers, and return to the Outfit (as the packaging says) *New and Improved!* Because the money laundry is so important, and because it's a family-owned business, a Strozzini has been the VP of Money for generations. That didn't mean StroBisCo wasn't proud of its place in food history; a photo of its first big seller in 1927, the Wonderfluff Caramel Bar, was displayed with a caption describing its significance in terms of penicillin or fire.

"Ms. Rispoli?"

A young woman with a gaze so chilly she looked like an

icicle in Prada beckoned from a private elevator. Tyler's assistant clicked on a perma-smile as we whooshed skyward, stopped, and the doors opened to a vast office. The furnishings were modern, thin, and Danish (like the assistant). Two enormous oil paintings dominated opposing walls. The rest of the space was ceiling-to-floor windows, with the widest view behind the desk, spreading over the StroBisCo plant. It was a panorama of factory buildings, smokestacks, eighteen-wheelers, and in the midst of it all, the enormous StroBisCo sign that was a Chicago landmark. Behind it, a jet inched noiselessly through the hot sky.

"That'll be all, Ursula."

I turned to Tyler behind me, grinning like a cat with a secret. He was dressed entirely in black—shoes, pants, shirt, and sport coat—which only made his copper skin seem creamier, his green eyes greener. He crossed his arms, sat lightly on the edge of his desk, and said, "Like what you see?"

"What's not to like?"

"I agree," he said, with a look both seductive and intimidating; I was being appraised while plans were formed for my acquisition. I touched the *T* pendant Max had given me, imagining his reaction if he could see me now, alone with the eighteen-year-old CEO of StroBisCo. "It's cool that you stopped by," he said. "I've only asked you to, what, a billion times?"

I looked around and dropped my voice. "Is it safe to talk here?"

"Ah. Business. Too bad," Tyler said with disappointment. "Of course. The office is everything-proofed. Shoot."

I told him that I was gathering information for an impending, confidential sit-down, and asked what he—Chicago's leading purveyor of junk food—knew about Mister Kreamy Kone. I asked without cold fury. So far, whatever was between us—simple flirtation or a deeper attraction—had proven strong enough that I'd never deployed it on Tyler. A single arched eyebrow betrayed his curiosity, but his reply was quick. He didn't know much, since MKK was tiny and local and StroBisCo was huge and multinational. I told him it was connected to an old Outfit front business called the Pure Dairy Confection Company, but he drew a blank. "Outfit rumors and anecdotes, I'm your man." He smiled. "But a nuts-and-bolts fact like that is clerical data. I'm the wrong guy to ask."

"Who's the right guy?"

"Let's start with him," he said, gesturing at one of the paintings. It was an oil portrait of an elegant man in a tailored pin-striped suit of another era. He had a regal bearing, with steely hair slicked back and a trimmed mustache beneath a hawkish nose. His square jaw jutted forward, challenging the world, but it was his eyes that stopped me; they were the same ocean green as Tyler's. "My grandfather, Genarro 'the Gent' Strozzini. The first VP of Money for the Outfit. Also, the founder of the Strozzini Biscuit Company and inventor of the Wonderfluff Caramel Bar," he said, nodding at the painting where his grandfather held one of the candy bars, presenting it to the viewer.

I moved closer and said, "It looks so real. Even the wrapper."

"Good eye," Tyler said, and pressed the painted *C* in the word *Caramel*.

The painting rose smoothly, revealing a hidden room. Tinted glass lights hung from the ceiling, giving the space a faint rosy glow. Rows of bulging file cabinets competed with high shelves lined with accounting ledgers, some reachable only by rolling ladder, while TVs tuned to financial news networks flashed silently from the corners. The room had a sweet smell—candy—and three distinct sounds: the pecking of keyboards, the whirr of adding machines, and the murmur of Mozart. In the center were two mahogany desks with cherubs carved into their corners, each occupied by basically the same guy, except that one was about ninety years old and the other around seventy. They wore sober vests, currency-green bowties, and thick glasses, and each had their hair parted in the middle. Besides computers and calculators, the desks were polluted with crumpled receipts, unsigned checks, piles of cash, and Wonderfluff wrappers. I inhaled deeply, realizing that besides candy, the room was perfumed with money.

I turned to the wall that had closed behind us. "Cool Capone Door."

"Classic, right? Like something out of an old movie. It was installed in 1960—"

A hoarse "ahem" interrupted Tyler.

Music from *The Marriage of Figaro* rode the air while the men stared at me as if seeing a polka-dotted unicorn. Tyler said, "Nino Rota and Nino Junior . . . Money's accountants, bookkeepers, and archivists. Guys, meet . . ."

"Sara Jane Rispoli," the elder Nino said, his voice like a thumbnail on sandpaper.

"Counselor-at-large," Junior said in a younger, no less grating rasp.

"A broad in the Outfit," Nino said. "A goddamn broad . . . how can it be?"

I was about to blink once, hard, and explain *exactly* how it could be when Junior bit into a Wonderfluff bar and said with a full mouth, "Ma coulda been in the Outfit."

"Your ma *shoulda* been in the Outfit," Nino croaked, taking the candy from his senior-citizen son, biting it, handing it back. "God bless her, she was tough as nails."

"Tough as shit," Junior affirmed, crossing himself.

"Tough as nails made of shit! Disgusting but true!" The old man chortled. He lifted the pop-bottle glasses, wiped his eyes, and looked at Tyler. "What do you need, boss?" Anything they had on the Pure Dairy Confection Company, Tyler replied, as Nino's fingers danced over a keypad. He stared at the screen and said, "Shelf A-six, row eleven, volume fifty-six, pages sixty-six through seventy-one. Get moving, kid."

I thought he meant me, but Junior was already hustling up a rolling ladder, glasses on his forehead as he inspected and pulled free a ledger. He flipped to the pages, made a disappointed sound with his teeth, and said, "Sorry, boss. It's a blackout."

"What does that mean?"

"Censored," Tyler said. "Covered up, so it can't be read."

"There's only one person in the Outfit who can issue that order," Nino said.

I looked at Tyler and said, "You mean . . . ," and silently mouthed the rest.

"Yeah, the Boss, Lucky. You can say it, the old man's not Lord Voldemort." He grinned. "It happens all the time for reasons that are, obviously, unclear. Some detail, a name or address or something that he wants to keep secret."

My mind raced wondering what it could've been and if it was something that would've helped me, but I remained cautiously silent. Lucky was the Boss; he could do whatever he wanted, and woe to the mope who questioned his decisions, especially around other loyal Outfit members.

Tyler said, "I guess there's nothing here to help you."

"Maybe a little something," Junior said, looking up from the ledger. "The back of page seventy-one. It was skipped." He clambered down, saying, "A few words."

He handed me the book and I looked at the page, which read:

. . . *only surviving heir is a grandson, Juan Kone, of La Plata, Argentina.*

Looking over my shoulder, Tyler said, "Does that mean anything?"

I shivered a little as two pieces of the frustrating puzzle finally clicked, and recalled Teardrop's words—*Él no es Dios*— he isn't God. Maybe not, but it was undeniable that Irving "Ice Cream" Cohen's grandson was angry and powerful enough to have snatched my family and sent his army of red-eyed freaks after me—and that he may have been *of* Argentina, but he was currently *in* Chicago. I was more convinced than ever that he and his creepy legion were holed up inside the old Pure Dairy Confection Company factory, and I turned to Nino the elder. "Check one more thing for me, please?" I said, straining to keep my voice steady. "A name. Weston Skarlov."

After a few taps and a return, he looked at the screen. "*Niente.* Nothing."

"Sounds like an alias," Junior said. "Like 'Jack McGurn,' Capone's bodyguard. You ever meet a Sicilian named McGurn?"

I shook my head, sure now that it was a fake name and an eternal dead end. If there were no trace of him in Money's archives, there wasn't one, period. I thanked the Ninos, Tyler pressed the reverse *C,* and as we stepped back into his office, I looked at the other painting for the first time. It was of a young, pretty African American woman. She was seated, smiling warmly, with a man standing next to her, his hand on her shoulder. He looked like a younger version of Tyler's grandfather, without the mustache, and I said, "Your mom and dad?"

He nodded slowly. "They died in a plane crash when I was fifteen. One minute they were here, the next, gone forever. Of all the terrible things about it, the worst was the simplest . . . I never got to talk to them again." He cleared his throat and put on a small, empty smile. "It's impossible for anyone to understand how it feels, so I never talk about it. I just try my best to remember them how they were."

I gazed at the painting, seeing how alive and confident his parents appeared, certain that more days lie ahead. Commiseration is such a sweet temptation—I wanted to tell Tyler everything about my family, since he was the only person on the planet who had experienced exactly what tore me apart every day. It made the connection I already felt to him as an Outfit kid even stronger, and I began to say something comforting when he pulled me close. I was suddenly in his arms, near enough to see what a perfect nose really looked like. He smelled earthy and lemony, and he smiled a little, saying nothing. I couldn't help but smile back because it was such a movie embrace, a little ridiculous but exciting, and because being so close to him was something I'd wondered about. It was also pleasant torture since Max was in there too—in my mind, my heart, hovering over my conscience. Tyler's lips began to move, and I froze, unsure if I was able to resist a kiss, when he said, "Remember that offer I made about taking you to Paris?"

"It's hard to forget."

He grinned, showing a major investment in dental work. "In two weeks. I have a meeting. We'll take the StroBisCo jet."

"What about school?" I said, wondering why I wasn't trying to break free. He held me firmly but with no force or pressure and I realized that was the reason—it felt comfortable, like we'd embraced a thousand times.

"I'm in college, remember? It's extra credit for me. Besides, we'll go over a long weekend. You'll only skip one day of classes."

"I'm skipping one now."

I waited, curious, but there was no kiss, only a gentle touch beneath my chin and a tease as he said, "You know what they say. After you've done it once, the second time is even better." The grin that followed bordered on irresistible, reminding me that it was time to go. After a quick friend-squeeze, we stepped apart and Tyler buzzed for his assistant, who accompanied me down to the lobby. We rode in silence, Ursula smiling so hard it almost came out of the back of her head.

When we reached the bottom, I stepped off and said, "Well . . . have a nice day."

"At StroBisCo, every day is *perfect*," she said as the doors closed slowly on her cyborg eyes.

A shiver moved across my shoulders as I left the building. The glass shrine to money was modernistic, sunny, and crisp, which made its concealed rooms and hidden agendas just as creepy as BabyLand. It felt good to be back on the train, headed to the Loop for my final appointment. One more transfer, and I got off at Washington and Wells, cutting through the people and pigeons of Daley Plaza, headed for the great, hulking Picasso. The steel masterpiece dominated the courtyard across from City Hall, which houses the Chicago Police Department headquarters. The area teemed with secretaries and clerks. The guy seated on a bench wearing a short-sleeved dress shirt and ho-hum tie eating peanut butter from a jar was indistinguishable from a zillion other mid-level, middle-aged bureaucrats. His face was as featureless as a marshmallow. Each time I met him and went away, I forgot what he looked like—in other words, the perfect Outfit mole. I'd called his cube in the records division of police HQ that morning and said, "J. Edgar Hoover wore women's underwear." A short pause was followed by a monotone voice asking what I needed. I told him, and I listened to typing fingers access the archive. After a little mouth breathing, he said, "Picasso, noon, peanut butter," and the line went dead.

I sat next to him now, and he didn't acknowledge me. His gaze was fixed on the statue, and the spoon never ceased in its continuous round trip from jar to mouth as I asked about Ice

Cream Cohen. He told me what I already knew and added nothing about Mister Kreamy Kone. Although it was a dead end, I brought up Weston Skarlov. "I couldn't find anything," he murmured, "but it sounds Russian."

"So?"

He turned to me with eyes like raisins in a bowl of tapioca pudding. Cunning pinpoints of light glittered at their centers. "The Russian mob has operated in Chicago for decades," he said evenly. "Small-time drugs and gambling, not even worth absorbing into the Outfit. They paid a street tax and we tolerated them. Recently, though, with waves of new immigrants, they've grown and begun to encroach on our turf. Word is they have a new boss with an old-fashioned appetite for violence as a way of doing business. Necks are being slit and skulls cracked, Capone style, except the Russians are the ones imitating Scarface Al. We're at the beginning of a war that is not going to end gently." He closed the jar, licked the spoon, put it in his breast pocket, and stood. "Like I said, Weston Skarlov sounds Russian. For what it's worth," he muttered, walking away. I watched him turn invisible in the crowd, realizing that with all I'd learned that afternoon, there was only one fact that mattered.

Cohen to Kone, to Juan Kone.

I whispered it over and over, realizing with sick wonder that the monster who took my family had a name.

16

THE NEXT DAY, I STOOD SILENTLY AROUND A
corner learning the once-and-for-all lesson that a person's incredible good looks do nothing to dampen her insecurity.

I heard it before I saw it, listening to Heather argue with
herself.

"I haven't attended school for so long, I don't know *anything*," she said, as I paused outside the front door of the
bakery, followed by a beat of silence, and then, "Plus, it's Chicago . . . I don't know *anyone*." It was after the next beat that
I realized how little she understood Fep Prep and my place in
it when she said, "Yeah, of course I know Sara Jane. But she's
so cute and confident. I'm sure she has, like, a million friends.
I'll be a total hanger-on." Dead air, and then, "Yeah, I know
it's shallow, but who doesn't want to be popular? Did it ever
occur to you that some people just *need* it more than others?"

Heather's anxiety made me like her even more.

It wasn't that I thought she was pretending to be nervous
about school when we'd spoken on the bakery roof. But the

way she looked, her natural gorgeousness, seemed as if it should endow her with the confidence of an Amazon. Now I saw that assumption was incorrect. She was as prone to insecurity as anyone else, and maybe more so, since she'd been constantly judged by how she looked. I was growing attached to her, maybe too quickly, maybe even dangerously (for her), but I couldn't help it; the weird, rough times we'd both endured, combined with her blue eyes, felt like the welcome appearance of not just a family member but a friend. I politely knocked and jangled inside, and was enveloped in the perfume of warmly baking pastries. For the past months, the place held only buried secrets, bittersweet memories, and stale air, but now it smelled like my childhood and I swallowed thickly, seeing Annabelle on one side of the counter and Heather on the other; she'd been talking to her mom, who'd answered silently with her hands. Heather said, "SJ . . . you're early."

"Security's strict about being on time," I said absently, looking at Annabelle and sniffing the air. "Rum cake . . . blackberry muffins . . . what else?" She grinned widely, doing her best Uncle-Buddy-in-drag impression, and moved her hands enthusiastically.

Heather said, "Biscotti alle . . ."

"Mandorle," I said, nodding. "Almond cookies. My dad loved . . . loves them." I swallowed again, ridding myself of feelings, and said, "Where's Uncle Jack?"

"At the hotel. He's having a bad day," Heather said. "The drug he's on, Remembra, has terrible side effects, which wouldn't be so frustrating if the shit actually worked." Annabelle reprimanded her, but Heather shrugged it off. "It's the truth. He loses more memory every day and all that stuff does is make him puke." She looked at me with a smirk. "When it comes to how drugs should work, I'm an expert."

Minutes later, as we stood on a crowded train, I said, "Sorry about your grandpa."

Heather lifted her shoulders. "What you witnessed back there was a Richards family tradition of talking around the truth." She looked at me with a sad smile. "He's boozing again. I found him last night, facedown over that story you gave him with a half-drunk bottle of whiskey at his side, and helped him to bed. He's done that over the years, quit and started and quit again. We thought Alzheimer's had put an end to it, but apparently not. I didn't tell my mom. She has enough on her plate with him."

I wanted to be encouraging and also ask if Uncle Jack had made progress translating the pages, but there wasn't a delicate way to do either. The probability that the old man would make no progress at all, combined with the rapidly approaching sit-down with Lucky, made my stomach churn. And then the train eased to a halt as the speaker announced Diversey Avenue. I scanned the street below for little ice cream trucks but instead spotted Max as he left Bump 'N' Grind. Heather and I would run into him if we continued our current pace, and I just didn't have the spine for it after the disastrous phone call the day before. I owed him credible explanations for my behavior and, as he'd said, for kicking him aside, but all I had was love, and it wasn't enough. I stopped Heather and said, "Hang on."

"What's the matter?"

I nodded at Max waiting for the light to change. "That's my boyfriend."

"Don't sound so thrilled," she said, with a teasing smile that sparkled. "Seriously, are you guys fighting or something?"

"It's complicated. Part family stuff and part, well, another guy. Not as in I've cheated, but more like I made him think that I *almost* cheated. It's hard to explain."

"Uh-oh. How'd he find out?"

"I told him." I sighed. When she responded with a you-are-an-idiot look, I explained how I only flirted with the guy now and then, but that I'd used him as excuse to make Max jealous after being away all summer, and now I was trapped in my lie.

Heather lifted an eyebrow. "Back up. You and this guy . . . what's his name?"

I didn't see any danger in a morsel of truth. "Tyler."

"Tyler likes you? He's into you?"

"Yeah, I think so. Anyway, he's way more into me than I am him."

"Do you like him back? Even a little bit?"

I paused, biting my lip, assessing my feelings. "A little, I guess," I said, washed with guilt at my own words. "But mainly because we have things in common, like, from a family-business standpoint."

"They have a bakery?"

"A big one."

"And you haven't been with him? Honestly?"

"Been with . . . ? No, of course not," I said, unable to suppress a blush. "I mean, even Max and I haven't done *that*."

"Who's holding back? You or him?"

"Us. We've talked about it, how nothing should happen until we're both ready, and that for now the most important thing is just being together. Or, it was the most important thing until yesterday, when I was a total idiot on the phone. Oh . . . ugh," I said, covering my face with a hand. "God. I tried to tell him for the first time that I loved him and even managed to screw that up."

Heather lit a cigarette and said quietly, "Do you?"

I sighed and nodded. "Yeah, I do. But I'm ruining it because I won't . . . answer certain questions."

"You must have a good reason."

"Absolutely."

"Then don't. If he can't respect your privacy, maybe he's not the person for you."

"No, he is," I said. "Sometimes I think I'm not the person for him. Like, I can't give him all that he wants."

"What a guy *wants* . . . the eternal mystery that keeps cheesy lady magazines alive." She snorted. "I've dated more than my fair share for a high school senior and frankly, since the incident with that producer perv and my dad's crappy reaction to it, I can tell you exactly what most guys want . . . a centerfold, or a trophy, or—ick—a mommy." She held my gaze and said, "Which one does Max want?"

"None of them. Just me . . . the real me."

"If that's true, you're lucky and he's rare." Her voice softened as she added, "Okay, so tell me. Why are you holding back?"

"Everything going on with my dad, my family." I shrugged.

"Just protecting myself, I guess. I love Max but need to keep my distance. The fact that he wants to get closer is threatening sometimes."

"I know how you feel," she said, a shadow crossing her flawless face. "Like I said, love junkie when it came to the adoration of millions of fans, but if a guy I actually *knew* felt that way toward me, I rejected it completely. Actually, I became turned off to the entire subject."

"Of love?"

"No, silly." She smiled. "Guys."

"Wait. You're . . . ?"

She held up a slim hand. "I hate labels . . . and hating labels is *very* L.A. So all I can say is that, based on personal experience, I'm in a phase where men turn me off," she said, lifting the corners of her mouth demurely. "It's a little complicated."

"Complicated is the word of the day," I said. "Like my thing with Tyler . . . really, it's not even a *thing*. It's just sort of there, you know?"

Heather nodded, lifting the nub of cigarette, staring at tendrils of smoke and then flicking it away. "The Brazilian martial arts thing I told you about, capoeira? It teaches you to kick some serious ass with punches, leg sweeps, and head-butts, set to a rhythm that you have to absorb, like, into your entire being in order to master it. Mind-body, remember? I was taught physical and mental control in order to prepare for the ultimate question: what will it be like to leave drugs behind forever?"

"Because it's a battle," I said, seeing the logic.

"Exactly. So when you leave Tyler behind, how does it feel?"

I thought for a moment, the truth blooming warmly in my chest. "It's no battle at all. I only want to get back to Max."

"Why?"

"Because . . . because, like I said, he wants me for only me."

"Then that's the answer, SJ. Don't allow Tyler or anyone to come between you and Max. And when you're ready, let him get closer," she said, squeezing my shoulder. A bump of family love went through me and I wanted to tell her that everything would work out for her too; that kicking an addiction to mass adoration would reward her with her own Max, or Maxine. Before I could speak, she pointed at Diversey Avenue and said, "Coast is clear." A few minutes later, we climbed the front steps of Fep Prep. Heather took a deep breath, and my identity shifted once more, flip-flopping from the lead in a gritty urban crime flick to an extra in a shampoo commercial.

The morning bell that summoned students to homeroom rang like trumpets heralding the arrival of a princess; as I accompanied Heather down a hallway, all that was missing was a red carpet and klieg lights. Time and space took on a slow-motion quality. Sunlight streamed through tall windows while her golden hair rippled like windblown corn silk. The tickle of a smile crossed her lips, blue eyes flashed with just a pulse of carnality tempered by shyness, and her lean, curvaceous body cut through a sea of gaping kids as gracefully as a schooner. I felt myself fade into the background as the new reality of "*the* Heather Richards who was the *original Becky*!" was projected into the student body's collective psyche. They liked it, wanted more, and Heather gave it to them. We stopped at her locker, and she bent to fix a sandal strap, showing the perfect hint of a lacy thong. The crowd gasped appreciatively, and she stood up, whispering how nervous she was on her first day, and how she really, *really* wanted people to like her. I wished her good luck and we promised to meet in the cafeteria at noon. She wove away looking tentatively at room numbers, and I turned and nearly knocked Gina to the floor.

"How do *you* know *her*?" she said, her eyes flicking from me to Heather.

"Oh. She's my cousin."

Gina narrowed her gaze. "I didn't know you had a cousin. Especially one who looks like *that*."

"Neither did I."

"She was the original Becky on *Two Cool for School.* Do you have any idea how valuable that information is?" She smiled accusingly. "Are you holding out on me?"

"No, I'm doing this weird thing called *it's none of your business*!"

"Don't split hairs. What else can you tell me about her?"

"You know I don't gossip, Gina, especially about my own cousin," I said. "If you have questions, ask her yourself."

"That's not how I work, but no worries . . . I'll know everything about her before the last bell," she said with a nose wrinkle. "Aren't you lucky, having her at Fep Prep. Your stock is going to skyrocket."

"What stock?"

Gina smiled with dimples. "Your popularity stock, silly."

I watched her walk away, silently scoffing at the notion, and then noon rolled around and I entered the cafeteria, realizing how wrong I'd been. First, there had been nothing to worry about in regard to Heather's first-day comfort level. She sat at the center of a table packed three kids deep buzzing like honeybees at a hive. Second, as I made my way there, uber-popular Walter J. Thurber moved hair from his eyes and said, "Hey, SJ," and then two Fep Prep cheerleaders waved, saying, "Hi, SJ!" in chipmunk unison, and then another kid who I'd never even seen before said . . . and on and on. I waded to the table, hearing Heather's giggle tinkling like wind chimes in a summer breeze. When she spotted me, her face opened in a warm smile and she asked Ken and Kendra White to move over and make room for me.

Ken and Kendra, who existed with invisible quotation marks over their heads as "the Most Popular Fraternal Twins at Fep Prep and Possibly in the World."

It would've been easy to dismiss Ken as a doe-eyed muscle-head if he wasn't also really smart, or simply a hunky blond mathlete if he didn't also have a sense of humor and dance well. But he was all of those things, and tall. And the same held true for Kendra, a raven-haired knockout and cheerleader (easy to categorize!) who won the National Teen Science Poetry award for her haiku on quantum physics and performed charity work for the blind (busted the stereotype). Heather was wedged between them with the twins jostling for her attention, and all I could do was stare, thinking, *Holy crap . . . it's* Two Cool for School *in real life . . . except Becky's the good guy!*

Everyone liked Ken and Kendra or wanted to be liked by them, but when I sat behind the duo each day in silent study hall, I came to despise them. My first reason was texting, which they never ceased doing, their thumbs a constant tapping blur. For some people, it doesn't matter who they're texting, if anyone—it's the act that matters. But that wasn't my issue with Ken and Kendra. It was *what* they texted, back and forth to each other. I squinted at their screens and read how everyone was an idiot, or an asshole, or a loser, or fat, or stupid as hell, or slutty, and the people they referred to were the ones looking at them with stars in their eyes as they beamed their "we're perfect but humble" smiles. There are few things I have less patience for than hypocrisy, unless it's my second reason for disliking Ken and Kendra, which was their pure, poisonous contempt for humanity.

That's why their competitive preening toward Heather caught me off guard.

Rarely separated, always conspiring, they were going nose-to-nose over Heather.

Even from where I stood, I could see hearts in their eyes for her, and daggers for each other. A competition had begun between Ken and Kendra for Heather's attention. The two people whom the Fep Prep masses admired, who secretly hated everyone, looked like they would kill each other to be her BFF, or GF, or some whole new BFFGF-I-HEART-U combination. Whatever situation was blooming between the trio, it was, to paraphrase Heather, not easily labeled. The three of them were staring at me now as Ken patted a seat between him and Heather, saying, "Hey-o, SJ! Park it!" while

Kendra slid her butt a bit and said, "Sit here, SJ! Plenty of room!"

I felt my fist curl into a rock at being called familiarly by my initials by people who, yesterday, hadn't even known my name. I stifled a desire to use their beaming faces as speed bags and turned to Heather. "Everything going okay?"

"So far, so good," she said breathlessly, with no trace of nerves.

I thought of the tense way she'd spoken to her mom, of her anxiety as we entered school. She was so electrified now, so coolly in control, directing the crowd's oohing-aahing attention with the flip of her hair or twist of her hip that she seemed like another person. Her voice hummed like a mermaid's, her smile radiated sex and benevolence, and *oops!*—there was that thong again. Heather hadn't been the focus of starstruck fans in a while (it had been three years since she was on TV) and the adoration was clearly energizing, transforming her right before my eyes. In fact, her own blue eyes glowed faintly, the gold flecks twinkled ever so slightly, and for a moment it was impossible to tear my gaze away. The world narrowed to an azure pinpoint, flattened out, and opened again, and I floated weightlessly into my subconscious. I shivered, staring at what was not my wildest fear but something more wrenching—my greatest desire. It wasn't a perfect nose or Ken and Kendra White levels of popularity, or even harmony with Max.

It was my family, safe at home, with me in their midst.

My mom smiled, caressing my face with her whole, delicate hand, and my dad pulled me close while Lou hooked my pinkie, eyes shining smartly as he whispered, "Remember, we're

Rispolis. We stick together even when we're not together. All or nothing." I felt my mom's touch, opened my arms to my dad's embrace, basked in my brother's presence. It began to seem possible that my family would actually materialize before me if I kept my gaze locked on Heather's—that she could make it come true, and if so, I'd do anything she commanded, anything at all because, God, she was perfect and beautiful and generous. I'd lie, steal, and kill for her if only she would—

By force of will, I broke free with a psychic-suction *pop!* gobbling fresh air as if I'd been trapped underwater but knowing that barely a split second had passed. When I glanced at Heather, she seemed as confused as she was dazed, having seen my desire and not understanding what the vision had been or what was happening to her. She may have been experiencing flickers of cold fury, but clearly she'd felt its full force when she connected with me. And then, slowly, her confusion softened like hot lava, ebbed, and began to harden into something like secret self-knowledge. I could see it—that blast of cold fury through her brain and body felt like the most vital, valuable part of her that had been absent until now—and she could see that I recognized it.

I saw something else, and it was as much about me as her.

A torrent of fear, rage, and desolation caused cold fury to flicker and burn inside me; it was those same feelings that drew my victims' worst fears to the surface and locked them under my control. Now, not only witnessing but *feeling* Heather's power, I understood that while ghiaccio furioso is in the DNA, the emotions that activate it are unique to the carrier. Heather wanted nothing more than to be desired, using people's greatest desires to place them in her mesmerizing command. I felt my legs moving, backing away in survival mode as she shook her head and licked at her lips, trying again to catch my gaze. By then I was pushing through a circle of admirers, enduring more greetings of "Hiya, SJ!" until I was alone in the hall outside the cafeteria.

After catching my breath, I peeked through a window in the door.

A throng of kids stared fixedly at Heather like she was a messiah relating the universe's most closely held secrets of showbiz and rehab. She had their complete, mesmerized attention—disturbingly similar to what I received from homicidal mobsters. The difference was that they weren't quaking with fear or silently sobbing as my audience did; they were worshipping her. It was plain now that she possessed ghiaccio furioso but wasn't in control of it, or even had a clue what it was. The oddest part was that her internal triggers were so obviously different than mine. Instead of duress, fear, and injustice, her flame appeared to flicker when she was overcome by the twin emotions that seem to drive so many actors—nerves and neediness—and was paid off not with subservience from criminals, but idolization by the masses. I was sickly fascinated at the display, feeling its inherent threat, hoping she wouldn't see me looking at her.

"What are you looking at?"

I jumped like a cat on a hot plate. "Max," I said, catching my breath. "I . . . where have you been all day?"

He looked through the window and said absently, "Who's that?"

"Her?" I said, unable to shake the guilt from my voice, unsure if it was from peeping or purposely avoiding him. "My cousin . . . Heather Richards."

"So that's her," he said flatly. "The one who's causing everyone to wet their pants. She was on TV or something?"

"*Two Cool for School*," I said. "The original Becky. She was . . ."

"I never watched it. It always seemed so stupid," he said. "She's pretty, I guess. In a Barbie doll sort of way."

"Yeah, she's . . . from L.A."

He faced me, a corner of his mouth lifting in a humorless grin. "Funny. I just got invited to move there."

"What? What are you talking about?"

He looked back through the window. "My dad wants me to live with him. My stepbrothers miss me, and my dad knows I don't get along with my mom's boyfriend."

"Gary the dentist? You don't? Why haven't you told me that?"

"It's not like you tell me anything that's going on in your life."

I was suddenly so tired of hearing that, as if I had any choice in the matter, and a wisp of electricity crept along my shoulders as I said quietly, "You know your problem, Max? You're a goddamn baby." He turned with anger and confusion in equal measure, his lips separating but nothing coming out as I said mockingly, "Why won't you tell me, why can't I meet your family, *why, why, why*?" I was shocked at the animosity behind my words, but continued with, "You're such a hypocrite . . . *you're* the one who actually cheated! How does

214

it matter if it was *with* me or *on* Chloe? Mister I'll-never-lie-to-you was perfectly fine lying to her! Maybe I flirted a little, but I didn't cheat!"

Max stood motionless and spoke deliberately, saying, "How the hell do I know *anything* you say is real? You're a shadow, Sara Jane. Holograms give up more information than you do." He took a step closer with his eyes locked on mine. "But I know one thing. Your little rant just helped me make up my mind."

Trembling, I squeezed my lips against my teeth, feeling the ridges of my braces. "So you're leaving? You're going to California?"

"You know that I . . . you know how I feel about you. I think you like me, but—"

"It's more than like, Max! I tried to tell you on the phone yesterday!"

"It's not enough. Being with you is like dating a stranger. So yeah, it's time for a change. When the semester ends, I'm gone."

"No . . . I won't let you . . . ," I muttered, feeling my jaw muscles ripple and my hands squeeze into fists, blinking once as the cold blue flame ignited deep in my gut. I snared his brown eyes, held tightly, and watched terror spread through them like fingers of blood in clear water. I refused to let him leave me—I'd force him to stay using power that he couldn't resist, and eventually we'd work out our problems, and—and then I saw his worst fear flickering like a black-and-white film that had been retouched in screamingly bright colors. It was myself as I am nearly every day, in jeans, Cubs T-shirt, sneakers, my dark hair long and loose, and eyes shining violently blue as the camera went close on my face. I smiled and said softly, "I love you," and moved in for a kiss.

When I pulled back, the boy I'd embraced was not Max.

He was tall, masculine, and faceless, and spoke deeply, saying, "I love you too."

Max's worst fear was me with someone else—I'd planted it there. What I knew then was what I'd always known, that like he'd said, he wasn't too good to be true, but he was *true*—Max was honest with me because he loved me. It wasn't complicated but I'd made it that way, and I blinked quickly, unlocking his gaze from mine. He bumped along the wall, rolling his fists in his eyes as if they'd been scorched by sunlight. I knew then that I would never use cold fury to force Max to do or feel anything.

Instead, I would let him go.

It was the moment I'd been dreading, and now that it had arrived, it wasn't anything like the poems or rom-coms said. There was no sense of freedom or relief, and no weight lifted from my shoulders. It was burdensome and painful, but I had to because he was right—I would never allow him into my deadly life and I refused to endanger his with the truth. And so I did the only thing left. When he opened his eyes, seeing me again, I pulled him close and kissed him hard, until it hurt.

It was so sweet, and it felt like death.

He parted his lips as if there were something to be said, but closed them again.

We looked at each other for a long time, and then the bell rang. Max went his way, and I went mine.

I didn't look back because I would've turned and followed him, apologized, and—what? Begged him to be patient without telling him why? Asked him to love me back, because I needed so badly to be loved by someone who really knew me, except that he had no idea who or what I really was? The old Sara Jane, the girl who occupied this body only months ago, would've chased Max down and made up an excuse just to stay with him, knowing it was flimsy and temporary but not caring.

Somewhere along the way, I'd left her by the side of the road.

My life is not my own—remember the chauffeur—my life is not my own, I thought, and I kept walking.

17

BREAKUP TUESDAY MELDED INTO SHOCK
Wednesday. Tomorrow was sit-down-with-Lucky Thursday,
but I was too preoccupied to worry about it. Instead, I spent
Wednesday drifting through school semi-blinded by thoughts
of myself and forlorn at breaking up with Max. We floated
past one another in the hallway and he lifted a chin in a slight
hello, and I responded with a mumbled "How are you?" but
nothing more.

The split had to happen, but he should not have walked
away in silence.

Maybe he believed there was time to reverse course, but
I knew that wasn't true. Time is a liar. Things end brutally,
quickly. In the icepick-sharp reality of my life, families vanish
in a zephyr of blood, uncles plummet from Ferris wheels, and
when you walk away from a boy, you don't look back, because
over is over.

Across a hallway of bobbing heads, I saw Max fumbling
at his locker.

From the curve of his shoulders and twist of his mouth, I knew he was hurting.

I tried to remember if the last words I spoke to Lou or my mom were uttered in love, anger, or indifference, but I couldn't. I recalled my dad's farewell as he crept away in the Lincoln, but louder and more lasting was that I said nothing in response. I wished then for Max that he would've said whatever he held back before I walked away. The way my life was going, he'd never have the chance to say it. Because he was sensitive and smart, I knew that irretrievable moment would cut him.

"Hey, SJ," Heather said, dragging a fingertip across the back of my neck, leaving a crackling trail as she passed by with the twins at her side. "What do you know?" Her voice was feathery soft and an aura seemed to flare around her. Kids gaped, genuflected, and one of them elbowed me to get near her.

"Heather!" Mandi Fishbaum barked as she and a pair of her look-alikes jostled past me. "We *really* need to talk about Saturday night!"

A pinched look crossed Heather's face, like a supermodel who'd sipped vinegar. Not loudly but rising above the din, she said, "You just bumped into my cousin."

Mandi licked her scarlet lips nervously. "Um . . . I did?"

Heather stepped up and put an arm on my shoulder. "Yeah. You did. You must not have seen her, because why else would you be so rude?" She smiled, showering the hallway with sparkles. "I like your hair, Mandi. Do you like it, SJ?"

"I guess so." I shrugged. "It's . . . big."

She squeezed my shoulder and said, "It *is* big, and you are too, Mandi. Not, like, from a body mass standpoint. I mean underneath all of that makeup and stuff, you're a big person with a generous heart who would love to invite my cousin to your party."

The hallway was as silent as an empty library. In the history of Fep Prep, no one had ever told Mandi Fishbaum what to do, or for that matter whom to invite to her (notorious) parties. Mandi put on a smile, it slipped, and then she blew air from her cheeks and rolled her eyes. Without looking at me, not even trying to contain a sour-lemon pout, she said, "So . . . I'm having a party this Saturday night and . . . Well, anyway, you can come if you want to."

"That's *so* sweet of you," Heather said in one of those amazing actress tones that convey pure sincerity, and that Mandi's a bitch, and that the only thing my cousin cared about was me. I didn't need to be defended—I could kick the world's ass if I was coldly furious enough—but Heather's regard for me, her concern, was like adrenaline to the heart, making me feel more alive. She lifted her perfect eyebrows in silent dismissal as Mandi obediently withdrew with an unctuous smile. Heather turned to me, grinning. "Get out your party dress, SJ. Have fun, fun, fun with the people who love you most!"

"I wouldn't be caught dead there." I smiled.

"I know. That's why I love you." She winked, walking away with the twins. At the end of the hall, she turned and waved, and instead of the real Heather Richards—former child star battling a virulent addiction problem—I saw the original Becky, reborn and projected into an alternate universe. It was as if she'd never been dumped from *Two Cool for School,* but rather the show had fast-forwarded to Becky's senior year where, in a reversal of her character, she'd become everyone's most beloved student. She had undergone less a transformation than an actualization of what she always wanted to be, not just on TV but in real life. I couldn't stop looking at her floating away like an electric butterfly, as a thought bubbled through the murk—how amazing it was that she'd attained that level of idolization so quickly.

She'd ditched the green contact lenses, her eyes glittering like blue diamonds.

It was obvious that she was using ghiaccio furioso to make people fawn and follow; her commanding popularity, begun with a trickle of cold fury, had grown into a tsunami. Although I'd been aware of the phenomenon since I was small, the flame didn't fully flicker and burn until months ago, and even then I had to dig through the old notebook to discover what it was. If Heather remained ignorant of its existence, perhaps she would do nothing more than crown herself Miss Fep Prep—except that experiencing cold fury came with an insatiable need to understand it, and oneself. It was clear she too felt a bond between us, and I couldn't help but think that I owed her an explanation, which carried innumerable risks. It was a perilous consideration, one that I'd normally talk through with Doug, and it occurred to me then that he'd become invisible.

Our last contact was Monday when he left a note about the creature's laptop. I knew he was around; he'd erased and re-scribbled the title of the Friday morning film on the

Classic Movie Club announcement board. It was his normal ritual, except this time he'd scrawled TBA, to be announced, which was very unlike Doug. Further signs that he hadn't completely tumbled off the planet existed at the Bird Cage Club, where Harry had been walked and messily fed, used clothes strewn on the floor, and his laptop plugged in to recharge, pinging provocatively. His absence should've made me nervous but I was trying to find my feet after splitting with Max, and when I wasn't at school, I was trying to track down information about Juan Kone. Wednesday night, long after the city exhaled its workforce, I sat typing with index fingers on Doug's laptop, staring at the glowing screen as if it were a crystal ball. First it revealed that Juan was some sort of genius and second, that he was fat.

Like, circus-sideshow fat.

I followed the trail of his academic and professional achievements, first at Universidad Nacional de La Plata, where he'd obtained degrees in pharmaceutical biology and food engineering. The Internet tagged him next when his dad, Oswaldo Kone, welcomed him into the family business, Kone Química (Kone Chemical), which produced additives for junk food; Oswaldo died a year later and left the operation to Juan. When Juan became CEO, a local newspaper, *El Día,* ran an interview. I scanned it, thumbing my Spanish dictionary, until Juan was asked about his influences and he named just one—his grandfather, Irving Cohen. Electricity tiptoed over my shoulders as I read how Juan's childhood was spent at Cohen's knee, "learning lessons from the injustices inflicted upon my poor grandfather that will guide me for life."

Uh-oh, I thought, *that sounds like Outfit talk for a vendetta.*

I double-clicked on a photo, watching Juan crowd the screen—one more oyster cracker and body parts would be hanging from lampposts. He accepted an award while smiling into the camera, his suit straining to contain legs like bulging sandbags and arms like sugar-cured hams, the corpulence creeping to fingers as taut as twisty balloons. His face—small dark eyes, babyish nose, and oddly delicate lips—seemed to float in a pool of tapioca that spilled into a neck, all of it framed by a mane of black, lustrous hair. A mustache as straight and thin as a thread of yarn sat on his lip, while farther below, somewhere between the first and second chin, a glossy goatee perched. The only other distinguishing characteristic was pinned to his lapel—a yellow rose. It had been the signature of his grandfather, proof left behind that Ice Cream Cohen had robbed the Rispolis. I knew instinctively then that Juan was aware of the deadly rift between his family and my own.

The Kone Química website had been shut down; a later blurb on the *El Día* website reported that the factory had burned and the insurance payout was huge, but it didn't mention Juan. In my mind's eye, I watched him waddling from a private jet at O'Hare Airport with a suitcase full of cash and a head brimming with knowledge about junk food and drugs. I sat back and twisted the facts like a Rubik's cube, from my family's abduction by tinkling trucks to the creatures' attempts to capture me to ice cream itself, both the slow-melting type and Sec-C. Step by step, the colored squares lined up—it wasn't a lesson of injustice Juan had been taught by his grandfather, it

was the limitless power of cold fury! Juan may've been after revenge, but what he really sought was contained in the brains of certain Rispolis. I had no idea how he could or would use enzyme GF, but there was no denying the fact that he wanted ghiaccio furioso.

I'd give it to him.

I would give him *me* in exchange for my family's freedom.

It was the only way left. There were too many layers between us—too many creatures, hidden headquarters, and Weston Skarlovs. It was time to step into the bear trap; maybe cold fury would free me from it and maybe it wouldn't, but either way, the standoff was over. I looked at the screen at Doug's Friendbook page and found messages he'd recently traded with another Mister Kreamy Kone fanatic.

GoalieMoley: You were the life of the party. God, you can really samba!

HotDoug: It's the life-saving S-C! Makes me feel like dancin'!

GoalieMoley: And romancin'???

HotDoug: You should know!

GoalieMoley: BTW, have you RSVP'd for the MKK Cubs game on Sat.? You can invite a newbie but you'd better not make me jealous!!!

Several things got my attention—Doug as the life of a party, Doug doing the samba—but it was the romance part that stopped me. I knew that a deep self-loathing made my friend believe a relationship with another person was impossible. All I could think was that Sec-C must be pretty potent for such a solid inhibition to be lowered.

The cursor flashed.

I leaned into the keyboard, typing:

HotDoug: I'll be there! Bringing a special guest that some in the MKK community may know . . . Sara Jane Rispoli. She can't wait to meet Juan Kone!

The message was as dangerous as the loaded .45 in my steel briefcase. Juan Kone had spun his sugary web in the shadows, but those few lines would force him into the open. I sent the message just as the elevator clanked to a halt. Carefully I closed the laptop, dropping the room into darkness. When footsteps and a murmuring voice drew near the control center, I snapped on the desk light and said, "It's about time."

Someone or something that resembled Doug shrieked, fumbling a phone.

"Sara Jane!" he said. "You're awake." He picked up the cell and spoke into it, yanking up too-large pants with one hand. "I've got to go. I have to get some sleep, and you do too. Because, silly, tomorrow's a school day and good boys go to school. Me too . . . bye," he said softly.

He turned with a smile creasing his sunken cheeks, as I whispered, "Doug?" It was a reasonable facsimile but one that looked more like a deflating bouncy house in the latter stages of collapse than my best friend. I hadn't seen him in a week and in that time he'd lost enough weight that flesh hung from his body in folds, making him appear loose and melted under his now tentlike clothing. He was still overweight, but his entire being was reduced in a way that revealed an actual skeletal system, and a neck, and a waist. I moved closer, gaping, and said, "Are you . . . okay?"

"Never better," he said, his eyes pulsing with a rosy glow. "Guess who's dating an athlete?"

It felt like I was strolling through someone else's dream. I mumbled, "Who?"

"Me! Doug Stuffins!" he trilled, holding the edges of his flapping polo shirt in his fingertips and curtsying. "A real, live *hockey player!*"

Doug had yet to absolutely self-identify as straight or gay, and I was sensitive about offending him. Tentatively, I asked, "Field or ice?"

He stepped forward and pulled me close. It was like being hugged by a bony bag of pudding. A sickly sweetness poked at my nostrils. "You're kind, and you respect me. You're an old soul," he whispered. "It's a stupid term, but true. Thank you."

"For what?"

"For this!" he said, sweeping his hands over his body. "For introducing me to Sec-C! It's saving my life!" I pulled back and took a closer look at him. His sudden relative smallness had been such a shock that I hadn't noticed that his face was as pale as freshly butchered pork, his eyes had turned pinkish, and when he smiled his tongue was lavender; all of that plus the model-thin body straining to emerge from layers of cellulite, and a chill went across my skin.

I was staring at someone morphing into a creature, and it was all my fault.

I'd sent him to that Sec-C party to find out about Mister Kreamy Kone headquarters, and those freaky fans recruited and then absorbed him. Every instinct cried out to act now, immediately, and tear him free of that cult and its toxic frozen treat, but the reality was that I needed Doug as an entrée to the Cubs game and to Juan Kone. I was taking advantage of the only person who had truly helped me; it was boldly selfish on my part, but I had no choice. I'd told Doug from the beginning that nothing was more important than saving my family, that I'd use any means possible, and now that included him. So, instead of warning him about the danger he faced, I told him only that I'd made a major breakthrough and that it was essential that I go with him to the game on Saturday.

That's when I knew for sure that Sec-C was affecting his body *and* his mind.

The world's most inquisitive kid didn't ask a single question.

Instead he listened with a goofy smile and random giggles while glancing at buzzing text messages. To get his attention, I reminded him vigorously that I'd been whistled in for a sit-down with the *Boss of the entire effing Outfit!* His response was a nod, texting thumbs, and a burble of laughter. I wondered if a slap across the face would snap him back to the moment, but before I could make a move, his eyes darted to mine as he licked his lips. "By the way!" he said excitedly. "I met your cousin! I can't believe the original Becky is in *my* history class! God, is she hot! A genuine L.A. firecracker!"

I paused. "Did you hear about Max and me?"

"No. What . . . ," he said, but his phone buzzed again and he glanced at it, chuckling and saying, "Oh, you dirty little . . . ," while texting back, and then looked up, surprised that I was there. "What were we talking about? Wait . . . Max, right?"

"Right," I said. "We—"

"Yeah, I saw him the other day. He had on the coolest T-shirt! It was this vintage motorcycle thing! I've got to get me one! Ask him where he bought it, okay?"

I nodded, taken aback at Sec-C's infiltration of the part of Doug's brain that allowed him to be impressed by the original Becky and cool T-shirts. I wanted to shake him until he became the old Doug again, but I couldn't. Not yet. Not until after the Cubs game on Saturday. All I could do is say good night as he rolled onto the couch and instantly began to make buzz saw noises. Harry tilted his head, looking at Doug's diminished physique, the body warmth minimized, and turned toward my bedroom. I rose from the control center and walked onto the terrace, where the city was disappearing behind waves of fog. I inhaled the atmospheric ice, feeling it burn my lungs.

Twenty-seven floors below, Frank Sinatra tinkle-crooned about Chicago through wet clouds, and I gritted my teeth, thinking, *We'll see whose kind of town it is.*

18

I WAS CAUGHT BY THE THROAT, TRAPPED BY rough fingers as the stench of rotten animal flesh—that sweet stink of maggot-covered meat—infiltrated my nose, lungs, and mouth. Trying to move only forced his grip to tighten, the angry thumbs digging harder against my pulsating arteries. I gaped at a pair of eyes inside woolen holes, expecting to see pinwheels of lunacy, but instead they blinked back like two cherries on fire. The ski mask lifted by a force unseen, lightly levitating. Beneath was a severe, angular face with a line of scarlet blood cutting across a cheek as white as a snow-covered field. Teardrop's head attached to Poor Kevin's bulky body seemed like a natural occurrence in that nightmare world. Its taut, gray lips parted, like slicing open a freshly caught eel, and the blackened, infected tongue uncoiled as it spoke.

"Answer me! Answer me! Answer me!"

One of the most paralyzing sensations hardwired into the human psyche is groggily waking up, assuming you're alone, and then realizing that someone is lurking nearby. My brain was still in dreamland Thursday morning, where everything loomed large and heart-stopping, and I froze, sure that a bleached-face mutant in a ski mask—a combination of one who haunts my night terrors long after his death and one who pursues me through the streets of Chicago—would materialize at my bedside. Both of my eyes opened at once, focused on the ceiling, and the only sound was me swallowing. It was quiet, and then the high-pitched, girlish tone spoke again, demanding answers through the keyhole, right outside my room.

"Answer me! Answer me!" it demanded, and of course I would. I always did.

Rolling from the mattress, I grabbed the sap and yanked open the door to nothing—no hybrid freak, face behind the voice, or Doug on the couch, only dust motes doing pliés through morning sunlight. Harry and his leash were gone, which meant Doug had taken him around the block. As I turned to my room, the voice spoke again, vibrating beneath a pile of papers on the control center. I remembered then that my (thirty-ninth) disposable phone had died. I'd activated a replacement, but no one had called until now. The ringtone was an actual voice, saccharine and babyish, like something you'd hear on an anime cartoon. I then spoke a cautious hello into the receiver, listening to a voice tinged with just enough whispery pain to make it sound suffering but sexy.

"SJ?" Heather mewled, each letter drawn out half a beat.

"Yeah. Are you okay?"

She took a deep breath. "I need help. Right now. Badly."

I waited, listening to static. "Help with what?"

"With what's going on inside my head. I have a terrible headache, behind my eyes. It started last night and hasn't let up. I thought . . . maybe you could help me."

"Headache," I repeated, breathing a little easier. "Maybe a migraine?"

"Rancho Salud. My capoeira therapist, remember? He . . . ow! Shit, that kills!" she spit like being touched by a live wire, as warning bells went off in my gut. "He told me it would hurt like hell when my mind and brain finally cleared themselves of years of toxins and chemicals. I thought it was the usual rehab BS," she said, her voice pressed down by pain. "The old 'power comes with freedom from drugs' line. But guess what? He was right. Because as bad as it hurts, I've been having these, like, flashes of clarity, where I understand myself. It feels like I can . . . well . . ."

I licked at my dry lips, feeling grit on my tongue. "What?"

"It sounds crazy, but . . . it feels as though I can make people do whatever I want them to do. Especially, well, like me."

"Uh . . . really?"

"Yeah, really. It's as if, somewhere in my mind, I command them to like me, not just in the moment, but forever. Ken and Kendra, for example," she said. "They called me this morning, literally both on the line, to make sure I'd meet them at Bump 'N' Grind. When I told them I wasn't going to school, it was like I'd canceled Christmas. They kept asking, 'Why? But why?'" She made me jump when she laughed, full and throaty, and then she was silent a moment. "It feels like it's coming through my eyes."

"Oh? Um . . . how through your eyes?"

"I don't know," she said, and paused, the phone crackling impatiently. "Do you?"

"Me?" I said, never sounding guiltier in my life. "How would I?"

I could almost hear her shrug. "Because we're cousins. Because we have the exact same color of eyes, with the gold thingies in them. No one on my dad's side of the family has them," she said, her voice dropping. "And because you promised that you'd always tell me the truth . . . if there's a truth to tell, that is. Because you're not a liar."

Nervy pinpricks attacked my body. "Really, there's nothing . . ."

"But it takes someone with secrets of her own to recognize a soul mate . . . sorry, that was a little *too* L.A. What I mean is, I felt a connection the first time we met, so indulge me, okay? Let's do the 'Trust Test,' and instead of my mom, you'll be you."

"Heather . . ."

"What do you know about my headache, SJ? What do you know about the power I feel? Can I control people? Can I, SJ?"

"There's nothing I can tell you."

"You have to tell me!" she shrieked. "I have a *right* to know!"

I didn't respond, since my denial would be obvious. The air was dense between us. She coughed once, clearing her throat of agony, saying, "Silence isn't an answer."

"You're tired. Headaches are . . . the pain makes people think things that . . ."

"Aren't true?" Heather said in a voice cut between anguish and determination. "Because I'd be, like, *totally* unhappy if I thought you were holding out on me."

I shook my head all alone in my room, relieved the conversation was taking place on the phone instead of eye to eye. "It's . . . sorry, it's a mystery to me. Really."

Her pause was so full of disbelief that all I could do was bite at the inside my cheek until she sighed. "It's probably a migraine, complete with hallucinations. I'm staying in a dark room with a blanket over my head. No school for me, which means I can't bring the cookies you asked for," she said dully. "You'll have to stop by the bakery. Who are they for, by the way?"

Three dozen of Rispoli & Sons' famous molasses concoctions.

A direct order from the Boss of the Outfit.

My sit-down with Lucky at noon felt like a hurricane about to reach shore.

"Oh, uh . . . my doctor," I said, "I have an appointment today. I'm not going to school either. So I guess I'll see you Friday."

"Sure. Well, good luck at the doctor," she said remotely. "It's important to know *exactly* what's going on inside yourself." She hung up without a good-bye.

I looked at the phone and then stared into a mirror, blinking my eyes, summoning and dismissing the blue flame. Heather wasn't in control of the phenomenon, but she was aware of it and suspicious of me. What struck me was her age, nearly eighteen and only now experiencing cold fury. I wondered if her therapist had been unintentionally correct, that part of Heather's brain had been clogged by chemicals and only now, more than a month drug-free, cold fury was able to trickle into her eyes.

It occurred to me then that it wasn't only cruel not to tell her who and what she really was, but potentially dangerous, if Juan Kone discovered she was a carrier. But then, danger was at the heart of all of my relationships; forced to weigh the safety of anyone else against the priority of finding my family, I'd decided long ago that my mom, dad, and Lou would always win. It was this dynamic that forced me to cut Max loose; the closer he got and the more he knew, the more he'd be in danger and slow me down. The same applied to Heather. Explaining cold fury meant revealing everything about my family and our life in the Outfit—*and, and, and*— with each fact more hazardous than the next. Divulging those things would put her in the same type of jeopardy as Max, and I didn't have the time or energy to worry about her, either. All I could hope for was that her use of cold fury remained unfocused and harmless, safely contained within the walls of Fep Prep, and didn't interfere in the quest to find my family.

Thinking of them reminded me of my sit-down with Lucky at noon.

I opened the notebook to the seventh chapter, *"Procedimenti"* ("Procedures"), for guidance on the meeting and came upon three blunt paragraphs:

> *Being whistled in for a sit-down with an Outfit superior*
> *should be taken with the utmost seriousness, as there are*

only two reasons for such a meeting—you have failed to do
something or a request will be made that you do something.

If it's a failure, apologize profusely, swear on your
mother, wife, or children (never a pet) that you will make
it right, quickly remove yourself from the premises, and
make it right!

If you're requested to do something, say yes.
Immediately.

I had no idea which one it could be, failure or request. I'd already gone far beyond my moral boundaries in deciding the fates of depraved criminals; being asked to do even more was unimaginable. I dressed in my standard counselor-at-large outfit of businesslike blouse and skirt, pinned back my hair, and sighed. I had so much grinding stress in my life, from sit-downs to cousins with cold fury to dementia-ridden great-uncles—and then I remembered the molasses cookies! I knew I'd be a fool to show up without them, so I left the Bird Cage Club without waiting for Doug to return. Traffic flowed quickly, the battered Lincoln roared over the pavement, and although the creatures seemed to be nowhere, I parked behind the bakery just to be safe. I glanced at the electrical box, tempted to enter via alley-vator, but chose the back door instead. I unlocked it with my key and stepped quietly inside.

First I heard the industrial stainless steel refrigerator humming.

Then I heard a whispering voice.

No—voices, plural, I was sure of it.

Moving with velvet steps, I peeked around the refrigerator into the white-tiled kitchen. I'd perfected the art of eavesdropping by listening to my parents' whispered conversations, and I stood perfectly still, barely breathing. Annabelle's back was to me, and Uncle Jack faced her, nodding, eyes troubled, but what struck me was that her hands were on her hips. She wasn't using them to talk. Uncle Jack spoke quietly, saying, "I told you, I *can't* remember. It's buried . . . too deeply to reach . . ."

"Try *harder*!" Annabelle said, and I realized that she wasn't whispering as much as shoving words out her mouth with a jagged, breathy effort.

"Too deep . . ." Uncle Jack whimpered, putting a hand over his face.

Quickly, with a boxer's speed, Annabelle grabbed him by the shirt collar and yanked him close, giving him a hard shake to punctuate her words. "No, you listen to me, *old man*! I didn't drag my *druggy kid* across the country to screw around in some musty old bakery, whipping up cookies for your *great-niece*!" she rasped. "*You* said there was something *incredibly valuable* here that would take care of Heather and me for *life*! You said coming all the way to Chicago would help you *find it*!"

"Remembra and my mind." He gasped. "They're failing me!"

"And you're failing *me*!" she said, shoving him away, stalking over to the baking table. I peeked around at the Xeroxed pages of *"Volta"* spread out on it, covered in Uncle Jack's translated scribbles. "All day long you stare at this fairy tale she gave you!"

"I—I think it's helping me . . . maybe," he said weakly.

"It's bullshit!" she croak-whispered, spinning toward him just as I pulled back behind the refrigerator. "Instead of doing her damn homework, rack that swiss cheese brain of yours for . . . what the hell did you say it was? Ultimate power?"

Hearing the words, everything stopped—my heart, my mind, time itself.

The secret inside *"Volta,"* the one Uncle Jack was digging for with Buondiavolese, unaware of what he was doing.

The one that I hoped and prayed could free my family.

At some point the old man had known ultimate power existed—he just didn't remember what it was or where it was located. Now the answer was literally at his fingertips, on those copied pages, and I peeked back as Annabelle gathered them up. Slowly, deliberately, she shredded them into thin, babble-covered strips. Uncle Jack started toward her, but she stuffed the paper down the garbage disposal and a whirring second later, it was all gone. I should've attacked her or shrieked like a madwoman or wept bitter tears, but instead I stood motionless, hearing her spit, "From now on, you think about the past, when you were a *Rispoli* instead of a *Richards!* You think about what you learned from your mobster father about ultimate power!"

It was silent for heavy seconds until Uncle Jack said, "I was a bad father. I should've given you . . . more."

"Oh, but Detective Keegan, you were far too *busy* with police work," Annabelle said in a tone so acidic it cut through the garble of her voice. "Besides," she said, pulling the scarf from her neck, lifting her chin defiantly, "you gave me this!"

I peeked at a ragged line of tissue scarring her throat; once revealed, it screamed for attention.

Uncle Jack's face darkened, and then went blank. "I did . . . something . . . but I can't remember . . ."

"Let me remind you for the hundredth time," Annabelle said wearily. "You were full of whiskey. 'Drowning old secrets,' as you used to say." She put the scarf in place, wrapping it in delicate folds. "You passed out with a cigarette between your fingers. Somehow you escaped the house unharmed. I wasn't so fortunate."

"There was . . . a fire," he said, his brown eyes welling up. "A terrible accident."

"With booze and drugs, there are no accidents," she said matter-of-factly. "Only things that conclude with blood or someone dead. That's it. No Hollywood endings."

"Annabelle," Uncle Jack said, opening his arms, looking lost and desperate.

She hesitated as the rage in her face went from red to pink to pale. Clearly, they'd covered this painful ground before, with the old man forgetting more of it and Annabelle forgiving him all over again. "Daddy," she sighed, slowly embracing him.

"I'm disappearing. Bit by bit. I want to take care of you and Heather before . . ."

"That's why we're here," she said, leading him from the kitchen.

I watched the door swing shut, hurried to a box on the counter filled with molasses cookies, and grabbed it. As I sped from the bakery, the tragedy of what had occurred sunk in—

the razor-thin chance of discovering the *"Volta"* secret of ultimate power gobbled away by a garbage disposal. It had been
just copies of the chapter's secret pages, but there was no way
Annabelle would let Uncle Jack work on another version. I
had no idea what Juan Kone knew about ultimate power—
I still had no idea what it was myself!—but if I'd hoped it
would serve as a defense against him and the squad of creatures, that fantasy was gone too. I pulled to the curb, trying to
figure out my next move, as my hand brushed the Rispoli &
Sons Fancy Pastries box. Looking down at it, I realized that
everyone is left a legacy by her parents.

Sometimes it's soft, sweet cookies and secret meetings with
gangsters.

Other times the legacy is a moment that scars your neck,
and soul, for life.

In the end, it's what she does with it that matters.

19

THE ADDRESS IN THE NOTE THAT SUMMONED
me to the sit-down was on a gray block right off Michigan
Avenue, between Oak and Elm, that I wasn't aware existed.

If I hadn't been looking for Poplar Street, I'd have driven
by without a glance.

Idling at the corner, looking from the note through the
windshield, I was struck by the blandness of the area, populated by faded brick apartment buildings, chunky Victori-
ans, and skinny mid-rises. Somehow the note had become
damp, and I realized my hands were sweating. I swung to
the curb and cut the engine, grabbed the cookie box, and
shut my eyes. To say I was nervous was an understatement;
it was full-soul trepidation, as if I were about to face a demon that knew everything I was hiding about my missing
family, especially my (possibly rat) dad. I thought, *What if
he does? What if that's why I'm here?* and realized that it didn't
matter—there was nowhere to run. The thought didn't calm
me down but it did get me moving, and half a block later I

stood outside a building that was neither shabby nor luxurious. More than anything, it was forgettable, an anonymous rectangle leaning toward the sky like an upended shoe box. A discreet brass sign affixed beside a revolving door read:

HOTEL ALGREN
Long-Term Residency Only

NO TRESPASSING—SOLICITORS WILL BE PROSECUTED

I looked skyward, seeing only sooty stone and stringy clouds. I was expecting the secretive majesty of the Commodore Hotel, with a red-carpeted entrance manned by a doorman in a bell captain's uniform. Instead I pushed through to a tiny lobby. A dusty palm tree wilted in the corner and circulars for pizza and Thai places were scattered under a row of mailboxes. There was no doorman; the entry to the home of the Boss of the Outfit was completely unguarded. I checked the address again—correct—and crossed to an elevator. It arrived with a groan and complained all the way to the thirteenth floor, leaving me in a hallway with worn carpeting and buzzing light fixtures. Somewhere nearby, a TV grumbled. The note read *Apartment 1306,* and I counted down until I came to the door. For luck, I kissed my mom's gold *R* signet ring and pressed Max's Triumph medallion against my neck. I barely knocked, and the door swung open to a guy who looked like an ancient Roman statue. He was as solid as poured cement, with cropped silver hair and penetrating eyes peering down an aquiline nose.

Slowly, with no question mark at the end, he side-mouthed my name in a Chicago accent that sounded like *Seer-uh Jee-un Riz-booli.* I nodded, smiled, lifted the cookies, received no smile in return, and slowly lowered the box. He made a clicking noise with his tongue and motioned me inside. I entered a small, plain room. A single bed covered by a thin blanket sat next to an old TV and chipped wooden chair. An oil painting of geese in flight hung on the wall, and plastic slats covered the window. The door closed behind me, locked, locked again, and locked once more.

I turned and said, "Lucky?"

He jerked his head at a door. "Bathroom," he said, sounding like *bee-ath-rum.*

"Pardon?"

"Go."

"I . . . don't have to . . ."

"Go," he hissed through clamped teeth in a way that made the hairs on my neck stretch. I entered a pink-tiled, bleach-smelling restroom and shut the door. A glass vanity etched with rose vines hung above a pink porcelain sink. I yanked a pull chain on the vanity as a frost-covered fluorescent light stuttered to life. There was nothing behind the shower curtain but a (yes, pink) tub, and then I looked over the toilet where a homey, hand-painted sign hung. Next to an image of an apple-cheeked little boy and girl holding hands while making their way to an outhouse, a verse read:

Be it ever so humble
For woman or man,
Whether pee-pee or poo-poo,

There's no place like the can!

I stared at it, seeing the raised *C* in *can,* and pushed it. The wall and false toilet attached to it lifted, revealing a concealed hallway. I stepped forward, the wall swooshed shut, and I moved cautiously toward a floor-to-ceiling barricade of riveted steel. A slot opened in it wide enough to reveal a pair of shifty eyes. I'd seen something like it before, thinking of the Prohibition-era door to Club Molasses. A voice said, "Password."

"Password? Oh, right!" I said, remembering the note, and I read, "'I refuse to answer on the grounds that it may incriminate me.'"

The slot slammed, a door rose, and I moved toward the owner of the eyes, which resided in a bullet-shaped head attached to a gorilla body. An Uzi was slung over his shoulder and a .45 strapped to his waist. His partner, a gawky dork with slick hair, ushered me toward a metal detector while Bullet-Head rested a hand on the pistol. Slick stared at me and removed a toothpick. "You're the Rispoli?"

"That's right."

He snorted, unpeeling a "big fragging deal" grin. As I entered the metal detector, he said, "Take off the ring. And whatever's around your neck. What's in the box?"

"Molasses cookies."

"Cookies?" he said with mock wonder. "Guess I didn't get the memo."

"What memo?" Bullet-Head said.

"That we were becoming a branch of the *Girl* Scouts!" Slick said as they guffawed together, two idiots with the same donkey laugh.

I blinked once, the cold blue flame leaped like a caged tiger, and I held Slick's wiseguy gaze until his forehead sprouted sweat and his chin quivered. When his worst fear was traveling between us (him modeling women's frilly underwear in front of a mirror and being discovered by Bullet-Head), I said, "You're making me late. I'll tell Lucky why."

"No . . . please, Counselor, *please*," he whispered.

I blinked, watching him collapse against a wall. Turning to his partner, I said, "How about you, cue ball? You get the memo?"

"Yes, ma'am. I mean, no, ma'am . . . miss . . . Counselor!" he said, vigorously shaking his head and pointing a finger. "That way. The viewing room."

I turned down a hallway wide enough to park a Cadillac in and stood outside glass doors where sad, sweet lutes and ululating angels played through the air. I knocked once, got no response, and put an ear to the door, hearing a muffled sobbing. I knocked again and entered a dark room flickering with Technicolor. On-screen, Bambi nosed the dead body of his mother. Two figures sat side by side in the front row. An explosion of sobs shook the room as the cartoon deer whispered, "Mother? Mother?"

"Oh God! It's *just . . . not . . . fair!*" the voice wailed, pounding the arms of the chair.

"There, there," a female voice said comfortingly. In the dark, I saw the spark of a lighter and smelled a cigarette.

"Why the hell does the poor mother *always . . . get . . . killed?*"

"'Cause Disney likes to kill mothers," the female voice said.

"Excuse me," I said softly. "I'm looking for Lucky."

It was silent, and then the crier blew his nose, calling out, "Cut the film! Turn up the lights!" Bambi disappeared, the room was semi-lit, and I hadn't even taken a step when he said, "We're coming to you." I stood nervously, expecting a specimen more intimidating than the thug who'd answered the apartment door. A metallic scraping preceded them as an elderly man emerged from the gloom, pushing a walker. He was not thin or fat, tall or short. The Cubs ball cap could've been brand-new or fifty years old, and his glasses, framed in black, were neither thick nor thin. He wore a dull dress shirt beneath a light-blue Windbreaker covering a soft potbelly, beige pants with no crease, and white Velcro tennis shoes. As he approached, he thumbed away tears with a handkerchief. His appearance was similar to the facade of the Hotel Algren—in one glance little impression was made, and he was forgotten. I knew enough about the Outfit to realize it was a purposeful effect. When you spend a lifetime carrying out brazen crimes and committing acts of terrorism, anonymity is a strategy for survival.

Then he drew closer, and I saw his eyes.

In contrast to the rest of him, they were impossible to ignore or forget.

They were iridescent black pearls, sucking in the light around them while giving out nothing, and I knew I was looking into the face of death. *A shark could try to disguise itself inside a dolphin suit,* I thought, *but its eyes would give it away.* He stared at me coldly and said, "Who'da thunk it? A girl got the *malocchio.*"

"*Malocchio?*" I said, my voice shallow.

"The evil eye. In the old days, guys used it for intimidation. They'd practice, squinting into a mirror." He chuckled, shaking his head. "Idiots. Only certain Rispolis got *malocchio,* right?"

"Yeah," I said. "That's right."

"I'm sure your pop told you, but as a gentle reminder"—he grinned wickedly—"use it on me and I'll slit your goddamn throat." My tongue went dry and before I could speak, he said, "But then, why would you? If I'm incapacitated, you are, as the poets say, shit outta luck. Symbiosis is a big word, but it fits—we benefit each other mutually. You sit in judgment over homicidal thugs and force them to behave, and I make sure the losers in those disputes don't kill you . . . and they want to, every last one."

Of course he was right. On some level, I was aware of being protected as counselor-at-large. The losers were harshly punished *and* highly vindictive, and after all, I had these cold, furious eyes in the front of my head, but not the back. The past four months had shown that I was as vulnerable to sneak attack as anyone; ghiaccio furioso would be useless if an Outfit enforcer got the drop on me, threw a bag over my head, and started in with a tire iron. Besides that, there was a question that occurred to me each time I used cold fury on a thug to settle a dispute—how long did the effect last? Was it temporary or forever? I had no way of knowing since I'd been deploying it for just several months. I could only imagine Lucky's bloody wrath if I used cold fury on him, and then the old man snapped out of it.

Quietly, I said, "I won't, ever. You have my word."

"There's a reason Nunzio and Enzo lived to be old men and your dad's suffering some disease instead of a bullet," he said, "and you're looking at him. I've been Boss a long time. Someone's always plotting, ready to slit my throat and take over, but I've survived it all. The counselor-at-large helped me do it—*helped*—but the real reason I'm still in charge is because I never make a threat I don't fulfill. *Tu capisci?*"

"Si." I swallowed. *"Capisco."*

"Speaking of your dad, poor Anthony Rispoli. So sick, he hasn't been seen on the street in months. So near death, a girl is doing his job. Back in the day, the Outfit wasn't always Italian, but it was always everything *except* female." He shrugged his thin shoulders. "Times change. One thing the Outfit does well is change with them. Just to be clear, I don't give two craps in a handbag if your dad is sick, healthy, or dead, as long as a Rispoli is serving as counselor-at-large."

"Good. That's good," I said, trying to keep the relief from my voice.

"The problem is, some people *do* give two craps. That's why you're here."

"I don't understand. What people?"

"Zip it. I never stay in one place while discussing business. We walk and talk."

"Or roll," said the woman at his side, and I looked at her for the first time. Lucky may've been seventy-five or ninety-five, and she was up there too, but showgirl sexy in a timeless way. Her hair was a platinum tidal wave swooping over one side of her face, while her curvaceous body was girdled into a va-va-voomish dress ending just above the knees. She smiled with ruby lips, scrunched a not insubstantial nose (it made me like her), and said, "Peek-a-Boo."

"Uh . . . the same to you?" I said.

"No, silly," she said, switching a cigarette from two French manicured fingers to the corner of her mouth. "Peek-a-Boo Schwartz. That's my name. Well, my stage name, anyway. If history has taught us anything, it's that nobody wants to see a broad named Irma shake her moneymaker."

"My girlfriend," Lucky said, "who left girlhood behind long, long ago. Everyone seems to know it except her wardrobe."

"You're no spring chicken yourself, you old bastard," she said as a horn honked softly. We moved out to the hallway where Bullet-Head waited with a golf cart, helped Lucky into the driver's seat, and disappeared. The old man pointed me into the seat next to him. Peek-a-Boo lifted the Cubs cap, kissed Lucky's head, and said, "Be nice."

"I was born nice," he growled.

"I ain't even sure you was born," she said as he and I whirred away.

The hallway seemed to go on forever. I cleared my throat, saying, "This is a huge apartment. I mean . . . it's the whole floor, right?"

"Whole damn building," he said. "Them cookies for me?"

I had a death grip on the pastry box. "Oh. Yeah."

"Open it," he ordered. One hand on the steering wheel, he grabbed a cookie and devoured it, jaws snapping, then burped softly. "Tastes like my childhood. I was pals with your grandpa Enzo . . . *amico mio*. We came up together."

248

My lips moved without permission, saying, "What about Giaccomo?"

The cart slowed to a stop with his eyes pinned on me. "Enzo's brother wasn't in the Outfit and didn't know nothing about nothing. The . . . *end.*"

I swallowed a mouthful of pebbles. "Right, so, uh . . . you watch a lot of movies?"

"A good film is like a well-made clock. All the parts moving in sync. Just like the Outfit. We supply addicts and perverts, and they pay us. We bribe bad cops and crooked politicians to protect us so we can keep supplying addicts and perverts, and so on. It's the circle of freakin' life." He bit into a cookie and paused, looking like he'd tasted spoiled milk. "Except all's not well in paradise. We got problems with the Russian mob. They're young, bold, and bloody, and their leader has *testicoli* of steel. He ain't shown his face yet, but his guys are encroaching on our turf, kicking inside our business, stealing our daily bread, and busting heads." He leaned in, the combination of rage and excitement unmistakable. "There's gonna be a war. Prisoners will be taken for leverage and revenge. You're gonna use that precious *malocchio* to get 'em talking—names, locations, stash houses—and then, according to the crimes they've committed against the Outfit, you'll make a crucial decision over and over again."

"What's that?" I said, my throat sandy.

He grinned with teeth as sharp as broken glass. "Torture or kill."

"Torture or . . ."

"According to my records, in all the months you've served

249

as counselor, that's one judgment you haven't yet passed . . . the death sentence. Am I wrong?"

"No," I said quietly.

"If I'm gonna order our soldiers onto the streets, I have to know the counselor-at-large will help us win, and that justice will be served," he said. "Fortunately, we got a test case. We caught one."

"One what?"

"A Russian! Our guy in Melrose Park has been assembling a weapons cache for the war—AKs, nitro caps, plastic X. Last week, he busted one of 'em hanging from the roof, gaping in the window. I don't know if the freak was doing recon or if he's a peeping Tom—Johnny Eyeball, I call him—hell, I ain't even sure he's in the mob!" Lucky leaned closer, his eyes inky dots behind the glasses. "What I am sure of is that Russians are a tight-knit bunch . . . they *always* know other Russians. If this SOB has even a shred of information on the mob, *you're* gonna get it!"

"You want me to use ghiaccio furioso?"

"We've cracked his knees, busted his head, but all he does is say 'I vant go home! I vant go home!' in that goddamn accent. He fell into our lap, and now I'm throwing him into yours," he said, nodding almost imperceptibly, although someone somewhere saw it. Seconds later, the sound of chains was followed by Slick and Bullet-Head dragging out a slumping figure in filthy jeans and a shredded hoodie, ankles manacled, head bowed. Slowly he lifted his neck, revealing a face covered in knuckle marks and bruises, but it wasn't the wounds that stopped me. It was his eyes—one red, the other glassy blue.

The guy from the church roof who'd hidden among the angels.

He was in his twenties and deathly pale, raw boned and shuddering with fear. It was plain that he'd been on his way to becoming an ice cream creature. The thugs threw him on the floor, kicking him for good measure as he groaned, eyelids fluttering.

"Well, what are you waiting for?" Lucky said. "Make him talk!"

"Now?"

"Why *not* now?"

Because a coincidence being incredible doesn't mean it's con-venient, I thought. *And because, just by looking at the poor half creature, I know he has nothing to do with the Russians but some-thing to do with Juan Kone. If he knows anything about my fami-ly, I can't risk him saying it aloud.* Tamping down panic, I said, "Because he's been beaten too badly. He can't even keep his eyes open. I can't do a thing if he's unconscious."

Lucky turned his predator gaze on Slick and Bullet-Head, hissing, "Idiots!"

"But . . . you told us to," Slick said feebly.

"Get the hell outta here!" the old man roared, sending them scattering. He moved his head side to side like a boxer twist-ing the rage back into place, and said, "You . . . you're taking him, Counselor! Back to Club Molasses or wherever the hell, and rip any information he has about the Russians right outta his head!"

"What? But . . ." And then I stopped myself, since it was exactly what I wanted; if I was going to get Johnny talking,

251

it had to be done in private. I also knew that an opportunity like this—a one-on-one audience with the Boss who'd been around forever and knew everything—was rare. "Yeah, of course I'll take him," I said, and gathered my courage, adding, "What you mentioned about symbiosis? How we benefit each other mutually? I've served as counselor for four months, and I haven't asked anything for myself."

Lucky smirked wearily. "Everyone, guy or broad, young or old, is always working an angle. What do you need? Guns, drugs, or money?"

I paused, aware that I was stepping into dangerous territory. "Answers to two questions," I said as calmly as possible.

The old man clicked his teeth, staring at me. "Ask," he snarled.

"Who is . . . or was . . . Weston Skarlov?"

Lucky's face was a desert of suspicion, outrage and confusion crossing it like shifting sands. It was plain he had no idea. But as chief spider at the center of the Outfit web for fifty years, he knew that he should, and he wondered if something was being put over on him. Almost grudgingly, he admitted that he'd never heard the name before. And then I asked about the Pure Dairy Confection Company and where its headquarters had been located. "Irving Cohen . . . the bookie with the ice cream business as a front. He owned the goddamn Catacomb Club," he murmured, eyes going to slits as he peered into the past.

"There's a rumor about my grandpa Enzo . . . he cut down all of those people with a tommy gun."

Lucky paused, jaws rippling. "That's what they said."

"Who?"

"*They,* you fool . . . long-gone Outfitters whose whispers and gossip died with them. There's hardly anyone left from that time, so what does it matter?"

He was right, it was dead history, and I asked again, "Where was Cohen's ice cream factory?"

"I don't know," he replied sharply. "I was just coming up then, making my bones by busting other people's. Cohen had been banished." He squinted his fathomless eyes, sucking in light. "That's it. No more questions. Now you take Johnny Eyeball and claw out whatever information he has. And if it just so happens there's nothing inside that ugly skull worth a damn? Kill the bastard."

"Me?" I asked quietly.

The old man nodded, his face rigid as stone. "Not that we got a trust issue between us, Counselor, but if so, I want hard proof you did the job," he said with a grandpa-vampire smile. "I want his red eye as a trophy."

I knew I could kill to defend myself; I'd proven it on Lower Wacker Drive. But that was when a creature had been trying to infiltrate my brain. Killing Johnny would be a type of self-defense as well, since failing to provide his eye to Lucky would be suicide. It was my turn to nod, since words wouldn't form in my cottony mouth.

"You see that?" he said, jabbing a finger past me. "That's an express elevator. It's a straight shot down, like going to hell. So take that freak and go," he said, speeding away. I watched him leave as something buzzed audibly nearby. My gaze moved across wallpaper decorated with velvety flowers until, squinting into the center of a bloom, I found the lens of a tiny camera. It whirred and dilated and I assumed that I was being observed on a screen in a concealed room. When I turned, Peek-a-Boo stood behind me, smoothing her skirt. "You were watching," I said.

"There's hardly a spot in the entire hotel where someone's *not* watching." She smiled. Her eyes flicked down at Johnny with disinterest and back at me. "You'd be surprised how many crooks never suspect it. Then again, most crooks are really dumb."

"How much did you hear?"

"Your conversation? All of it." She produced a cigarette like a magician, flicked a gold lighter, and blew smoke between crimson lips. "Lucky has me listen in on all his walk-and-talks so no details are missed or forgotten. He says I have a great pair of ears," she said. "He's wrong, though."

"Yeah?"

"I have a great left ear," she said, pushing back her platinum swoop, "and then I have this." The right ear was a ragged nub of flesh, mostly gone, and Peek-a-Boo patted her hair back in place. "It got shot off a long time ago," she said, lifting an eyebrow.

I didn't need any prompting. Knuckles told me that there had been one survivor of the Catacomb Club massacre—a woman who played dead after having her ear removed by the tommy gun. "You were there," I said.

"Peek-a-Boo Schwartz and her Feather Dance," she said grimly, striking a pose. "I was the entertainment . . . me, a few discreetly placed peacock fans, and a snare drum. Stripping, they called it. Pantomime dancing, I called it. Never showed more than thigh-high." Her eyes fluttered beyond the moment and her chin quivered as she lifted the cigarette to her lips. "That night . . . what I remember is the unending clatter of the gun, and how no one had a chance to scream. Until then, I didn't know that blood had a smell. I can still smell it. But I never *think* about that night, I do everything *not* to think about it, and I wouldn't have, but you asked Lucky about it."

"You saw him. You identified my grandpa Enzo as the shooter."

"No," she said, the steel back in her voice. "I said it was Nunzio Rispoli's *son*."

We stared at each other for a moment until I said, "Giaccomo?"

"I was lying on my side as he walked through, kicking bodies, and his bandana slipped. The two of them looked so much alike that at first I thought it was Enzo. Then he put it back in place, isolating his eyes, and instead of cold blue, they were brown and troubled." She shrugged, saying, "After I said it was Nunzio's son, the Outfit assumed it had been Enzo, since Giaccomo was a civilian. Before I could correct the mistake, Nunzio and Enzo spoke to Lucky about it. He and Enzo were close allies, and he knew your grandpa would become counselor-at-large someday soon. It was good business to help the Rispolis hide Giaccomo's secret. So, Lucky told me never to utter a word about it. And I haven't, until now." She sighed and said, "It's a dirty old episode, but you must have a reason for wanting to know. And in this business—hell, this *life*—if one broad won't help another, no one will."

I knew then why Lucky had blacked out information about Ice Cream Cohen and the Pure Dairy Confection Company; it must've contained damning evidence of Uncle Jack's vengeful shooting. I also realized that history had repeated itself, with Great-Grandpa Nunzio protecting Uncle Jack just like Grandpa Enzo tried to protect Uncle Buddy.

I wondered if Uncle Jack had suffered the same frustration as Uncle Buddy after being forbidden to be a member of the Outfit; if so, like Uncle Buddy, it made him want it even more. Without Nunzio's permission, he'd taken revenge against Cohen for the robbery of the Bird Cage Club, making the worst mistake of his young life. Both incidents added up—he'd been Nunzio's transcriber of *"Volta"* when the old man was going blind, recording his father's secrets in Buondiavolese, but barred by Nunzio from any further Outfit participation, which made him lash out in a horrific manner. There was no other way he could've known about ultimate power. It also explained his ability to record such a detailed description of the dispute between Ice Cream Cohen and the Rispolis, and the resulting massacre—it was a first-person account.

Why Uncle Jack concealed it between the pages of *"Volta"* remained a mystery.

Was he fulfilling the purpose of the notebook by including every possible Outfit secret—or was it the confession of a guilty mind, hidden where only another Rispoli would discover it? I thought of his battle with alcohol and what I'd overheard between him and Annabelle about "drowning old secrets." Maybe he couldn't drown them all, even after going deep into the fictional world of acting. Maybe Giaccomo Rispoli, a.k.a.

Jack Richards, a.k.a. Detective Ned Keegan, was unable to forget what he'd done until the gift of Alzheimer's did it for him.

"In the viewing room," I said carefully, "was Lucky . . . ?"

"Crying?" she said, flicking an ash as a sad smile blipped and faded. "That's why he watches so many movies. So he can sit where no one can see him but me and blame the story for making him weep like a baby. That old man has an infected soul, shot through by all of the things he's done. He's hidden in movies for a long, long time. Most everyone in the Outfit knows about it. Not one of them is dumb enough to talk about it," she said, as the elevator arrived. "Call it remorse, guilt, or low-grade insanity, but weeping in the dark is the only way he can get any relief."

I threw an arm around Johnny, dragged him onto the elevator, and turned to Peek-a-Boo. "Maybe this is an understatement, but he doesn't seem like the crying type."

"Nobody is completely one person, honey," she said as the doors began to close. "You of all people should know that by now."

20

IT'S A GOOD INDICATOR OF HOW FAR OFF THE rails my life has gone when the most positive thing about my day is that handcuffs aren't necessary.

Hours after I'd hauled Johnny up to the Bird Cage Club and snapped an end of one onto his ankle and the other to a radiator, it was plain that restraint was not an issue—he was still unconscious. I knew he was alive because I'd checked his breathing when I put a pillow beneath his head, and again when I covered him with a blanket. I wouldn't be using cold fury to draw out information about my family or Juan Kone until he was alert. With a sigh, I sat on the couch and sunk into thought—Uncle Jack was the Catacomb Club shooter, and it was shocking, perhaps unanswerable, but at least it hadn't been Grandpa Enzo.

In other words, my possession of cold fury did not mean I was predetermined to be a killer. Even gripped by the electricity and the pleasurable endorphins it released, I still had a choice. Thoughts of death and dying made me consider

how much damage Irving Cohen had done so many people, and how his grandson was continuing the legacy. Hopefully, by this time on Saturday, either from details gleaned from Johnny or at the Cubs game, I'd come face-to-face with Juan Kone. I imagined what I'd do when I finally got my hands on the bloated monster, and I blinked and yawned. The last thought I had before falling asleep was where the hell I'd ever get a red eyeball to satisfy Lucky.

I awoke Friday morning, still on the couch, as sun gushed through the windows.

Snapping to attention, I looked over at Johnny, still amazingly asleep. Harry sniffed tentatively at his face as he groggily lifted a hand, snoring. Doug hadn't returned the previous evening; I assumed he was with his hockey player, hoped he was safe, and felt an instinctual need to discuss everything with him. I prepared for school quickly and then unsnapped the handcuff from Johnny's ankle. Before leaving, I scribbled a note indicating the restroom and then made sure to lock the elevator cage behind me. Compared to the other surreal details of my life, having a half-formed creature as a prisoner didn't seem so odd. A fast train ride later, I hustled up the steps of Fep Prep, swiped an ID card, hurried through a metal detector, and then slowed, watching gleeful, glowing faces bounce by, hearing cheerful chatter, feeling the sugary air vibrate across my shoulders.

Then came the bared bellies.

Navel after navel, abs after abs after flab, each girl I passed had her shirt rolled up just enough to show some stomach. It was as if a secret fashion message had been passed to every

female in school but me. It was Friday, which meant Classic Movie Club met during first period. I rushed to the theater room, anxious to talk to Doug, and was stopped by high, tinkling laughter. It was followed by a throatier response, and I entered the room cautiously, wondering, could it possibly be—

"Oh my *God,* that's *so* funny!" Doug roared, squeezing his hands together. Heather sat onstage, long legs crossed, arms thrown back, button nose crinkled, as he beamed up at her like a starstruck fan. "And you're totally right . . . that's *so* L.A.!"

"How would you know?" I said. "You're from Lincoln Park."

"SJ," Heather said, sliding from the stage, and I saw the Dodgers T-shirt cut high enough to show the wink of a belly button above crenulated stomach muscles. I couldn't believe it—she'd started a schoolwide trend before first period! "You're just in time for the film," she said. "We didn't think you were going to make it. Did we, Doug?"

"No!" he said, jumping to his feet, as jittery as a cockroach. The whites of his eyes were pinker and his body was even more shrunken, as if he were wearing a Doug-skin suit. "She is so cool and so funny and so *hot!*" he said, jabbing a finger at my cousin. "If I had to describe *exactly* what I wanted to look like, it would be *post-rehab Heather Richards*! If I were a girl, that is! Or *not!*"

"I decided to join the club." She shrugged, flipping her hair. "I thought I could offer a showbiz veteran's insight. After all, I spent my formative years being watched by millions of fans."

"It prepared you perfectly for high school," I muttered. "Headache's gone, huh?"

"Yeah. I spent some time with my grandpa," she said. "Funny how the wisdom of an old man can help get your mind right."

"Careful," I said, nodding at her belly. "You don't want to catch a cold too."

"You mean my mini-shirt? Showing a little skin is *very* L.A."

"Dying of exposure is *very* Chicago."

"If knives in the back don't get me first," she said sweetly, smiling with eyes that were narrow, sharp, and as blue as a summer sky. Every warning in my body and brain flashed code red and gonged like church bells, pealing *"She knows! She knows!"* At that moment, the door banged open and Max entered. I was surprised to see him, as if our breakup should've voided his normal routine. Timidly I said, "Hey, Max."

"Hey," he mumbled, folding himself into a chair and staring at the screen.

"Have you guys met? I mean formally?" Doug said, sweeping an arm from Max to Heather.

"No, but I've heard *a lot* about you, Max. Gosh . . . I feel like I know you," she purred, turning a poison look at me into a honey-dripping one at him. "We should get together and have a *long* talk sometime."

"About what?" Max said without looking at her. "Crap TV shows for kids?"

Her angelic features darkened, but she smiled through it and turned away, saying quietly, "You two *deserve* each other."

261

I looked at Max, but he wouldn't meet my eyes. Doug was busy with his laptop, setting up the film, flitting like a hummingbird; there would be no opportunity to speak with him privately about Johnny. Usually we sit in the front row while Doug projects the film onto the screen behind the stage, but today I climbed to the last row of seats, trying to get as far away from the three of them as possible. Doug clambered onstage, made a sweaty steeple with his fingers, and said, "So, normally we just turn on the movie and watch, but today is special because we have a new member. Everyone, I give you the original Becky . . . Heather Richards!" He clomped his hands together, Max remained motionless and Heather did a faux curtsy while I tried not to puke. "Also, I know we never talk before a movie," Doug said, "but *this* one is really special! It means a *lot* to me! It's almost *autobiographical,* with the whole *she's-one-thing-that-blossoms-into-another* theme! And so, without further ado . . . *All About Eve*!"

He almost leaped to his laptop, his huge, flapping shirt making him look like a flying squirrel. The lights dimmed and for the next forty-five minutes, I watched a young, ambitious actress ingratiate herself to an older, more accomplished one, then imitate her, and then displace her and shoplift her fame. The younger woman, Eve, lies, cheats, and even attempts to steal the husband of the older actress, Margo. Doug's underlying point seemed to be that he was determined to move into his own personal spotlight, and that was okay—I'd encouraged him to claim his own life—but the fact that he was doing it by using Sec-C was anything *but* okay. We'd reached a scene in which Margo was becoming loudly inebriated, realizing that Eve was encroaching on her career. I almost jumped out of my skin when Heather whispered, "Now *that's* a realistic drunk."

I turned to where she perched one seat away from me, chewed back my nerves, and said, "Let me guess. You're speaking from experience."

She nodded, and I saw a tiny azure star explode at the center of each pupil. "Real drunks tell it like it is. That's why alcohol and drugs are called 'truth serum.' It's the clean-and-sobers like you who tell the real lies." I could smell her perfume and see her lips glistening with gloss, but her beauty was undercut by the sorrow in her voice. "You lied, SJ, by *not* telling me something. You withheld the truth from someone who trusted you . . . maybe too fast, but I did. And that's *worse*." All I could do was stare at her in flickering shadows. "What's ghiaccio furioso?" she said, pronouncing it with a "juh" at the beginning, "cho" in the middle, "ozo" at the end, like someone who speaks Italian.

I thought for a split second, saying, "Uncle Jack."

"I guess a cocktail of Remembra, whiskey, and Chicago unearthed something stuck in that sick old brain, because he was babbling about it today. I walked into his room searching for aspirin after talking to you on the phone and got a healthy dose of family history instead. I wasn't going to come to school today, but I was just *dying* to have a little chat with you," she said, just above a whisper, as Doug shushed her. In a faint, accusatory tone, she said, "He was pacing the room, tearing out his hair, saying how his father and brother had used it on him decades ago to force him to leave Chicago.

'The fury in their blue eyes,' he kept saying, over and over again, 'was impossible to resist.'" Heather's eyes glowed like sapphire pools filled with goldfish. Something crackled nearby, and I smelled the rich burn of electricity. "He said that power was in some of the Rispolis, the ones with blue eyes. That's what's tearing my brain apart and putting it back together, right?"

"You have no idea what you're talking about," I whispered numbly.

"But you do, SJ. You know *all* about it. Ghiaccio furioso . . . cold and furious, and completely in control of everyone," she said. "It's how I've felt in blips and flashes since the drugs drained from my brain." She inhaled deeply, looked at the screen and back to me, washing the dim room with a cobalt shadow. "Since I can remember, I've been the center of attention. I was either being pursued by producer pervs, or used by my dad, or gobbled up by fans, or dissected by therapists. But you know what?" she said, focusing on me with luminous teeth. "I *adored* being the center of attention. In its freshest form, attention is pure, hundred-percent *love,* and it makes you a billion feet tall and able to do anything . . . kick down buildings, conquer audiences, trash hotel rooms, hook up with anyone you want when you want them, flip your son-of-a-bitch dad the bird, and wrap your whole damn family around your little finger! That's love . . . I mean, that's *attention*! It's better than love because I don't have to give it in return! It's unfiltered *power*! I had it when I was Becky . . . with ghiaccio furioso at my command, I can have it as Heather!"

She sat back, panting. On-screen, Margo lowered heavy eyelids and murmured, "I'll admit I may have seen better days, but I'm still not to be had for the price of a cocktail, like a salted peanut."

Quietly, Heather said, "Me too and me neither. I'm a has-been, but I can be a still-am. I'll go back to all of those producers in L.A. armed with ghiaccio furioso, back to my own dad who said my time was past, and regain my rightful place while making sure every one of them suffers like I did! I'll own that town! Hell, I'll own the world and crush anyone who tries to stop me! Who needs drugs when I have *this*!" She flipped her hair, which moved in a silken cascade. "Tell me how to use it on demand, whenever I want, instead of in fits and starts! Tell me what the crackles and shocks mean across my shoulders and inside my head!" she hissed. The terrible mistake I'd made by not telling her about cold fury at the very beginning was suddenly, painfully obvious. I'd realized that an overt display on her part could possibly attract the lethal attention of Juan Kone, but ruled by ceaseless concern for my family, I'd set her aside. I'd convinced myself that, like Max, she was safer in ignorance.

Except she wasn't like Max.

She was like me, a carrier of enzyme GF, which had dangerously manifested itself.

I should've helped shape her understanding of it, just as my dad should've helped me. How had I forgotten that sting of betrayal? But now the desire for power had rooted itself in Heather's insecurities like an uncontrollable weed, smothering logic and reason. For her, the ability to not only punish those who'd hurt her but to neutralize anyone who stood in her way was the quest. I wanted to dole out revenge as well, to the people who'd hurt my family, but I didn't want to own the world and was certain that anything I taught her about cold fury would hasten the course she was determined to follow. Quietly, eyes pinned on the screen, I said, "I can't, because you'll use it for . . . for . . ."

"Who are you, Spider-Man?" She snorted. "Are you really going to say *evil*?"

Her tone, offended and pleading seconds ago, now dripped with acid. In one day we'd gone from friends to frenemies, and I turned to her face, twisted into a mask of Gorgon freakishness—gray movie shadows quivering over a too-wide smile, eyebrows dancing on her forehead, her teensy nose like a vampire bat's. "You're right, I should've told you," I whispered carefully. "But it's too late now, and I won't be responsible for helping you hurt anyone. What I will tell you, what you deserve to know, is that there are very bad people searching for it, and they'll teach you exactly what evil means. Please, Heather, if you feel the power surging in public, on the streets of Chicago, don't use it. They're watching." I rose to leave, but her hand clamped viselike on my wrist as she squinted through the gloom.

"I see it now . . . you're *selfish*! You don't want anyone else to control ghiaccio furioso like you do! You want it all for yourself!"

"You're a fool," I said, trying to free myself as she held tight. "I wish I didn't have it at all."

"Tell me how to turn it on and off," she said hoarsely, "or I'll never leave you alone. I'll follow you, *plague* you, until . . ."

Using my left hand, opening my fist into a hard, flat palm, I slapped her so fast that all she could do was sit back and gape. Her face crumpled into a mask of pain and abandonment, and I saw how badly I'd violated the bond that was between us.

"Tell me, please. We're family, SJ . . ."

But I couldn't, it would be like uncaging a wild animal, like tossing grenades.

"Aren't we . . . at the very least, aren't we still friends?"

Yet she really did deserve the truth.

"Tell me, you little bitch, or you'll *regret* it!" she hissed.

And then I remembered my mom, dad, and Lou, and almost of its own volition, my hand darted like a cobra, grabbing her by the collar and yanking her surgically perfect nose to my Sicilian one. Through clamped teeth, I said, "I don't have *time* for regret."

"I'm . . . warning you." She gasped. "You won't even see it coming . . ."

"Bring it," I said, tossing her back into the seat and walking away as Margo drunkenly warned the other party guests, "Fasten your seat belts! It's going to be a bumpy night!"

And I pushed through the door into fluorescent brightness, hearing my name called as I charged down the hallway. Max pulled me to a stop and said, "What was that? Were you and Heather fighting? It sounded like someone got hit."

"I was applauding the movie with one hand and her face got in the way," I said, shaking free. I was nearly gone, almost to the double doors that led to escape, when he called me again. I stopped but didn't turn.

"There's a party tomorrow night," he said, the words drifting toward me. "I don't like parties, but my cousin Mandi is having it. I don't really like Mandi much either, but . . ." I could almost hear him shrug. "I said I'd go, and I try to do what I say. I want you to go too, Sara Jane. Show up and we'll pretend like we're meeting for the first time so we can start fresh, with no secrets between us. Okay?"

It was quiet, and when the weight of the question became too heavy, I turned.

The hallway was empty, only the lights buzzed, and Max had gone away.

As usual, he'd done the right thing for both of us, since he didn't want to hear me say no, and I didn't want to lie.

21

IN THE MONTHS FOLLOWING MY FAMILY'S disappearance, I learned that the surest way to kill sorrow was by burying it.

After leaving Fep Prep and blowing off the rest of the school day, I threw myself into infiltrating Johnny's mind. I needed what was locked inside, but even more, I needed to smother the despair from the scene between Max and me. Only an intense diversion would do it, which was waiting on the couch when I entered the Bird Cage Club. Johnny sat catatonically, looking at nothing. He paid no attention to the food I offered, but drank a steady stream of water, his hand reaching for the glass with a mind of its own. He sipped now, wiped carelessly at his lips, and mouthed something silently. When I leaned in and asked him to repeat it, the words blew past my ear like a dying breeze.

"I . . . vant go home," he said in an accent like the one Lucky put on when imitating him.

"Where is home?"

Johnny turned toward the wall of windows and rose from the couch. Jagged shards of glass still hung in the window frames here and there, and he stared past them out at the city. "I vant go home . . . home . . ."

I stepped to his side, watching his eyes flick from building to building, first one, then another, desperately combing the landscape. His brow wrinkled and his nostrils flared as tears formed in a look of helpless frustration. It was a sensation I knew well, and a realization opened then like a slowly blooming flower—Johnny wasn't uttering a constant plea for freedom. Instead, he was simply lost. On the church roof, and at the house where the Outfit guy snatched him, he'd been aimlessly searching for where he came from. I asked his real name and if he could recall family or friends, but he just kept scanning the steel canyons.

Sec-C had done its job, chewing away portions of his memory.

If he couldn't recall the most important people in his life, how could I expect him to know anything about the most important people in mine?

His scrambled mind meant Lucky was right; I'd have to use cold fury if I hoped to learn anything. One eye was as red as Teardrop's, which meant it was impenetrable; I hoped cold fury would affect Johnny's blue eye and allow me access to his troubled mind. Standing so near, I realized now how bruised and filthy he was. Before doing anything else, I had to clean him up. Sitting him back on the couch, I removed his grimy hoodie and paused, staring at his pale arm and torso, each bearing a clue. The scars on Johnny's left wrist were not new but precise and indelible, permanent reminders of having once tried to kill himself. It made me think of Chloe, adrift without Max, and also of the feelings that possessed me when I thought I was a natural-born killer. The scars fit with what I knew about people drawn to Sec-C, racked with loneliness and pain, desperate for a miracle to make them feel connected and whole.

His sweat-stained T-shirt told another story.

Of course Lucky and his guys hadn't seen it; why bother to take off a disgusting hoodie just to kick someone's butt?

The flag it bore was white and red, with a screeching bird inside a coat of arms, its emblem reading *Chicago-Polonia Soccer Club*. Most Chicagoans, even one my age, knew *Polonia* was another word for Poland, since so many Polish people emigrated from there to here. If so, it explained Johnny's accent; Lucky, a paranoid old criminal who suspected Russian mobsters lurking around every corner, had mistakenly heard the Slavic sound of his enemies in Johnny's voice.

It added up to a guy from one country who came to another, and who, for pitiful but unknown reasons, gave himself over to Sec-C.

Until he freed himself—before his transformation into a creature was complete—and escaped into the wilds of Chicago.

I drew his attention, held his gaze, and blinked the cold blue flame to life. The blue eye widened in terror as we both observed his worst fear—him, staring at his own image in a large mirror, confusedly touching the taut, bleached skin on his face, pulling back an eyelid and regarding with horrified awe the scarlet pupil staring back. I couldn't tell where he was—the surrounding area was out of focus—but other people moved behind him, some fully formed creatures in black, others like Johnny, dazed, in street clothes. Slowly, an angular, hard-edged face pushed from the gloom, gazing at him in the mirror. It was Lou, reflecting all the calcification prisoners undergo to survive. He whispered to Johnny, "You're halfway to becoming one of them. Soon you won't remember anything, and after that you'll just turn off . . . like a plug has been pulled. Unless you stop eating that frozen shit. Unless you run." Lou's eyes were dark and hollow, boring in on Johnny. "We have a savior. We have to wait for her." His lips tightened into a mad grin that sent icy knife pricks down my spine. *"Run!"* Lou shrieked, and I fluttered my eyes, breaking the connection.

Tears streamed down Johnny's face.

My heart pounded in my head, an excited drumbeat that said *He's seen my brother! He knows where my family is being held!*

I yanked him close and yelled, "That place—where is it?"

Cringing, he muttered, "Home . . . I vant go . . ."

"Tell me!" I barked, but cold fury was muted, half its strength—Johnny's fear was visible through the blue eyes, but like the other creatures, the red one must've blocked the part of his brain that forced him to do as I ordered. The location of my family was right there, inside his nodding head. I just couldn't make him tell me where it was.

"Oh, SJ! I'm ho-*ome!*" Doug's voice rang out as he rose up the elevator. "And guess who's *super* excited about the Cubs game *to-morr-o-o-ow?*" I looked at a clock above the control center, seeing that hours had passed and it was nearly mid-night. He came dancing by, slowing as he spotted Johnny. "Hey, who's your friend? I heard about your big breakup and—*whoa!*—are you off the Max train *already?* Hey, I know how it feels! *Choo-choo,* here comes the Sec-C express, *chooka-chooka!*"

"Doug, I need to talk to you."

"Hey-hey, whatya say, Cubs are gonna win today . . . or tomorrow . . . whatever!" he sang, doing a sloppy pirouette.

"Doug!" I bellowed, freezing him in mid-spin. His eyes were wide and rose colored, his gaunt face bright with sweat. Sec-C was taking its toll, and it gave me a tinge of apprehension at telling him about Johnny. What I really wanted was to get between him and those deadly friends, but I couldn't, not yet. My inability to draw information from Johnny meant that I definitely needed Doug for access to the Cubs game. And then guilt over the blatant exploitation of my friend burbled up in my gut again. Sec-C or not, I had no right to doubt his loyalty. When I had his attention, I told him all about Lucky, the sit-down, and the poor damaged kid whose fear reflected my family.

He nodded, listening closely, and said, "Super important question: the game tomorrow . . . do I wear my new red silk shirt or something less flashy? I have to look my Dastardly Doug best. That's what my hockey player calls me . . . Dastardly Doug!"

"Did you hear anything I said? There, on the couch . . . do you see him, Doug?"

"Yeah, so?" he said, glancing quickly. "He's a zombie. That's what we call the losers who can't handle Sec-C. They sit around and stare and then disappear to wherever his kind goes. None of my concern."

"None of your concern," I murmured, trying not to sound as disturbed as I felt. "Okay, well . . . at the least, we should make a plan for when trouble starts at the game."

"You mean if," he said. "These are cool people. No one wants trouble . . . we just want to par-*tay*! This Kone guy sounds like a major tool, but . . ."

"Doug," I said in a flinty tone that at least momentarily drew his attention. "He's not a *tool*. He's the maniac who took my family. There *is* going to be trouble."

"Well," he said, nodding, "if that isn't just so-o-o Sara Jane! It's *my* turn to have fun, *my* turn to shine, and all you can think about is you and your little quest!"

"Knock it off, will you? This is no time to try and kick-start the electricity. Trust me, it's barely beneath the surface. So, here's what we should do . . ."

His head bobbed as he mocked me, saying, "Here's what we should do-o-o!"

"I'm not kidding."

"I'm not kidding either, because I'm Sara Jane Rispoli, and I *never* kid!" he brayed madly. "And I never laugh and I never joke and never, ever, *ever* have fun! Because why have fun when I can get punched in the face and then brood about it? Why have fun when I can lick my wounds while pondering the injustice of the universe? Chase, fight, whine, *repeat*!

274

Chase, fight, whine, *repeat*! Jesus, you know what you are?" he announced, pointing an oddly bony finger at me. "You're a bore!"

Coldly, feeling alone on Earth, I said, "I'm just trying to find my family."

"*Screw* them, Sara Jane! You're *never* going to find them! This whole thing has been a *fool's* game!" Doug exploded. His pronouncement expanded between us, dangling in the air like iron balloons. His jaw slackened, showing those teeth and that tongue. Regret flashed across his face, and he stared at the floor for a moment before looking directly at me. "I've been consumed with *your* life and *your* problems, but now I care about *me* more. I want to become that slim, sensual thing I've dreamed of," he said. "It's becoming real, and nothing else matters. Not you. Not your family. Nothing."

All I could do was absorb the words like a body blow. "It's not you talking," I said quietly. "It's Sec-C, doing something terrible to your brain. You want to see what you're becoming? Look . . . it's sitting right there on the couch."

Doug held out his arms crucifix style, a scarecrow billowing with loose padding and empty cloth. "No, Sara Jane. Look at *me*. Sec-C has made me almost normal sized for the first time in my life," he said. "You don't know what that means or how it feels."

"But it's not healthy. It's hurting you."

"I don't care," he said. "When you're as overweight as I am—was . . . whatever—you're two terrible things at once: a freak everyone stares at, always in the worst type of spotlight, and a complete outcast. They gape, but they won't come near. They gasp sadly when you bend to tie a shoe, or look piteously when you yank a huge T-shirt over an exposed acre of belly, but they grimace if you dare to sit near them on the El. They stare, fascinated, as you sip a large coffee something with whipped cream, but act like you have the plague if your hand accidentally brushes theirs, like they're going to catch your fatness . . ."

"Doug—"

"That's the worst part . . . human contact doesn't exist. It's not natural, never being touched or caressed, and it hurts worse than being called some idiotic name. Even the people that quote-unquote love you are secretly repulsed and hug reluctantly, or only when it can't be avoided. They think you're a self-indulgent glutton, unworthy of affection, when really you're trapped and smothering beneath a landslide of yourself."

"I never thought that you were a glutton."

"I know," he said. "All you thought about was *you*. Well, this is *my* life now. This shrinking body, my growing group of friends, and yeah, Sec-C. And don't tell me it's the drug talking, because we're one and the same. It's me, and I'm it . . . I'm Sec-C. And I'll do *anything* not to lose it." He turned away, ignoring Harry whining at his feet, unzipped a backpack, and began throwing clothes inside. "There are other places where I can shower," he mumbled.

"It's after midnight."

"So? My friends and me . . . our party never ends."

"What about the Cubs game tomorrow?"

"What about it?"

"After all we've been through," I said, standing over him while he sniffed shirts and rolled up socks, "do I really need to tell you how important it is? It could be the life or death of my family. I can't get anything out of Johnny, so now all I have left is me. I'm trading myself to Juan Kone in exchange for my family's freedom."

He stood motionless but didn't face me. "What if he doesn't let them go?"

"I have to try. I've got nothing left. I need you to get me into that party suite."

"But why?" he said, and then paused, tightening his jaw. "Why *this* way? Barging in on all of those people. Why do you have to . . . ?"

"Ruin it for you?" We stared at each other, and he knew what I would say, and then I did, softly. "I don't care about ruining it for you, Doug. I don't care about ruining fortunes, futures, or lives if it helps me find my family. If I cared, I couldn't take action. You know that . . . you've always known it."

Doug exhaled, jaw tightening, then rifled through the backpack and handed me a ticket. "That will get you into the game. The party is in suite sixteen. That's all I can do," he said, slinging the backpack. He went quickly to the elevator and pushed the button.

"So you're leaving? For good?" I said.

"I think so. Probably." He nodded, the back of his head rising and falling as the arthritic elevator announced its arrival. "Yeah. I'll get my other stuff later."

"What about remembering the chauffeur, Doug?"

He boarded the steel box and stared at the floor. "Forget him. That's my advice."

"Okay. Well, thanks . . . for all of your help." The cables clunked as the elevator descended, and I crossed the floor, saying, "Wait! Not just for your help! For being my friend!" I reached the cage but he'd fallen away as I said, "My only friend," hearing the words tumble into darkness. Something cold and insistent touched my leg, and Harry stuck his nose toward me with a disappointed look. "Only *human* friend," I said, trudging back to Doug's laptop. My gaze drifted to his Sec-C friends having an excited conversation, and I noticed an improbable name nestled quietly among the chatter:

GetUrLicksIn: Perfect day tomorrow for sunshine and S-C at Wrigley Field!

IscreamUscream: MKK fans are pumped! Go Cubbies!

MeltMyHeart: Forget the Cubbies—go S-C!

AbeFroman: Be careful, S-J.

SuperScooper: Hey, Sausage King of Chicago . . . typo! You mean S-C!

MeltMyHeart: Sausage and soft serve?! Eww . . .

IceQueen: With S-C, I never crave encased meat anymore! Miraculous!

I stared at it—*Abe Froman!*—as blood rushed in my ears like Niagara Falls. There was only one person in the world who knew that name would mean something to me. It was Lou's favorite part of *Ferris Bueller's Day Off.*

It meant that he was still alive.

I was so flooded with love that I nearly wilted from enervation, like a battery running dry, but shook it off as an urgent thought came to mind—it also meant he knew I was going to the Cubs game. For Lou, the scene in which Ferris impersonates Abe Froman is a perfect cinematic example of taking a risk to seize an opportunity. His message seemed to acknowledge that I was about to do that, as if he were being informed of my plans. But how, and how had he gained access to a computer? I touched the keyboard, hesitated, and then used Doug's online name.

HotDoug: AbeFroman is right! MKK fans—be careful at the game! S-C is not for all!

IscreamUscream: Only the enlightened few! Like ex-alcoholics!

IceQueen: Regretful potheads!

MeltMyHeart: Former fatties!

HotDoug: Thanks for the thoughtful reminder, Froman! You must have lots of friends!

I drummed my fingers impatiently, heard the *ping!* and read:

AbeFroman: One friend in particular, whom I'm with now.

MeltMyHeart: Boyfriend or girlfriend? Come on, Froman. Share!

IceQueen: MKK fans share everything! Especially life-changing S-C!

AbeFroman: Can't say.

MeltMyHeart: Froman's shy! Loosen up, Abe! You need some S-C on a sugar cone!

AbeFroman: Can't because I don't know. Impossible to tell.

IscreamUscream: Sounds like some other MKK fans I know!

AbeFroman: Signing off. Friend must go, right now. Please be careful, S-J.

SuperScooper: Instead of the Sausage King, Froman's the typo king!

A crackle of electricity crossed my shoulders, and I attacked the keyboard.

HotDoug: You be careful too, Froman. If I could say thank you in German, I would.

My eyes held the screen, nearly dilating, and then a tiny *ping!* as I read:

AbeFroman: It's danke schoen, like the song. I still sing it now and then with my parents.

My parents—the most beautiful words I'd ever read; Lou confirming that all three of them were still alive. I inhaled tears, swallowed them away, and looked over at Johnny's slumping form, one hand wrapped around the glass of water. I eased him back and turned off all of the lights. The room was enveloped in grayness, the only illumination rising from the city far below. I gazed out the window, feeling the cutting loss of Max combined with the deficit of Doug. For every step forward I took to find my family, I'd taken two steps back in losing the other people who were part of me.

I cracked all ten knuckles percolating with a perfect hatred for Juan Kone.

Love could wait.

22

SATURDAY MORNING I CLICKED AWAKE LIKE an alarm clock, fully alert to my surroundings and what the day could hold. I spoon-fed Johnny cereal and helped him guzzle more water like a big pliant baby as he gazed past me. Afterward I secured him (cuffed but comfortable) to the couch. At the last minute, I scribbled instructions of what to do if I didn't make it back and pinned it to his chest. I didn't know if he could read it or if anyone would find him, but it made me feel better to do it.

And then I rode the subway alone, despite the fact that Cubs and Cardinals fans stood shoulder to shoulder or sat butt to butt as the train burrowed from the Loop toward Wrigley Field. The presence of so many people barely registered. I was inside my head, blotting out the world and formulating a plan for when I encountered Juan Kone.

The train emerged from Chicago's clay belly, morphing from subway to El.

Minutes later, it eased to a stop at the Addison Street station.

There was nervous jostling as people debarked, fearful that the train would whoosh away before they got off. I was the last to step on the platform, looking up Addison, across Sheffield Avenue, squinting down Waveland Avenue, straining to hear the tinkle of ice cream trucks. It was crucial to scout the adjacent streets, since that's all there is around Wrigley Field—bustling boulevards, grimy alleys beneath the El, and overparked residential lanes. It's the last of the urban ballpark neighborhoods, with a billion places to ambush the unsuspecting. All I saw were fans competing for sidewalk space with vendors, scalpers, and cops, and the only sound was the hum of a crowd converging in an enclosed space for a public spectacle—voices and shouts, horns and brakes, and an express train that roared north, leaving airborne scraps of litter in its wake. I pulled the cap low and descended to ground level, hurrying up Addison.

An enormous pair of black-rimmed eyeglasses undulated outside the main gate.

It was as large as a school bus, pumped up by loud industrial air blowers.

Cubs fans wearing the same type of glasses posed for pictures next to the giant bouncy rubber thing, and a nearby sign read:

Dominic Hughes Day!

Honoring the Cubs Center Fielder's Gold Glove Award!

First 10,000 Fans Receive
Commemorative Eyeglasses!

Hughes had been my dead uncle Buddy's favorite Cubs player, known for his speed on the field and thick glasses on his face; it felt like an omen, but I was unsure if it was good or bad. And then I joined the throng, allowing it to give me cover while being swept up a ramp leading to the party suites. It didn't take long to find number sixteen. I took a deep breath, blew out any lingering fear, and entered. Cubs memorabilia hung from the walls, overstuffed furniture covered the floor, and a huge window looked out over the bright-green field, just now being populated by both teams.

What the empty suite lacked were people.

What did not belong there was a hospital gurney.

I spun for the door as fingers like iron squeezed a cloth over my face. I inhaled sharp chemicals, took a step to turn, kept turning, or maybe the floor was spinning, and then my head was not attached to my body. The world became a carousel twirling with color—red eyes, snowy face, black gloves lifting my neck, my arms—as I tumbled into weightlessness. I was unconscious for three seconds or a year, it was impossible to tell, pushed into the abyss by Doug's betrayal.

When I opened my eyes, I was strapped to the gurney.

Two electrodes trailing thin tubes sucked at my temple, one connected to a laptop, the other spitting crimson droplets into a plastic bag. A nearby tray held a scalpel, hypodermic needle, and five glass vials filled with my blood. I wasn't constrained but my limbs were as useless as the tentacles of a dead squid and my head was filled with a million stinging marbles. Woozily, I lifted it toward the picture window. Outside, the old scoreboard announced the bottom of the sixth inning, Cubs in the lead, two to one. With great effort I looked to the left at a commemorative bat hanging from the wall, and to the right, where Teardrop stared at me with devil eyes.

"You're not a freak, you know. There's nothing the least bit paranormal about you," a voice intoned behind me, rippling with an Argentinian accent. "You are simply a human being . . . *un mortal* . . . with a neurological abnormality." I knew who it was but couldn't turn, so I flicked my eyes at the laptop, seeing my brain composed of colored lines, the middle area pulsating with a blue glow.

"My limbic system," I slurred, "where enzyme GF is produced."

"*Muy bueno.* Very good, yeah," Juan said, his tone like a concerned physician. "Enzyme GF cannot be extracted from the normal bloodstream. It must be harvested within inches of the source."

A moist suction noise, like a thick milkshake through a thin straw.

The muted crack of a bat, muffled cheer of the crowd, my breaking heart.

"My friend, Doug. How did you force him to sell me out?"

"You're partly correct. No force, but plenty of selling out," Juan said. "He's nowhere near the transformational stage . . . one eye must turn completely red to indicate the halfway point. But since he demanded unlimited Sec-C in exchange for you, perhaps he'll get there sooner than expected."

Washed with pity and hatred for Doug, I said, "He didn't betray me. It was that sugary poison."

He ignored me, saying, "Ah, see there, the blood bag is nearly full. I've already collected five vials from you. This beautiful plastic pouch comprises the sixth vial."

"Wait—that's what all of this has been about?" I said. "Six vials of Rispoli blood? Then why . . . why did you keep my dad . . . my whole family, for so long?"

"I need only six *more* vials. Isolating the enzyme requires *gallons* of blood, to separate plasma from red blood cells, but this is of no concern to you. I drew nearly the full amount from your father. These six glass tubes finally fill the quota." The suction noise sounded, and Juan's tone turned accusatory. "It was a bitter disappointment to learn that your brother was not an enzyme carrier. It nearly caused me to drain your father dry. His blood supply regenerated, of course, but it took time, which is the sole reason I kept your mother and brother alive . . . to provide comfort, hoping to speed the process of his heart refilling his body. But then he did something with his brain. When I tested fresh samples of his blood for enzyme GF, they contained less and less, and recently, none at all. It was as if he were locking down his limbic system so nothing could leak out. Six small vials away from my goal! That's when we came after you."

"What is it?" I asked, feeling a whispery itch at the end of a toe. "What's your goal? After what you've done to my family, I have the right to know."

"You have the right to nothing. You're less than human . . .

a tree yielding sap, a mine giving up ore. Then again, every genius likes to hear himself talk." He chuckled.

Teardrop came alive, pushing away from the wall. *"No le diga cualquier cosa!"* (Tell her nothing!)

"Hear me, you vile thing," Juan said in the icy, assured tone of master to slave. "Speak out of turn again and your silver cone will remain decidedly empty. *¿Entienda?*"

Teardrop stared over me, dipped its head subserviently, and stepped back.

I felt a finger jump and then a thumb, the digits slowly re-awakening.

Juan cleared his throat. "I learned of ghiaccio furioso when Abuelo Cohen told me about his spat with your great-grandfather. 'Spooky Sicilian phenomenon,' he said . . . valuable enzymatic mutation, I said. Years and countless experiments at Kone Quimica later, I realized its origin had to be in the limbic system, where fears are formed, memories made, and pleasure and addiction frolic. I tried and failed twice to create a synthetic version of enzyme GF. In fact, I was my own *first* lab rat," he said as the suction noise grew louder and he drew up alongside the gurney.

The NASA-like wheelchair Juan sat in whirred, elevating him to my level.

I turned to him, unable to stifle a gasp.

To say that he had lost weight was a grotesque understatement; he'd lost almost everything. His face, pale with piercing eyes, glossy hair, and goatee, stuck to his skull so tightly that it looked sprayed on. He was dressed in a black suit that clung

like snake skin to a narrow, pointed cage of brittle bones. Arms like breadsticks, fingers like pencils, and legs thinner than broom handles were a shocking warm-up to the tight ball of stomach that visibly rose and deflated beneath his suit, making the suction noise with each revolution. Slowly he opened his coat, revealing a rubbery pump where his stomach should have been. "Disgusting, yes? This is the result of my first failure to create a Rispoli-like enzyme. I injected an experimental chemical into my bloodstream and *voila,* the little bugger ate away most of my guts. Without a steady stream of what I so deliciously call 'blue goop' forced into my digestive tract, my body will eat itself. Inconvenient, but at least I'll live. Unlike Primero and the others."

Hearing his real name, Teardrop—Primero—lifted his head.

"Real brilliance lies in the ability to merge surplus with need," Juan said through papery lips. "On one hand, every country on earth has a surplus of human leeches, chemically dependent castoffs, and the generationally impoverished. On the other hand, dictators, terrorists, and criminals around the world require a continuous crop of fresh hoodlums to carry out their dirty work. When I isolate the Rispoli enzyme, the need will be met. I will happily sell it to the highest bidder."

"The enzyme?" I asked.

Juan shook his head. "The hoodlum. An endless supply injected with a hybrid of Sec-C and enzyme GF! In other words, a thug with no moral consciousness or memory, but fully equipped with the electrifying power of ghiaccio furioso!"

"Sec-C," I said, putting it together, "was a failed attempt to

create supercriminals out of addicts, and the lost and lonely. You snuck it into ice cream, and by the time they started to feel good about themselves, they were hooked."

"Recycling the planet's human garbage as weapons, yes. I failed with Sec-C alone. But mixed with enzyme GF—only six more vials!—and I'll achieve it!"

"And then," I said hopelessly, "you'll let us go?"

Juan pinned his eyes to mine, his mouth a bluish line. With a sigh, he said, "Catching you was tiresome. I realized that I would have to be prepared to extract your blood on the spot, as you have a nettlesome habit of escaping. But now that I have you, why would I ever release a reliable source of enzyme GF? With a snip of the brain stem and a reliable life-support system, you'll be my lobotomized fountain of Rispoli blood."

Mine ran cold at the thought of it—lying in a motionless coma as my heart filled and refilled an endless line of plastic bags. I swallowed back the horror of it and said, "But my family. They're of no use to you now. You could set them free . . ."

"I suppose," Juan said vacantly. "Of course this is a money-making venture . . . I expect to earn billions. But all great achievements grow from emotion, and mine took root in revenge. Your great-grandfather ruined my grandfather's life and made exiles of our family. So you see, I have the best of both worlds. I keep you, and when we've finished here—in a perfect act of vengeance—I'll kill yours."

The blood bag was filling like a crimson hourglass. I felt feeble life in my limbs but had little control and needed time, a few precious minutes, and said, "Sec-C was a failure, so Primero was a failure too?" I felt Teardrop's laser gaze and sensed its coiled body ready to pounce, yet the force of Juan's admonition held it in place.

"Oh yes. Completely," Juan said. "Sec-C goes directly to the limbic system and suppresses memory, fear, hunger, and pain, so a user grows amazingly thin and can fight without feeling a thing! At the same time, it heightens pleasure and addiction zones, so the user feels sexy and always wants more."

"*¿Puedo? ¿Por favor?*" Teardrop said impatiently.

"*¿Qué?*" Juan said, tapping a finger at the bag, which was nearing capacity. "*Sí* . . . you may begin." He buzzed closer, pushing his skeletal face at mine. "Apparently, you killed a companion of his. Primero loved it obsessively . . ."

"No! It drowned while trying to kill *me!*" I said, as Teardrop inspected the scalpel's pinpoint blade.

"And now Primero hates you with the same passion. That's why Sec-C is a bust," Juan said. "With every miracle drug comes side effects. It destroys pigmentation, rots the mouth organ, blots out sex characteristics, and erases short-term and most long-term memories. With too much Sec-C, users become infected, androgynous, amnesiac albinos. But wait, there's more," he said with a salesman's grin. "Sec-C also drives love and hatred to explosive levels. Primero adored that sexless mummy . . . *verdad,* Primero?"

"*Sí, verdad,*" Teardrop whispered as a red droplet pooled in the corner of its eye, plopped on my shirt, and it swung the scalpel, nicking my earlobe.

Oh God, oh no, oh Dad! Daddy, please, I don't want to be sliced to pieces!

"The problem is that all of the intense emotion causes too much blood flow, burning right into the ocular capillaries . . . the eyes," Juan said, pointing at his own face. "Very special contact lenses, my design, to keep ghiaccio furioso out. The addicts, however, are immune to your power. The more blood-soaked their eyes, the less you can penetrate them. Ah, but again, there is a downside . . ."

Teardrop jammed the small knife into my forearm, flinging my blood on the wall, and harpooned the scalpel into my leg, slicing flesh through my old jeans.

Oh God . . . oh Mom, help me, I pled silently. *This isn't how I want to die!*

"So listen now, Primero," Juan said, "and learn how you will die."

Teardrop paused with the scalpel pressed behind my ear, ready to drive it into the vein that throbbed there.

"Eventually, too much blood will burn through, and then . . . *hiss-boom* . . . brain implosion," Juan said coolly. "You will expire, just like the hundred Primeros that came before you. No criminal organization would pay for hoodlums whose heads blow up. But for those fueled in part by long-lasting ghiaccio furioso, there won't be enough money in the world. And all that my customers need to keep their armies under control are a simple pair of rose-colored contact lenses like mine . . . for an extra fee, of course."

Outside, a loudspeaker announced Dominic Hughes coming up to bat.

Uncle Buddy . . . I don't hate you anymore. I need you. Help me, please . . .

Juan buzzed to the window, looked out at the field, and said, "The bag is full. Primero . . . kill her." The creature leered down with its eel tongue, and I uttered it once more—*Please!*—as razor-sharp steel pierced my neck.

The muffled crack of a bat sounded close by.

The window exploded and Hughes's foul ball caromed around the suite.

I threw my dead-weight arm at the wooden tray, clumsily grabbed the hypodermic needle, and drove it through Teardrop's gloved hand. It had a high tolerance for pain but not for watching six inches of pointed steel bisect its hand. While it gaped in shock, I lunged at the five full vials, knocking a pair to the floor, where they exploded like tomato-juice bombs. Juan shrieked again, manipulating the wheelchair toward me as I grabbed the other three vials and tumbled to the ground, a savage boot nearly crushing my skull. I rolled away from Teardrop and awkwardly got to my feet on one side of the gurney, woozy and wobbly. Teardrop and Juan were on the other side with Juan scrabbling at the blood-filled bag. As I raised my hand to smash the three vials, the commemorative baseball bat on the wall grazed my knuckles. I turned, groping for it, dropping and crushing the three vials underfoot. Teardrop sprung over the gurney, the hypodermic piercing one of its hands and the scalpel firmly in the other as it hissed, *"Ahora usted muere!"*

I felt the blade rip between my shoulder blades as I pulled the bat from the wall.

I turned, swinging, cracking Teardrop across the face with the fat end, watching it twirl on one heel, gasp, and fall. The floor was drug-wavy beneath my feet. Juan was trying to free the blood bag from the IV stand, but his spindly fingers were too slow. I lifted the bat, assumed a home-run stance, and said, "Step away from it or I'll knock your goddamn head off. It won't take much."

Juan buzzed backward, seeing truth in my eyes. "I still have *them*. You came here to trade, *sí*? Okay, more blood from your veins for your family."

"So you can create an unstoppable army of criminals?" I said, unhooking the bag. "Screw that. This curse stays in my family."

"It's a *neurological abnormality!*" he bellowed, bobbling his head like a jack-in-the-box. "You will give me that blood or *they . . . are . . . dead!*"

"With only six vials to go?" I said, shaking my head. "You're lying."

"I mean it! I'll throw away the whole grand scheme and kill them one at time!"

"I was a fool," I said. "My family would never want me to sacrifice myself, because it's not fighting. It's surrender. What the Rispolis are to the Outfit, who my father is . . . who *I* am . . . it's sick. But it's *our* sickness, and Chicago's. Not the world's."

"I'll murder them," Juan chanted, his voice like wind carrying a distant scream. "I'll start with the boy. So intelligent and sophisticated. He deserves a long life, and society deserves the goodness he would bring to it." He buzzed closer, pupils jiggling. "First I'll burn the soft flesh from his eyes, and then . . ."

And then I punched a guy who cannot walk.

A man with bones like straw and organs the consistency of rotten mushrooms.

I used my mom's signet ring to brand Juan's huge white forehead with the Rispoli *R,* the diamond teeth biting the letter into flesh for time immemorial.

His jaw swung from its cranium, his eyes rolled back, and he slumped like a scarecrow in the wheelchair. He looked dead, but then he hadn't looked quite alive, and I didn't have time to worry about it; experience informed me that few organisms recovered from a blow to the head like Teardrop. I pulled out the electrodes, slid the blood bag into the waist of my jeans, and with the bat at my side, slipped through the door. The walkway was empty, but I knew it wouldn't be for long; someone would come on the run to check the window shattered by Hughes's baseball. I hurried along, realizing how brilliant Juan's plan had been—they couldn't get me in a car chase or on the street, but I never suspected they'd infiltrate my best friend's head. The ramp to the main gate was nearby, and I was passing a closed door when I heard something that stopped me.

Samba music.

I turned and looked at a card next to a suite, which read *MKK Fan Appreciation Day.* I'd known there was a party for Sec-C users, but the shock of Juan's chamber of horrors had pushed it from my mind. Now I stood bristling at the fact that Doug was partying while, if circumstances were different, I might be dead. I gripped the baseball bat and kicked open the door as the rhythms of Rio scratched to a halt. Across the room, a crush of jittery people buzzed and slurped in front of a soft-serve machine like a crush of ants attacking a piece of candy. Doug saw me, and his sticky mouth opened and shut before he said, "Oh. Sara Jane. You're . . ."

"Alive," I hissed as the crowd turned with a rose-colored glare. Every race and sex was in that jumpy crowd, but not every age; Juan hadn't targeted anyone much older than twenty, from an acne-scarred redhead in an oversized Bulls jersey to an African American beauty with piercings and tattoos to a scruffy Latino dude who looked like he slept in alleys, and on and on. As they stared, I saw something that I'd seen in Doug's gaze since I'd known him—a hungry need to be part of something. Almost every kid in America learns the dangers of controlled substances in grade school, sees classmates smoking weed and taking pills in middle school, and is fully versed on recreational use versus addiction by high school. A fact taught along the way is that, among other emotional triggers, people are drawn to the drug culture because it's a social institution, like square dancing or a street gang, where the most forgotten loser can find acceptance.

That's how I saw Doug now—a kid who had been systematically ignored by unfeeling, vodka-swilling, dope-smoking parents. He wanted not to be fat—to be liked, even adored, perhaps caressed. His mind was being fooled by Sec-C into feeling sexy while his brain prepared to explode inside its skull. I couldn't allow that to happen. I would *not* allow it happen. I threw the bat on my shoulder and strutted inside, Outfit style.

"Um . . . pardon me," a voice chirped. I turned to a cute,

freckled face with chipmunk teeth and pinkish eyes. She crinkled her nose, lifted a clipboard, and said, "Welcome, newbie! I'm Konnoisseur Colleen! Name, please?"

"Is that Sec-C?" I said, nodding across the room. Through a glass window in the machine, it folded over on itself, pink, white, and slimy.

"Indeedie!" she chirped. "Good and good for you, as they say!"

"How much of it do you have to eat before your tongue falls out?"

Her eyes narrowed and smile evaporated. "What's your *name*?" she brayed.

"Let me spell it for you," I said, hocked deeply, and spit in her face. She reeled back, and I cut through the crowd, knowing I was an interloper and worse, a buzz kill. Doug huddled behind his fellow addicts, whom I shoved out of my way. His eyes jiggled as I quoted one of his favorite films, saying, "I'm *ba-ack*."

"Uh . . . hey, Sara Jane," he said, and broke for the door. He didn't take a step before I got him by the collar into a walking headlock.

"This is called tough love," I said. "You don't like it? Tough."

The crowd pushed behind us, gaining momentum, as Konnoisseur Colleen cried, "She can't have him! He's ours now! One of you—*stop her!*" And then it was a crush of humanity, but I was first out the door, hauling Doug, who was trying to slow us until I gave him a hard shot to the kidneys. He howled but moved, with both of us running up the ramp instead of down to the exit, trailed by MKK fans. As we headed for the nosebleed seats, a sunshine-filled entryway opened in the walkway. I pulled him onto the stadium rooftop with its junk food and beer stands, and its smoking fans who want a break from the game. It overlooks the main gate on Clark Street, and I hustled Doug to the edge, looked down eight stories to the sidewalk where people were having pictures taken wearing big, silly glasses, and back at MKK fans streaming onto the rooftop. I wrapped my arms around Doug's waist and said, "Over you go! Move it!"

"What? What are you talking about?"

"Hurry!" I said, fighting him as he scrabbled to stay on the roof, and saw I had no choice. I blinked the cold blue flame into existence, grabbed his gaze and said, *"Jump!"*

"No! You can't make me do *anything!"* Doug said with a crooked smile, his eyes redder than I'd ever seen them. "I can actually say *no* to you!"

"Say no to this," I said, clipping him with a left hook on the chin and pushing him over a low railing and off the roof. I was about to follow when Konnoisseur Colleen snagged my ankle.

"Got you!" she yelled, tasting the heel of my shoe as I hammered her mouth, lost my balance, groped at nothing, and fell through the warm air over Clark Street.

Below, Doug lay on his back gaping up at me. He scrambled and rolled, giving me just enough room to land next to him on Dominic Hughes's huge inflatable glasses, which huffed and bowed. He lifted his arms and squealed, "I'm *bleeding!"*

"That's my blood!" I said.

"*You're* bleeding!"

"No, a bag of blood broke. I was carrying it in my . . ." I hesitated, knowing the MKK fans were regrouping inside Wrigley Field. "I'll tell you about it later! Let's get out of here!"

"No!" he said, sliding to the ground. I followed, looking at Doug's dancing eyes, jumpy hands, and sticky face, as he said, "*Those* are my friends! *This* is my life!"

"Those are junkie wannabes and you're wasted. I just punched their leader in the head, maybe killing him. And this?" I said, showing off my blood-soaked self. "It came out of my veins. It was the culmination of that maniac's master plan, which I destroyed. Are you sure you want to waltz back in there, since I was your 'special guest'?"

He absorbed it through a drug-addled brain and said, "Let's get the *hell* out of here!" We sprinted to the El station like our lives depended on it and darted onto a train. When it was safely barreling toward the Loop, I realized something.

Besides an "abnormality," Juan never told me what cold fury actually is.

It meant that I still didn't understand the greater part of myself.

I was alive, though. Brain intact, Doug at my side. And for now it was enough.

23

A PRIMER ON WHAT HAPPENS WHEN AN
addicted friend is deprived of drugs.

First he'll get pissed off and start babbling nonsense, kicking over furniture, and being abusive to small Italian greyhounds. Second, he may seem like a life force, but in fact he's suffering from withdrawal, and it could kill him if he doesn't kill himself first. Finally, and most important, he will call you every vile name under the sun, including a few you've never heard before. If you're going to save his life, you must turn off your feelings. Ignore everything he says and call 911.

Of course, I couldn't do that. I had to take care of Doug on my own.

All Saturday night and into the early hours of Sunday, he raged around the Bird Cage Club pinkly foaming at the mouth, damning me to hell for ruining his new, svelte life. I cracked the notebook to chapter six, *"Metodi"* ("Methods"). Not finding what I'd hoped for, I flipped to chapter seven,

"Procedimenti" ("Procedures"), came up dry again, and nearly gave up when I decided to try to chapter five, *"Sfuggire"* ("Escape"), and there it was, a short, scribbled section that read:

> *How to Shake Free of Hooch, Horse, and Nose Candy*
> *Addictive substances are good business but STRICTLY FORBIDDEN for Outfit members; incapacitation affects one's ability to earn. To kick a habit, mix and administer three quarts of "Screaming Banshee," as indicated below; you will need:*
> *A) Vinegar, six raw eggs, ginger, cayenne pepper, and one medium-sized herring*
> *B) Lots of towels, and a bucket*
> *C) Handcuffs*
> *D) Someone large to apply the handcuffs, as juiceheads and junkies hit, bite, and claw*

I removed the steel bracelets from Johnny, who sat benignly, gazing past the scene; Sec-C had left him in a constant state of compliance. Doug, on the other hand, was in a boiling tantrum, and when he turned to scream about the size of my nose, I was standing there. He looked at what I held and said, "Those are *my* handcuffs!"

"Remember when you locked me to a chair? Seems like yesterday."

Doug's eyes glowed like neon strawberries as he took a step backward. "So?"

"So now it's your turn, slim," I said, and the struggle was

brief—he slapped while Harry nipped at his pant leg, and I kneed him in the gut, taking away his breath, and dragged him by his collar, whimpering. When I had him secured to a chair, I said, "It's time to puke for a while." Doug let loose with ear-bleeding invective, quieting only when I yanked back his head and filled his big mouth with the (aptly named) Screaming Banshee, clamping my hands over his face to make him swallow. He did, his eyes went wide, and I barely managed to catch the crimson explosion in a bucket. The next hour was brutal, disgusting, and necessary as we repeated the process half a dozen times. Doug was as weak as a kitten in a storm drain when his stomach was finally, completely empty. I threw him on my mattress and fed him water. His eyelids fluttered to unconsciousness. When I was sure he was out, I reapplied the cuffs, attaching him to the radiator in my bedroom/office. It was the most painful way to kick a drug—do-it-yourself rehab—that brought to mind Heather, and further, Uncle Jack and Annabelle.

I sat on the couch next to silent Johnny, who sipped water and nodded off. Harry laid his head on my lap, and I thought about my cousin glowing with the crushing force of beauty while pulsating with a power she barely understood. The old man, with the facts from *"Volta"* swimming around his plaque- and guilt-ridden brain, all that vital knowledge unable to be collected or remembered. And his middle-aged daughter, mute with regret and resentment but able to voice deep-seated greed. All of their secrets, desires, and failures—I felt the weight of them because I'd grown to care about them. The problem was that caring is dangerous. Sentiment and emotion had no place in my life—they were deadweights and anchors. Rolling Harry aside, I resolved to ask them to leave the bakery, to pack up and be gone by the end of the day tomorrow. Johnny would be dealt with too, probably left anonymously with one of the city's many Polish social clubs. Grimly, I wondered if he might be so generous as to donate his red eye to satisfy Lucky.

I stood and crossed the room, watching Doug snore, knowing I had a decision to make about him too. He'd betrayed me in such an egregious way that it had almost gotten me lobotomized. It was becoming more and more imperative to allow no one to threaten my existence as I fought to free my family from Juan Kone.

And then I made the mistake of talking to Gina.

By Monday morning, Doug was sweating like a lawn sprinkler and misquoting movies in his sleep ("Frankly, my dear, I *do* give a damn . . .") but wasn't thrashing about anymore. I unlocked the handcuffs without waking him so he could use the restroom, and told Johnny that he had to stay inside the Bird Cage Club. He blinked his different-colored eyes. I told him to eat anything he wanted and not to touch anything sharp. He yawned and shivered from his well-worn spot on the couch and fell back asleep. As usual, I had to go to school so as not to raise suspicion, and glanced back at Johnny as I left, hoping that both he and Doug would politely not die while I was gone. As rattled as I was by my encounter with Juan, as hollowed out as I felt about my separation from Max, I resolved to make it an uneventful day.

That resolution was kicked in the face the moment I walked into school.

Talking to Gina knocked it out cold.

Kids whispered and pointed as I walked down the hallway, and it continued until last period. It was with my head turned, tracking a group of oglers, that I plowed into a pair of Mandi Fishbaum's look-alikes. The first one flipped her hair and said, "Better keep your eyes open, SJ. *Wide* open."

"Speaking of," the other one said, "I never noticed before, but you and Heather have the same color of eyes."

"That's not all they share!" The first one smirked, giggling and turning away.

My instinct was to squeeze their throats until they choked up whatever it was they were cackling about. Instead, I went straight to the nucleus of all gossip. The hallways were emptying as kids hurried for the exits. When Gina saw me coming, she slammed her locker and hustled in the other direction, but between her heels and my determination, she never had a chance. I grabbed her, and when she turned, it was something I'd never seen before—her face etched with pity. Without preamble I said, "What?"

"What what?" she replied, trying on a smile that slipped.

"Don't bullshit me, Gina. People are whispering. What's going on?"

"SJ . . . ," she said, biting her lip. "Sara Jane, please. I don't want to tell you."

"How is that possible? You always want to tell everyone everything." I leaned in, cornering her against a locker. "I want to know. Whatever it is."

She sighed, shaking her head. "The party Saturday, at Mandi Fishbaum's? There's a rumor, unconfirmed . . . Supposedly Heather slept with someone."

Of course people knew we were cousins, but I wondered what it had to do with me, and said, "Okay, big deal. She finally chose between Ken and Kendra, or she chose both, like an Olympic sex event, Ken to Kendra to Kendra to Ken. Who cares?"

Gina looked at me, face pale, eyes moist. She wiped her nose, saying, "I always liked you, Sara Jane, but you're so, like, clueless to how the real world works . . ."

"I don't get it," I said, my mind thick, the pieces coming together too slowly.

"The someone," she said nearly inaudibly, "was Max."

My brain pushed against my eyes, my throat clogged, and my heart stabbed itself with something sharp enough to die. I touched tears and realized that part of me was a flimsy lie. So sure I'd disconnected myself from love, so stupidly positive that nothing could pierce the emotional shell I'd constructed from scar tissue, and now I stood weeping and weak. All I wanted was for it not to be true, but I knew something had happened between Max and Heather, since something *always* happens for a rumor to ignite. Besides a self-destructive desire to find out exactly what occurred (I didn't *want* to know but *needed* to), the only other sensation coursing through my veins was the worst one known to human beings—a smothering combination of physical rejection and emotional abandonment, imagining the person you love touching someone else, kissing someone else, whispering things to her he'd spoken only to you. And how all of your intimacy—so precious and protected—had been destroyed by one secret moment that *never* remains secret. It can't, because it's infused with carelessness and disregard for the third person, the one for whom no concern is shown. Me.

Gina hugged me and I stood rigidly in her perfumed embrace as she murmured, "At least you're not boring anymore."

That's all it took to understand that I'd been wrong; *plenty* of concern had been shown to me, but of the treacherous kind. I remembered Heather's threat, hissed in semi-darkness—*You won't even see it coming!* How better than to steal her cousin's ex-boyfriend? It cut deeply and also created the sort of humiliation that would stick to me until I graduated. The only part that gave me comfort was knowing that it had been a plot, and Max a pawn. It wasn't lust or charm she'd used to seduce him, but ghiaccio furioso. It didn't mean he hadn't done anything, only that he'd been powerless. And then my lifted heart fell, and I was enraged for myself and for Max, and mumbled, "He couldn't resist."

"Oh honey, I know," Gina said, hugging me tighter. "She's too hot."

"It's time to cool her off," I said as electricity snapped across my shoulders.

"Ow!" Gina cried, jumping away. "You shocked me!"

"I'm just getting started," I said, sprinting down the hallway and bursting through double doors into screaming daylight. I knew Heather would be heading to the El by now, and I ran for it, hitting the platform just as a train shuddered to a stop. I looked left and right as people flowed off and on, the cars pulled away, and my name was called, dancing behind the rumble.

She was there, waiting for me, slim hips swaying as she moved languidly. A small, secret smile plumped her lips. "Gotcha," she purred.

"You shouldn't have done it," I said. "I mean . . . did you? Do it?"

"Gee, SJ," she said, using a pinkie to smooth her lip gloss, "that's kind of a personal question. Between Max and me, I mean."

"Remember when you asked me to tell you when you were being an asshole?" I said, cracking all ten knuckles. "It's now."

The platform was empty except for us, and she moved within arm's length, saying, "Max is a sweet boy, by the way. Not a lot of experience, but developing new talent is *very* L.A., so I was happy to—" And then she went silent, since it was impossible to talk with my fist in her mouth. She hit the boards hard on her back, skidded to a stop, and rolled to one knee. Holding her jaw, she spit blood, and said, "You sucker punched me!"

"It's *very* Chicago. An old tradition when someone talks trash," I said, curling my fists and facing her shoulder-forward in a boxing stance, ready.

She rubbed her jaw, shaking her head, and said, "I should've known. You're half a liar and half a cheat. No help when it's really needed. Just like the rest of the family."

"You know *nothing* about my family," I spit, feeling the cold blue flame flicker in my gut. "All we share is DNA."

"This could've been avoided if you'd helped me understand

306

ghiaccio furioso. By the way, the 'Trust Test'? You failed," she said, rising carefully to her feet, kicking off her shoes. "Did I mention I was the capoeira champion?"

"Of Rancho Salud? Must've been some tough opponents . . . you versus ninety-pound crackheads."

Heather smiled, drawing a pointed tongue across white teeth. "Of L.A. County. My therapist thought competitive mixed martial arts would be, quote, 'a positive channel for an untamed life force,' end quote. That's rehab talk for I'm going to kick your skinny ass."

"I was right, wasn't I?" I said as we circled slowly. "You used ghiaccio furioso in a sick and twisted way, just like I predicted."

"You call it sick and twisted. I call it a beautiful act between consenting adults."

"Except Max didn't consent," I said, lining up my fists. "That's how you get that precious attention you need? Bending the will of a guy who loves someone else?"

"Funny, he didn't mention anyone. Then again, he was busy having his will bent," she said, dropping and sweeping my ankles out from under me. I hit the boards and tucked and rolled, her hammering heel missing my face by inches as I leaped to my feet in time for a sharp cracking backhand to my face. I reeled, spit blood, and ducked. Her next punch swooshed overhead and I drove a fist into her solar plexus, knuckling the oxygen out of her lungs. As she gagged for air, I jabbed her twice in the face and she went back on her butt. She lost no momentum, rolling to her feet as I blinked, giving full, furious life to the blue flame, and my gaze scrabbled for hers.

"Stop," I said calmly, and she did, like playing freeze tag, seeing what was burning behind my eyes.

And then she stopped me too, blinking just once, mirroring my gaze.

"By the way, I don't need your help after all. I think I'm getting the hang of it," she said, drawing near, and it was like pointing the tips of magnets at each other, the power repelling each other, each of us unable to wholly grab the other's mind—me trying to locate her deepest fear, her trying to wrangle my most closely held desire. All I saw were blips and scratches of what was buried in Heather's brain—her dad screaming at her to *Be prettier! Be cuter, happier, more peppy, zestier and bouncier and more TV-worthy, goddamn it, or no one will love you, ever . . . ever!* and her mom, Annabelle, turning away from it all silently, doing nothing as Heather's dad pointed a finger and called her *Stupid girl! Clumsy girl! Big-nosed and too tall and too skinny and too this, too that!* But I couldn't hold or contain those terrible old feelings, and suddenly Heather was so close that I smelled her acrid sweat, salty blood, and curdling perfume. Contemptuously, she said, "Oh look, how sweet, all at home together . . . perfect mommy and daddy who love their daughter unconditionally, and a smart little brother who's so devoted to big sis that he wants to link pinkies . . . *awww*," and she was right, there they were, the image of my family between us, real and alive, and I desired it so badly that love rose up and crushed my heart, squeezing it to death. I was so weak I could barely move. And then the image peeled away in wet, gray strips, revealing another underneath. Heather's face was so close that our noses touched as

308

she hissed, "That's right, SJ. Throats slit, bodies cold, staring into nothingness for eternity." She'd seen it, that nightmarish image of my parents and Lou buried in my mind, and she was trying to use it to disable me, but all it did was start a *sizzle-crackle-buzz!* and then I could not have cared less if they were dead, since I could kill *her.*

My hands moved with minds of their own to her perfect throat.

I squeezed soft flesh, thumbs digging at a fibrous trachea— it was delicious to murder her—as her eyes popped with screaming, vibrating flecks of gold.

And then my fingers were being bit and burned by a live wire, like touching an exposed, thrumming outlet, and Heather grinned with shark-blue voltage behind it. I freed her, screaming in pain, my palms scarred as I stood swaying, barely on my feet, like being punch-drunk. "Tell me!" Heather shrieked. "How does ghiaccio furioso *work? How* am I able to do this to you? Tell me about *me!*"

The words spilled like water over a dam as I babbled, "It begins with extreme emotions . . . love, anger, hatred, loneliness . . . igniting a cold blue flame in my gut. But now I can will it into existence. All I do is think and blink."

"The really powerful part, the electricity . . . where does it come from?"

"I don't know."

"Liar," she hissed, grabbing me roughly at the neck. "Tell me. *Now!*"

"All I know," I rasped, "is that those intense feelings . . . have to evaporate . . . they have to die inside me. What's left . . . is the overwhelming urge to kill someone who I believe has done me wrong."

"Yeah. I know the feeling," she said, as the squeal of an approaching train sounded. I was lifted into the air and Heather grunted delicately before throwing me onto the tracks. I was mostly paralyzed, but I was also from Chicago, where people stumbled, leaped, or were pushed beneath the steel people-movers weekly, so I curled into a human burrito, clumsily pulling in my appendages. The train's horn blared, tenor-high and apologetic for killing me. The train clattered overhead, spitting oil and snapping sparks as it complained to a slow, rusty stop, not crushing me, not cutting me to pieces. I lay on the tracks, inhaling the impossibility of being alive, licking petroleum, knowing without a doubt that the preordained time and date of my death had been wrong. There were voices on the platform, desperate to help but certain I was dead, as I clawed myself to freedom, seeing no more Heather. From the street below came the merry tinkle of an ice cream truck as Frank Sinatra rose up, singing the anthem of a city he loves.

Or maybe this time it was a celebration at finally bagging his prey.

24

I ROSE SLOWLY TOWARD THE BIRD CAGE CLUB
in the elevator, smelling like someone who'd gotten run over
by a train.

After the fight with Heather, I still was unsure of how cold
fury worked *against* cold fury, although it was plain she'd
grown stronger by the day. After seeing my fear, she was also
aware of my family's precarious situation. I gnawed a thumbnail, knowing it didn't matter since the ice cream creatures
had almost certainly taken her. I was appalled by what she'd
done with Max and tried to do to me. But if she'd been carried away to the same horrific place as my family, then I'd try
to save her too.

It's possible to dislike someone for who they are, but not
how they became that way.

The *who* part is up to the person, constructed from con-
scious decisions she makes as she grows older, each resulting in a (sometimes bloody) consequence. But *how* a person is
shaped and molded has nothing to do with the person herself.

Where she's born, to whom, and whether or not those people love and protect her, or abuse and use her, just isn't up to the person. In all of those categories, Heather got a bum deal. Still, there's a point where everyone has to stop being a kid and decide who she's going to be.

That's why I didn't hate Heather.

I saw now that she was weak and damaged.

Maybe because of how she'd been raised, the universe had bestowed upon her a level of gorgeousness that caused the general public to flirt, fawn, and sometimes faint. But she had a responsibility to decide what to do with that ethereal gift, and she had chosen the most selfish and manipulative path.

I shuddered, knowing what Juan Kone would do to her.

He had my dad's blood but lost mine, and he needed those six precious vials.

I wondered if they'd begun to draw them yet from Heather's brain.

The end would come soon afterward, not just for her, but for my family too. Juan would finally have collected enough blood to isolate enzyme GF, Heather would be lobotomized, and the services of the Rispoli clan would no longer be required. The trail would go cold, since Juan wouldn't need me anymore, either. The creatures and their little black trucks would disappear, along with any chance of following them to the Mister Kreamy Kone factory. All of my desperate efforts had failed miserably, and now I was out of leads. When those six vials were full, the cosmic hourglass would be empty.

I had only one supremely dangerous card left to play.

I would get Lucky alone. I'd use cold fury to force the

old man to order the entire Outfit—every killer, pimp, and bookie—to tear Chicago apart searching for my family. It meant admitting that they'd disappeared, which would expose my dad to life-threatening charges of being a rat (and me too), but there was nothing else to do. I was in that moment of silence before a dam broke, and if I didn't act immediately, it would carry all of us away, forever.

I closed my eyes, visualizing my parents, asking them to help me do the very thing I'd spent the last four months trying to avoid—putting us all at the mercy of the cold-blooded Outfit—and whispered, "Please . . . help me . . ."

"Please . . . say something. Anything," Doug murmured.

I walked around the corner, seeing him sitting across from Johnny on the couch. "You're awake," I said.

"More than this poor guy, even though his eyes are open," he said. "Actually, sort of open. The red one is like a searchlight but the blue side is pretty droopy."

"I think Sec-C cut really deeply into his brain. It's like he's teetering on the edge of recovery or . . . you know." I shrugged.

"Could've been me," Doug said quietly.

"How do you feel?"

"Like I've been turned inside out, tongue first," he said, sipping the Screaming Banshee and shuddering. "By the way, this earns its name. I've been screaming out both ends." He tried to explain how he felt, physically and emotionally, describing the first like a savage flu—his guts rejecting everything, all of it pouring out deep red—and the second as being trapped in a wonderful dream that became a hellish nightmare, then a dream again, over and over. "Taking Sec-C, all of your happy emotions are intense, like you love someone to *death,* and flowers are *beautiful,* and sex . . . ," he said, pausing, "is actually a possibility someday. And that's life-saving! It's a release from being the unattractive fat kid, and because you stop eating, you're really *not* him anymore! Except the drug ebbs away, and then you are again, at least in your head. You crash like Wall Street, and it's brutal. The unhappy emotions take over, and you hate yourself to *death,* and flowers are *disgusting,* and sex does not occur because you love someone or even like them. Instead, it's raw manipulation. It's telling a terrible lie with your body. And then you slurp more Sec-C and it starts again."

"Are you done with it, Doug?"

"Maybe. Probably," he said. He added sheepishly, "Are you done with me?"

I petted Harry vacantly, scratching beneath the little dog's chin. "That sort of betrayal . . . allowing me to walk into that suite?" I said, shaking my head and looking directly at him. "The only reason I'm not dead is because of a wild baseball."

"I know," he said, welling up, "I hate myself for it. I'll *always* hate myself."

"Everything I've fought for, every inch I've clawed toward my family, could've ended right there," I said. "So yeah, the more I thought about it, the more I realized that Doug Stuffins, Mister Popularity, was totally unforgivable."

"Sara Jane . . ."

"That's why I'm forgiving *you.* Those internal suspicions you have, those mental whispers that you're unlovable and destined to be alone forever? The ones that made it easy to take Sec-C? I know they're nonsense," I said, "because I know the real Doug. The smart, loyal person who would never have done that unless his mind was twisted by some very bad drugs. So there's no 'maybe' or 'probably' when it comes to being done with Sec-C. If you want my friendship and confidence, there's 'definitely' and 'forever.'"

Doug pinched moisture from his eyes. "Definitely. Forever," he said quietly. The way he looked at me wasn't pleading or hopeful; it was resolute, full of truth, and meant as much to me as his declaration. He patted his deflated belly and said, "I get to keep the body, right? My version of post-rehab Heather Richards?"

"Speaking of," I said with a sigh, and I told him about her and cold fury, her and Max, and her and the ice cream creatures. With a shudder, I repeated Lucky's request—correction, *demand*—for Johnny's red eyeball. Doug had a million questions and observations, convincing me that he was finding the best parts of his old self. Finally, I explained my last-ditch effort to save my family by using cold fury on Lucky.

When I finished, he said, "What if?"

"They're already dead? Well . . . then at least I tried."

"Then you would have outed yourself for nothing. The Outfit needs a counselor-at-large, I get that, but not so badly they'd allow the daughter of a dead rat—no offense—to mediate their dirty business. Besides, you know what Lucky will do if you get him in a cold fury headlock," he said. "Look, if your family is . . . not here, there's still a whole life left for you to live. If you can't help them"—he shrugged—"maybe it's time to step back."

"No. Never. I'll keep at it until there's nothing left . . . them or me." I sighed. "It's just that I've wasted so much time trying to comprehend a dead language—"

"Hey!" Doug said, taking the Screaming Banshee away from Johnny, who'd lifted it like a glass of ice water and gagged down a mouthful.

"So much time trying to crack the code of Ice Cream Cohen and Weston Skarlov . . . ," I said, the words trailing off as Doug and I watched the effects of the noxious concoction on Johnny, who was shaking all over, staring at me as his lips began to move.

"Weston," Johnny mumbled through a foamy dribble, "west . . . on . . ."

"Wait a minute," Doug said. "Are you . . . trying to talk?"

"Skarlov. S-s-s-karl . . . ov," he said, dissecting the words with his teeth and tongue. "S-s-s-karl . . ."

We moved closer as his eyes widened, seeing something terrible that wasn't there. "It must be Screaming Banshee," I whispered.

"Please don't let them take me back," he gasped. "There's blood in the air . . ."

"Where?" I asked.

"Weston," Johnny said, biting down on the syllables, "west, on . . . skarl . . . s-s-s-south karl . . . ov . . . av . . ."

"Avenue," Doug said slowly.

I put it together, saying, "West . . . on South Karl Avenue?" Doug attacked his laptop as I thought aloud. "Uncle Jack's scrunched handwriting, recording the location of the Pure Dairy Confection headquarters so long ago. His small o—

ov—looks just like a small *a*—av. The phrases that faded away between the word *partner* . . . I assumed it was a name, but it was directions to a place."

"Then who helped Ice Cream Cohen rob the Bird Cage Club? Who was the partner?" Doug asked, pulling up a map.

"Who knows?" I murmured, looking over his shoulder. "Another dead secret."

"Here it is, South Karl Avenue!" He pointed. "A dead-end near Back of the Yards! It has to be the place!"

After all of this time, seeing the tiny digital street as an actual place was unreal. Joy and relief flared and faded, replaced by regret as I asked myself, *What if I'd been smarter reading Uncle Jack's hidden pages, or faster tracking down Juan Kone? What if I hadn't been so fearful and had told Heather everything about cold fury?*

And then, before my eyes, South Karl Avenue began to glow with possibilities.

I turned for the elevator and the Lincoln, yelling for Doug to bring Johnny.

It had to be the place because there were no other places left, and no more time for what-ifs. There was only now, before it was too late.

25

NOT LONG AGO, MANY OF THE NATION'S hooved and cloven animals were turned into meat in a small neighborhood on the South Side of Chicago. This bastion of butchery, called the Union Stockyards, spawned numerous side businesses since something had to be done with all of those animal carcasses. In the world of recycled snouts, bones, organs, and tails, one institution rose above all others when it came to stinkiness—the rendering plant, where leftover parts became lard or tallow through a process of boiling and straining, which smells exactly like what it is—animal corpse soup. It's a putrid stench that assaults a person's senses, conjuring up images of milky maggots, of flies swarming roadkill. Although the majority of Chicago's South Side rendering plants have closed, the odor lingers, especially on warm afternoons.

It was unseasonably hot when we crept westward on South Karl Avenue.

The humidity made it smell like driving through the rancid sweat sock of a giant.

It was a dead end on the south fork of the Chicago River, that notoriously foul stretch nicknamed Bubbly Creek. A chain barrier blocked the end of the road where, a few feet later, water the consistency of yogurt belched up pockets of methane gas from a century of decomposing animal carcasses on its muddy floor. I creaked to a stop, seeing the burned-out shell of a factory on one side of the street, its brick walls still black from a fire that must've happened decades ago, and a boarded-up warehouse on the other, its windows covered in warped wood. "That's got to be it," I said, feeling my heart beating in my throat. I'd be going in there with cold fury that didn't affect Juan Kone or his creatures, and the presence of my family—my intense love for them—deactivating the electricity. I looked at Doug and said, "The answer is no."

"Because there are dangerous things that only you can do in there, you want to protect me, blah-blah-blah," he said. "Listen, I'm *always* going with you, no matter where it is. So why waste the words?"

I saw the determination on his face, nodded once, and turned to the backseat, where Johnny sat staring straight ahead, rigid but not completely disconnected from the present. We'd given him an additional dose of Screaming Banshee, which had drawn him out of his walking coma even more. Softly, I said, "Stay here, okay? If something happens, take the car . . . if you can drive." I nodded at the boarded-up warehouse. "How do we get inside?"

A tremor crossed his shoulders. "Not there. There," he said, pointing at the torched shell of a building across the street.

I looked at the structural skeleton through which the moving river was visible. "Is there a basement or something?"

He pointed into the brown water. "The boat. Touch it." I looked through the building at a red skiff in the distance, then back at Johnny. "The boat," he whispered, and sat back with his eyes closed.

Doug and I exchanged a look and then slipped out of the car. As we crossed the cracked, weedy street, I could've sworn that everything—the burned-out structure, river, and red boat—moved slightly in the breeze. We approached the building and, cautiously, I poked at the scene, which rippled softly beneath my finger. "It's digital," I whispered, amazed. "A huge, flexible screen, draped over the whole thing."

Doug licked his lips. "Push the boat."

I did, carefully, and a section of the screen—a digital door—popped open softly. My mind was going like a hummingbird, and I heard Doug's hurried breathing as we stepped inside and looked up at the hidden building—three stories of white brick with the words PURE DAIRY CONFECTION COMPANY over the facade. There were no cameras looking at us, no touch pads to gain entry; the building was well hidden, of course, but the lack of electronic safeguards spoke more to Juan's ego and arrogance than airtight security. I gripped the .45 as we entered the building, Harry's claws tick-tacking on the floor, and paused outside the only door. I turned to Doug. "Ready?"

"No," he said seriously.

"Here we go," I said. I counted to three and pulled it open.

It was a room as deep and vast as an airplane hangar, purely, hygienically white, illuminated by enormous hanging light fixtures. The floor was cut into four quadrants. In a far corner, a fleet of black trucks sat gleaming, ready for a chase. In another was a steel vat bearing the words SECODAL CORTEXITRATE. Tubes ran from it into a large, droning pump, while sticky red puddles pooled at its base. A third corner held a sophisticated laboratory behind glass walls. It was outfitted with a computer bank attached via hundreds of slim wires to a large, industrial refrigerator marked simply ANTHONY RISPOLI; instinctively I knew it held gallons of my dad's blood.

A steel box as large as a small house, with a narrow door and single barred window, squatted in the fourth corner—my family's prison.

I wanted to sprint for it and tear the door off by its hinges.

I would've, if it weren't for all of the bodies in my path.

I stood with my feet cemented to the floor, looking at a scene eerily reminiscent of the Catacomb Club massacre.

It was twenty or thirty perfect-looking dead people with chiseled features and gray, parted lips, staring into eternity. Their slim model bodies lay where they fell, as if it were a big game of musical chairs and they'd all lost. A smeared red trail of Sec-C led from the vat to them, the dead, right into their hands holding empty silver cones. It was so still—being around so much fresh death made it feel disrespectful to move, but I had to, there was no way I couldn't. I gave Doug the .45 and said, "Find a safe place and cover me." He didn't seem to hear me, his gaze pinned to the bodies, until I touched him roughly. He turned with tears in his eyes, nodded, and led Harry away. I tiptoed through the corpses to the steel box and stepped inside, whispering, "Mom? Dad? Lou?"

Nothing, silence, a muted gasp of breath.

I felt along a wall, found a light switch, and stared into a nightmare. All of those simplistic movies show a prison cell as a little home away from home with a tidy shelf of books, sparrows landing at the window, and a spare but clean toilet and sink. Instead, I looked at a dank, dirty hole where people were thrown to die. The complete inventory—stained mattresses with handcuffs; a jug of brown water; bits of moldy bread and bowls of slop; cases of empty baby-food containers, the labels marked *High in Iron!* to fortify my dad's blood; a heart-wrenching message scrawled on the wall. Seeing it written in something thick and auburn, looking at the crude drawing of a Ferris wheel, I became murderous hatred incarnate. The words spoke only to me:

We are alive
in Sara Jane
Each day we wait
for Sara Jane
Our daughter, our sister, our savior
Sara Jane

"Creepy, huh? It's like a . . . a prayer," someone slurred, and I spun to see Heather emerging from a dark corner of the cell, except it wasn't her. It was the alternate-universe version of her—a staggering living-dead with red, leaking arteries and burn marks seeping at her temples, painfully visible since her golden tresses had been shorn away. She was wrapped in a hospital gown fouled by scarlet streaks and spatters. Her eyelids fluttered, and if I hadn't thrown out my arms, she would've fallen on her face.

I eased her onto a mattress, asking urgently, "Where are they? My family?"

She parted her lips, her voice rustling like dry grass. "You're too late."

Three little words—the summation of my quest—made me want to scream in her face, to run for the door. Instead I shook her lightly, trying to keep the insanity strength out of my grasp. Heather's eyes opened slowly; the irises weren't blue anymore but ashen gray, drained of an essential element. "Gathered them up. Took them away," she said, her words a garble. "Wouldn't take me . . . told me to die. Said it's better for a junkie like me." Her gaze shifted to nothing. "Made me drink something . . . made me sick."

My heart raced and my body surged, knowing I'd missed them by torturous minutes. "Who took them? Juan?"

"One of them. With the red eyes, but different . . . ," she murmured, as a line of spittle leaked from her mouth. "Your dad, so weak, barely moving. Your mom asked where they were being taken but it hit her, oh God, hit her so hard . . ."

"Sara Jane!" Doug bellowed, his voice rolling across the floor.

I stared at the inscription on the wall, inscribed it on my heart, and carried Heather across the floor, trying not to look at the bodies beneath me. Doug stood outside the laboratory, waving me over. He did a double take when he saw Heather, dropped the .45, and helped me carry her into the lab and onto a gurney. He nodded past me then and said, "Look." I stared beyond the computer screens glowing with digitized brains and alphanumeric data at a plush velvet chair and ornately carved desk. Juan sat crumpled behind it like a large-headed spider on a spindle body, greedily sucking a straw jammed into a bag of life-sustaining blue goop. Empties were scattered across the desk like squashed jellyfish.

When he glanced up, the *R* I'd punched into his forehead winked painfully red. His eyes were crazed, the only part of him besides his lips that moved. I moved closer, cautiously, seeing his reedy shoulders and concave chest folded in a jack-knife, nearly touching his paralyzed hips and legs, while he clutched at his middle with a bony hand. Things were leaking out of him between his fingers, some red and bloody, some blue and goopy, and that's when I understood—the pump in his stomach was gone. He removed the straw from his smeared lips, squealing, "Judas! *¡Renegado!* Look what it— that traitor!—did to me! It worked among us, lived among us, disguised as one of my very own creations . . . and then tried to *kill* me! Oh, my beautiful pump. The murderous thing ripped it right out of my body!"

"What about them?" I said, unable to look out at the massacre.

"I worked my fingers to the *bone* creating that workforce! And *it* had the *audacity* to wipe out every last one of them!

Murdered them all with a tasteless, odorless poison . . . slipped it into Sec-C!"

"Oh no," Doug murmured, glancing at Heather, who was barely alive.

"And then—*¡hijo de puta!*—it took *my* test subjects!"

"My family," I said. "Who was it? The person disguised as a creature? The one who betrayed you?"

"I'll tell you one thing," he said, his voice dropping conspiratorially, "unless I install a new pump quickly, I'm in trouble *muy grande*! Without a consistent source of this pulpy protein, my body will eat *me*!" His gaze moved to Heather as he drank. "So the traitor poisoned her, too? Ah well . . . she was useless. Years of substance abuse had compromised her enzyme GF. But you . . . you're as pure as the driven snow! Lay on that table and I'll draw the blood, six small vials, which we'll add to your father's, *sí*?"

"How do you plan to make me do that?" I said.

"Not me. It," Juan said, and I turned to Teardrop entering the lab like a deadly skeleton in a crisp black uniform, eyes glowing like hot coals. "I sent you out to snatch her, and instead she came to us!" Juan said cheerily. "*Es maravilloso,* yes?"

I was without a weapon; Doug had dropped the .45 somewhere. I pushed him aside, as far out of harm's way as possible, while blinking cold fury to life. My hope was that the electricity would follow before Teardrop ripped my head off.

Instead, the creature stared out at the bodies. "They're all dead," it said quietly.

"What? Oh, yes, an unfortunate incident. A rat in the

woodpile, so to speak," Juan said. "Never mind that now. Let's get to work."

The creature turned to him, its face pale and empty. *"Muerto. Todos."*

"Primero," Juan said sharply, as if disciplining a child, "I can *always make new ones*! Now, *put* her on that table and *open* a damned artery in her head!"

Teardrop turned to me, and I pointed at Juan, saying, "The things you've done for him? Terrible things. All you're going to get for it is sudden death, like them. He told you all about it. Did you forget so soon?"

"¡Mi creación! Do as I command!"

"Él no es Dios. He doesn't create things," I said. "He only destroys them."

"He made me who I am," Teardrop said. "He said I was broken and discarded . . . forgotten . . ."

"But human," I said. "Now you're less than that, and still all of those things. Look at them out there and *remember* what he told you . . . you were made to *die*!"

"¡Bastante! Enough!" Juan shouted, and it snapped Teardrop from its reverie. It began moving toward me and then hesitated, veering toward Juan. "Yes, of course . . . save me first!" he said. "The replacement pump is just there, on the shelf. *¡Rápidamente!*"

A red line creased Teardrop's cheek. "You killed them. You killed us all."

"No, no . . . I was *betrayed,* don't you see? By someone disguised as one of you!"

"We're all disposable . . . human garbage, like you call the street people, the ones I help you recruit. I was one of them once, but I've forgotten so much," Teardrop said, swatting the blue-goop-filled bags from Juan's grasp and lifting him like a rag doll.

"You're taking me to the pump, *sí*?" Juan pled, his head wagging violently, the only physical protestation he could make. "You're saving me, *sí*?"

"It's too late to save either of us," Teardrop said, hurrying past with his quivering cargo, exiting the lab, headed out of the warehouse.

"Stay with Heather!" I said to Doug, and ran after them. "Who was it? The one who took my family?"

"Help me!" Juan said, looking over Teardrop's shoulder. "Please, help me now, and . . . and we'll be partners, you and I! With your blood and my brains . . ."

Teardrop advanced toward the dead end of South Karl Avenue like a robot on a mission, and I asked again, "Give me a name! Please!"

"I don't know who it was, you silly bitch!" Juan spit, his head vibrating. "A ghost, a phantom, and now it's gone, just like your family! Save me, damn you!"

I slowed, knowing Juan was right, that my family was gone again, and I stopped in my tracks. "No," I said softly, the blue flame puffing out. "Damn *you*."

Teardrop stepped over the barrier into the marshy grass and paused. *"Soy belleza y belleza es yo."*

Juan turned to Bubbly Creek, gas blisters burping to the surface. "No . . . no," he said, trying to put authority into his voice, "you listen to me! *¡Escuche!*"

Teardrop looked down at the wasted body in its arms. "My Beauty drowned. Swallowed dirty, cold water, and died. *Mató la Belleza . . . you* killed Beauty."

"No, stop! I *command* you to stop!" Juan screamed. *"¡Monstruo! ¡Diablo!"*

Teardrop looked back with its eyes less red and more human, and walked slowly into the creek. Juan's head battered the creature's chest, pecking and biting like a trapped bird, too busy fighting to scream, and then he was underwater with only Teardrop's shoulders and head visible. And then, with a determined plunge, it went all the way under. The sludgy water swallowed them both, belching mud. I stared at the swirling surface, waiting for nothing, and turned back to the warehouse.

Doug was standing close to Heather, holding a thick black folder. "It's about you. And your dad," he said. "It explains cold fury." I nodded, and we pushed Heather toward the door, pausing at the field of bodies. Doug glanced beyond, at the vat of Sec-C that had done it. There were chemicals everywhere, in green bottles and tin drums. "Let's burn it down," he said.

"In a minute," I said, looking at a dead creature staring past me blankly, its red eyes focused on nothing. I remembered Lucky's command, returned to Juan's lab, and came back with a scalpel. I bent over the creature and paused, murmured an apology, and then removed its eye with a delicate flick. Lucky would have his ghoulish, ocular trophy and never suspect that it came from anyone but Johnny. I wrapped it up carefully and said, "Okay. Torch it."

It took only a few minutes to soak everything with flammables.

After a moment of silence for the dead, Doug dropped a match.

Dancing flames caught the chemicals and when everything was burning—victims, my dad's blood, Sec-C—we hurried out. South Karl was weedy and deserted. There was no sign that anyone was aware of the rapidly growing conflagration. Bubbly Creek oozed past, smelling like death. The Lincoln looked empty until Johnny's head appeared, lifting slowly into view. His face softened, like seeing an old friend. "I dreamed of home. I saw it." We moved him in front, placed Heather in back, and I climbed in beside her. Doug started the car, and when he turned the wheel, driving away, she leaned into me woozily, head on my shoulder, and stayed there. I touched her cold hand, and it moved.

"I heard Juan talking about your dad," she said, "mocking his weakness."

I was quiet, looking out the window, seeing the sooty South Side speed past.

"It's the part of your brain where love exists. That's your weakness too."

"Because of how I feel about my family . . . about Max."

She coughed thickly and took a deep breath. "He didn't do it. With me, I mean."

I looked into Heather's gray gaze, her beauty intact but infected, and my heart clutched, seeing her more dead than alive. "We were alone," she said. "I was ready to use ghiaccio furioso when he began talking about you. I saw the love in his eyes . . . it was right there, a living thing. And then I remembered something and the flame blew out."

"What was it?"

"We're family. We're Rispolis . . . and I . . . love you too," she said, blood leaking from the corner of her mouth, spattering her gown.

"Doug," I said to the front seat, "we have to get to a hospital, now."

She looked at me pleadingly, her eyes searching mine. "Don't hate me."

"I don't. I never will."

She laid her head against my shoulder and closed her eyes. Her mouth curled into the ghost of smile as she whispered, *"Break away to where the sun shines every day . . . at Family Fun Town, we wanna be your host . . . have fun, fun, fun . . ."*

"With the people who love you most," I sang, without music in my voice.

Heather shivered once, and the car was quiet. I stared at her a second longer, willing her to open her eyes. When she didn't, I looked out the window, seeing nothing, letting a piece of my heart drift away.

The rest is predictable, I suppose. Sometimes there's nothing as tragic as things turning out as you could've guessed they would. I couldn't risk exposure, so as respectfully as possible, we left Heather's body at a hospital along with contact information, and sped away. Juan's poison turned out to be formulated from diamorphine. A pathologist ruled her death an overdose of heroin. Annabelle assumed that her addicted daughter had fallen off the wagon, all the way to nowhere. I stopped at the bakery the day before she and Uncle Jack left for good, taking Heather's body back to L.A. I've never seen a person cry as hard or deep as Annabelle. The sorrow unstopped her voice as she sobbed brokenly for her only child's wasted life. I held her, standing in the kitchen, and when she pulled back, her face was filled with the same devastating disappointment—in fate, in life, in herself—that used to crease Uncle Buddy's. I guess things other than cold fury run in our family. She tried on a smile, licking at tears, and handed me a sheaf of bound papers, croaking painfully, "Take this. Uncle Jack wanted you to have it. He has no use for it now." I looked at the title, reading:

The Weeping Mafioso
An original screenplay by Jack Richards
June 26, 1966

I turned to the old man sitting on a stool with his back to me. Besides the hum of the refrigerator, the kitchen was quiet. All of the reassuring smells of freshly baked cookies and cakes had dissipated. Something had broken inside him in the past few days, either a severe worsening of Alzheimer's or the terrible shock of Heather's death—or maybe unearthing an old memory filled with guilt, self-hatred, and subterranean bodies that was better off dead and buried beneath the disease. Whatever it was, he was still alive but as far away as his granddaughter. I touched his shoulder lightly, and he turned, his warm brown eyes searching mine. A showbiz smile lit his face as he touched my arm, saying, "And who are you, my dear?"

It was the perfect line, delivered perfectly.

I thought about what had happened in less than a month and all I'd been through.

I said nothing, since sometimes I knew who I was, and other times I had no idea.

26

SOMETIMES THE ONLY WAY TO GET AWAY FROM yourself is to leave the place where you're the most yourself. Becoming immersed in a different city or country requires a person to conform to its rhythm and language, creating new layers of identity. Unfamiliarity is like a psychological bottle opener that pops you out of a groove.

I was out of the groove now, thirty thousand feet in the air, getting as far away from myself as I could.

It was time to go because I'd failed miserably at the last, best chance to save my family. I hated Chicago, the Outfit, and myself, and I was unable to separate the three. I was losing my mind pacing the Bird Cage Club, not knowing if my family was alive while driving knives into my heart by repeating that verse over and over again.

We are alive
in Sara Jane
Each day we wait
for Sara Jane . . .

Until something happened that nearly drove me over the edge. Dressed in formal sit-down attire, I visited the Hotel Algren carrying a small cooler filled with ice and presented it to Lucky. My explanation was simple: something had been wrong with Johnny's mind that cold fury could not affect; I was unable to extract information and killed him as ordered. The proof shone up from the cooler, glistening red. Lucky nodded as I spoke, lifted the eyeball from ice, and placed it on the table between us. "This war is just beginning. You'll have plenty of opportunities to torture or kill. The Russians think they can beat me, an old man," he said, dropping a fist like a hammer and squashing the eyeball into crimson pulp, "but *I'll* crush every last one of them."

I was driving away in a daze when Tyler called.

He was charming and witty, but it all sounded like mud in my ears until I heard one word. I made him repeat what he'd said, staring out over the gray, hateful city for a long moment before answering with a quiet, "Yes. I'll go to Rome with you." And that's where I was now, on the StroBisCo jet, in a thick leather seat sipping something bubbly, looking down at Chicago growing smaller and farther away. Tyler's proposition had been flattering—he'd moved his business meeting from Paris to Rome just so I'd go with him—and also grasping, since it was plain he'd go to great lengths to draw me in. I leaned into the aisle, looking at the back of the plane where he sat meeting with three rapt employees, issuing orders to the trio of underlings only slightly older than himself. Sitting back, I removed a piece of lined paper, unfolded it, and read it again.

Dear Sara Jane,

By the time you get this, I'll be on my way to California. My dad says there's a good high school nearby and that I can ride my motorcycle every day. So I guess there's an upside to everything.

I got your voice mail. Thanks, I appreciate your words. It meant a lot to me that you were finally ready to talk. The thing is—and I don't want to hurt your feelings, only tell the truth—it's too little, too late. We started out strong and true, and I tried to keep it that way, but you didn't. Your voice mail seemed to acknowledge the ever-present element of . . . well, I guess the only word is dishonesty.

This letter isn't about love.

For us, that was the easy part.

It was about all the things you wouldn't tell me, all the weird situations you refused to explain. And when you didn't show up at Mandi's party, it changed something. I went from not understanding why you wouldn't talk to me truthfully to not caring anymore. But I do care about your happiness, Sara Jane, I want you to know that.

I hope you find what you're looking for.

Best, Max

I stared at the words *find what you're looking for,* feeling their unintentional sting. My message had been simple and, I saw now, heartbreaking for him. I'd left it after dropping off my cousin at a hospital, when I was finally alone in my dark room at the Bird Cage Club, whispering earnestly into the phone, "I heard about you and Heather. She told me the truth. And now

I'm ready to tell you the truth, Max . . . about everything."

And I had been. I was so devastated at losing my family again, so bereft at the futility of Heather's death, that I wanted to give away part of myself—to unload the burdensome secrets, lies, and classified criminal information I carried like a tumor. If Max had picked up instead of letting it go to voice mail, he would know everything now. But just like my inability to save my family, I'd missed that opportunity too. And now that he'd done the brave thing, removing himself from a broken relationship, I had to let him go free.

I was trying to free myself too.

All I knew was that my family had been taken by Lou's "friend"; otherwise, the trail was cold, leading nowhere. It seemed certain now that they were gone forever, and as heartbreaking as that was to accept, I was being whistled in, sit-down by sit-down, decision by decision, by a larger, criminal family. I couldn't fight the tide any longer. I also didn't want to be completely alone, and if I were with anyone, he'd have to understand my life without requiring an explanation. And then he was leaning over me with an arm on the back of my seat, smiling with perfect teeth, green eyes set off by copper-colored skin. Tyler wears a type of cologne, lightly, that smells of lemon and spice, and his thick, dark hair is cut to frame his face like a fashion ad. He's half African American and half Sicilian—he refers to himself as "Africilian"—and really is one of the best-looking guys I know, and smartest too.

Smart enough to know that our respective roles would make us a power couple.

The Outfit has a long, sensible tradition of keeping the things that matter—secrets and profits—as strictly in the family as possible. As long as Tyler and I fulfilled our responsibilities, our relationship would be regarded favorably, like the prom king and queen of organized crime. It may seem self-serving, but dating Tyler also strengthens my position. Of course, he comes with all of the inborn Outfit traits—suspicion, double-talk, duplicity toward enemies, mistrust of friends—but he's also of my generation. As far as I can tell, he has no issue with the counselor-at-large being a woman.

He's also not Max.

But I resolved to get past that.

So when he leaned closer, gingerly touching Max's *T* medallion at my neck, I tried not to flinch. He said, "I like this. From now on, it can stand for Tyler," and before I could respond, he kissed me lightly. It was pleasant, soft, non-threatening, and still not Max, which meant no sparks but nice. Very nice. Definitely something I could get used to, like fat-free cupcakes. And without the element of love, I'd never be in the position of weakening myself, suppressing cold fury and the electricity, which I'd need more than ever as my role as counselor-at-large expanded. Which reminded me of the thick black folder in my backpack, the one Doug took from Juan's lab marked *La Ciencia de Ghiaccio Furioso* (The Science of Cold Fury). Doug read it (his Spanish is a million times better than mine), saying that if Juan had done anything good in his life, he'd at least provided a simple neurobiological explanation for cold fury. My reaction was that "simple" and "neurobiological" don't belong in the same sentence, but I realized how important it was to understand myself, and I resolved to read it on the flight.

Doug had looked at me then, silent a beat before saying, "You're really going?"

I nodded without speaking, tossing clothes into a bag.

"Max is already gone, huh?"

"Yep. Gone."

"Hard to believe it's over . . . that you're giving up the search," he said quietly.

"Not giving up as much as moving on," I said, lifting the bag over my shoulder.

"I wish things were different . . . ," he said, letting the words drift since there were too many things to wish for. Instead, he opened his thin arms. "What about this place? Am I still a resident of the Bird Cage Club?"

"As long as you help take care of Harry. Oh . . . ," I said, remembering something. I dug in my pocket and came up with car keys, flipping them to him.

Doug looked at the key chain with an image of a stallion on its hind legs. "Really? The Ferrari?"

"It'll get you around Chicago faster than the Lincoln. It's good of you to help Johnny try to find his way home." I shrugged and said, "Keep giving him Screaming Banshee. Maybe it's not too late."

"When I look at him, I see myself if I'd gone a step further. If he has any chance at all, he'll need someone who really loves him. Or tough-loves him. Whatever," he said, punching my arm lightly. "Anyway, it's the least one ex-junkie can do for another." He pointed at the folder and said, "Promise you'll read it on your way to Rome?"

I did, I promised, so when Tyler went to speak with the pilot—"my airborne chauffeur," he called him—I reached into the backpack for *La Ciencia de Ghiaccio Furioso* and my Spanish dictionary. Instead, a sheaf of papers caught my eye. It was Uncle Jack's screenplay, *The Weeping Mafioso,* bound by brass tacks that had gone green with age. I flipped it open, intending to skim a few pages.

An hour later I sat back, dumbstruck.

Uncle Jack wrote it in 1966 when Nunzio was counselor, Enzo was in training, and Lucky had recently become Boss.

It was part family history, part Outfit lore, and it completed part of the puzzle in a way that the notebook never could.

The story centered on Uncle Jack's protagonist, a sort of super-gangster called Renzo "Rumrunner" Nispoli. Renzo runs a bootlegging operation, and as the years pass, his fortunes and power increase based on a singular talent for brutality. He kills, kills, and kills again at the behest of his superiors, first freezing victims with "the Look," squinted ferociously through sky-blue eyes. Renzo was a composite of Nunzio's and Enzo's cold fury, Nicky "Daggers" Fratelli's ability to murder without guilt, and Lucky's emotional peculiarity— the weeping part—which even Uncle Jack would've known about. After Renzo kills a club full of innocent people (the Catacomb Club massacre fictionalized), he hides out in a theater showing *Snow White and the Seven Dwarfs.* When the witch murders Snow White with a poison apple, Renzo bursts into tears. He's overcome by what he's done, weeping away the guilt in the privacy of a darkened theater.

So many old, dead secrets mixed up in that screenplay, just like Uncle Jack's mind, and I kept reading until my eyes froze on the page.

I blinked, but the words were still there.

All I could hear was the vacuum-hum of jet engines, the chatter of my teeth, my heart punching my chest, as I whispered the dialogue spoken by Renzo.

"I know the secret to ultimate power . . ."

And there it was, lifted from *"Volta"* all those years ago by Uncle Jack, transcribed as a throwaway plot point in a movie script that no one wanted to make. It was Renzo speaking furtively to the only person he trusted and who wouldn't betray him, someone near the Outfit but not allowed inside. His wife.

RENZO
I know the secret to ultimate power—*potenza ultima*—and where it's hidden! All I need to get my hands on it is one little brass key . . .

WIFE
How? How do you know where ultimate power is, Renzo?

RENZO (grinning like a fox)
Because my old man helped put it there, a long, long time ago. He told me when he didn't think I was paying attention. But I *always* paid attention.

WIFE

Tell me . . . where is it?

RENZO (cautiously, whispering)

It's in a vault made of brick, deep beneath the streets of Chicago. Right under what the old-timers used to call the "Troika of Outfit Influence."

I read all the way to the end but no further mention was made of ultimate power.

None was necessary.

I knew beyond all reason that the "Troika of Outfit Influence" was the heart of *"Volta,"* the hidden nugget I'd been searching for. So long ago, when Uncle Jack was a young man transcribing Nunzio's words into Buondiavolese, the poetic phrase must've stuck with him. He was paying attention—he *always* paid attention—and had recycled it decades later for his script.

"The Troika of Outfit Influence," I said, tasting the secrecy of it.

I licked my lips, feeling my brain spin like a roulette wheel, wondering where in Chicago it could possibly be. And then the little white ball click-clacked to a stop on the only possible answer, where everything began and ended—the notebook.

Ultimate power in its physical form resided inside the earth, but the meaning of the elusive phrase—the actual, pinpoint location—had to be contained within the creased and tattered collection of old secrets. *"Volta"* provided the *what,* and now I was sure that some other chapter, or yellowed letter or blurred snapshot, contained the *where*. All I had to do was examine each page, line by line and word by word, for the last elusive link to finding and freeing my family. Whoever had taken them hadn't cared about my dad's blood or Juan Kone's plan for a genetically engineered army. They'd cared about my family, the Rispoli clan, Outfit counselors-at-large for four generations.

They cared about ultimate power.

I nearly had it in my hands.

What I did not have was the notebook, which I'd locked in the steel briefcase and hidden where no one would find it back in Chicago. I wondered suddenly what I was doing on a plane to Rome—what I was doing *anywhere* outside the city while my family was still there—and I waved at Tyler. I met him the aisle, where he said, "Hey, sorry, I'm not ignoring you. He's a chatty one, my airborne chauffeur."

Remember the chauffeur, I thought, dismayed at how easily I'd been sidetracked by disappointment. "Listen, we have to turn the plane around."

"Huh? You're kidding, right?"

"I'm not much of a kidder, Tyler, you should know that by now. I need to get back to Chicago right away."

A slow smile spread over his chiseled face. "You almost had me there. Turn the plane around, my ass . . ."

"Do it now or it's gonna be your ass," I said, blinking once, grabbing his cool green gaze with my cold furious one, seeing his worst fear—it was his parents waving good-bye to Tyler from the steps of a private jet that would soon crash. I blinked it away, too ashamed to watch, and when he was able to face me, I said, "I'm sorry, but it's really important. I wouldn't ask if it weren't." He thumbed sweat from his lip, nodded obediently, and turned toward the cockpit. Watching him go, I thought of the movies where the girl—me—would utter Tyler's name. He'd look back, and I'd take his hands, pull him toward me, kiss him tenderly, and tell him to continue on to Rome, where the golden light of Italy awaited.

This isn't a movie.

This is real life, where families are kidnapped, brutalized, and lost, beautiful cousins overdose, loyal boyfriends leave you, and smart friends become stupid junkies. And where the answers you need most are never out in the open but always buried, sometimes within worn notebook pages, sometimes beneath Chicago.

The Outfit concealed speakeasies, massacres, and vaults far below the earth.

Muddied and bloodied, I was about to discover its biggest subterranean secret.

"Our daughter, our sister," I whispered, feeling the plane make its slow, determined arc through the clouds. *"Our savior, Sara Jane."*